Praise for
USA TODAY bestselling author
Jordan Dane

"Jordan Dane is a fresh new voice
in young adult paranormal fiction."
—P. C. Cast, *New York Times* bestselling author
of the House of Night series

"Dane's first offering in her new series, The Hunted,
is sensational. *[Indigo Awakening]* has strong characters
and a wild and intense story, matched only by the emotions
it will generate within you. Readers will love this book and
eagerly await the next adventure. Fantastic! A keeper."
—*RT Book Reviews*

"Galloping suspense turns out to be the main attraction of the book,
along with a few romance episodes and some pathos....
The Indigo children also stand out as interesting characters. Exciting."
—*Kirkus Reviews* on *Indigo Awakening*

"In her first YA novel, adult thriller writer Dane pens a macabre
slow-burner.... Thoroughly eerie, the plot includes flashbacks
and nightmares involving crossing over into the spirit world,
while Dane's well-developed characters provide an authentic
exploration of guilt, loyalty and belonging."
—*Publishers Weekly* on *In the Arms of Stone Angels*

"*On a Dark Wing* is a gripping paranormal thriller
with all the emotion of budding teenage romance,
and Abbey brings plenty of attitude to the story. Intelligent,
emotive storytelling offering a very different side to death."
—*The Cairns Post, Entertainment News*

Books by Jordan Dane

from Harlequin TEEN

In the Arms of Stone Angels
On a Dark Wing

The Hunted

Indigo Awakening
Crystal Fire

CRYSTAL FIRE

Jordan Dane

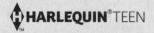

HARLEQUIN®TEEN

Recycling programs
for this product may
not exist in your area.

ISBN-13: 978-0-373-21093-0

CRYSTAL FIRE

Copyright © 2013 by Cosas Finas

This edition published by arrangement with Harlequin Books S.A.

For questions and comments about the quality of this book, please contact us at CustomerService@Harlequin.com.

Printed in U.S.A.

To my mother and father, who taught me the importance of family

{ 1 }

West Hollywood
10:20 p.m.

A sane person wouldn't think about going inside—alone—but Caila Ferrie didn't have a choice. She wasn't a stranger to darkness. She'd spent much of her life sinking into it, forced into the shelter and anonymity of shadows by her own choosing. That realization hit her as she stared at a deserted old warehouse from a murky alley across the street, believing she'd be better off inside than where she was. Brick walls were scrawled with veins of graffiti and glutted by neglect. Light from the street reflected off the jagged glass of busted windows and made the pitch-black broken parts look as if the building had eyes.

It was the third location she'd tried tonight, her last shot at finding Oliver Blue. She shut her eyes and took a deep breath. *Please let this be it,* she prayed. If she came up empty, she had nowhere else to go. Before she cut across the street, she looked over her shoulder and listened hard. She'd been careful and thought no one followed her, but it never hurt to be sure. Caila stuck to the shadows, even if it meant she had to take the long way around to cross the street. She took the precaution as much for Oliver as she did for her.

The guy was a loner. That's why few people knew anything about him. She'd met him only once through her friend Zack, who'd said that if anything bad happened, Oliver would be a guy she could trust. Zack never said why he had such faith in him, but he'd been adamant.

Because she trusted her friend, Caila had listened when he told her where to look for the guy, but the one time she'd met Oliver, he put her on edge. He didn't say much and barely made eye contact. He looked irritated that Zack had brought her. After her friend pulled him aside to explain, Oliver nudged his chin and mumbled the only words he'd directed at her. *"Zack's a good guy to watch your back. Hope you do the same for him."* Oliver left without saying another word. At the time she never thought she'd see him again.

If she wasn't desperate, she wouldn't have come.

It took Caila time to check every door and the loading bay for a way into the abandoned building. Everything on street level was locked tight. She almost gave up until she spotted a fire escape that led to the upper floors and the rooftop. Climbing those steps would make her a target for anyone watching the warehouse. If she found a way in, she wouldn't have much of an escape if she needed one, and metal stairs made noise. She debated her options, but the fact was that she didn't *have* any. She hadn't risked searching for Oliver to give up now.

Caila climbed the rusted steps and didn't look down. She kept her hands on the filthy railing, even in the spots riddled with gross chewing gum. With a bird's-eye view, she took comfort that she hadn't been followed and felt safe enough to crouch on a step in the dark. She reached into her jacket pocket and pulled out her last can of Cheez Whiz and squirted it in her mouth. She had to take a hit to keep her stomach from growling. After she emptied the can, she left it on the fire escape and got moving.

Zack had always kept her supplied with the stuff, that and spray whipped cream. Cheez Whiz reminded her of him. She'd found Zack when she'd needed someone to look after her, but memories of him were blasted out of her skull by an absurd habit she had almost no control over. Whenever she got nervous, random Disney songs earwormed her. An outburst from the French chef in *The Little Mermaid* erupted in her head like a brain itch.

Not now!

Whoever had control of the Disney MP3 in her brain took weird pleasure in torturing her with a music doodle when she least expected it. The habit had come from a distant memory, something she should have remembered as important, but couldn't quite recall. It usually signaled something bad, but not always. After she found a metal door with a broken lock on the second level, she stepped into the crushing silence of the abandoned warehouse—and even the French chef quit singing. A tingle raced across her skin like the chilling touch of a cold hand. Caila wasn't alone. Someone watched her. Her gift of second sight had sent her a warning, a rippling sensation that had started in her chest and raced down her arms. Being psychic, she relied on her instincts for everything. The impulse to run grew stronger, but she fought the push.

Her promise to Zack made her stay.

It took time for her eyes to adjust to the darkness as she searched every corner for anything that moved. The oppressive silence felt as if no one was there, but she knew better. Her bad case of warning tingles had intensified and felt as if jolts of electricity shuddered through her. Even though her throat felt parched and raw, she took the risk of calling out his name.

"Oliver? It's me, Caila. Zack's friend."

She winced at the sound of her own voice. It echoed in the belly of the old warehouse and made her feel stupid for yelling like an idiot. Caila had never been brave.

"Oliver?" She wrung her hands and kept moving with her eyes alert. "Please... I need to talk to you."

She crept between old wooden crates and rusted barrels, peering through the darkness for any signs of life—or any reason to run. She got both when a guy's low voice came from nowhere.

"This better be important."

Caila stopped dead still, with her heart throttling in the red zone. She fought hard not to show that he'd almost given her a heart attack. When she turned, she spotted Oliver staring down, crouched in the metal rafters above her. She only saw part of his face in the dim light coming from a cracked window.

"I wouldn't be here if it wasn't." She returned his glare but backed off on the attitude when she remembered why she'd come.

"Anyone follow you?"

"No, I was real careful...and I didn't see anybody below when I climbed those stairs."

He stared at her and didn't say anything for a long time. Caila didn't move an inch—or breathe.

"Why are you here?"

"It's Zack. He's missing. I haven't seen him in three days."

"Maybe he doesn't want to be found."

"Not Zack." She crossed her arms. "He wouldn't do that to me, unless something bad happened."

Oliver glared at her for another strained moment before he finally stood. "I'm coming down. Stay put and don't move."

When the guy vanished into the shadows, she listened for him but heard nothing. Not a creak of a floorboard or a scuff of a boot. He simply reappeared from behind a pile of tossed empty boxes. Dressed in worn jeans with holes in the knees and a black T-shirt with a bloody yellow smiley face on the chest, Oliver walked toward her with his eyes fixed on her.

Those eyes.

That's what she'd remembered most about him. His eyes were smoky green, intense and unforgettable. When they first met, she wanted him to look at her, but whenever he did, she felt raw and exposed as if he knew all her sins. Seeing him in the shadows magnified that feeling.

He was bigger than she recalled and towered over her with his broad shoulders and long legs. His scruffy black hair and bristled chin made him look older, even though Zack had told her that he was nineteen—only three years older than her. He had an upward turn to the corners of his lips that made her believe smiling had once been easy for him, but an unshakable sadness in his eyes weighed heavier now.

In another life she could picture him being a good son, tolerable brother and anyone's trusted best friend, but too much had happened to change him. Most girls would go bat shit if he even looked at them—normal girls who lived in an alternative universe light-years away who wouldn't recognize the walking wounded on sight as she did. She couldn't afford to let a guy like him get to her.

Letting her guard down made her vulnerable, especially now that Zack was gone. She hadn't lived on the streets of L.A. that long. Without Zack to run interference, she didn't know if *she* liked being alone with Oliver.

He kept his distance and said, "Tell me everything."

Caila stared at the blood-splattered smiley face on Oliver's T-shirt as he crossed his arms, and she thought of Zack. The tattered fringes of her life frayed apart as hunger and exhaustion from her sleepless nights made her feel light-headed. She'd have one chance to convince Oliver to help her.

Running on empty, she had nothing left—*only the truth*.

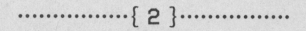

{ 2 }

West Hollywood
10:50 p.m.

"Why do you think he's in trouble?" Oliver asked.

He stood in a wash of moonlight coming from a broken window that silhouetted his body. His black hair covered one eye and shone under a bluish light that made him look like a ghost. Caila shoved that morbid thought from her mind.

"That time we met, you said that Zack was a good guy to have my back and I should do the same for him." She felt the burn of tears and had nothing left to fight them off. "Zack got the raw end. When he needed me, I wasn't there. If that makes a difference to you, I'll leave and never come back, but Zack needs help."

Caila didn't know what she'd do if he kicked her out. She needed someone to talk to, but when a rush of emotions hit her hard, tears came and carried a weight of their own. Her face grew hot and she felt dizzy.

Oliver cocked his head and lowered his voice.

"Took guts to come here," he said. "You look wiped. This wasn't the first place you looked, was it?" After she shook her head and lowered her chin, he said, "I'd say you have his back. Talk to me."

Oliver pulled two wooden crates over and made a spot for them to sit. Caila took it as a positive sign that he hadn't kicked her butt to the street. She joined him and filled Oliver in on the days before Zack went missing and told him everything. Thinking of Zack used to make her smile. Now all she felt was guilt.

"The last time I saw him he had a few dollars and went to buy us a couple of burgers. I get headaches and wasn't feeling good. He was always doing nice stuff like that for me." She rubbed the back of her neck. "He never came back."

Oliver nodded and kept listening, but he clenched his jaw as if he was stewing on something.

"I went looking for him," she said. "No one at that burger place remembered seeing him, but you know how that goes. I checked with other kids he knows, even went to a couple of hospitals and clinics. He hasn't turned up. Not anywhere."

Caila looked him in the eye. "I'm scared, Oliver. Zack always told me to find you if something happened. I got no one else."

Oliver grew quiet and glared into the dark. She had an awful feeling about what he'd say next, but he surprised her with a question she never saw coming.

"How did you two hook up?" he asked. "Zack never said."

"Oh, we're only friends. We never… I mean, it wasn't like that with Zack."

"Like what?"

Caila stammered and racked her brain for what to say as heat rose to her cheeks. When he shot her a half smile, she realized that he didn't expect an answer.

"You remind me of him. He liked making me squirm. Guess I made it easy," she said. "Can you help me find him?"

"I don't know. Maybe. Did Zack ever talk about me and my freak-show talent?"

"Not really. Guess he figured that was private."

"Yeah, good man. You have anything of his, something he touched?"

"No, he never told me about bringing anything." She dug through her pockets but couldn't even come up with coins that he'd touched, until— "Wait a minute. Yeah, I got something."

Caila jumped off the crate and raced back the way she had come. When she got to the fire escape, she grabbed what she needed and came back.

"Here. He touched this." She handed him the empty can. "Will this work?"

Oliver scrunched his face when he stared at the Cheez Whiz.

"Don't knock it," she said. "Squirt cheese is genius."

He smiled without a smart-ass remark and got down to business. Oliver shut his eyes and held the can tight. When he started to shake and breathe funny, she edged closer. His face twisted as if it hurt to hold the can. When he opened his eyes and had a hard time looking her in the face, Caila knew it wouldn't be good news.

"You know what happened to him, don't you?"

Oliver set the empty can at his feet without saying a word. It took him a long time to answer her. He got up and leaned a shoulder against a brick wall. Eventually he slid down and crouched near the floor.

"I only got glimpses of him, but I saw enough. Guys in uniform took him and they weren't the police." He shook his head. "Ever hear of the Church of Spiritual Freedom? Some kids call 'em the Believers. I call 'em fuckin' soul vampires."

She'd heard Zack say something similar. At first she

• 15 •

thought that those stories were nothing but urban legend. Zack never wanted to scare her. He only shared enough to make her cautious with strangers and be aware of people following her. But from the expression on Oliver Blue's face, she had a bad feeling that everything Zack had told her had been true.

"They're for real?" Caila had a hard time breathing. She shook her head and tried to remember stuff Zack had said. "Who could help us find out if they have him? I mean, there's gotta be a way of getting him back."

The look on Oliver's face told her plenty when he came to sit with her again.

"They got resources and money and cops on the payroll. We can't trust anyone. These bastards are high-tech. I hear they can hack into the city's surveillance and traffic cams. Makes it harder to keep ahead of 'em and hide, you know? You don't even feel a push until they're right on top of you."

"But why? Why would they come after…kids?"

Oliver stared into the dark for a long moment before he answered.

"Fear is a drug. They're afraid of us…of what we can do. To them, we're freaks." He turned back to her. "When people believe God is on their side, they think that gives them permission to do anything. They see us as a threat."

"But Zack… He wasn't dangerous. He never hurt anyone." Caila felt the darkness in the warehouse closing in on her. "Could you tell where he is now?"

"Normally, yeah, but not this time." He sighed and ran a hand through his hair.

She didn't know him well enough to tell if she'd gotten the whole truth about what he saw.

"Does that mean he's…" She couldn't say it.

"I don't know."

When he answered too fast, she got a bad feeling. All she could think about was Zack.

"Look, don't jump to conclusions," he said. "This freak show thing I do, it doesn't work like GPS. Tomorrow, I'll try it again."

When a fresh tear trickled down her cheek, Oliver reached over and squeezed her hand.

"You're tired. I can fix you a bunk for tonight. We'll figure out something tomorrow. Okay?"

His invitation surprised her, but it was late and since she had nowhere else to go, she nodded.

"You hungry?" he asked.

If cheese from a can didn't count, Caila hadn't eaten much since yesterday, but before she could say anything, a familiar sensation hit her hard. From the look on his face, Oliver felt it too.

"I got shoved, big-time," he told her.

"Yeah, me too."

Oliver didn't have to explain what he meant. Caila knew. She felt the mind push. Her gift gave her instincts she couldn't ignore. A psychic ripple could come for any reason, but she'd learned to expect the worst.

"Follow me and stick close," he said.

He grabbed her hand and ran toward the rear of the warehouse, dodging broken glass and piles of garbage. The mind shoves swept over her in waves. The surges hit her so fast she couldn't tell where they came from. When they got to the back wall, it looked solid with no way out and the floor had a gaping hole. Caila had no idea why he'd taken her here.

"Do as I do. No questions. You won't get a do-over."

With eyes wide, she watched him drop feet first through a dark hole. The sound of rumbling metal echoed in the cavernous space.

"Come on. Do it. Trust me." His voice came from below, but she couldn't see him.

Without hesitating, she closed her eyes and jumped feet-first. When her butt hit metal, she couldn't stop. She slid down and spiraled out of control through the shadows until she felt his strong hands catch her.

"Good girl."

She caught a glimpse of his smile before he grabbed her hand and pulled her with him. When she looked over her shoulder, she saw the makeshift metal slide he'd made to get him to the ground floor, but when a flash of red hit her, she slowed down.

"I saw something. Over there." She pointed, but Oliver didn't stop.

"No talking. We gotta book."

The bellow of pounding metal echoed through the warehouse as if it came from everywhere at once. She remembered the doors had been locked on this level, but whoever was out there sounded determined to get in. Caila ran wherever he took her, until her lungs and throat burned and sweat drenched her body.

Beams of red laser lights strafed the walls around them and she heard voices outside. They were close, but Oliver didn't hesitate. He headed for another corner of the first floor and stopped over a manhole in the floor.

"This is our only way out now," he told her. "They probably have the roof covered, but no matter what you see down here, no screaming."

No screaming? Oh God. She cringed. *Lion King.* Weird flashes came to her and the music started.

"Hakuna matata," she mumbled under her breath.

"What?"

"No worries." She stared down the hole and shook her hands. "I can do this."

Like last time, Oliver went first and crawled into the manhole. She heard his hands and boots on the rungs of a metal ladder, her only hint of what she'd have to do. Caila didn't wait for him to get to the bottom. She followed him, pulling the cover back over the hole and praying she wouldn't find out why he'd warned her about not screaming.

Belowground everything turned pitch-black and she felt her feet sink into water.

"I got you," he whispered.

She heard his voice and felt his hand in hers, but the moldy stench of something dead made it impossible to breathe. Oliver moved as fast as he could with her slowing him down. They slogged and splashed through the water, but when she felt her leg hit something that slid through the puddle and shrieked in a high pitch, she finally understood what Oliver had meant about not crying out. *Rats.* She winced and kept her mouth shut and her feet moving.

When they emerged from the tunnel to street level, she finally breathed fresh air as he lifted her through the maintenance shaft. They were free. Oliver had gotten them out, but when she dared to smile, he shook his head.

"We're not clear yet. Only one way out of this alley," he panted.

Oliver grabbed her hand and never slowed down, but after he rounded a corner, his boots slid and he skidded to a stop.

"Holy crap!" he gasped.

They came face-to-face with a wall of muscle in uniform—a SWAT team of cops or an army of storm troopers in black. Like in the warehouse, bloodred beams blinded her and painted over their heads and hearts. Oliver didn't wait to see what these men would do. He lunged and turned the other way, pulling her with him.

"I thought you said...th–this was the only—" Caila never finished.

When she saw movement to her right, she heard the menacing sound of boots on the ground and shadows eclipsed street lights. More of them were coming. They were surrounded.

"Shit!" he cursed. "I'm...sorry. I can't believe they knew about that tunnel."

"Why are they doing this? We're just kids."

"Damned freaks," he whispered, only loud enough for her to hear.

They had nowhere else to run. They were outnumbered and faced an army of men with weapons. Caila raised a hand to shield her eyes from the lights. She gripped Oliver's hand with her body shaking.

Did I do this? Did I bring them down on Oliver?

She had a bad feeling that her connection to Zack had earned her a target on her back. Now her bad luck had put Oliver in danger. They backed up and headed deeper into the alley until they had nowhere else to go. With her back to the wall, Caila couldn't think.

Flashes of terrible images bombarded her from the many waking nightmares since she'd lost Zack. She pictured him dead. Caila didn't want to end up like that, abducted by the same heartless people who must have taken Zack. They'd stolen him off the streets as if they had a right to take his life. They'd kidnap her and now Oliver too. She'd never see him again and she'd be alone.

The dark core of her gift burned inside her. She knew what that meant. It started deep in her belly and welled up in her chest until her skin flushed with heat. Her heart never slowed down. Her psychic gift had its own will to protect her. At times it forced her to do things she fought against and she had to struggle to control her body, but what came next shocked her.

She turned toward Oliver, looking for an excuse to touch him the way her gift demanded. She needed time to do what must be done. Without thinking any more, she pulled him into her embrace and kissed him. In front of all those armed men—the ones who were whistling and laughing now—Caila wrapped her arms around him and pressed her lips to his. If she had a last wish, kissing Oliver was as good as any, but she needed the intimacy and precious time.

The move stunned him.

At first Oliver resisted her and started to pull away, but it didn't take long for him to give in. Caila made sure of that. She felt her gift surge from her body into his. Tears came now, as they usually did, when she fought the regret of doing what she had to do. She cried for Zack and now for Oliver. When he lifted her off the ground into his strong arms —to school her on kissing—the sensation intensified and raged hot. She stopped thinking about the danger, the fear and the never-ending nightmares over Zack and her past.

She flooded Oliver with a life she'd always wished for and now might never have, things she'd given to Zack too. Sweet forever dreams she wanted to give Oliver because she couldn't count on taking them with her. She'd never known what it felt like to be loved by anyone, not even her own family. How could she let her life and Oliver's end in an alley, trapped like stray dogs?

Her gift took over and she didn't fight it. She couldn't. It invented a life they could both see and feel—a normal life where they were free. As she'd done with Zack, she gave Oliver a reason not to be afraid when fear was what had brought them together. None of it would be real, but she didn't care.

Whatever her gift made her mind see would soon become hard-wired into her brain as if it were true. The life she'd infused in both of them would feel as real as their first kiss. That had to be enough, but when she pulled away and gazed up at him, she realized what she'd done. He stared down with his incredible eyes brimming in awe of her and a deep-rooted connection between them that he didn't have a minute ago.

"Don't…forget me," she whispered as she touched his cheek.

She felt as close to Oliver as she'd been with Zack, but one thought tainted everything. Caila had taken his life as surely as the Believers had hijacked Zack's.

Somewhere in L.A.

Oliver Blue fought the men off, even with guns pointed at his head. He had to protect Caila and because she felt the same way about him, she screamed for him to give up and not get hurt. They were outnumbered, but he had to do something.

When one of the men slugged him and hit him with a Taser, Oliver's world went black. He awoke to the sound of an engine and the jostling of a moving vehicle. His head lay in Caila's lap and she stroked his hair. His hands were cuffed behind his back. They'd left her free to move. That had to mean something. They'd come for him, not her.

"Are you okay?" Her whisper came to him through a fog. It almost didn't register, but before he could answer, a stern voice broke through.

"No talking."

After his head cleared, he saw they were being held in

a windowless van. He tried to ask her questions, but a guy kicked his boot and grunted the universal sign of "Shut up, freak!" For her sake he kept his mouth shut. He'd gotten her in enough trouble, but if they were after him, maybe he could convince them she was normal.

The vehicle stopped and he was hauled from the van. Caila got the same rough treatment. She looked scared, and that killed him. They bound her hands behind her back with zip ties, and black hoods were put over their heads. Before everything went dark, Oliver saw a glimpse of his surroundings and smelled grease and gasoline. They were in a garage loading bay. An automatic door opened with a hiss. When cool air hit him, it filtered up the hood to bring a medicinal odor with it. It smelled like a hospital or a clinic. He counted his steps and tried to sense where they were being taken.

But when the girl cried out, he knew they'd be separated.

"Caila. Tell them you're not like me," he yelled. "They made a mistake taking you. Tell them."

Oliver shoved the men who held him, but when her voice faded, he knew they'd taken her behind a door and down a hall in another direction. After the shoving match, he'd lost track of his count. If he didn't know where Caila was, he wouldn't be going anywhere, not without her.

They took him down an elevator. When the doors opened, he felt a chill and smelled dank humidity. Water ran through pipes over his head. A basement. They hauled him down a long corridor before they made a right and two lefts. After he heard a card key swipe, a beep and double doors open, Oliver got hauled into a room and pushed into a chair where they strapped down his legs and hips. Before they secured his arms and chest, they took off his cuffs. By the time they were done, he couldn't move.

"You bastards. That girl has nothing to do with this. I

swear she's not like me." He felt the thick fabric puff away from his face when he yelled, but no one removed the hood.

When they finally yanked it off, the bright lights blinded him. He squinted and felt his eyes water. Before he got oriented, two men dressed in white uniforms tightened a strap across his throat.

"Hey, they kidnapped me. Call the cops!" Oliver yelled to no one in particular. He only made noise. "Fire! Please help me."

The two men only laughed and one of them said, "Give it a rest, kid. No one is gonna help you. Not here."

When the door opened, Oliver let himself hope that someone had come to save him, but that didn't happen. A nurse came into the room carrying a tray with a syringe and other stuff on it. Without a word or even a look in his eyes, she forced an IV into him by sticking a needle into a vein on the back of his hand and taping over it. She injected the IV with whatever she had in the syringe. It didn't take long for him to feel the drugs take hold.

The lights became brighter and hurt his eyes. Everything he did felt as if he were doing it in slow motion. The nurse moved across him and his eyes didn't track her. He'd lost his edge and barely noticed when she stuck patches to his chest and head that had wires running to a machine.

Caila. He should have worried about what they were doing to him, but all he could picture was the girl's terrified face. He didn't even notice another woman enter the room until she spoke.

"My name is Dr. Fiona. I'm in charge here." She stepped close enough for him to feel her breath on his cheek. She stared at him as if he were a rash. "When I am done with you, dear boy, I will know you better than your own mother."

"That's not saying much." He smirked. "You look like someone who'd aim higher."

"That attitude won't serve you here."

"Attitude is all I...got."

His words slurred as the drugs flooded his body and his world dulled to a somber gray.

"That's not true. You have no idea of your full potential. I have plans for you, Oliver Blue."

"You know my n-name."

His lips felt as if they weighed a ton. Every word, every thought became a challenge.

"Your arrest record made it easy. It seems you have a temper and resort to your fists, but you'd be surprised what I know." She backed off and looked down at a chart she held in her hands. "This girl, Caila Ferric, what's she to you?"

"Nothing. We just met." He didn't flinch at his lie. He couldn't. "She's not a...circus act l-like me. You sh-should let her go."

"Just like that, on your word?" When the woman smiled, that chilling look demanded all his strength not to react to it. "She's the reason you're here. Not the other way around."

He struggled to make sense of what she said, but a growing numbness inched up from his toes toward his chest and arms and carried a chill.

"It would appear that Caila has a way of endearing herself to everyone she meets. We have an interesting dossier on her. Quite a gift she has. Think about it, Oliver. Doesn't it seem odd that you're willing to sacrifice so much for someone you just met?"

The woman cut open his T-shirt with scissors, but after she peeled back the fabric to expose his chest, she got quiet. Her eyes shifted down his body until they settled on his face and she leaned closer.

"You should've been more careful who you associated with. I'm sure whatever she told you, it wasn't the truth. She's a pathological liar. Personally I'm grateful she brought you to me. I think you're destined to be one of my shining stars, Oliver."

"I don't sparkle, lady." He jerked at his restraints. "Where's Zack? That's how you got Caila's name. You have him. I know it."

"I suppose that would be a correct statement, but how is it that you're so certain? I'm curious."

"Caila gave me a can Zack touched. I saw him in a Cheez Whiz vision. He grabbed a couple of In-N-Out burgers and you nabbed him."

"Ah, impressive. You have an amazing gift to connect with others, Oliver. Psychometry, is it? I can work with that. You're perfect, in fact." She smiled before she upped the dose of drugs into his body. "Strip off his clothes and scrub him down. My work isn't done. I have special plans for this one."

Dr. Fiona was done talking to him. She gave orders to the two men in uniforms. They heaved something heavy onto his head that covered his eyes, and his world went black. He gasped for air when the gear clamped over his nose.

"Can't...breathe."

He fought the restraints but couldn't move. When hands invaded his body, no one talked to him. They scrubbed his bare skin with cold soapy water that made him shiver, but he couldn't see what they did to him. He couldn't see *anything*.

The last thing he remembered hearing was the pounding of his heart until it faded to nothing.

Weeks later

When people die, do they know it? In his present predicament, Oliver Blue had nothing but time to ponder the question. He breathed through his mouth—at least he thought he still did. He couldn't hear his breaths and he'd lost the ability to feel them.

For all he knew, he had died.

The mask that covered his head cut off air to his nose to block his sense of smell. Goggles and earmuffs made his prison absolute, isolating him in darkness and a never-ending white noise. The only sleep he ever got came when inky black snaked through his hallucinations to smother him in silence. Between his countless nightmares, he'd lost track of how long he'd been lost, strapped down until his body had grown numb.

He gave up screaming. No one ever came. No one ever touched him. He could still remember what his hands and arms looked like, but the rest of him had been harder to imagine—or feel. Isolation and lack of stimulation left him a prisoner, trapped in his own body.

Dr. Fiona knew what would happen to him. She *must* have known. After he gave her attitude, she knew he'd refuse to cooperate, so the doctor had found a way to force him. At first he hated her experiment. Hated *her*. Eventually—from the hours of solitude—he learned to appreciate what she'd done. Dr. Fiona had shown him the truth. His brain had to adapt. It was the only part of him that he *felt* now, except for—

Caila. He let his mind picture her face, the girl who'd been taken with him, by the Believers. He sensed her and knew they still had her. As long as the Believers had the girl, they had him. She was the only thing that kept him alive and struggling for every breath.

Caila.

Oliver imagined whispering her name in the dark and pretended to hear his voice doing it. Her name stirred something in him. *Something real, something he could truly feel.* He remembered her hesitant smile and the way her ice-blue eyes lit up when she looked at him. She'd planted a piece of her in him like a precious seed. Caila had branded him, using her gift. It'd been the only thing she could do before the Believers separated them. He had plenty of time to remember what happened.

The night they were taken, they'd been trapped in that dark alley outside the warehouse, surrounded by armed men who moved with the precision of a SWAT team. Some of the details were fuzzy, but the girl's face remained sharp in his mind. He remembered everything about her, and when he'd lost all hope for their escape, Caila took away his fear. She wrapped him in her arms and kissed him. That kiss shocked him, but something powerful overcame his panic. She made him forget the danger. For that split second all he saw—all he felt—was her. A fragile part of her, trapped in that frightening and intense moment, had stayed with him.

Now the seed of Caila's memory had sprouted even more and deepened its roots in him when he needed her most. He wanted to be with her and pulled every memory he had of her to trigger his senses. When he felt her as if she were with him, a change began. A tremor started deep in his brain— the source of his power—an excruciating, glorious pain. A dim light in the distance pierced the darkness. It stabbed his eyes and blinded him. His head ached from the false light.

Like dust adrift on the wind, his body splintered into countless tortured pieces. He welcomed the agony, as he would've welcomed death.

Oliver lifted from the weight of his body and became free of its pain. Still tethered, he hovered over his empty shell and looked down at it. What he saw shocked him. Only his lips and chin showed. Beads of sweat covered what little skin he saw. His lungs gasped for air and his muscles fought the restraints that held down his arms and legs. He couldn't feel any of that. *Nothing.*

He was strapped to a weird lighted table in a dark room. Parts of his body were covered by a slick black material that adhered to his skin as if it were painted on, hooked to tubes that drained and fed him. Machines in the room tracked his vitals and scanned the colors of his brain activity.

He didn't look or feel human. Not anymore.

But after his initial shock—of seeing his failing body—he realized Dr. Fiona had given him a gift. She'd freed him and forced him to leave his body. He felt stronger. She'd turned him into something far greater than he ever thought he could be. Oliver didn't think about what he looked like now and he didn't care. He only focused on one thing.

Caila.

This time when he thought of the girl, he felt her inside him and knew where to find her.

Haven Hills Treatment Facility
Ward 8
After midnight

Caila Ferrie sat in a corner, locked in a darkened cell. With her head down, she let her dark hair fall over her face as she wrapped her arms across her chest. Nothing warmed her, and every echo outside her door made her skin crawl. Soft footsteps and the hushed murmur of voices kept her edgy. She thought they'd take her again. People in white uniforms came for her, day or night, giving her tests and taking blood. They never explained what they did or answered any of her questions. They took, and gave nothing in return.

Ever since they had separated her from Oliver, she couldn't stop thinking about him. What were they doing to him?

She rocked against the wall until her shoulders and spine felt bruised. Through the shadows of her mind, Oliver's mesmerizing green eyes consumed her. She'd brought this on him. The Believers had come for her, something she'd instinctively felt after Zack went missing.

That kiss. She'd betrayed Oliver with a kiss. She could blame her gift, but what would be the point? She was the carrier, the one who had done it to Zack and now Oliver. What she'd done to them hadn't been the first time.

After her parents divorced, that's when her troubles got worse. She remembered countless hours alone and she got shipped between her mother and father as if she were a punishment. Her mother remarried a drunk and her sperm donor was a verbally abusive man who reinvented his life by living with women who had kids. Being a stupid kid, she got attached to her new pretend family until her father found a way to crush her hopes of normal. Overnight he'd force them to leave and never tell her so she could say goodbye. When she cried over losing a sister named Ashley she adored, words she'd heard her father say came back to her in a rush. *"Shut up and quit your crying. Shit happens."* She'd given up any hope of having a real family. It hurt too much.

After she lost Ashley, she quit trying.

When the isolation got to her, her gift took over in subtle ways and in measured pieces that she never saw coming. Little by little she stole memories from other people—normal memories, better ones, to smother those in her real life on days when she felt bad. Her mind filled with faces and smells and the homes of others until those images and sensations replaced her pathetic life. It didn't take long for everything to get mixed up in her head.

She used to keep a diary to remember stuff, until she simply stopped writing it down. After she gave up fighting it, she lost track of what had been real and eventually she forgot where home was. Even if she wanted to, she didn't know how to get back or who she'd be going back for.

Ashley was gone now.

That's when Caila's survival instincts kicked in and she hit the road to search for a place where no one would judge her secret life. She couldn't imagine a future where her happiness depended on people who only hurt her. For a girl with nothing to lose, anywhere else would be better than where she'd been, but now she'd brought her troubles to Oliver.

Oliver. Forgive me.

When she called to him and didn't feel him, Caila jumped to her feet. She ran for the small mattress in her cell and curled under the blankets and covered her head. Her skin prickled and sent chills over her body. It felt as if tiny spiders crawled over her. Big spiders she could tolerate, but something about the little ones terrified her. She couldn't stop rocking and her whole body shook.

But when the small room lit up, she saw the light through the covers and she felt the weight of a presence in the small space. She held her breath and stopped rocking. She didn't dare move. She couldn't remember hearing the cell door open. *How did they get inside?* When no one grabbed her, Caila pulled the covers from her head and peered out from under the blanket.

Her eyes grew wide when she saw Oliver. He looked dead. *No, it can't be.* She'd had this nightmare before. He'd come to her in her dreams, bloodied and mutilated, but this time he looked real. Caila couldn't believe what she saw.

"Oh my God. What—?" She couldn't finish.

Oliver had come to her. At least she thought it was him. He wore the same thing she remembered from the first time they'd met through Zack. Oliver stood tall in worn jeans and an unbuttoned chambray shirt that left his chest and stomach exposed. She had a memory that she'd picked out that shirt for him from a donations bin, but she didn't know if that was real or something she'd done with Zack. When Oliver cocked his head, his long hair fell over his eyes, the way Zack's used to do. She wanted to brush it from his face as an excuse to touch him.

But something was different about Oliver.

His hair, dark as a raven's wing, shone in blue shimmer as if moonlight dusted its magic over him. The light came from inside him. It pulsed and felt warm against her skin. Seeing the strange unnatural glow wedged her throat tight. Until he smiled a fragile shy grin and she realized it was really him. She wanted to run to him, but a horrifying thought stopped her.

"Are you…dead?" Her voice cracked.

Oliver didn't answer her. He opened his mouth, but nothing came out. The effort looked as if it pained him. Caila trembled and her eyes burned from the tears she held back as she stared at Oliver. His gentle blue light shone and lit the shadows of her room. *My fault. This is all on me,* she thought. When he took a step toward her, she flinched. Caila couldn't hide her fear of him, and from the expression on his face, that hurt Oliver.

"I don't understand. How can you be here with me…like this? How did you get in here?" She didn't expect him to answer, but before he tried, she had a desperate urge to ask, "Can I touch you?"

She didn't wait. When she stood and reached for him, her fingers drifted through his body, yet she felt something odd. She felt the sucking pull of gel, as if he were almost solid, and her small hand left an impression on his stomach like pressing into clay. When she looked up at him, to see if he felt her touch, she got her answer. He shook his head and a tear trailed down his cheek.

He felt nothing.

"What have they done to you?" she asked.

What have I done?

No matter how hard she tried, she couldn't hide the shock on her face. He pulled away from her—looking hurt and alone—before he vanished into a swirl of mist that lingered. Caila rushed to where he'd stood and breathed in his vapor and felt his chill on her skin like a winter fog.

She didn't know if Oliver was alive or dead...*or something else.*

"No, please..." she cried, with her arms clutched around her as she crumpled to the floor "...don't leave me."

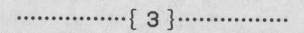

{ 3 }

Rayne Darby had on her lucky stuff, a black Guns N' Roses "Sweet Child O' Mine" T-shirt with her favorite jeans that were shredded on the thighs and her dark brown café racer motorcycle boots. Both wrists were laced with leather, and beads coiled around them. She wanted to kick ass today in her best gear. If her parents had been alive and knew she planned on declaring war on a church, they would have totally grounded her.

A spotlight shone down on her as she stood in the cool darkness of a large room and stared at a man's lighted silhouette twenty-five yards away. The tiny details of his face didn't matter to her. Only one guy haunted her mind whenever she held a gun in her hands, like now.

The Stewart Estate had a firing range located in its basement, along with other rooms Gabriel and his uncle Reginald had dedicated for training. The Stewarts came from a long line of Indigos. The family had taken every opportunity to hone their abilities because they knew they'd need every protection possible. The others had powers that made weapons unnecessary. Rayne was the only one who clocked time at the firing range. At first Gabe had resisted the idea of her with a gun, but when she told him that he might not always be around to be her white knight in blue flames, he reluctantly agreed to lend her a handgun and show her how to use it.

She'd come alone to practice with a Glock 21, but Gabe's ghost dog Hellboy had followed her. She welcomed the company, but the dog must have sensed her jittery mood and paced the floor behind her, whining.

"Settle down, boy. I can't kill you, remember? I'm the only one in danger here. I could shoot my eye out."

Guns made her nervous. She had to get over that. Not long ago, she'd pointed a gun at Boelens, a cruel man who hunted kids for the Believers. He'd made fun of her for not knowing about the gun's safety. She was determined that wouldn't happen a second time. If she ever had that man in her sights again, she'd know which end to point and how to wipe the smirk off his face.

Staring at the paper target of a man's silhouette, she imagined facing someone who could shoot back. She got the cold sweats every time she pictured standing in front of Boelens again. With her eyes on the target, she slipped on her protective goggles, but before she donned her ear muffs, a low voice with a faint British accent sent shivers down her arms.

"You look quite fetching in those goggles."

When she turned to see Gabriel standing on the edge of the spotlight, she smiled and put down her weapon.

"That's something a girl doesn't hear every day."

He walked up and pressed his warm body against her back. He fit in all the right places as if he'd been made for her. Rayne couldn't help it. She stifled a gasp when he ran fingers through her hair and she felt his breath on her skin.

"Protection is important," he whispered in his sexy British accent as he nuzzled and kissed her neck.

"Are you here to give me a...lesson?" She leaned back against his chest and let him wrap his arms around her.

"You need one?" He put his lips next to her ear. "Anything you want, I'm your guy."

Rayne heard the smile in his voice. She fought a grin too.

"Give me the rundown one more time and do it slow. I want to remember everything."

It would have been easy to stick with the flirty teasers and kiss Gabriel all afternoon, but he took weapons seriously and she did too. Too much was at stake and she hadn't forgotten the reason she wanted to practice. After Gabe pulled away, he stayed at her back and spoke in her ear as she stared at the target, the *second* object of her growing obsession.

"You must do one very important thing before you ever pick up a gun," he told her.

"Oh yeah? What's that?"

"Read the manual. Not everything comes with instructions, but firearms do. Take advantage of that."

After she moaned and flashed back to high school, she said, "Okay, I got a homework assignment. What comes next?"

"Find a suitable target, preferably very bad men. Not me," he said. "And don't fire at Hellboy. You'll only piss him off."

"I'd never shoot your dog." Rayne winced. "Not on purpose."

"Ah...your confident assurance makes *me* feel much better, but my four-legged friend is another matter."

When she looked down at Hellboy, the phantom dog cocked his head and perked a blue shimmering ear.

"I swear he understands every word you say." She smiled.

"Funny. He never listened when he was alive. Being dead has improved his disposition."

"Okay, don't shoot dead dogs. Got it. What's next?"

Gabriel went down the list, cautioning her to keep her finger outside the trigger guard unless she was ready to shoot. He had her practice holding the gun until she felt more comfortable and watched her rack the slide to load the chamber.

"Spread your feet, shoulder width." He moved his fingers along her arms as she aimed and repeated what he'd told her, about where to place her feet, knees and elbows.

"Firm grip and lean forward a bit," he said. "Now align the front sight with the rear one and aim for center mass. No fancy head shots, Annie Oakley. When you're ready, take a deep breath and let it out before you squeeze the trigger."

Gabe slipped her earmuffs over her head and put on his own gear before he stepped out of the way. When he gave her the thumbs-up, she took her deep breath and aimed her Glock.

Rayne squeezed the trigger and blasted the target. This time she didn't close her eyes.

Stewart Estate
Afternoon

That's it! You're there. Don't stop.

Lucas Darby kept his eyes shut and strained to hold on as he listened to the voice in his head. His body shook as if every fiber of his being were about to shatter like a frag grenade.

I can't do this, he argued.

Yes, you can.

He stood alone in a training room belowground on the estate. When the acoustic tiles on the ceiling and red carpet under his feet shifted, his stomach reacted to the unsettling vertigo. In seconds everything went black and he didn't feel the floor under his feet. Streaks of white bombarded him like blowing snow, but each particle made noise. Shrieks and whispers echoed by him as if he were speeding past.

His outstretched arms ached as his mind raced through the blur of entities too countless to truly feel. He didn't know if the minefield of souls was dead or alive. The act of sifting through them felt like drowning. They squeezed in on him and smothered him with their maddening need to link to him.

He sensed the spirits of the living and the dead, both human and animal. They pinged off him as light would reflect across countless mirrors, building speed. Everything came fast and nothing made sense. His strongest instinct was to protect himself, as if he were under attack.

Not ready. I can't breathe.

Hold on! You're almost...

Lucas stopped listening. He couldn't slow down and he couldn't stop the pain. Heat burned in his belly and burst through his arms and legs, detonating him into splinters of hurt. He hated it. He should have been in control, but every second felt as if he'd been free-falling through hell. An outsider had crawled into his skin and wore it. That stranger, who punished his body from the inside out, was Gabriel Stewart.

Hang on. Don't...

"Shit!"

Lucas shut the voice off—shut down everything—and dropped to his knees. He couldn't take it anymore and let go. The release hurt almost as much. His abrupt freedom sent agonizing waves of energy coursing through his body like the sudden stop of centrifugal force. He could breathe again, and everything slowed when his muscles released their tension, but the aching hollowness of his failure replaced the worst of it.

For days Gabe had been running drills that tested the hive connection they shared. Lucas got pushed harder than the other dozen Indigo children who were staying at the estate. Gabriel and Kendra believed he was on the path to becoming a Crystal child like Gabe. That was another evolutionary step beyond the more warriorlike Indigo children. A Crystal child was a peaceful protector as well as an incredibly strong psychic. Lucas was pure Crystal child, unlike Gabe, who had developed his hybrid abilities first as an Indigo before he transcended into becoming a Crystal child, encompassing the best and most powerful of both worlds.

As it turned out, Lucas had a lot in common with his counterpart, but their psychic muscle and aptitude for the bizarre were the only things they shared. Linking to the Indigo warrior rage in Gabriel—the violence he was capable of—made the drills pure agony for him.

On his knees, Lucas doused his face with bottled water. Sweat poured off him, and his whole body felt weak as if he'd run a marathon without a day of training. Being held in a mental hospital for years had made him soft.

"What happened? You broke it off before you got to the shotgun part. You had it, Luke. You were almost there." Gabriel barged into his training room where he'd been isolated on purpose.

"No, *you* were doing it, not me. This is insane. I can't do it." Lucas got off the floor and wiped his face with the towel he had draped over his neck. Mental sparring with Gabriel had turned into a fierce workout that went beyond the physical. Gabe would expect him to sacrifice his beliefs. It was bound to happen, but he wasn't sure he could do that.

"This isn't just an exercise to build up my abilities, is it?

I know where this is heading…what you expect me to do, but I'm not made of ice like you, Gabe."

"What's that supposed to mean?"

The silence between them became deafening. Lucas gulped water to give him time to figure out what to say. When the Effin twins came into the room, along with a few others, Lucas should have stopped for Gabriel's sake, but he didn't.

"Harnessing this kind of power is meant…to destroy. I don't think I can kill another human being to save my own life." He blurted out the words, not caring how they sounded. "That would make me no better than them."

No one said anything.

The glare that Gabe had on his face softened, but it didn't go away. He took a deep breath and heaved a weighty sigh that reverberated off the acoustics of the training room.

"Damn it, Luke. You think this is easy for me?" Gabe's voice was low and barely above a whisper. "Contrary to what you might believe about me, I've never killed anyone, but you don't know what we'll be up against. You've only seen a fraction of what they can do. They'll learn from their mistakes. They already killed Benny, but things will get worse."

Luke crossed his arms. He felt like crap, especially after he saw the disappointed look in Gabe's eyes. He respected the guy. He just didn't have to agree with him.

"Look, the church will see most of these kids as expendable, but I can't tell them that," Gabe said, only loud enough for him to hear. "I understand your view and it's brave and commendable, but this isn't a theoretical discussion about violence and how men should live. The reality is that we've got to step up. We're the only ones who can protect them against men who don't have your scruples."

Lucas hadn't thought about how vulnerable the others were. It was one thing to put his own life on the line and accept the consequences, but could he sit back and watch the Believers launch another attack like the one that killed ten-year-old Benny? The homeless kid had just wanted to belong to some kind of family—and Kendra and her group had taken him in. Until the Believers flushed them out of their tunnels like rats, killing Benny without provocation. For Lucas, the act of killing another human being—no matter how justified the reason—would tear down the foundation of his humanity. But so would sitting on the sidelines and watching others around him dying without doing a thing. Doubts waged war in his head.

Gabe turned to walk away before he lost his temper, but when he stopped and turned back, Luke braced for more.

"What would you die for, Lucas? Would you kill to protect your sister?"

Lucas felt the heat rush to his face.

"I shouldn't have to," he said.

"Yeah, exactly." Gabe dialed back the attitude. "In a perfect world, human beings don't kill their own kind and they don't hunt kids in secret. Pull your head out and open your eyes, Luke. Perfect doesn't exist."

Gabe stormed from the room and never looked back. As he left, he said, "Training's over for today."

Lucas felt like shit.

Midnight

Gabriel Stewart had awakened from a restless sleep, drenched in sweat with his sketchbook in his lap as he sat on the floor next to his bed. He flipped on the lights to see the face of another kid in trouble staring back, and his drawing triggered flashes of his nightmare vision. Gabe knew sleep would be impossible, after the intensity of the dream. He had to get out and breathe fresh air. After he splashed water on his face, he got dressed in jeans and a hoodie sweatshirt and took the sketchbook with him.

He'd drawn more faces over the past week. His connection to those kids had come through Lucas. He felt it. In the quiet of the mansion at this hour, Gabe was alone with his dark thoughts as he crept up the winding stairs of the highest tower that overlooked the estate grounds, one of his favorite places to think. When he got to the rooftop of the mansion, he leaned against a parapet to look out over the valley. The night sky flickered with countless stars, and a sliver of the moon dappled its sparing light over the rolling foothills. A cool breeze tousled his hair as he faced into the wind. As a child, he'd felt as if he stood on the top of the world here, but now the weight of that world felt crushing.

Being alone with his thoughts, he felt the magnitude of what he was doing. He'd spent weeks training kids to use their psychic gifts to fight—to defend themselves against people who could kill them. At first he made it an amusement for the little ones, to give their minds a chance to process what he eventually wanted them to do. He didn't know how to explain human cruelty to kids, especially when they were the target. The dark way his mind worked now, to anticipate what the Believers could do to them, wasn't something he ever wanted to share with anyone. That reflected more on *his* disturbing nature.

The death of his mother, at the hand of his father, had changed everything. His childhood ended the day she died. With everything she gave him, she'd prepared him as best she could and opened a door to his future. But thanks to his father, he'd have to live that future without her.

The beauty of the Bristol Mountains at night wasn't enough to distract him from thoughts of his father, the stress of the training or his argument with Lucas. It was bad enough that he had to look into the young faces of the Effin twins and ask the brothers to concentrate on the hypothalamus gland of the human brain and give control over to him. He didn't want the boys to know how deadly he could adapt their gift. That gland controlled the four Fs—the instincts to fight, flee, feed and fuck. Only one would be an excellent way to die.

But if it came to it, he'd be the one to kill, not the twins. He had to insulate them from the violence somehow and he hoped Rayne's brother, Lucas, would feel the same. As a Crystal child, Luke had equal potential for channeling and amassing the Indigo powers of the collective, but in training today he deliberately shut Gabe down. He refused to use his abilities to test his limits and he didn't agree with his tactics. The kid was only fifteen and had spent his last few years in a mental hospital. Gabe should have cut him slack, but he couldn't afford to, not when innocent lives were at risk.

After they had words, he hadn't seen Lucas and he hadn't talked to Rayne since he'd seen her at the firing range. The stress of the long hours of training had taken a toll on them. The gravity of what they were doing—and what they prepared for—had worn them down.

Rafael Santana had it rough too. He was still dealing with his gunshot wound, but an even deeper injury to his heart had been caused by the death of little Benny, a kid he loved like a brother. Rafe had an inner strength and resolve Gabe could use. He was eighteen and had the respect of the others, but he wasn't a team player. Gabe wasn't sure he could count on him.

Between Rafe and Kendra and Lucas and the twins, Gabe had more people counting on him for safety and a future than ever before. He wasn't used to caring for others. But he also knew that they wouldn't be able to hide out here for long.

Taking the fight to the Believers had to happen. Gabe couldn't sit back and watch from a distance anymore. Not when he knew that it was *his* father who was the leader of a legion of religious fanatics bent on destroying their kind. His father's maniacal mission to eradicate Indigos and Crystal children had been instigated as a reaction to Gabe's own manifesting powers when he was a boy. From what Lucas had told them, through his nightmarish mental links to the kids being experimented on in Ward 8 of Haven Hills, the church would stop at nothing to destroy what they feared. They didn't believe that the Indigo kids—the teens with growing mental powers and connections—were the next evolution of mankind. Instead they thought these kids—mostly innocent, mistreated by family and misunderstood by a world not yet ready for them—were an abomination that had to be wiped out, enslaved or turned into nothing more than controllable human lab experiments.

His father had an agenda, wrapped in dogma, to justify persecution and genocide. In his father's mind, the ends justified the means. Not a new concept in man's history, but explain *that* to the kids who were on the receiving end of such atrocities. His father had to be stopped. Gabe didn't have to be clairvoyant to know he'd soon have to confront the man—face-to-face—but one question stopped him cold.

If it came to it, could he kill him?

The man had taken everything that truly mattered from him, but would revenge for his mother's death be enough? His mother wouldn't agree. She'd never want him to use his abilities to kill, but he still had the children to think about. Their lives were in his hands now.

He'd been so intent on his deadly thoughts that he didn't

hear Rayne walk up behind him. She had to speak to catch his attention.

"Hey," she whispered. "I'm getting good at finding your hiding places. I hope you don't mind company."

When he turned, Rayne gave him a shy smile, tinged with the uncertainty that she'd intruded on his privacy. She had on plaid pajama bottoms and a SpongeBob T-shirt and stood wrapped in a blanket draped around her shoulders. Even with all the fancy clothes in the armoire in her room— the offerings for the guests at the estate—she chose Sponge-Bob, something of her own to wear, and Gabe loved her all the more for it. He opened his mouth to say something, but Rayne shook her head and raised a hand to stop him.

"You don't have to explain what you're doing here…or why you can't sleep." She smiled and crossed her arms to brace against the cool night air and tugged the blanket around her. "Is that your new sketchbook?"

"Yeah. At this rate, I'll have to buy a new one soon."

"Mind if I take a look?" Rayne held out her hand.

She'd learned to ask permission since the first time she'd seen his visions on paper, the ones he drew without fully being awake. His sketchbook was out of bounds and private. He flipped the artist's pad open to his latest rendering, the one he wanted her to see. The drawing disturbed him so much he couldn't say anything.

"Oh my God. You saw this?" she gasped with her eyes on the dark vision. "No wonder you can't sleep."

She stared at the tortured face of a boy in a helmet, with his mouth gaped open in a silent scream. The kid's head and eyes were covered and his body was strapped down. The sketch reminded Gabe of the horrors and mutilations of the Inquisition, a disturbing period in history that he'd learned about from his mother when she'd homeschooled him.

"The guy in the helmet is in real trouble, and things are getting worse. I feel it. These Indigo kids aren't asking for the world, Rayne. They only want what should be theirs—a home where they can be safe with people who love them, a normal life where they aren't judged…or hunted for what they can't help being. I feel responsible for what happens to them now."

"I know you do. I can see that. But you saved my brother and these kids once. I know you'll find a way to help them again. If it makes a difference, I believe in you."

Gabe wished that Rayne's faith in him would be enough to cut through his doubts, but it didn't. He felt like a poser. Before he could say anything, she pulled him into her arms and kissed him with his sketchbook pressed between them. When he pressed his lips to hers, his fingers ran through her hair as heat rose from his belly and spread. Loving Rayne had been easy. He only wished that one day loving her would be his whole world.

After Rayne kissed him, she looked at the sketch he'd drawn of the screaming boy and said, "Just hold me." She burrowed into his arms and nuzzled her warmth to his chest. He kissed her forehead and breathed in the smell of lavender soap and something uniquely Rayne. The minute he held her in his arms, Gabe knew that he'd kill to protect her—even if his father stood in his way.

With that thought, a familiar anger stirred in his belly and burned like a seething, hot ember, braced by the never-ending love he had for his mother. For him, all the wrongs of the Believers had a face, the man calling the shots in Los Angeles. He closed his eyes and fixed on his father.

Alexander Reese.

Los Angeles, California
Hours later

Gabriel had finally come to face the past he could no longer outrun.

The boy felt his way through the darkness as easily as if it were daylight. Inside the formidable walls that surrounded the secluded estate, Gabriel kept watch of the men who patrolled the grounds. Dressed in black uniforms and armed, guards patrolled the posh residence in pairs, but Gabriel sensed every turn they made and anticipated their moves even before they made them. In evasive and fluid maneuvers that looked more like perfectly timed choreography, he ducked behind shrubs and crept through the deep shadows cast by the trees pushing too hard, risking too much. It was as if he dared these armed men to catch him.

The moon shed little light, but the boy navigated the dark using his powerful gifts of second sight. A reckless kid playing a dangerous game. The darkness would be a handicap only for the men who protected the estate—defending the man he'd come to confront.

Gabriel melded into the shadows and vanished as he got close to the house. He dissolved like mist that drifted in the night. But when a floorboard creaked on the grand staircase, his heart pounded in his chest. He couldn't stop his body from reacting. Gabriel crept toward the master suite. When the bedroom door opened with only a whisper of warning, everything had come to that moment. A boy would face his father. For the first time in years.

He wanted to move but couldn't. He stopped breathing. His lungs burned as if they were on fire. The years of Gabriel running, hating and grieving had gathered force to drive him here. The boy stood over the bed and glared at the man who had ruined his life and destroyed his mother.

A commanding power stirred in Gabriel. It seethed like a festering heat and he shook with its magnitude. When he couldn't contain it anymore, shafts of searing light burst from his mouth and eyes and hurled energy into a rising force. Gabriel fixed his preternatural eyes on the one he'd come to finally confront, and the man winced in terror at his son and cried out.

Alexander Reese finally understood what his boy had become.

"No!" He jolted off his pillow.

Alexander Reese sucked air into his lungs like a drowning man and stared into the darkness of his bedroom. With his body drenched in sweat, he searched the room looking for anything that moved. At first his eyes played tricks on him. Shadows stirred his worst imaginings and even noises that should have been familiar made him strain to listen harder. He had to blink to make sure he was awake.

"Gabriel," he whispered. A tear trickled down his cheek. That nightmare felt as real as if it had happened. A part of him wanted his runaway son to be there for purely selfish reasons. Except for a blurry surveillance photo, he hadn't seen his eighteen-year-old boy since his mother had taken him with her in the middle of the night too many years ago. Beyond wanting to see the young man he'd become, Reese never wanted to lay eyes on the boy again—for Gabriel's sake.

Even though he still felt the enduring presence of his son in his memory, he sensed that he was alone. Only his shame lingered, over what had happened to Gabriel—and what fate would have in store for the boy. His mother, Kathryn, had been to blame for how his child's life had turned out. Her deceit had pitted father against son. A twist in Reese's gut always came when he thought of Kathryn. She'd destroyed his happiness and tested his faith in his church.

Yet something more disturbed him than a past he'd been ashamed of.

Given the security at his estate, Reese knew breaching the defense measures of his home and grounds would be hard for anyone to crack. He found it odd that in his hellish nightmare he believed that Gabriel had done it.

"Damn."

With a shudder, he sank back onto his damp sheets and stared at the ceiling with the sound of his breathing and the thud of his heart filling his head. Ever since he'd found out that Gabriel had come back to L.A., nightmares were his constant companion.

In truth, he dreaded seeing his son again. Not merely for what the boy had become, but Reese didn't want to face what he'd be forced to do to his son in the name of his faith and his duty. How far would he go to sacrifice what he fervently believed, that these children were a new plague, a mutation that could destroy mankind? His faith demanded that man be held to a different standard—a far superior ranking— than any other living thing. As believers in God and made in the Creator's image, man had a duty to survive and defend his right to life against anyone who would threaten his future—even if that menace came from beings masquerading as human. His son's "condition" did not hold him harmless from blame. Innocence would not be justification for allowing his kind to coexist. They'd be an affront to humanity, especially if they believed they were superior.

Gabriel hadn't asked to be a genetic mutation. Reese blamed his dead wife for what happened. She'd tricked him into fornicating with her to create a child. He'd come to despise her for what she'd driven him to do—to correct his "mistake." Fathering Gabriel had become his secret and also the reason he had volunteered to head up operations in L.A.

He'd given the boy life. Who'd have more right to take that life away? It wouldn't be easy for him, but he would make the personal sacrifice to fix what he'd done. Kathryn had deceived him with her mockery of love in order to procreate a new enemy of man, spawning more like her.

Reese couldn't think of Gabriel as his child anymore. He had to forget his responsibility to the boy, because he had a greater purpose now. He had done his best to distract his organization from finding his son after he'd disappeared. When the boy went into hiding, it had made his job easier, but now it would appear Gabriel was flaunting what he knew. He had threatened to expose his secret by sending him a peculiar message through one of his mercenaries.

Even Fiona had seen the odd drawing his son had made— a picture of *him*. As leader, Reese relied on his anonymity within his compartmentalized organization. Few knew his face or name. That sketch had sent a clear message. Gabriel intended to stir things up. He'd been seen with the Darby girl. He wasn't keeping a low profile. It wouldn't take much for anyone in his organization to realize their relationship if Gabriel got caught and talked—especially if he accused him of being responsible for Kathryn's death.

Reese had covered his tracks, but shining new light on a closed case wouldn't be good. A car accident could turn into a murder investigation and detectives would open his life up to public scrutiny. The way he saw it, he had no choice now. If he wanted to keep his secret, he had no recourse but to kill the boy.

After he took a deep breath, he almost dismissed the lasting remnants of his bad dream, but something made him sit up and search the darkness again.

"What the hell?"

His nightmare could have merely been triggered by his chronic humiliation over Gabriel and Kathryn—except for one, hard to ignore, undeniable fact. Something very real had been left behind.

The smell of Kathryn's perfume.

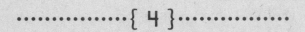

{ 4 }

West Hollywood
Morning

Dr. Fiona Haugstad had spent the night tossing and turning. She blamed her lack of sleep on eating too late and an overindulgence in red wine at dinner the evening before that left her with a morning headache. She'd hoped to share her meal with Alexander Reese, but after he declined to join her, she wallowed in a pity party of one. A heady merlot had kept her company instead.

"One day, Alexander," she muttered as she ran a hand through her blond hair and stretched.

In a bleary-eyed fog, she tossed off her bedcovers and slipped a silk robe over her pale blue nightgown before she headed for her bathroom. She turned on her shower on high and let the water heat as she stared into her mirror. If she were younger, Alexander Reese might not have resisted her invitation for a very private late-night dinner at her home, but she refused to succumb to any feelings of inadequacy.

The man simply didn't know what he'd missed. His loss, not hers.

Fiona stripped out of her robe and nightgown, letting the

garments drop to the floor at her feet. Naked, she turned toward the steaming shower, but something made her stop.

She caught a glimpse of something dark —behind her, reflected in the mirror. Fiona gasped and covered her bare breasts with her hands. As she stared into the fogging mirror, she saw a face with startling eyes and a peculiar smile.

Oliver Blue.

His body flickered like a sputtering candle, only partially covered in slick black strips of prototype material designed to prevent bed sores. Dark goggles and the sensory deprivation helmet flashed in and out to reveal his tortured face trapped inside it. It was as if he'd breached a barrier, yet couldn't stay.

"Is it...r-really you?" she stammered. He didn't answer.

A deep contusion on his belly caught her eye. The shape of the bruise looked odd. The scientist in her wanted a closer look, but when tortured screams erupted all around her, she covered her ears and collapsed to her knees. Fiona felt sure the cries were his, but when she looked at him, his haunted face only flinched into a pained grin.

"How did you...?"

Fiona couldn't stand it any longer. She got to her feet and rushed toward the door with her heart hammering in her chest, but when she looked over her shoulder, Oliver had vanished into the billows of steam from her shower.

"Oliver?" she whispered.

Fiona waited for the wild-eyed boy to chase after her and terrorize her in her own home. When nothing happened, she dared to step back and peer into her bathroom. She only heard the rumble of her shower.

No shadow. No Oliver Blue.

Fiona blinked and leaned against the counter with her legs feeling weak. Anyone else, in any other line of work, might have blamed the hallucination on alcohol...or guilt. But Fiona wasn't delusional and she didn't *do* guilt. She chose to think like a scientist on the verge of a great discovery.

Although her heart hadn't calmed down, Fiona actually felt a strange exhilaration over what had happened. She'd set the whole thing in motion weeks ago. Oliver had been her very private experiment. Not even Alexander Reese knew what she'd done to the boy.

Fiona rushed to get ready. She had to see Oliver. Her next steps with him would be critical.

Stewart Estate, Bristol Mountains

Lucas had been plagued by doubt ever since his confrontation with Gabriel Stewart during training yesterday. Feeling restless, he'd gotten up early and gone for a cross-country run on the estate. The steep mountain climbs had been challenging and he'd worked up a sweat, but the intense workout didn't make anything clearer.

After his run, he doused his head with water from a garden hose before he toweled off and went inside to clean up. Training with Gabe made him realize how weak his body had become after being locked up and drugged for years in a mental hospital. While the other kids improved their mental gymnastics, Lucas had to get his body in shape too.

Gabe went with him most days. The guy was in much better shape, but he never showed off. He kept Lucas going when he wanted to quit. Only today, Gabe didn't show and Luke couldn't blame him.

What would you die for, Lucas? Gabriel had asked him. *Would you kill to protect your sister?*

Those questions struck him like a punch to the gut. Until now he'd been a kid having others take care of him. No decisions required. Although it felt good to take charge of his life now, he hadn't realized how hard that would be. Others looked to him, as if he knew what he was doing. He didn't feel strong like Gabriel.

Even Rayne had surprised him. She'd risked her life for him and ignored his warning to stay away when he told her that it was too dangerous for her to search for him after he'd escaped Haven Hills. Instead she'd saved him—saved them all—when she refused to give up and had brought Gabriel with her. Lucas only remembered Rayne as a kid, before their older sister, Mia, committed him to the treatment facility. Seeing Rayne grown up reminded him how much of his life that he'd lost.

After he showered, he didn't bother to dry his hair. He got dressed in jeans and a blue T-shirt and went looking for his sister. The door to her room was open and Lucas heard voices. When he poked his head into the bedroom, he found her stirring a small red plastic bowl with a spoon, talking to the Effin brothers. Frederick, the life-challenged butler, hovered near her shoulder. The twin boys had their faces pressed to a tall glass cage that was lit with UVB heat bulbs, peering at Rayne's pet.

"He's an iguana. His name is Floyd Zilla," she told the twins and smiled.

One of the Effin brothers glanced to the other with a quizzical look, communicating telepathically in their usual fashion.

Should we tell her that he prefers Carl?

Lucas blurted a laugh as he joined them, but when Rayne shot him a look, he covered up his amusement with a cough.

"What?" she asked.

"Nothing." Luke shrugged. "Something in my throat."

Rayne shot him a look before she went on with her lizard lecture.

"Floyd is vegan. I made him dinner. Fruit and parsnips mush," she told them. "Want to taste it?"

Both boys grimaced and shook their heads. They couldn't leave the room fast enough.

Lucas glanced into the bowl she had and smirked. "Whoa, he eats that shit?"

"It's good for him. He doesn't have teeth."

"What he *doesn't* need is a nose. That stuff smells like feet."

Frederick winced. "Good Lord, you've made me grateful to be dead."

The ghost butler popped from sight, sounding like a cork rocketing from a champagne bottle.

"Guess we both know how to clear the room." Lucas chuckled.

It felt good to laugh, even though it didn't last long. While he watched Rayne fill Floyd's water dispenser and feed the iguana, he'd been quiet. Too quiet.

"What's up, little brother? You look like you've got something on your mind."

"What? Are *you* psychic now?"

"Mia would freak if *that* was contagious." Rayne meant that to be funny, but she didn't even smile. Neither of them did.

"What do you think Mia's doing…now that she doesn't have your digits anymore?" he asked.

"I have no idea." Rayne stopped what she was doing and Floyd cocked his head, watching through the glass. "I thought I would like the peace and quiet, but…it's almost worse not knowing."

Lucas knew that Rayne had to ditch her old phone because of their sister's persistence. Mia hadn't given up searching for both of them. She had sent threatening text messages and recorded voice mail until Rayne had no choice but to get a burner phone. She'd prepaid for a cell so it couldn't be traced. She hadn't made that decision easily. Cutting off Mia meant his sister didn't trust her either.

"Stay strong, Rayne. It wasn't right that she worked with her church to find me. She didn't even go through the police, at least not the legit cops. Family doesn't do that. She chose them over me."

"I know you don't trust her," she said. "I don't either, but it feels...wrong to cut her out, without at least letting her know we're okay. She's still...family."

Lucas didn't know what to say. Rayne had spent more time than he had with their older sister. Meds had robbed him of years from his life. His memories of his older sister had been tainted by Mia's insistence on locking him up as if she'd been embarrassed of him.

"What she did, it hurts, you know?" he said.

Mia's face lurked in the shadow of Luke's memory. He had no desire to see her again, at least not until he gave it more time.

"I understand. I really do."

Rayne didn't bother to justify what Mia had done and Luke appreciated her for that. He didn't want to believe Mia could have betrayed him by turning him over to the church she worked for. Maybe she'd been brainwashed to think he was really dangerous, but Lucas couldn't afford to risk everything on her motives. He had only his gut instincts to rely on when it came to Mia and he needed to make sure Rayne understood.

"She would've let them send me to Ward 8. Even if she didn't know what they'd do to me, that doesn't mean I should trust her." He ran a hand through his damp hair as flashes of his worst dreams came at him, even in broad daylight. "I believe those nightmares I've been having about that place.

JORDAN DANE

They're too real. I think I'm seeing through the eyes of kids who are being tortured. Bad things, Rayne. That could've been me."

Luke crossed his arms. The nightmares were too fresh and never-ending.

"Gabe's sketchbook is filled with new faces. They scare me," she said. "He thinks he's channeling your dreams."

"Yeah, my visions are getting worse." He fixed his gaze on her. "It's safer for us to assume Mia works for the Believers. She's the enemy now. Even if she's oblivious of what they're doing, letting her in on anything could put all of these kids in danger. It's not just about our family. There's more at stake."

The look of sympathy on his sister's face reassured Luke that she understood, but when she put her arms around him, that sealed the deal. She'd been the only one who hugged him for real. It felt good to have Rayne back. She might be the only family he had left.

"You said Gabe's been drawing?" Luke asked. "He hasn't said anything to me."

"Yeah, about that." Rayne pulled from his arms and forced a smile. "Whatever's been going on between you two, I think you need to talk about it. That's all I'm saying. Please don't put me in the middle."

Lucas sighed and said, "Okay. Thanks for letting me know."

Taking charge of his own life would have to come one step at a time, but that didn't mean there wouldn't be days when he felt like shit doing it.

Gabriel squinted into the sun as he stood with the other Indigos by the fountain in the courtyard, enjoying the warmth on his skin. A beautiful day in the Bristol Mountains was impossible to resist, and Uncle Reginald had planned to take advantage of it. They'd all been working hard, and tensions were starting to show. Instead of keeping them in the training rooms within the basement of the manor house, he had asked Gabe and the other kids to meet him by the trickling fountain in the cobbled patio garden.

Uncle Reginald wore pressed khakis, a pith helmet and binoculars hanging from his neck, as if he were on safari. Coupled with his thicker British accent, his apparel made him look like Rudyard Kipling's Gunga Din in a *Monty Python* skit. Uncle Reginald had a dressing room full of unusual clothing that he'd collected from his travels. Gabe fought a smile when he saw the man's somber expression under his lion tamer hat.

After they were present and accounted for, his uncle simply said, "Follow me, please."

Not even Gabriel knew what his uncle had planned when he took them for a hike into the foothills, along a worn dirt path. They climbed under a dense cover of trees until the trail hit a high meadow filled with wildflowers. Gabriel breathed in the cool air, filling his mind with countless memories. The grassy clearing held a special place in his heart. It had been a favorite spot to picnic with his mother, Kathryn. She always had him carry a basket filled with treats she'd especially prepared for him to try. The goodies were often exotic, yet never the same. His mother believed everything should be an adventure, especially picnics with her only son.

When Gabe got to the open field with the others, near a huge boulder that had meant something to his mother, Uncle Reginald stopped and stood at the base of the stone, waiting for them to gather round him.

"I'd like to try something a little different today." The man waved an arm. "Make a circle please."

The children did as they were told. Rayne had come along,

even though she didn't have the psychic aptitude that her brother, Lucas, had, and Hellboy stayed close to Gabe's heels. Rafael leaned against the boulder behind his uncle, looking completely bored, ignoring "Dead Fred." That's what Rafe had started to call Frederick, hoping the insult might dampen the dead butler's keen interest in him. No such luck. Frederick had become Rafe's occasional companion since the troubled boy could actually see and hear him. He figured the kid needed a friend, and Gabe couldn't argue, even though Rafe might disagree.

In solidarity with the occasion, the butler wore camo hunting gear, a wide-brimmed Indian Jones fedora and hiking boots and had an elaborately carved wooden walking stick for a touch of panache. Why a ghost had to wear camouflage, Gabe wasn't quite sure.

"I'd like you younger children to pair up and work on extending your contact reach." Uncle Reginald grinned, always making the little ones feel as if they were playing a game. "For the fun of it, one will hide and the other will search using your cognitive abilities, then trade off. But please stay within sight of this big rock here. When I blow my whistle…" His uncle pulled a whistle from his pocket and blasted their ears with a shrill demonstration. They all cringed. "Run back and we'll have lunch. Cook has prepared a treat for us. Understood?"

He pointed to the kids and paired them up but kept Rafe, Kendra, Lucas and Gabe behind. He had special plans for them.

"Rayne, be a good girl and watch over the children, will you? These binoculars are for you." He took the binoculars off his neck and handed them to her. "Be my eyes and ears, if you don't mind. Children always find a way to do things they shouldn't."

Before she took off, he put his pith helmet on her head. It hung low and covered half her face. When she laughed, only her teeth showed, and that made Gabe grin.

"Will do," Rayne said, and ran off to locate her charges.

When they were alone, Uncle Reginald fixed his gaze on Gabe and the others and didn't say anything until he had their full attention. Even Rafe closed the circle around him.

"I'm asking each of you to do something that won't be easy. We must learn to rely on one another, to become a real family now. That requires trust."

Gabe should have known their training would come to this. Trust had always been difficult for him. Living life on the run with his mother had meant secrecy ruled. They trusted no one except each other, but his uncle was right. Real trust was the next step.

"Out of necessity, we've all learned to build mind shields to block our private thoughts from being read," the man said. "Being connected to others as we are, it's self-preservation to strengthen our shields and it's a good skill to build upon."

Gabe knew his uncle and he knew there was a "but" coming. The somber look on his face was a dead giveaway.

"There's a reason I bring this up now. There will come a point where we'll leave this home and confront the Believers," he told them.

Gabe hadn't missed the fact that his uncle had used the word *we*.

"Having strong shields may sustain us if we're taken by the Believers," his uncle said. "I know that's not a pleasant thought, but given what we know about each other and this place, it would not be good if we break under pressure. Being able to block...the pain of torture might help us survive and keep these children safe."

Gabe looked at Lucas. They'd shared the same nightmares

of the tortures on Ward 8 at Haven Hills. He hadn't talked about it with Luke, but eventually he'd have to.

"The other side of the exercise will be a challenge. That's why I want you in pairs."

"Pairs?" Kendra asked.

"I'd like you to partner with Lucas, my dear. I'm proposing a test of your mind shields."

"What?" Kendra crossed her arms. "We have shields for a reason. What's private should be off-limits."

"Believe me, I understand your concern. I wouldn't ask any of you to do this if I didn't think it was necessary."

Not even Gabe liked the sound of this. From the looks of the others, they didn't either.

"As we grow stronger, it will require us to establish rules," Uncle Reginald explained. "Ethics, if you will. There will be times we break those rules with others to defend ourselves. In an ideal world, we would all want to live in respectful civility, but the world we live in isn't ideal."

His uncle gazed at each face and let his words sink in before he went on.

"I'm talking about psychic attacks, memory invasions, altering dreams and manipulating the behavior of others."

Gabe glanced at Lucas and Kendra. They'd seen him cross the line of psychic attacks and manipulation after he confronted Boelens and his men in the tunnels. He didn't feel bad about that. Not even a little.

"These tactics have grave consequences, even with the best intentions." His uncle sighed. "Unfortunately, in order to up our game, we must learn how to do these incredibly invasive things. The most responsible way to practice is on each other, the people we trust most."

"On each other? What are you asking us to do...exactly?" Kendra didn't look happy.

"One of you will resist the mind probe by reinforcing your shield while the other will try to break through. Then you will have a go at your partner by switching roles. I don't expect all of you to be successful. Given your abilities, each of you will pose a unique challenge."

"How do we prove that we got past the shield?" Gabe asked.

"Yes, good point." His uncle nodded. "So we can respect each other's privacy, the one breaking through should only take a short glimpse and get out fast. Find a harmless memory and confide that to your partner, no one else. You should not talk about what you see...with anyone. Understood?"

What his uncle had asked them to do wouldn't be easy. Everyone looked worried, but when Lucas shrugged and looked ready to try it, he glanced at Kendra. She clenched her jaw and shook her head, stopping him cold.

"No," she said. "I can't do that. I won't. Not with Lucas."

Luke looked utterly confused. Uncle Reginald could have pressed Kendra for a reason, but he chose a different way.

"I know this isn't easy. I won't pressure any of you, if you're uncomfortable with this method. Like I said, this will take trust and—"

"I didn't say that I wouldn't try," she explained. "If Rafael is okay with it, I choose him."

All eyes shifted to Rafe. He clearly didn't like being the focus of attention, but eventually he shrugged.

"I'm game, I guess," Rafe said. "I got a shitload of crap in my head, but if you can get at it, it's yours."

Before Frederick budged an inch, Rafael pointed at Dead Fred and said, "I got this." The butler only raised an eyebrow and watched him leave with Kendra.

Lucas's face turned red as she left with Rafael. The kid looked lost.

"Don't read into it. Letting someone behind the curtain of Oz for the first time… It'll be hard for all of us," Gabe told Luke under his breath, so no one else heard. "She's known Rafe longer. That's probably all it is."

Lucas nodded, but he didn't look as if he bought his explanation. Gabe felt sorry for the guy, but that didn't mean he'd go easy. Luke was a Crystal child, like him. If they were meant to survive, the kid had to step up. They all did.

Haven Hills Treatment Facility
Ward 8

Fiona had been so eager to see Oliver that she pulled through garage security with only a wave and didn't bother to slow down to show her badge. Everyone knew her on sight, no matter what time of day she came. She went straight to Ward 8 without a detour to her office.

She would never dare admit it to anyone, but as she stepped out of the elevator at Haven Hills, the humid odor and darkness of the corridor outside Ward 8 got to her. It was creepy. She deserved better than to operate out of a basement. Still, the magnitude of her work benefited from absolute secrecy, and within the secured walls of the ward, everything was state of the art. She came and went at all hours, without anyone second-guessing her reason for being there.

Not even Alexander knew how far she'd gone with Oliver. As she walked under the red and white sign of Ward 8 and headed through the double doors of the secured facility, the face of Oliver Blue—and his striking green eyes— obsessed her with every step. The anticipation of seeing him sent adrenaline coursing through her veins.

Fiona had done it. She'd finally achieved something truly remarkable.

She and Alexander and the most dedicated Believers were the only defense against an enemy who lived among them. As a scientist she had to act, especially when she knew that 99 percent of all species that inhabited the earth before man were extinct now because they never saw the end coming. They simply weren't prepared for Armageddon. Fiona felt the threat of kids like Oliver and she was in a unique position to do something about it.

Lately Alexander Reese had different ideas.

He had targeted Lucas Darby as a greater threat because he'd manifested into a Crystal child early at fifteen. If the transformation of Indigos were on the rise, he saw that as a warning sign that they should focus on those kids at the expense of everything else. Fiona didn't have blinders on when it came to viable targets.

She saw all these kids as potential threats. Lucas Darby had turned into a priority for Alexander, but a distraction to her. That's why she had to keep the man in the dark on her diverging agenda with the Indigos. He wasn't a scientist. He wouldn't understand such scholarly pursuits. It took vision and a keen intellect to see the future as she did and have the guts to do what must be done to these children in order to defend against their potential superiority.

Fiona had always wondered. If she deliberately sense-deprived one of these kids, what would happen to their already responsive brain? Could she escalate their abilities in a controlled experiment? If this were true, they'd be like clay in her hands. She could control evolution, manipulate it or stifle it.

The possibility of that was staggering, especially if she could achieve even a fraction of success with a normal human being. Would that be possible? Could becoming the next evolution be achievable by anyone? Her work could level the playing field, and her vision had the potential to alter the future of all men. She marveled at her impending contribution to history as she headed for the boy's locked cell.

"Oliver, I knew you had potential, a strong boy like you," she said. "Now we'll see how special you really are."

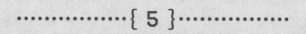

Haven Hills Treatment Facility
Ward 8

Fiona stood outside Oliver Blue's locked door, but she couldn't go in. She stared through the small wire-mesh window to look at him, reassuring her that he was still under her control. After she'd seen him in her bathroom that morning, it had been a very mixed blessing.

Had she manipulated Oliver into exhibiting the first signs of teleporting or had she triggered something darker in him? When she looked into the shadowy room, the boy's legs and torso were strapped to the light table. His mouth gasped for air like a dying fish, and his body jerked as if the erratic twitching was beyond his power to control it. She forced her eyes away from the boy and shifted her focus to the machines that tracked his vitals and brain activity, something easier to watch.

What she'd done had been necessary, to advance science and sustain her faith. The church placed humanity above other creatures, including Oliver Blue and those like him. Seeing the boy and knowing what he'd done to haunt her in her home, she felt justified in her actions to safeguard mankind from a kid like Oliver. Even if she had a hand in making him a monster, the potential within him had given her plenty of reason to do what must be done to control his kind.

Fiona took a deep breath, unbuttoned her suit jacket and opened the door with her ID passkey. She didn't have to be careful about not making a sound. Oliver couldn't hear or see her.

The backlighting of the table cast an eerie glow onto his body, making his twitching more unsettling up close. Fiona couldn't see his face. Only his gaping mouth struggled to breathe. He moaned with the effort, a sound that would only vibrate in his head and not be heard over the white noise she had programmed to play in his ears to control his sleep patterns. As she stood over him, her eyes trailed down his body toward his stomach. His muscles flinched and quivered as he gasped.

But something else caused her to bend closer to see a mark on his shuddering belly. A bruise. Fiona shouldn't have done it, but she couldn't stop her urge. She slowly reached down and placed her hand over the mottled flesh of his stomach. His skin felt warm to her touch and she pressed down to hold him in place as he struggled under her hand.

The boy jerked and cried out, "Who's th-there? H-help me."

The bruise was in the shape of a small hand, smaller than hers. As Oliver called out to her in his delirium, begging for her help, Fiona stroked his belly to calm him, but she didn't say a word.

He wouldn't have heard her anyway.

Minutes later

After Fiona had questioned her staff about the mark on Oliver's body and no one shed light on what had happened, she knew only one way to get to the bottom of the mystery. When she got behind closed doors in her office, she hit the speed dial to the head of security, Stan Caulfield. She never bothered with anyone else.

"I want the surveillance footage for Oliver Blue's room and the corridor outside, plus the card key reports for anyone accessing his room. Top priority, Mr. Caulfield."

"How far back do you want to go, Dr. Haugstad?"

Fiona slumped back in her chair with the phone to her ear. She had no idea and had to think. Oliver had been held in that room for over a month, isolated by sensory-deprivation gear, but the bruise looked fresh. Could someone unauthorized have visited him? Staff had been told not to touch him. Any interaction would have been minimal. Although she hadn't seen him in a week, reports from the nursing staff had kept her apprised of his condition, but those records would not account for something remarkable like what she'd witnessed in her bathroom.

"Send me the last week," she told him.

But before she hung up, Fiona thought differently about the bruise that looked like a small hand on Oliver's stomach and played a hunch.

"Give me the same for Caila Ferrie."

"Anything else, Doctor?"

"No, that'll be all."

She hung up the phone and got up from her desk to walk toward the large floor-to-ceiling window in her office. A lovely day. The incredible view overlooked the pristine grounds of Haven Hills, near the back of the property where the secured private delivery bay was located. Whenever she stood by that window, she could look down to see the new Indigo children being delivered—or the bodies being disposed of afterward.

Fiona oversaw everything that truly mattered at Haven Hills. Alexander Reese had seen to that. But now as she faced a critical part of her experiment with Oliver, she had to decide.

When would she let him out of the headgear? And once he was free of it, what new things would she discover in the boy? Despite the ultimate sacrifice Oliver was bound to make for science, he would only be a footnote to history—a practice run for the real thing. Fiona knew her real accomplishment was yet to come. She hadn't forgotten about Lucas Darby. They needed a new lead and good fortune to find him. Alexander Reese's man O'Dell had escalated his efforts to find the boy, without results so far.

Because of Oliver, she couldn't wait to get her hands on a Crystal child—Lucas or that other mysterious boy she'd found on a surveillance camera, traveling with Rayne Darby. Either would do.

Stewart Estate

Kendra Walker knew she had hurt Lucas, but she had her reasons for choosing Rafael to test the strength of her mind shield instead of him. Lucas was too powerful for her to survive his mind attack, and she didn't want him digging around in her head again. She had too much to hide.

When Lucas had been sick with a fever from his concussion—from an injury she had a hand in causing by grandstanding with the Believers—he'd tapped into her memory against her will. He repeated words she'd said and it felt as if he mocked her pain.

"I didn't mean to do it, Daddy. It just…happened. Please don't hate me."

Hearing those words again shoved her right back there, as

if it were yesterday. It was as if he'd read her mind, down to her darkest secret. At the time she tried to reach him in the only way she knew how—with her mind.

No. Stop, Lucas. You don't know what you're saying, she'd told him. *Please don't...*

But he didn't stop. He said it over and over and everything he mumbled brought back a terrifying crush of memories. She felt betrayed, even though he denied doing it and didn't remember what he'd done. She wanted to give him the benefit of the doubt that his delirium had caused it, but the truth was that she didn't know him well enough to trust him with the one thing she couldn't let anyone know.

That dark memory was the only thing she kept from her beloved Indigos.

In a community where privacy of thought was fragile, she had vowed to keep that secret—until she fell in love with someone special. A life should not be built on lies. If she ever fell in love that hard, Kendra would have no choice. She would have to risk losing everything to tell the truth to the one person she hoped would understand and love her in spite of what she'd done.

But Lucas had threatened that vow and her right to choose. Whether he had meant to or not, Lucas had *taken* that memory from her. That was reason enough to avoid him and his ability to get around her shield, but she also felt the strained relationship between her and Rafe, ever since she'd kissed him at Benny's funeral.

That kiss had changed everything.

Once they got under a shade tree in the mountain meadow, Rafael stopped and turned to her. He had a serious expression on his face and Kendra knew he had something on his mind, beyond the psychic exercise they'd been asked to try.

"You can see anything I got. I have no secrets from you," he said.

Kendra had to smile. She'd expected a confrontation, but his honesty and willingness to let her in had surprised her. Mostly she felt like crap for being the complete opposite.

"The point is that you're supposed to block me, make it hard for me to see what you're hiding." She trailed a finger down his arm before she held his hand. "You can't make it that easy."

She caught the twitch of a rare, shy smile. When his face flushed, she knew she'd embarrassed him.

"I know, but if you don't want to do it, I understand," he said. "I'll back you up. You need me to lie and tell them that we did it, I'm good with that."

Rafael knew how to read her. She didn't know if this came from his Indigo nature or it had always been a part of him. He respected her beliefs about Indigos, listened quietly to her rants on injustice and supported her radical ways without much complaint.

But after they both lost everything—Benny and the home that the Believers had destroyed—it had opened her eyes to how much her feelings for Rafe had changed. He'd been the strong one, the one who had his head on straight. They'd been punished because of her arrogance. Her defiance had cost them all, but Rafael never made her feel bad over what happened—not even when she wanted him to blame her for Benny.

What happened made her doubt everything she'd been fighting for. Rafael had been her rock all along. She wasn't worthy of his loyalty, or anyone's, but she had to do her part now.

"No. Gabe's uncle is right," she said. "We gotta do this."

"Then you hit me first. I can take it."

Rafe took a deep breath and turned his back on her. He walked out from under the sprawling tree and headed toward the edge of the meadow and a steep drop-off that overlooked the rolling hills of a valley. She followed him and watched as he sat on the ground and closed his eyes to concentrate.

Kendra didn't sit. She paced through the tall grass at his back. She'd never invaded his privacy before. It felt wrong. He sat there and waited for her to attack him.

I gotta do this.

When she was ready, Kendra stopped directly behind him and found balance in the blue sky that filtered through Rafael's dazzling Indigo blue aura. She centered on the largest cloud and felt her way to him. Connecting to him had always been easy. She sensed him everywhere and gasped at the beauty of his essence, the parts he let her see and feel. She saw God in the Indigo soul.

To attack Rafael, a guy who had seen too much pain in his life, felt like a sin, but she did it for the good of the others. Whatever she would do to him, she knew it would hurt her too. How could it not?

Kendra winced as she ramped up her hit on him, for real. The cliff, the blue sky and even Rafael shifted into black and white, like an old photograph, until everything shrank to a pinpoint and got replaced by total darkness. The birds, the wind and the sound of the Indigo children laughing behind her had shut down fast, like a sucking vacuum that popped her ears. It took time for her eyes to adjust to the void. When swirls of gray broke through, she saw her first glimpse into Rafael.

Massive walls took shape with clangs of metal, strong and impenetrable. They glistened like black obsidian. She stood in the dark at the center of a shadowy maze. Wherever she turned, the labyrinth shifted to form new patterns, like formidable chess pieces blocking her way. Each path reflected back, slick as glass.

In the dim light, she saw her face projected across countless mirrors. Every image captured a different memory she'd shared with Rafe—a smile, a touch and quiet conversations after midnight when neither of them could sleep. She saw her face everywhere, images that had been captured through his eyes.

Rafael? What are you showing me?

She projected her thoughts and reached out to him. He didn't answer her, but more images came in rapid succession. There were more of the same, until she finally understood. Rafael was showing his love for her. He wasn't hiding or shielding how he felt. He meant for her to see and feel it.

Kendra finally saw the countless ways he showed his feelings for her, in everything he did, every small gesture, the gifts he'd stolen to give her, pretending he'd bought them all. Why hadn't she seen it before? She'd been stupid and thoughtless, but most of all, she didn't deserve his love.

Please…stop. I can't…

Kendra felt her heart beat faster as she ran through the black chasm of mirrors with her face staring back, a face she didn't recognize anymore. She should have let the warmth of Rafael's love embrace her, but she didn't deserve to be happy. She ran for the darkest corners of his mind and pushed through the shields that he'd placed in her way, until she broke free.

Deeper in the darkness she heard angry voices and the crush of fists smacking flesh. The grating sounds were muffled in the distance and masked by the voice of a child. It shocked her that the child's laughter made her anxious. Her skin prickled as if fingernails scratched across a chalkboard. She'd heard the laugh before, yet couldn't quite place it.

When she turned to look for the child, a billowing swell of shadows edged closer. A wall of black rain rumbled loud and swallowed everything in its path. Kendra knew she'd never outrun it, but instinct took over. As she ran through the harsh thick rain, it pummeled her with oozing, dripping oil. The smell was toxic and ugly. It clung to her hair and coated her face.

The stench smothered her and made it impossible to breathe. She had to stop running. Her lungs burned with every gasp. When she looked down at her arms and hands, the beads of thick black oil magnified to reveal what they held inside. Every drop glistened with an awful memory that cut into her with a sharp sting, while the child's laughter grew louder.

Kendra knew she'd broken through his shield. He wouldn't have opened this door for her to walk through, not if he loved her. The dark waters of Rafael's past rushed in fast and swept over her, threatening to drown her. She thrashed in panic and she panted for air as if it would be her last breath, but when a new reality exploded in a rush, she wanted to scream. No storm. No dark waters or putrid-smelling oil. She was in a dark, messy room and a man came at her swinging a baseball bat. Kendra cringed and ducked.

No! Stop! she called out to the man, but he didn't listen.

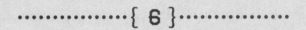

{ 6 }

Stewart Estate

When the angry man in Rafael's memories rushed into Kendra—colliding and slicing through her body as if she were invisible—she felt his rage cut through her. She turned to see where he'd gone and stared into the terrified face of Rafael when he was only a boy. *Stop! Don't do it,* she begged, but the man couldn't hear her.

Whatever she saw now had already happened. All she could do was watch.

Kendra heard the pounding. The smell of blood made her sick and she shivered at the gut-wrenching crack of bone. She collapsed to her knees and covered her aching stomach with her arms, but nothing could distance her from the abuse. Rafe had fought back. She felt his defiance and his shame. He survived his father's assault and ran away from home, barely able to walk, but flashes of his memories, homeless on the streets of L.A., were worse. Rafael had done unthinkable things to survive.

Kendra broke down, sobbing.

"I got a shitload of crap in my head, but if you can get at it, it's

yours." Rafael's voice came to her and reminded her of the risk he'd taken…. *"Hit me first. I can take it."*

She wanted to stop and get out, but when she remembered where she'd heard the laughter of the child, she stayed for Rafe's sake…*and her own.* That's when she saw Benny again. Seeing the dead boy's sweet face, alive and happy through Rafael's memories, broke her heart. She ached for his loss, but she now understood why the child's voice, contaminated by the anger of Rafe's father, had disturbed her so much. The boy who had been Rafael's greatest strength—and his salvation—could now destroy him.

Kendra felt the suffocating heat of Rafe's intense grief all around her as she drifted through the shadows of his darkness. Feeling his pain only reminded her of what she had done—the secret that no one else knew. Rafael was far stronger than she had ever known. He didn't talk much about his past and neither did she, but maybe this was his way of letting her in.

She wandered for what felt like hours, but time had no meaning here. She had to find her way out. When she couldn't take any more, she stopped moving and shut her eyes tight.

She clenched her fists and felt her body stiffen as she pictured the Bristol Mountains—and Rafael waiting for her on the other side. When she broke off her connection to his hellish memories, the sudden shift from darkness to bright sunlight blinded her and a rush of sound punished her ears. She collapsed to the ground and felt the prickling sting of grasses against her skin.

"Oh God," she panted.

She squinted into the sun and held up her hand to shield her eyes. After she realized she'd come back, she stared at Rafael in stunned silence. He scrambled to his feet and rushed to her side to hold her hand.

"What did you see?" he asked. "Did you get in?"

Kendra still felt haunted by the darkness in Rafael. She took a deep breath and struggled to calm the pounding of her heart as she stared into his dark eyes.

"No." She shook her head. "You were too tough. Maybe next time."

She chose to lie, for his sake and for hers. How could she describe what she'd seen and felt without hurting him?

"Yeah, next time," he said.

After Rafael helped her up, he looked as if he wanted to ask her more, but he stopped. An abused and broken boy reflected in his eyes. Why had she never seen that before? Rafael had survived his father, endured his life on the streets and risen to a better place because of his love for Benny. Kendra hoped there was a heaven for him. He deserved it. He'd already done time in hell.

But did he have it in him to keep fighting?

"You wanna try it on me?" she asked.

She tried to sound up for it, but from the look on his face and the slump of his shoulders, she knew what he'd say.

"No." He shook his head. "I gotta...get out of here."

Rafael left her standing on that cliff, watching his back as he left. *Rafael.* She called out to him, telepathically, but he never answered her. What should have brought them closer— her seeing every secret he had and even how he loved her— only made her feel that they were further apart.

He needed to be loved by someone special and deserved someone whole, who could help him get over his busted life—not be a reminder of it. Even if he didn't blame her for what happened to Benny, *she* did. As she watched Rafael walk away, she realized she was as crippled as he was.

How could she help him...*or anyone?*

★ ★ ★

Gabriel led Lucas through the trees to a small pond so they'd have privacy to conduct their psychic attack exercise. The kid didn't say much. He looked distracted by what had happened between him and Kendra. Every time Gabe glanced over his shoulder at him, Luke didn't look happy. He even ignored Hellboy, who had latched to his side like an unearthly shadow. Getting Luke far away from Kendra and Rafe had been Gabe's priority.

When they got to the spring-fed watering hole, the pristine surface reflected the sky like glass. Gabe's mother had always loved this spot, calling it heaven's mirror, and she saved it for occasions when she wanted his mind clear to teach him something new about his abilities. Bringing Lucas here meant a great deal to him. He hoped it would become special to Luke too.

Gabe shrugged out of his plaid shirt and tossed it over a shrub. He left on his vintage black T-shirt for the Slayer Reign in Pain tour and stretched his arms and back. By all accounts, he looked as if he were preparing to work up a sweat.

"You go first," Luke told him. "Offense or defense. Your choice."

"Very considerate of you, Lucas. You're quite the gentleman, but sorry to say, I'm not."

Lucas winced when Gabe cracked his knuckles.

"I was just being…"

"Polite?" Gabe grinned as he circled Lucas with his eyes fixed on the kid. "There's no Boy Scout merit badge for psyche assault. Toss the good behavior and let's improvise."

"How?"

"Let's save time. We'll both go offense."

Luke furrowed his brow and took a moment to think about what he'd proposed.

"You mean we do both? Attack and defend at the same time?"

"Yeah. Let the Indigos do it their way. We should set the bar higher, don't you agree?"

"Uh, yeah. Sure."

The guy nodded and said, "Yeah," but he didn't *look* sure. That made Gabe smile.

"I've got another idea to make things interesting. You game?"

This time, Lucas didn't answer.

The minute Lucas agreed to try something different, Gabriel took off running. It didn't take Lucas long for him to figure out what the guy had in mind. If he wanted to snake his brain and steal a memory, he had no choice. He had to keep up.

"Come on, boy. Let's go." Luke called Hellboy, but the dog only sat on his haunches and looked up into a tree, ignoring them both. "Suit yourself."

Lucas chased after Gabriel. When he broke out in a sweat, he peeled off his windbreaker and tossed it aside as he ran. The guy didn't use the path around the lake either. That would've been too easy. When Gabe cut through the rough hilly terrain and the dense vegetation that surrounded the water, Luke had to leap over shrubs and careen through trees that cut his bare arms.

"Damn."

Before Gabe got too far ahead, Lucas had to make his move. Chasing the guy wasn't getting the job done. He focused his mind on Gabe for a push and fought his way into the essence of his unwilling target. The sound of his boots pounding the ground and his quickening pants faded to a rhythm in his mind as the edge of his sight turned dark. The last thing he saw of his reality was Gabe's back as he glanced over his shoulder.

The guy had a smile on his face.

Inside a murky vision Lucas got a strong odor. Completely disgusting. Intense colors spiraled around him like Christmas lights on a slow spin. The beams streaked through the shadows to give him only brief glimpses beyond the dark veil. He heard voices that felt more real than the Indigo hive, but that smell became annoying and made it hard for him to breathe.

What the hell…?

He felt his body slow down and when he stopped, the colors quit spinning and blotched together in a massive puzzle around him. A huge canvas circus tent took shape with empty bleachers positioned around a center ring. After that happened, the smell had grown too pungent for him to ignore.

When the shrill call of an elephant broke the silence, he looked down to see where the stench came from. Lucas stood in a pile of—

"Crap."

Elephant dung, to be exact. From the size of it, that's what it *had* to be. Luke sidestepped the mess and scraped off the bottoms of his boots. The distraction almost made him miss the soft murmur of a boy's voice coming from outside the tent.

Luke forgot about his boots and went looking for the source of the noise. From the sounds of gurgling and a heavy huff, Lucas knew he would find more than a boy behind the curtain in front of him. He slowed down when he saw a dark silhouette moving on the other side. A gigantic beast shuffled to the gentle coaxing of a young boy's commands.

Lucas inched closer, gripped the curtain edge and pulled

it back. A huge elephant, with faint pink freckles on its flapping ears and a wrinkled head, lumbered around to face him. When the animal turned, Luke saw a boy straddling the elephant's neck. The kid wore a red cape and a glittery feathered turban. He smiled back and Luke knew it was Gabriel when he was a child. He recognized him from the huge circus billboards mounted on the walls of the great room at the Stewart mansion.

Luke had done it. He must've broken through Gabe's mind shield to catch a childhood memory. But when he raised his hand to wave, the elephant squared off in front of him with water dripping from its coiled trunk.

Lucas didn't have time to duck. The elephant heaved its massive trunk like an accusing finger and delivered its payload. It spewed a never-ending stream of water directly into Luke's face. He fell back with eyes shut and gasped for air. Luke expected to hit the dirt, but that didn't happen.

Like a harsh slap, he opened his eyes to find he was flailing underwater. A wall of glistening bubbles and the dark fingers of undulating pond grasses had replaced the circus and that damned elephant. Lucas kicked his legs and stroked his arms, desperate for his next breath until he realized. All he had to do was stand. The water was shallow near the shoreline, but the sudden chill and his survival instincts had broken his concentration. He wasn't in Gabe's head anymore.

What the hell happened? The big top tent was gone and he was drenched. Luke trudged to shore, feeling more than a little confused. Hellboy stood onshore and wagged his tail until his whole body got into it.

"Not funny, Gabe," he yelled.

"Now, that would depend on one's perspective. From where I am, I find it quite amusing."

Lucas hadn't gotten his hearing back, not with water in

his ears. Gabe's voice echoed around him and made it difficult to pinpoint where the sound came from.

"The elephant shit was a nice touch." Luke had to keep him talking.

"I call that sensory stimulation."

When he got to dry land, Lucas spun around and peered through the trees until he heard a soft laugh and looked up. Gabe was straddling a tree limb. The guy had the balls to grin back. It didn't take long for Luke to figure out what must've happened. Gabriel never ran. He'd climbed the tree nearest the spot they'd started their psychic attack exercise. No wonder Hellboy never got into the chase. The dog knew better.

"But how...?"

"I made you think that I ran. I used memories of our morning runs and embellished your senses with some of my own experiences. I created an illusion inside an illusion."

Gabe explained that he respected Lucas's abilities and went on the assault fast to get a jump on him and keep him off balance. Since he couldn't be sure Luke had ever been to a circus, he'd used images from the billboards displayed in the great room to make him think he'd broken through to his real memories. The guy had outclassed him so badly that Luke didn't know where to begin to compete with a mind that thought the way Gabriel did. He had a lot to learn.

"How did I end up in the water?"

"I didn't push you, if that's what you're asking." Gabe leaned back, propped against the tree trunk. "You fell in, I'm afraid. Be assured, I wouldn't have let you drown in two feet of water."

"I never got beyond your mind shield, did I?" Luke stood by the pond, soaking wet. "You let me see the circus so I'd think that I'd broken through."

Gabriel dropped down from the tree.

"That was human nature and the merits of a strong offense, Lucas. I let you see what you expected to see so you'd stop and give up your assault." He shrugged. "I've been at this longer than you, and my mother was a good teacher."

"Did you get by my defense?"Lucas already knew the answer from the blushing smile on the guy's face.

"The last Christmas that you spent with your sister, Rayne, before the hospital, she gave you a framed photo of you with your dad and that Harley. The three of you worked on restoring that sweet vintage ride. You were quite touched. You must have loved your father very much."

Lucas nodded. The memory of that Christmas had rooted in his heart and helped him survive Haven Hills. Gabriel had definitely gotten by his shield.

"Was Rayne really that cute, even back then?" Gabe asked. "Sweet girl."

Lucas grinned and said, "I wanna rematch."

"Yeah, I figured you might. Good man."

With Hellboy at his side, Gabriel slapped him on the back as Luke heard the sharp trill of the whistle, Uncle Reginald's signal that it was time to eat. Lucas gave in to his hunger and followed Gabe back to the clearing, but his mind wrestled with everything that had happened. Gabriel had given him plenty to think about and work on.

Haven Hills Treatment Facility—Ward 8
Hours later

Two men in white uniforms came to Caila's cell and woke her from an exhausted sleep. She had no idea what time it was. They shoved the door open and went straight for her. One guy yanked her covers back and the other grabbed her by the arm.

"Where are you taking me?"

The men didn't answer her. They didn't say anything and barely looked at her as they hauled her by the arms down a hall. Caila's feet were bare and cold. Her skin puckered in goose bumps. All she had on were the yellow top and pajama bottoms they'd given her to wear. The thin material made her feel naked.

They took her to a large exam room. She'd been there before, when they took more blood and hooked her up to a machine that measured something in her brain. This time when they opened the door, a woman in a white lab coat was waiting for her. Caila didn't like her. Her pale eyes were the color of glacier ice and her ashen blond hair was pulled back tight to her head. She looked mean.

"Caila Ferrie. My name is Dr. Fiona," the woman said. "Good of you to come."

"Did I have a choice?"

The words were out of Caila's mouth before she even thought as the men strapped her to what looked like a dental chair and secured her arms and legs. When they were done, the doctor ordered them to wait outside.

"Is that any way to show appreciation for my hospitality?" The doctor smiled. "You were living on the streets of L.A., not a safe place at all. Here you have a bed and food and medical care."

"I'd rather eat garbage."

Even though the exam room was ice cold, Caila felt sure the chill came from the doctor.

"If that's what you want, that could be arranged, but you aren't leaving here. You're a danger to society. You're not... well."

"That's a lie and we both know it." She heard the hostility in her voice but couldn't stop it. She had nothing left to lose.

"I'm the doctor. You are what I say you are and you're in my hands until you cooperate."

Caila glared at the woman until the doctor's words sank in.

"Does that mean I can get out of here?" She didn't wait for her to answer. "How? When?"

"That depends."

"On what?"

"On your willingness to help me. You've been a good patient. You haven't objected to any of my tests and—"

"You're holding me against my will. I'm your prisoner."

"A mere technicality." Dr. Fiona grinned and looked smug. "Tests and lab work can only tell me so much. I'd like you to fill in the gaps so I can pinpoint my examination. Your freedom will depend on how forthcoming you are with me."

Screw cooperation. Caila had lost her patience for promises from this woman.

"Where's Oliver?" She fought against her restraints. "I wanna see him."

"Tell me what I want to know and I'll consider letting you see Zack. Would you like that?"

Caila almost choked. *Zack? My God, yes.* The faces of Zack and Oliver sprang from the darkness of her worst fears.

"What do you want?"

The doctor pulled up a stool on wheels and sat close to her. "Tell me how your gift works, but don't bother lying to me. I've got data on you. A thick file. If I catch you in a lie, you won't be the one I punish. Your friends will pay the price and I'll be sure to tell them you're responsible."

Caila didn't trust this woman. Not even a little, but she couldn't stomach any more cruelty heaped on Zack and Oliver because of her. She lowered her head and shut her eyes tight as she talked. "My gift acts on its own. I can't always control it, so I'm not entirely sure how it works."

"You expect me to believe that? Do you care about Zack and Oliver at all?"

Caila jerked her head up when the doctor raised her voice to let her true colors show. Her face had pinched into a taut grimace.

"No, it's true. I'm not lying. When I get stressed, I can't stop it and I don't always know what will happen."

The doctor glared at her, considering what she'd said before she asked another question. "What did you do to Zack? Exactly."

There was no way she could explain what she'd done and have this woman—or anyone—understand. Caila's mind raced with what she'd say. Her usual justifications were things that she'd repeat in her head when she couldn't sleep. It was all she had.

"When I came to L.A., I had no place to live and not much money. My first night at a shelter, I got robbed. They took everything while I slept. That's when I met Zack."

"Sweet, but get to the point."

"He seemed nice. He talked to me and let me hang with him."

"Yeah, I'll bet. I'm sure it had nothing to do with sex."

"It wasn't like that with Zack. We never—"

Dr. Fiona laughed and shook her head. "Oh, don't bother. I can understand you trying to control Zack with sex, but that's not the kind of 'gift' I'm talking about. What did you do to him? Tell me and make me believe you."

Caila knew this woman wouldn't understand. No matter how she explained what a decent friend Zack had always been to her, this cynical woman would never believe how it was. But saying what she actually did to him would never come out right either. She couldn't look the woman in the eye when she blurted out her answer. This time it had to be the truth, for Zack and Oliver's sake.

"I gave him memories, good ones of another life with… *me* in it. I made him feel safe and loved. I was afraid he'd leave me and I needed him. My gift did it, not me. I swear."

"You made him love you?"

"Not…love, exactly. I shared my dreams with him, of a life we could have. We both needed that. He was scared too. I didn't do anything to hurt him."

"Sugarcoat it all you want, honey. You wiped out his free will and got a white knight in the process. How does it work? Tell me."

Caila did her best to describe what happened in her body when her gift took over. After the heat welled up inside her, she felt an uncontrollable urge to touch and make a connection. Her fingertips on Zack's cheek. A kiss for Oliver. Hearing the words coming from her mouth—to the delight of this hideous woman—made her feel like a worse monster.

"So you have to summon your ability, through an emotional reaction? Fear, for example. It doesn't come from a random touch. Is that it?"

Caila lowered her head and nodded.

"Did you do the same thing to Oliver?"

She felt the heat on her cheeks when she said, "Yes."

"Well, that explains a lot."

The doctor stood and walked over to a door. She unlocked it using a key she had dangling on her ID badge. Caila had noticed the key before. Inside the smaller room were a desk, a computer and some file cabinets. The woman unlocked one of the file drawers and pulled a file that she tossed on the desktop, before she swiveled a computer monitor around. She made sure Caila could see a split screen of four colorful scans of the human brain.

"The brain is a complex organ. There are one hundred billion neurons passing signals to each other over one thousand trillion synaptic connections. The brain gives us the ability to think, communicate, create, dream and experience our emotions. Memory is a huge part in this process. What we learn and feel, we retain as memory and it changes how we behave in the future. It becomes instinct. Memory can also be manipulated. A rather simple process, really. Using the power of suggestion can—"

"Why are you showing me this?"

Caila had no patience to listen to this woman talk about science, not when Oliver and Zack were her lab rats. She stared at the screen, looking for a label that showed Zack's name. All she wanted was a connection that meant something to her.

"I thought you'd want to know about Zack…and you."

The woman smiled when Caila couldn't hide her strong reaction. She had to know where Zack was.

"You see, in Zack, whenever I stimulated his mind with suggestions of you, I observed different lobes in his cerebral cortex become highly active, regions dealing with his memory. These are his scans and here are the hot spots I'm talking about." The woman pointed to the screen. "The long-term memory had me puzzled, especially when I knew you didn't know him for very long. Our people had begun tracking you in L.A."

"Tracking me. Why? What does this have to do with me?"

"You're my latest science riddle, that's why." The doctor looked smug. "If memory is simply what a person sees, what if new memories can be infused into someone's brain by showing him a different past? Would it change him? It would seem that you, my dear, can control anyone's future by manipulating their past. You did it to Zack and now Oliver. That's extraordinary."

"I don't know anything about that."

"No, I guess you wouldn't. A gift like this is wasted on someone like you." Dr. Fiona narrowed her eyes. "So let's talk about something you do know about. Oliver came to see you the other night. Tell me about *that*."

Caila felt the heat rush to her face. "What? No, he couldn't have. I was...locked up. So was he, right?"

She had only one instinct when it came to Oliver's visit. She had to lie. It was one thing to talk about her gift, but telling this woman about Oliver felt like a secret that wasn't hers to tell. She didn't want to get him into more trouble.

"I thought you wanted to see Zack. The only way that will happen is if you're honest with me. Did you see Oliver the other night?"

Caila felt the sting of tears and fought them. She gritted her teeth, not sure what she'd say. "Yes, I saw him, but that was only a dream. There's no way he'd show up in my room." She raised her chin. "That's the truth. I swear."

"Yes, I suppose it is, according to you. Surveillance recordings show something else. We see everything that happens here. Cameras are everywhere." The woman glared at her. "Oliver is remarkable. On our surveillance cameras, he shows up like a beautiful glimmer of light. Pure energy. What did he look like when you saw him?"

"Like a ghost. What did you do to him? If what I saw was really him, is he dead? How could he appear to me like that? You did something."

"I only released him to become what he was always meant to be." The doctor smiled. "Of course he has me to thank for that. And now that I know what you've done to him, I can use that."

"Why are you doing this to us?"

"You really don't know? Or do you think we're just stupid?" the woman said. When Caila couldn't answer her, the doctor shook her head. "You may think you're human, but you're not. You're a diseased limb that should be amputated. You, Zack, Oliver. You're all the same."

"You promised I could see Zack."

Dr. Fiona looked confused by the shift in topic, but she quickly recovered. "Yes, I suppose you've earned that right. I see no harm in it and a promise is a promise." The woman nodded. "I'll have Zack brought to you."

Caila swallowed hard as the doctor ordered the uniformed men into the room to escort her back to her locked cell. She kept her face from showing how excited she was about seeing Zack, but she couldn't stop her heart from reacting. His face and his eyes flashed pictures in her head. She didn't care if her memories of him were real or not.

Zack would finally know she'd come for him. She had his back.

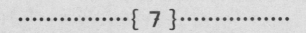

{ 7 }

Stewart Estate
Dusk

Gabriel had nervous energy that needed to be worked out of his system. Whenever he couldn't settle down and his senses got shifted into overdrive, he had to find a release. After he'd taken a long run, he went to his uncle's well-equipped gym to finish up on weights and an abusive round with a seventy-pound punching bag. After he stripped off his T-shirt and got down to wearing only his sweatpants, he bound his hands in elastic wrap, donned boxing gloves and got to work.

In no time he shifted into high gear and battered the bag in blinding succession, sidestepping and circling it with each driving blow. The muscles in his legs burned and his fists ached with every jab.

Stay focused and keep moving. Use the pain.

His gloved punches had a rhythm that intensified as his underlying anger toward his father stirred the demons inside him. He missed his mother, missed his life and missed a dead ten-year-old boy he'd never met. He picked up his pace and circled the bag, focusing his whole body on every blow. His lungs were heaving and sweat trailed off his arms and back as he bobbed and weaved. He switched up the speed and varied his combination punches—left jab, straight right, left hook. Gabriel had hit the zone.

When he saw movement in a wall mirror, he shifted his eyes to see his uncle at the doorway to the training room.

"You've s-saved me," he panted. "The bag…has a keen right cross."

Panting, Gabe yanked off his gloves and left the white elastic wrap on his hands. He'd worked his way toward exhaustion and it felt good.

"Your mother used to tell me about your penchant for boxing." Uncle Reginald brought him a white towel and bottled water. "Rocky would be very proud."

"High praise indeed." Gabriel grinned and wiped his face with the towel. "And who couldn't benefit from a solid theme song, eh?"

"Sorry to disrupt your workout, but I had to know. How did Lucas *do* this afternoon? I wanted your assessment."

"He's amazing," he panted.

"Tell me something I don't already know."

"Okay, if you insist. A pig's orgasm can last an astonishing thirty minutes."

His uncle grimaced. "Good Lord, you don't say. Now I have another reason to appreciate bacon." The man smiled. "I noticed Lucas came back a bit damp. Seems to me that your mother gave you a similar swimming lesson. Did you breach his defenses?"

"Some lessons are classic and worth passing on. I got by his shield this time, but he'll make that harder in the future. Exactly the point of our exercise. He's clever, that one." Gabe grinned, cracked open the water bottle and drank. "The power I feel from him, I can barely contain it. He has no idea how incredible he is. He's holding back. I know he is and I don't know why."

"You were like that at his age. Your mother worried over you too."

"What? She never told me that."

"She didn't know how hard to push you, to achieve what she knew you could do. Sound familiar?" Uncle Reginald winked. "Guiding the young can be a test of patience."

"Yeah, I get that. But I've been having more visions. Violent ones. I'm channeling them through Lucas, and he doesn't seem to feel them like I do. Maybe drawing the faces makes each one stick with me. Lately they're haunting me even when I'm awake."

"How do you *know* Lucas isn't feeling the same? Have you talked to him?" His uncle crossed his arms and cocked his head. "You have to remember that he just got out of the hospital. This is all new to him. These visions must be frightening, yes?"

"You're probably right, but I have a bad feeling. These visions are escalating for a reason. He may not sense that like I do."

"What are you feeling?"

Gabe only shrugged and took another pull of water.

"Tell me exactly, Gabriel. Come on."

"I feel like I'm alone on a dark ocean, treading water without land in sight. When I'm not haunted by the faces of terrified kids, that's what I see in my dreams." He sighed. "We're not ready. Not even close, but it feels like…"

"Like what?"

"Like we've run out of time."

He couldn't look his uncle in the eye. In his heart, he wondered if Lucas had a point. He didn't know if his intention toward his father was about revenge or something else, but he couldn't say that. He simply wasn't prepared to share that much with his uncle, not when those thoughts were so muddled in his head. He settled on telling his uncle a fraction of the truth.

"Am I pushing them too hard...or maybe not enough?" he asked. "The truth is that I won't know any of those answers until it's too late...until I can only watch things happen like I did the last time."

"No, Gabriel. You did more than watch. You stopped the bleeding and you stepped in when it would have been easier to stay in hiding. I'm proud of you."

His uncle tried to make him feel good, but Gabe had to make him see.

"Before, when it was only me, I had nothing to lose," he told him. "That was my edge, but I've lost that. All I have now are...doubts."

"Oh, my dear boy. Don't you see?" His uncle held Gabe's face in both hands, as he used to do when he was a boy. "You think having nothing to lose gives you an edge, but I think it's better to have something worth living for. I think you've found that. Don't you?"

His uncle smiled and let go. "With an undertaking like this, it's natural to have doubts. But you must have faith in the human spirit, Gabriel. These children could surprise you." He forced a halfhearted smile. "They have you, and Kendra, Lucas and Rafael will do their part. You'll have your army when you need it. Now get some rest. Tomorrow will, most assuredly, be brighter."

Uncle Reginald had said what he'd come to say. Gabe had no doubt that the man sensed the troubles between him and Lucas and wanted to reassure him. As he watched his uncle go, he wanted to believe the man was right.

"Have I told you how much I like having you here, Gabriel? You and your new friends have brought life and purpose to this old house…and me. Besides, how else would I have learned about the carnal exploits of swine?" Without turning around, his uncle called out to him as he got to the door, as if he'd read his thoughts.

I love you too. Gabe shot him a message without opening his mouth.

His uncle raised his hand and waved goodbye. He'd gotten his message, loud and clear. They both had.

Haven Hill Treatment Facility
Ward 8

Caila paced the floor of her cell, wringing her hands until her fingers ached. Randy Newman singing "You've Got a Friend in Me" looped in her head to punish her. The maddening sweet lyrics about friendship with its upbeat rhythm tortured and mocked her with how wrong it felt. She was no one's friend.

Dr. Fiona hadn't brought Zack yet, and the longer it took, the more she believed the woman had lied to her. If she had, there wasn't anything Caila could do about it. She went to the far corner of her room and sank to the floor, rocking and waiting, until she heard rolling wheels in the distance. From the sounds of it, the gurney would come by her room. Zack.

Caila leaped to her feet and ran for the door as Randy Newman mercifully stopped singing. Being too short, she had to jump to catch a glimpse out the wire-mesh window of her cell. When she saw Dr. Fiona with two orderlies wheeling something down the hall outside her door, she knew they had Zack. Caila backed away from the doorway and cringed in the corner. She couldn't breathe and sickening bile rose hot from her belly.

Would Zack blame her for what happened to him? How could he not, when she blamed herself? She heard the card key swipe the lock and the click and buzzer of her door as it opened.

When they rolled Zack in, Caila gasped and collapsed to her knees. Her eyes filled with tears. "What...? No, please... No."

She repeated those words over and over as she stared at a large glass jar that held a human brain.

"Zack didn't have much to offer, I'm afraid. For the sake of science, I kept the best part of him," the doctor said. "Oliver is quite another story."

Caila rocked with her arms wrapped around her. She couldn't take her eyes off the jar that held Zack's brain. The doctor's words from earlier replayed through her head.

"We'd been tracking you," she'd told her. *"Sugarcoat it all you want, honey. You wiped out his free will and got yourself a white knight in the process."*

My fault, Zack. I'm so sorry. She couldn't stop thinking it until the doctor tortured her more.

"Oliver is a fine male specimen. Truthfully, he's pleasing on a woman's eye, but to a scientist like me, what's inside his skull can be more fascinating. If he outlives his purpose, he'll earn a spot next to Zack." Dr. Fiona stroked the glass where Zack's brain floated in cloudy liquid. "What happens to Oliver will be up to you."

"He could...already be dead." Caila's throat wedged tight and her eyes burned. She didn't want to cry in front of this terrible woman, but she couldn't stop.

"That's true, but you don't know that, do you?" The woman didn't try to hide her disdain. The games were over.

"In case you missed it, you don't have an option," the doctor said. "You may not care what happens to you, but you got Oliver into this. Shouldn't you do everything you can to keep him breathing?"

Caila had been tricked. The cruelty of this woman had stunned her, but that was the very reason she had to do as she said. She couldn't help Zack anymore. All she had left was Oliver.

"Whatever you want, just don't kill Oliver."

Stewart Estate
Hours later—after midnight

Raphael Santana paced the grassy hillside behind the Stewart Estate—dressed only in jeans and boots—too restless to kneel by the grave he visited every night. A cool mountain breeze swept through his dark hair. It should have chilled the bare skin of his chest, but the fire in his belly kept him stoked with heat.

He still felt the remnants of having Kendra in his mind, and she must've stirred up his memories of Benny, the family he never got to keep. A growing emptiness filled him until he couldn't get the kid from his head—and he didn't want to.

When his boot struck a rock, he picked it up and tossed it in his hands as he stared into the gloom. His heart searched this world and beyond for the spirit of a small boy who had left an ache in his soul, a gaping wound no one else could ever fill. With the moon hording its light—nothing but a razor slash across a pitch-black sky—the dark became a part of him. After living in the tunnels beneath the streets of downtown L.A., Rafe craved the hush of shadows.

For him there was darkness even in daylight now.

"Haunt me, Benny. Torture me. I deserve it."

He flung the rock into the dark and heard it hit trees. The move made his side hurt where he'd been shot, the same fight where Benny had been killed.

"You should be the one standing here, not me."

Rafe collapsed to his knees at the grave. He winced when he hit the ground and clutched his side. The others had left trinkets for Benny—a worn teddy bear, flowers and a toy that spun in the wind. Every time he came to the grave, he had to face what had happened to Benny. He wanted to remember the kid smiling and funny, but that would let him off a hook he deserved.

"I miss you, little man."

He ran his fingers over the name etched on the headstone—*Benny Santana.* He had given Benny his own last name and had it carved into stone forever. The kid didn't deserve to be buried with the family name he got stuck with, so Rafe claimed Benny as the little brother he wished he had.

"I don't know what to do." Tears cooled his cheeks. "I don't know who I am anymore."

He glared over his shoulder and stared up at the mansion that had become his new home by default after the Believers had destroyed the tunnels. Kendra Walker and the others, like him, had come to live here. It would only be a matter of time before Kendra would ask if she could start her garden. That would mean she wanted to stay. Kendra was an Indigo healer. Tending her plants kept her more connected to the voices in her head. She heard them best through her garden. She needed that garden and her voices, but she could do without him, especially the way he was now.

This place wasn't home. Not to him. It looked more like a fancy castle, built on the peak of a mountain. He'd grown up on the streets of L.A., carrying everything he owned on his back.

"I don't fit," he whispered. "Not here. Not anywhere."

Rafe got to his feet and took off his black leather "forever" bracelet—the one that used to mean something—and left it on Benny's headstone. He stared down at the grave marker and wiped his eyes with the back of his hand. They'd buried Benny in the ground, but Rafe didn't feel him here. He could think of only one place that the kid's spirit might linger—the place where he died—the only real home that either of them had known.

If he had a shot at "seeing" Benny again, he had to risk going back to L.A.—and stealing Rayne's Harley.

Downtown L.A.
4:30 a.m.

In the early morning hours, Rafe sped down the interstates on Rayne's Harley with his body pummeled by the wind and his blood fueled with a rush of adrenaline. He'd hot-wired her ride, stolen cash from Kendra, ripped off a bottle of liquor from Gabriel's uncle and when he didn't take a helmet, he wondered if he didn't have a death wish. All he had on were the clothes on his back—jeans, boots, a T-shirt and a worn jacket.

Everything he had done felt like a one-way trip. He hadn't given any thought to what he'd do next. He kicked the bike into high gear with the wind lashing his hair. *Speed.* He couldn't get enough.

When he got to one of the tunnel entrances—the location where the Believers had staged their attack—he downshifted and hit the throttle to rev the Harley. If the bastards had staked the place out to see if anyone would come back, he had made an unmistakable announcement of his return.

Rafe killed the engine and hid the bike in the bushes, near

a thick stand of trees. He headed into the darkness of the tunnels, cracking the seal on the bottle of liquor and downing a long pull. It burned his throat, only the start of the abuse he deserved. He felt the alcohol burn into his body and kindle a fire in his chest. His old man only drank the cheap stuff. He had no idea what he'd ripped off from the estate. Probably some fancy shit. As long as it got the job done, the kind didn't matter.

Drunk or sober, he knew the danger of returning to the very place where the church freaks had hunted them and destroyed everything. He didn't care. If they came after him again and wanted a fight, he'd give them one, but as he wandered into the tunnels alone, he felt numb. He didn't recognize the place. The Believers had come in afterward and burned everything. Kendra's garden—the beautiful oasis she had created that had fed and healed them—had been uprooted, doused with gasoline and torched.

Their home had been wiped out as if they'd never existed.

He sucked down more liquor and wiped his mouth with his jacket sleeve as he stumbled over the old railroad track that led to the Cyclops, the old locomotive that had been abandoned in the tunnels. The metal beast loomed in the darkness as he rounded a corner, half-buried in old brick rubble caused by the explosion that had killed Benny. Its bared teeth of steel hovered over the rail and its blinded eye—a broken headlight—still breathed a fierce life into the old engine that was covered in dust and debris.

Benny loved the steel beast. Rafe stood in front of the dead train and looked up at its busted eye as he drank—remembering one of the last times he saw the boy.

"Yo, Benny. It's me. I got something for ya."

"For me?" A little head had popped out from the engine compartment. *"What is it?"*

"I got you something to bring you luck. Your own piece of magic."
Not nearly drunk enough to forget, Rafe shut his eyes tight and willed the kid to come to him. Little man had played on every inch of the old rusted train. His fingerprints were still on every gauge and lever, the only mark of Benny left behind. Rafe couldn't settle for that.

"No one's ever gotten me anything before," the kid had said in a shaky voice. With little fingers, he stroked the leather bracelet with Kendra's infinity charm on it.

Rafe pictured Benny sitting on the train's step with that crooked grin on his face and his eyes welling with tears. The kid had broken his heart that day, but he didn't know how much worse he could feel until he held Benny's dead body in his arms days later. Rafe stared at the spot he'd tied the bracelet to the kid's wrist, and his eyes burned with tears.

"Screw infinity!" he yelled to no one. "What happened... t-to forever, Kendra?"

He didn't feel Benny, not as he sensed the dead. Who was he kidding? He wasn't worth sticking around for. When he took another gulp, he felt dizzy and sick. Nothing killed the hurt. He grabbed the bottle and smashed it against the train. A shard of glass cut his cheek, but he didn't care.

He'd come to the tunnels—a place where he could be closer to Benny—but that place didn't exist anymore. Rafe stumbled back the way he'd come, not knowing where he would go. He only knew it wasn't here.

When he hit the night air, he wanted to puke. Bile churned in his stomach, mixed with the burn of alcohol. He wouldn't outrun his booze slug to the brain. Heading for the Harley, he half decided to sleep it off, but when an arm grabbed his neck from behind, he couldn't breathe. He kicked and fought to break free, but every move forced a crushing weight against his chest. His stomach felt on fire. The bullet wound had ripped open.

Rafe couldn't see faces in the dark. Men grappled with his arms and legs until he couldn't move. He sucked air into his lungs in fitful gasps. When he saw stars, his body gave out.

"Boss man said you'd be the weak link, kid."

Rafael felt the sharp sting of a needle stab his neck. It spread a burn under his skin and his arms went limp.

"Guess he got *that* right."

The gruff voice was the last thing Rafe heard before he drifted into a deeper darkness than he'd ever seen. Only one thing gave him comfort.

He felt Benny with him.

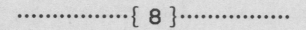

{ 8 }

Stewart Estate
Morning

Kendra woke the next morning with two sets of blue eyes staring down at her. The blond Effin brothers had blank expressions, as if they were vying for the top contenders in a staring contest. She wouldn't have been startled if the identical faces had been her only wake-up call.

Inside her head they talked at once—and not quietly.

Wake up. We can't find Rafael.

He's gone. His bed is...

One tugged at her arm. The other got louder.

Yeah, he never slept in it.

We gotta find him.

"He could be...with Benny."

Kendra said the words aloud to calm the boys. She didn't want them to panic the others before she checked it out. The twins had grown closer to Rafe. They'd been Benny's best friends, even though they never spoke a word to him. Benny had done all the talking.

"I'm sure he's okay. Where else would he go? We're in

the middle of nowhere. Let me get dressed and I'll meet you downstairs."

The twins nodded, looking like out-of-sync bobble-head dolls, and left her alone to change. She had a big fancy room, but some of the kids slept in her bed and on the floor. They'd been used to that in the tunnels, but bad dreams and the strangeness of a new peculiar place had drawn them together. She folded back the bedcovers, careful not to wake Bethany and Sarah. After she got a fresh change of clothes from a dresser, she stepped over Little G and Domino to get to the bathroom.

Rafael. Where are you?

She stared at her face in the bathroom mirror and sent out a message to him. When he didn't answer her, she closed her eyes to focus and extend her reach. She let her mind and instincts search for him, but when she came up empty, it frightened her. The last time she'd lost Rafael like this, she thought he was dead.

The twins are in a panic. They're scared. Hell, I'm scared. Please… talk to me.

When she didn't hear or feel him, she rushed to change. Something was wrong. Really wrong.

An hour later

"He's not at Benny's grave. I checked." Kendra rushed in from the courtyard with her face flushed. "I can't feel him anywhere."

Gabriel had a roomful of eyes on him. They'd gathered in the great room near the cold hearth. Their voices filled his head with questions and their darkest thoughts for Rafael. They looked to him for answers now and he had none. He stared across the room at the colossal circus billboards that adorned the walls, a faded display of the former life he'd lived with his mother, Kathryn, when they were fugitives hiding out with a traveling circus. The act they'd perfected—Hellboy and the Third Eye—Letters from the Dead—seemed like a lifetime ago. His mother had made him feel safe, even when they weren't. He wished he had a fraction of her ability now.

"The liquor cabinet is open and it appears that a bottle is missing." Uncle Reginald broke the mind chatter when he entered the room. "Perhaps he's sleeping it off…somewhere on the grounds."

Gabriel prayed his uncle was right when he turned toward Kendra.

"If he was unconscious, would you feel him?" he asked.

"No. I didn't in the tunnels, after he got shot." She wrung her hands and her voice shook. "He could be…hurt."

"What about you, Lucas?" Gabe asked. "You have any visions about him?"

"No, sorry." He shook his head. "Nothing."

"I didn't sketch anything new last night. Maybe that's good news," he told them. "I know you're all worried, but try to stay positive. If he's passed out from finishing that bottle, the worst that could happen to him is he'll find a new religion on his knees, praying for redemption at a porcelain altar. We'll have to search the grounds to be sure."

"I don't think that'll be necessary." Rayne walked into the room, a little out of breath. She must've heard enough. "My Harley's missing. He didn't take my keys, so he had to hot-wire it. Where would he go?"

The hive chatter filled the room again, even though Gabriel knew that Rayne couldn't hear it. Kendra shut it down when she chose to speak aloud, for Rayne's benefit.

"I think I know where he'd go," she said. "He went looking…for Benny."

Kendra didn't have to explain to Gabe what that meant. Rafael had a special link to the dead as he did. After his mother died four years ago, Gabe wanted his sixth sense to mean something. He wanted his mother to haunt him. He needed to feel her soul and to know that, if she still existed in some reality, he'd see her again. When that didn't happen, he'd spent hours walking the roadside where she'd died. If Rafe had felt the same, there was only one place he'd go.

"They could be watching those tunnels," he said. "Didn't he know that?"

"I don't think he cared," Kendra said.

Gabe nodded. He didn't have to know Rafe the way she did to figure out what might've happened. He only had to know what it felt like to lose someone he would've traded places with.

Haven Hills Treatment Facility
Ward 8

Fiona stood over Oliver Blue and stared at his shuddering body. He gasped for air from under the black helmet that she'd created to rob the boy of his senses. Even though he was still strapped down by restraints on his arms and legs, she took the precaution to have security guards with her. She had no idea how violent he could become once she got the sensory-deprivation gear off him and he felt the world again for the first time in weeks.

The truth was that she would've preferred no witnesses to her success or failure. Oliver had the potential to be her greatest achievement or nothing except a tortured mind that she'd created from her failed experiment. She didn't know what Alexander Reese would think of her rogue tactics. That's why she kept separate the real patient files locked away in Ward 8, in an exam room where she kept a second office. Her research was too important to be confiscated and misinterpreted by anyone, including Alexander.

There was only one reason Alexander would find out about Oliver now—if the boy became her triumph. If he turned out to be an utter failure, he would end up like Zack and remain her secret. Fiona reached out her hand to touch his bare belly. She let her fingers linger on his skin, even while he cried out for help.

"Shh. I'm here, Oliver."

She knew he couldn't hear her, but her gentle strokes over his body made him stop thrashing and crying out. By the time she touched his chin, he'd stopped fighting. Fiona put on latex gloves. She would check his vitals before she detached him from the equipment that monitored his vital signs and hydrated and fed him. She also administered a mild sedative to keep him calm. After she took off the helmet, no telling how he'd react.

"Come on, Oliver. Take a deep breath for me. Be a good boy," she whispered.

Fiona touched his bare chest with her stethoscope and listened to his heart and lungs. He wouldn't be able to hear her from under the helmet, but talking to him made the boy seem less like an animal. Every breath was a struggle for him. His body shook and his lips quivered. When she was done with her examination, she tossed the latex gloves into a sterilized waste receptacle and fixed her gaze on the uniformed guards.

"Turn the lights off, please. Once I get this helmet off him, his eyes will be sensitive."

One of the guards flicked off the overhead lights while the other hit the switch for the lit table under Oliver. The only glow came from the corridor and shone through the small window on the security door. When she reached for his head gear, both guards exchanged looks and one of them stepped closer. She saw the tension in their bodies. They were ready for Oliver to fight.

"I've given him a sedative, but if he becomes violent, I'll need you to hold him down so I can give him something stronger."

In the shadowy room, Fiona took a deep breath before she made a move toward Oliver. When she unlatched the black helmet, the clasps let out a sigh of air as the seal broke. She removed the section over his nose so he could take his first full breaths.

Oliver gulped air like a drowning man. When she got behind him, she pulled the helmet and goggles off his head and the boy writhed in pain and gagged. His eyes watered and tears streaked his face. He couldn't stop blinking and an agonizing moan came from deep inside his chest. The haunting noise didn't sound human, and the boy fought like a trapped and panicked animal.

"Oliver, can you hear me?" She dared to reach for him and touch his cuffed arm. "Please stop. I can't release you until you're calm. It's for your own safety." She lowered her voice and muttered under her breath, "And mine."

The boy turned his head and shielded his eyes from the light. His tremors didn't stop and neither did his miserable groan. He heard voices for the first time in weeks, and the sudden rush of his senses had to be overwhelming.

Fiona knew she had to be his savior. If she wanted her plan to work, she had precious moments to become his lifeline back to the living. "Please let me help you. Are you cold?"

He kept his face in the shadows, and his body quivered, but he didn't answer her. She wasn't sure that he could.

"Keep your eyes closed. I know your vision must be blurry. Don't fight it. Your sight will come back. I promise." She stepped closer and stood at his side. "Are you thirsty? Can I get you some water?"

Oliver fought his restraints as if he hadn't heard her. Fiona took a risk and went to the small stainless sink in his quarters and poured water into a disposable cup. When she returned to him, she raised his head to help him drink. He didn't refuse.

"Only a little or you'll get sick," she said. After he took his last sip, she tossed the cup. "You must be cold. Let me see what I can do for you."

Fiona went to the sink again and came back with a bowl of warm soapy water and a sterilized towel. She drenched the cloth in the sudsy water and started on his cheeks with gentle strokes. Since he still wouldn't turn toward the light, she moved into the shadows and leaned closer to him. She wanted her voice to be the only sound he heard.

Fiona ran a warm, moist towel over his face and neck with her voice barely above a whisper.

"Does this feel good?" she asked. "I imagine it's hard for you to speak. That may take time."

After she brushed the damp cloth through his hair and dabbed his forehead dry with another towel, the boy opened his eyes.

"There you are." She lowered her chin to meet his gaze and she smiled. "You're okay, Oliver. I'm here to help you."

The boy's tremors slowed as she soothed his cold skin with warm water and wiped him dry. When she bathed his chest and arms, he didn't resist the intimacy and his eyelids grew heavy. The sedative had done its job. While she had him in a twilight state, Fiona needed privacy with the boy.

"I'll be okay alone with him. Please leave us, but don't go far," she told the guards. "The sedative is working, but I may need you."

"Yes, ma'am."

After the men left the room, Fiona was free to talk.

"Oliver? You still with me?" She touched his cheek. "Don't try to talk. Just listen. I need you to understand what's happening."

She soaked the cloth again and gently ran it over his body. Oliver let her touch him without flinching. The boy was very weak. She saw that in his eyes and the way his atrophied muscles trembled. He looked like a junky in withdrawal. In his confused state, Fiona had to convince him that she cared what happened to him. He let her wash him, and that had been a good first step, but he had to trust and believe her.

"You came to me. I saw you in my bedroom. Do you remember that, Oliver?"

His jaw clenched, but he didn't answer her.

"It's okay. You made me very happy when you did. I knew you'd be strong enough. You're special, but it's your friend Caila who's got me worried. She won't let me help her."

Fiona brushed back a strand of his damp hair and fixed her gaze on him.

"What I'm about to say won't be easy for me to tell you or admit, but I see no point in lying to you. Not now. Too much has happened and Caila's future is at stake. It's up to you and me, Oliver. We have to help her, even if she doesn't want to get better. After I tell you the truth, you can decide. Are you willing to at least hear me out?"

Even in his weakened state, Oliver Blue fixed his forceful eyes on her and stared for a long moment before he finally nodded and choked out his first words.

"Yeah. Th-thanks...for h-helping...us."

Fiona smiled. "When this is all over, I'll be the one thanking you, Oliver. Trust me."

Twenty minutes later

Fiona had rehearsed the lies she'd told Oliver, but she'd been surprised how adept she'd gotten at stretching minuscule facts into bombastic lies. The more Oliver bought into her charade, the more outlandish she got. She told him they'd taken Zack for testing and blamed Caila for the target on the boy's back.

"Yes, we took Zack, but I saw him leave the hospital."

She hadn't completely lied about that. Part of Zack *did* leave the premises.

"What he told us about Caila, I don't blame him for not wanting to see her again."

She'd set the hook and Oliver took the bait by wanting to know more. She used his feelings for the girl against him.

"Caila implants fake memories into people she touches. She makes them love her so they take care of her. I tested Zack through a brain scan, and with his help, we figured out what she did to him. That made him mad, but can you blame him? Did she touch you like that, Oliver? You may not remember what she did. That's part of it too."

When he didn't answer her, she knew the boy was gradually buying in to her manipulative version of the truth. That's when Fiona laid it on thick. She told him that Caila had run away from a loving home and that her parents were still looking for her.

"Yes, a very sad state of affairs," she'd said. *"She stole memories from other kids. I suppose she didn't realize how harmful that would be to her."*

Of course the boy *had* to know how stealing memories could harm Caila, and Fiona was quick with an explanation. She told him that the girl had simply lost track of her lies and her fake memories. She made him imagine how tragic that could be for Caila to fill her head with the lives of other people until she couldn't remember what was real for her anymore. Fiona explained how memories were things people saw and that they shaped a person's future. The best way to describe Caila was *"an addict, jonesing for what other people had."* The girl needed psychiatric help. That's why she had to be confined at Haven Hills.

After the time they'd spent talking about the girl, Oliver finally got around to asking why *he'd* been taken. He choked on every word. He wasn't used to using his voice. Fiona saw in his eyes that he'd grown to trust what she'd told him and that he was still listening to her, but she had to come up with a good reason for what she'd done to him to cinch the deal.

"We had to take you because of Caila. We've been tracking her and anyone she crossed paths with. Her parents asked us to look for her, but once we saw what she was doing, we had to help those she touched, otherwise her abusive pattern would ruin their lives and crowd hers with false and confusing memories." She touched his arm. "We had to isolate your mind to be certain she couldn't reach you. That's why we resorted to using sensory-deprivation technology. Her link had to be broken for your own good…and hers. Do you feel her now?"

Oliver thought about it and eventually said, "I don't know. I'm…tired. Can't think."

"You must fight her pull on you, like Zack did. It got better for him, but I must admit that we had you in the headgear much longer. Her hold on you was stronger, I'm afraid."

Fiona saw how exhausted Oliver was. His hands shook and he winced in pain, even under sedation.

"If I release you from these restraints, will you promise not to hurt me? I trust you, Oliver. I hope you have the same faith in me."

After the boy nodded, she undid the straps one by one,

starting with his legs. When he was free, he rolled from the light and tried to stand, but collapsed to the floor when his muscles failed him. He crawled to the darkest corner of the room and huddled there, shaking. His mind and body were spent.

"The muscle weakness is only temporary. It will take time to build your strength. I'll help you with that, but there's one thing that concerns me." Fiona took a deep breath and knelt by his side, speaking to him in a soft voice. "Do you have feelings for this girl, Oliver? A girl you've only just met?"

When he didn't answer her, she made her case.

"The first step to reclaim your life is acknowledging what she's done to you. I know it will be hard," she said. "It was for Zack too, but you can't trust her. Poor thing, she doesn't even know she's lying anymore. Her gift takes over and she's mentally too weak to fight it. Her condition will only get worse if we can't help her break the pattern. Trust me. She needs to be here. I've seen cases like hers before."

Oliver looked pale and sick. He cowered in the corner unable to look her in the eye, but he surprised her when he said, "That helmet...did something...to me."

Fiona knew she had his trust when he openly admitted that his gift had changed, without her asking him about it. He'd confided in her willingly. A very good indication that she could push him for what she really wanted. "That came from you. Your psychic ability is really strong. I saw that on your brain scans. That's why I need to ask your help to find someone. A boy. He's someone else that Caila hurt, but he isn't as forgiving as you and Zack."

Oliver turned his head toward her, but before he made the effort to ask her more questions and drain what little remained of his energy, she touched a finger to his lips and got him to stop.

"You probably have questions about this boy and how you can help Caila, but I know you're exhausted. Save your strength and don't try to talk. I'll fill you in on what I know about him."

She stroked his cheek to keep him under her control while she went on. "I don't have the boy's name. I've only seen him once on a blurry surveillance camera image, but he's hiding from us. He's the last one I need to find before I can send Caila home to her parents and the loving care she needs. Either he doesn't believe we can help him break the hold Caila has on him or he doesn't want to be free of her. Desperate, sad people sometimes cling to love, even the manipulative kind. But if we can find him, we can break the unhealthy bond they share. She'll have the freedom to make new memories with her family and start over."

Oliver barely kept his eyes open, and his breathing settled into a normal rhythm. She kept touching him to force him to listen and to reinforce his trust in her.

"We haven't gotten close enough to talk to this boy. You might be our last chance at locating him."

It might have been easier for her to ask his help to find Lucas Darby. The church had more history on the Darby boy and could trace him through their facial recognition tracker system. But Fiona couldn't resist looking for the "other" Crystal child—the mysterious boy who had been with Rayne Darby at the L.A. County Museum of Art reference library—the boy who had tried to steal a picture book in his knapsack. She had that book and one of his original sketches, something she'd held back from Alexander Reese after he gave her the order to keep her focus on Darby.

If Oliver had used his gift to "see" what happened to Zack at the hamburger stand by simply holding something his friend had touched, he might glean vital intel from that library book and the sketch to give her a lead on a boy she believed to be more powerful than Lucas Darby.

"Whatever you do to help us find this boy, you'll have to earn his trust, even if it means lying to get close to him. He's a cagey one, but I have faith in you, Oliver. I'll guide you in your search so I can keep you safe. The sooner you help me, the sooner I can…release you. Nothing would please me more than you leaving this hospital the way Zack did."

Fiona fought to keep a smile off her face when she saw how much Oliver had bought into her story. Poor gullible Oliver, used and abused. She'd played his male jealousy strings with this mystery boy's involvement with Caila and counted on his pathetic need to help the girl.

"I knew you'd do the right thing, Oliver," she whispered. "You're a good guy. When you wake up, I'll give you a way to find the boy."

After Oliver sank to the floor and shut his eyes, Fiona got a fresh blanket from a cabinet and covered him. She'd have his help to find the nameless Crystal child—and her new motivated ally to track him would be one of them.

Perfect.

Downtown L.A.
Dusk

Gabriel crouched beside Rayne, Kendra and Lucas as they stared down a hill to an abandoned railroad tunnel. They had parked his uncle's Lincoln Navigator at a safe distance and walked the rest of the way to a secluded location that brought back terrible memories for all of them.

The Believers had staged their attack in this very spot, the night they killed Benny and destroyed their tunnel home.

Kendra was adamant about starting their search for Rafe

at the worst possible location, the one with the most danger, because that's how Raphael would think. He didn't care what happened to him anymore. Kendra had been right about the railroad entrance being the most dangerous.

Gabriel felt a strong push, a warning sign that something wasn't right.

"If he came here, he was daring them to find him," Gabe whispered to the others, but when he fixed his gaze on Kendra, he knew she felt the same. He saw it on her face.

"Wait a minute. I see something shiny." Rayne used Uncle Reginald's binoculars to get a better look below. When she stopped moving, Gabe knew she had eyes on something.

"My Harley. I see it." She pointed through the trees. "Maybe Rafael tried to hide it, but I can see one of my mirrors and a handlebar."

"Rafe could still be inside," Lucas said. "I can't feel him, but maybe Kendra can do better. I can sense the Believers. They're here and watching this place."

"Yeah, I feel 'em too. You got anything on Rafe, Kendra?" Gabe glanced over his shoulder at the Indigo healer. They all did.

The worried look in her eyes said it all, but she shook her head and said, "No, nothing."

"Rafe may have hidden the Harley, but we gotta assume these men left the bike there as a trap, to draw us in," Gabe told them. "That's why they're still here and hiding."

"I gotta know if Rafe is inside, even if he's...dead," Kendra said. When her eyes watered, she cleared her throat and wiped her face. "They got one man in the tunnels and two others are hiding near the Harley. How are we gonna get by 'em?"

"We're not." Gabriel locked his gaze on each of them.

"We're going straight through them. No more hiding. If they're here for us, we'll give them what they want."

The moment had come. No more drills and exercises. It was time to confront their enemy head-on.

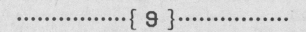

{ 9 }

Near Downtown L.A.
Dusk

Gabriel peered down from a ridge that overlooked the abandoned railroad tunnel. His vantage point had the cover of trees and thick brush to keep him and the others hidden. With his gift of second sight he felt the presence of the Believers, three men who stood in the way of their search for Rafael in the destroyed tunnels, the place the Indigos used to call home.

He might've taken pity if these men were innocent pawns caught in the middle, but they weren't. No matter what motivated them, money or religious beliefs, he had no mercy on anyone who would knowingly hurt children. In this place where the Believers had caused such destruction and the death of Benny, Gabriel felt justified in unleashing their growing abilities.

These men were the enemy.

"Lucas and Kendra, you're with me. No more training exercises. Time to conjure a nightmare these men won't forget," he told them. When he turned to Rayne, he said, "You've got the keys to the Harley. We'll create a diversion. When we do, take your ride and don't look back. We'll meet you at the SUV."

"But what if you need me?" she asked. "I could help."

Gabriel saw the fire in her eyes and knew he could count on her. Rayne had always shown a quiet strength. Even though she was only sixteen and didn't have psychic powers, his brave girl had more guts than the cowards hiding below, but he needed her for something far more important.

"If anything happens to us, you'll be the only one left to warn my uncle. He'll have to relocate the children. They won't be safe if…we're taken. If they have Rafe, we may not have a choice."

Kendra was the first to speak up.

"Rafael would die before he'd say anything. He's tough too." When her resolve faded, she said, "Besides, he may already be dead."

"We don't know that," he said.

From the look on Kendra's face, she understood his concern. Uncle Reginald had talked about what might happen if any of them were abducted. They knew too much. No one would talk willingly—especially the grief-stricken and rebellious Rafael Santana—but what if the Believers had ways to force the truth? They *had* to know what happened to Rafe. If he was dead, they'd mourn him and give him a proper burial next to Benny, but if he was in the hands of the church, they'd have the safety of the children to worry about.

Gabriel shifted his gaze to Rayne. "Once we stir things up, don't…watch. Do what you have to do for the sake of the children. You're our backup plan, a very necessary one," he told her. After Rayne nodded and didn't argue, Gabe said, "We've got to find out what might've happened to Rafael. We hit 'em hard, take a quick look round and then we leave. We won't have much time. Everyone know what to do?"

They nodded and waited for Gabriel to make the first move. When he stood, bathed in the fading light of the sunset, he didn't bother to hide anymore. He started his climb down the hill near the shadowy entrance to the railroad tunnel.

"Let's do this."

It didn't take long for him to feel Hellboy's fierce kinetic energy jolt through him when his ghost dog broke through the barrier of his existence to join him. With Kendra and Lucas at his side, Gabe felt his connection to the Indigo collective grow stronger.

"Don't hold back, Lucas," he said in a low voice. "Follow your instincts. Do it your way."

After Hellboy sensed the men hiding in the mounting darkness, the animal growled. Part wolf, the phantom dog gave in to his predator instincts and stalked his prey with ears perked and eyes alert, ready to attack. The blue shimmer of his body crept low and hovered next to Gabe.

"Come on, boy. Hook me up," he whispered, feeling a surge of power from Hellboy's realm of the dead.

Once Gabe reached the base of the slope, he headed straight for the tunnel entrance, ignoring the psychic push that warned him of danger. Two men cowered in the bushes and one remained in the shadows underground. Gabe felt the chill of the blue fire when it erupted over him. Shivers flooded his body, and a preternatural wind whipped through his hair. His breath turned to vapor from the cold. He felt the power of being connected to everything at once through the dog's spirit.

Now it was time for him to boost his transformation. Gabriel summoned the rage he felt toward his father, the man who had ruined his life. He fortified that anger with his enduring love for his mother, who had died protecting him from the man. The mix turned explosive.

Gabe held on as long as he could. Containing such power amplified it tenfold. When he couldn't restrain it anymore, he unleashed its fury and his consciousness splintered him into a million fragments. The sweet agony of straddling his world and Hellboy's had come in a rush and blew him apart.

After he shattered through the barrier between the living and the dead, he sensed a river's rush of life forces sweep through him. Their light reflected off him as if he were made of crystalline. As he tapped in to other Indigo souls, they released their power to him and fueled his strength.

Every trace of him vibrated and filled him until he heard a low hum that intensified. *The sound of many voices.* The clamor throttled the night air with a palpable feeling of dread. Something was coming. Even Lucas and Kendra turned to gape over their shoulders, searching the shadows. The drone of a menacing chainsaw grew louder and resonated a one-word warning to the men who lay in wait for them.

Run!

The deafening buzz manifested into a black swarm of bees. They blocked the dying sun and descended in a sinister cloud. Gabriel felt the hive's consciousness as if it were his own and he knew he could control them. When he lifted his arms, the swarm swept aside and made a void to shield them. Where he pointed, the bees launched their assault.

When one man stepped out from behind a tree and aimed a gun at them, Gabriel felt Kendra grow stronger.

Rayne crept through the trees and stayed low as she headed for her Harley. She had her keys. Once she got the signal from Gabriel, she'd hit the ignition and meet up with them later. Her part seemed simple enough, but when she heard the sound of a loud buzz, she had to do the one thing Gabriel asked her not to do.

She watched.

Lucas, Kendra and Gabe were meant to be the distraction she'd need to make her escape. If things went as planned, they'd rendezvous later. If not, she'd be on her own. Rayne came armed and understood how important her role would be. Someone had to think about the others, but hearing a swarm of bees amassing over them, she stopped. Rayne looked through the trees to see Gabriel, Lucas and Kendra confronting an armed man dressed in camo fatigues.

Oh, please, God. Don't let any of them die, she prayed.

Gabe glared at the man, looking fierce and angry. She'd seen that expression before and it always scared her. How could such a remarkable and kindhearted boy morph into someone that intimidating? But when Kendra stepped in front of him and Lucas, she raised her hand at the armed man and something happened. The guy's hand trembled and he couldn't pull the trigger. Rayne saw him try. He dropped his weapon as if the gun burned his fingers.

"Shoot. No prisoners," the man yelled, and ran toward them.

Rayne felt sick when another man raced from the bushes, holding an assault rifle on Lucas. In seconds, it could all be over.

No, not Luke!

Because of Gabriel, Lucas got swept into the vortex of Indigo souls. Something took hold of him and he let it happen this time. He had to know what Gabe felt and what he believed.

When a big man in camo gear rushed from the trees and aimed an assault rifle at him, Lucas didn't react as he would've done before. In another life he would've been afraid. Instead Luke trusted his gift and followed his Indigo instincts as Gabriel had taught him.

He didn't have to feel the same anger as Gabe to tap into his power. He radiated the light coming from inside Gabriel and drilled into the mind of his enemy to exploit his human frailty. With no mind shield to stop him, prying into the man's past came in a flash. Luke got a glimmer of a dark memory and didn't hesitate. He flung his arms out and hurled what he saw to plunge the man into his worst nightmare. He used a psychic push so extreme that it heaved the man off his feet and sent his weapon flying. The guy thrashed on the ground, flailing his arms and gasping for air in an all-consuming panic.

Only Luke, and the guy under psychic assault, knew what he'd done.

Lucas had read his mind and knew the man had awakened to countless bad dreams about drowning in a lake when he was a boy. He'd relived his near-death experience many times and it always sent him spiraling back to when he was a kid and couldn't breathe or reach the surface. He'd drowned that day and would have died if someone hadn't saved him.

Imagining what that felt like hadn't been hard for Luke.

After Gabe played his prank, which left Luke splashing in the shallow edge of the high meadow pond on the Stewart Estate, it didn't take much for him to summon a worse scenario and inflict that on the man. In another life Luke would have felt bad for what he'd done to a total stranger, but not today. Not after what the Believers had done to Benny and countless other children.

Today for the first time, Luke felt...*powerful*. He felt stronger than his Indigo nature. He had a notion of what it meant to be a Crystal kid. Gabe and Kendra had been right about what he could do. When he released the man's mind to let Gabriel's bees do the rest, he grinned until he realized he'd only taken advantage of Gabe's extraordinary gift.

He had so much to learn without the luxury of time to do it. His psychic shove that sent a man into the murky waters of an imaginary lake paled in comparison to the real terror of the unmerciful bee attack. The insects swarmed the two screaming men. They rolled through the brush in agony with their hands covering their blotchy faces.

But when Luke saw a third guy running from the darkness of the tunnels—and heard the Harley engine rev—he had to let go of his doubts and focus. Rayne was supposed to wait until they had control. Now the engine noise would draw the armed man's attention to her.

"Rayne."

Rayne saw what she needed to do and did it. She had no one to ask and there was no time.

The last man standing in their way had raced from inside the dark railroad tunnel to join the fight. She had faith in Gabe, Luke and Kendra, but if the man was more of a coward than the rest, he could retreat into the tunnels and set up an ambush in the dark or call for backup and bring more men.

She'd had enough.

Once the man cleared the tunnel entrance with enough distance, she revved the Harley, hit the gas and barreled through the underbrush to cut him off. After she came to a grinding halt, she spun the back tires and spewed gravel. The guy squinted and blocked the spray with his elbow. The distraction gave her time to pull her Glock and aim.

"You came out for air, tunnel rat. Drop your weapon and don't even think about going back in there."

Rayne glared at him and held her gun rock steady with

adrenaline punching through her veins. The man blinked once and considered his options, but Gabe's bees didn't wait. After the guy got stung, he dropped his rifle and ran off with his loser buddies, wearing his share of bees. She doubted these men would want a round two after they tended to their swollen faces, but they couldn't count on having much time.

Lucas was the first to reach her. He didn't look happy. "What were you thinking? You could have been hurt?"

"Oh, and what were you doing? Playing it safe?"

Still jacked with adrenaline, Rayne squared off with her brother, but regretted doing it. She was only glad they were okay. Kendra looked relieved that it was over for now, but when Rayne saw Gabriel, she had a hard time reading him. She holstered her weapon and turned off the Harley as he approached her.

"We won't have much time to search for Rafael," Gabe said to the others without taking his eyes off her. "Let's get to it."

Without a word, Lucas and Kendra shot her a sympathetic glance before they headed into the shadows. Rayne wanted to calm down and take a deep breath, but when she saw Gabe, she couldn't move.

Gabriel waited for the others to get out of earshot and made use of his time by staring at her without saying a word. His beautiful eyes were a mix of emotions that she couldn't figure out. She braced for what he would say.

"You didn't exactly follow the plan," he said in a quiet even voice.

She straddled the Harley with her fingers tight on the handlebars and said, "No, guess not."

Gabe stepped closer and brushed back a strand of her hair that had blown across her cheek in the evening breeze. The intimate whisper of his voice sent a rush of goose bumps over her skin.

"I'd be a hypocrite if I asked *you* not to put your life in danger...when I can't follow my own advice."

What he said surprised her. Rayne appreciated his honesty.

"We're in a fight that could cost us," he said. "Playing it safe isn't always an option, but that doesn't mean we should embrace the dark side and go Rambo."

"Rambo... Seriously?"

"The point is that I won't lecture you, but you can't stop me from worrying about you."

Gabriel pulled her into his arms and held her tight. He didn't say anything and didn't kiss her. His hug carried a different message that Rayne was only just beginning to understand. They were fighting for a better world, but until that happened, she had to trust her instincts and he did too—no matter what the cost.

Blinking back tears, Rayne squeezed him harder. She didn't want him to see how much it would kill her to lose him, not when she'd gotten him into the fight in the first place. *God, please keep him safe.*

Haven Hills Treatment Facility
Ward 8

When Dr. Fiona looked through the wire-mesh window of Oliver's cell, she saw him still asleep on the floor. That meant she wouldn't have to bother with security guards. The boy was in no condition to be a threat to her safety.

She had the library book and surveillance photo of the mystery Crystal child in her hands and couldn't wait to see if Oliver could track him with a touch of his special gift.

She had to see if sensory deprivation had enhanced this boy's second sight.

The exam room door shed light into the murky room as she entered. She flipped on the overhead light. He would need it.

"Oliver?" She knelt by the boy and brushed her fingers through his hair. "It's me, Dr. Fiona. You promised to help me, remember?"

Oliver opened his eyes. When he saw her, he pushed off the floor and sat up. He didn't say a word. His silence and the raw magnitude of his stare made her realize. His half-naked body and the intensity of his eyes up close made her uncomfortable. It reminded her that she was alone with him—locked in a cell with a boy she had tortured and lied to.

She took a deep breath and held out what she had in her hands. The library book. "You help me find this boy and you'll walk out of here. You have my promise."

What was one more lie?

{ 10 }

Two hours later

Rayne had hoped for more, but the search for Rafael at the old tunnels turned out to be a bust. Kendra didn't sense his presence. They found nothing of him except for a broken liquor bottle that looked free of dust and smelled fresh, with a brand label that Gabe recognized from his uncle's stash.

When Rayne saw the destruction again, it was an ominous reminder of what these kids had been through and the struggle that lay ahead. The Indigos' fight to live free had become her fight and not just because of Lucas. It was the right thing to do. They all walked through the tunnels in silence—as if they were on sacred ground—remembering what had been lost because Benny had died here. She knew they couldn't go home without trying harder to find Rafael. None of them would give up on him. They'd lost too much already.

After they escaped the tunnels using a different exit strategy and returned to where they'd parked the SUV, Rayne felt down and none of them did much talking. Gabe was the first to bring up Rafe's name.

"Take heart, Kendra. At least we didn't find Rafael's body.

That's something. We must take hope where we can find it." Gabriel put his hand on her shoulder. After she nodded, he shifted his gaze.

"Where's Ward 8, Lucas?"

Luke looked surprised and more than a little disturbed by Gabe's mention of the ward, the source of their connected visions. Rayne had seen her brother's reaction before and hated that he'd always be tortured by his hospital nightmares.

"Why? We can't just walk in and look around." With his voice raised, Lucas crossed his arms and leaned against the SUV. "Why would we want to go there?"

Gabe stayed calm.

"We don't have to go in, exactly. If we can get Kendra close enough to sense if Rafe is there, we'd at least know more than we do now," he reasoned. "So, tell us about Ward 8. Where is it?"

When Lucas stared at his boots and hesitated giving an answer, his reaction surprised Rayne. She'd always assumed Ward 8 was part of the church hospital where Luke had been confined as a patient.

"I'd say Haven Hills, but that's a guess," her brother said. "Whenever I see a vision of the ward, it's only a red-and-white sign over an entrance with double doors. I get a feeling that it's...familiar. I keep seeing a medical facility with security. There are guards and a woman in white. She's the one who brings the pain, but I can't picture her face."

"Anything else?" Gabe asked.

"When I was at Haven Hills, I remember hearing nurses talk about me getting transferred to Ward 8. They called it a one-way trip for hopeless cases. I escaped before that happened, but I can't rely on my memory. Between my visions and the drugs, I can't tell what's real."

These days Rayne knew it didn't take much for Lucas's

mind to yank him back to Haven Hills. He'd lost years of his life, and his dark past was rooted deep.

"Mia talked about some miracle doctor." Rayne sidled up to Luke and nudged him with her shoulder. "She told me her name. Fiona something, but I can't remember the rest. A foreign-sounding one, I think. I asked her if this doctor was the one doing the transfer or saving you from it. She never told me. Do you remember that doctor's name?"

"No, sorry. I barely remembered my *own* name back then." Gabriel heaved a sigh.

"A transfer could mean they'd do it by ambulance and take you to a separate location," he said. "The church has a great many resources, I'm afraid. But since we have to start somewhere, that hospital might be our only option. Let's give it a go while we're here in L.A. I'll ride with Rayne. Kendra, you've got the Navigator. Don't wreck it."

He tossed the keys to Kendra and they hit the road. After Gabriel climbed on the back of her Harley, Rayne took comfort when he put his arms around her. She'd never get tired of the way he made her feel when he got close. But when she caught an odd glance from Luke as he got into the SUV, Rayne did a double take. The haunted look in her brother's eyes gripped her hard.

She didn't have to be psychic to know that Lucas would hate being anywhere near Haven Hills.

West Hollywood
10:45 p.m.

After Gabe had Rayne make several passes around the Haven Hills complex on the Harley, Kendra asked if she could park the Navigator and watch the hospital. She wanted time to warm up her Indigo mojo. She and Lucas parked two blocks down so they could have an angle of the front of the facility. Gabe chose a spot not far away—an asphalt strip between two warehouses—where he and Rayne would have a good view of the rear entrance, a private patient loading zone. The alley smelled of trash and piss, but Gabe hadn't picked it for the ambience.

He got off the Harley and made sure he saw the cab of the Navigator. Luke had the passenger window down with his arm out, drumming a fidgety thumb on the door. Kendra was a shadow, backlit by the red neon sign for a laundry. Rayne stayed on her bike and kept her eyes alert for anything, including the murky alleyway behind her. They all were on edge.

Gabriel looked through his uncle's binoculars as he waited on Kendra.

I don't sense him, Gabe. Damn it. Kendra sent him a telepathic message.

Lucas, what about you? Could Ward 8 be here? Gabe asked, the Indigo way.

When the kid didn't reply, he tried again. *Luke?*

After a long moment of silence, Lucas eventually replied, *I don't know. Can't be sure. I feel…something. Just not sure what exactly.*

Although Luke hadn't offered much, Gabe knew what he meant about feeling something he couldn't figure out. Kendra had the true gift of feeling other Indigo souls, but inside the walls of the hospital, Gabriel sensed the despicable secret of his father. The staunch fanatics of the Church of Spiritual Freedom—the Believers—hurt Indigo children here.

"I don't know if Ward 8 is here," he said to Rayne as he lowered the binoculars. "But there's true evil behind those walls. This place is wicked. I can feel it."

Ward 8

Oliver Blue awoke in a dark room. A chill had left him numb, but he was too worn out to do anything about it. He lay sprawled on his belly, atop a mattress on the floor of his cell. With his face planted into a thin pillow, he could only open one eye.

Lifting an eyelid felt like an ordeal.

Different. The word kept him awake until he glanced over his shoulder and realized that his room had changed and he wore lame hospital pajamas. He didn't remember any of it. Someone had moved him to another room and really messed with him when they stripped him naked and made him wear pastel. Oliver felt like a drunk after a bender who discovered a girl's name tattooed on his ass.

Dr. Fiona must've ordered the change after he passed out cold, when he couldn't help her find the kid. Maybe she'd drugged him again. His brain was too fried to care. He saw that the doctor had left the surveillance photo and the book with him, but the exam room was gone, where she had monitored his brain activity and plugged him into machines to keep his body functioning. In this new room he had a sink and a toilet. No mirror. No more restraints.

No more thoughts of death.

No Caila.

Oliver shut his eyes tight and burrowed into the pillow with a moan. He forced the girl's face from his mind—and felt a hole where she had fit. He fought that feeling as the doctor told him. He wanted his life back. He wanted to be left alone.

His only hope to make that happen was to do what the doctor told him—if he could. The first time the doctor had given him the book and the photo, he'd been too groggy. He barely remembered what happened, except that he couldn't focus through his exhaustion and the effects of the meds, but maybe that was only an excuse.

His gift had changed. He wasn't sure how or why, but he felt different. He sat up and reached for the book the doctor had left him. He closed his eyes and clutched the hard cover to his chest until the edges pressed into his fingers and hurt. He even smelled the coppery tang of blood.

Caila had complicated his life with a trick. He didn't want to care about anything. He didn't want to be responsible for anyone else. He sensed truth in what Dr. Fiona had said. The doctor was…

True evil…wicked.

I can feel it.

"What?" Oliver jolted awake when he heard a guy's voice as if it came from inside his head. He searched his cell, but no one was there.

"Hello," he called out, and felt stupid doing it. His room was empty except for him and this blasted book.

Had he dreamed the voice? Or was it a fake memory from Caila? Exhausted and alone and fresh from Dr. Fiona's treatment of sensory deprivation, he couldn't trust his new reality. He was different, yet a bizarre feeling lingered like a twilight sleep dream that seemed too real.

The voice he'd heard had a British accent.

Oliver stared into the shadows, listening. He didn't hear the voice, yet there was a presence in the room that he felt. Like the way a stray cat stares over your shoulder to make you think it sees someone behind you, that's how it felt. Even the hair at his neck prickled. *Shit. Grow a pair.* Living the way he did, Oliver had seen plenty to make him scared, but he hated how it felt to live with fear every day.

He made up his mind to do something about it. He shifted

his eyes to the glow from the hallway that leached under his door and he centered on it. Blocking out his shadowy room, he focused on the light as if it were a tunnel he could walk through. The barrier of light anchored his body while his mind ventured beyond it, free.

As he'd done before, the walls of his room disappeared and he let his consciousness reach outside his cell like a wisp of smoke. Oliver's lungs sucked air as his awareness snaked beyond his body, the way Dr. Fiona had forced him to do when he escaped the black helmet.

His essence drifted out of his room and down the hall. He got by guards who didn't see him, seeped under doors and blew like a feather through ductwork and vents. He didn't have to know where he was.

Oliver kept his focus on one thing now. He had linked to someone through the book, in a way he'd never experienced before. He couldn't be sure it was the guy he had to find, but whoever it was, he felt sure of one thing.

His gift had been changed forever—because of Dr. Fiona.

Outside Haven Hills Treatment Facility

"Does Kendra sense Rafe yet?" Rayne asked.

"What?" Gabe got hit with a sudden déjà vu. He heard Rayne's question, yet it felt as if he'd heard her say it twice. "Sorry. I had a strange…brain cramp, or something equally peculiar. What did you say?"

"I asked if Kendra has sensed Rafael here yet," she repeated.

"Sorry, no." Gabe shook his head. "But that doesn't mean Ward 8 isn't here. They could have Rafe somewhere else. Another of their torture chambers."

The minute he said it, Gabe regretted it. He saw Rayne

tighten her jaw and she had a hard time looking him in the eye. She still felt guilty over what had nearly happened to her brother. If he'd been transferred to Ward 8, she might not have seen him again...ever. Gabe knew she hadn't been the one to commit him. Her older sister, Mia, had done that, but nothing consoled Rayne when it came to the missing years Lucas had spent in hell.

"I'm sorry," he said. "I didn't mean to stir up bad feelings."

"I know you didn't. Guilt isn't an easy thing to shake."

Her eyes filled with tears and she wiped them. When he saw her struggle to hold it together, he went to her. Gabe ran a finger down her moist cheek and kissed her forehead.

"It scares me how close I came to losing Lucas to this snake pit." Her voice cracked. "I thought they were helping him, but one thing scares me more."

"What's that?" He pulled her into his arms and held her.

"If my sister, Mia, knows what her church does to kids like Luke, how could she let them do it? I can't believe she was willing to sacrifice Lucas. For what?"

"I don't know, Rayne. When people believe God is on their side..."

Gabe suddenly stopped. He pushed away from Rayne, a move he never would've done unless he had a reason. In a rush, it struck him. Gabriel felt a strong urge to protect her.

In his head he heard the sound of someone else's voice mirroring his own in an eerie echo. He didn't know if the words were his at all. Every word carried anger and he felt his body being invaded. He staggered back a step and fell against a brick wall, panting for air. His chest felt on fire and he couldn't catch his breath.

"Hey. What's happening, Gabe?" Rayne's words came in a muffled slur. She leaped off the Harley and ran to him.

They're fuckin' soul vampires. Fear is a drug. They're afraid of us. A low voice channeled through his head with all the subtlety of a rushing train.

When people believe God is on their side, they think that gives them permission to do anything. They see us as a threat.

Every word came like a punch to his gut, an attack he'd never felt before. He lurched forward and stumbled toward the hospital, shielding Rayne with his body. His eyes burned and tears streaked his cheeks as he reached out a hand to no one.

Make it stop! He blasted his message to the collective.

Make what stop, Gabe? Lucas had heard him. *Gabe's in trouble. Punch it, Kendra!*

Whoever had invaded Gabe's mind, the powerful entity had a link to Haven Hills— and something more. Flashes of a tortured face flickered from the shadows of his memory. A familiar vision that he'd lost sleep over—the screaming guy in the black helmet with dark goggles. He'd drawn him in his sketchbook. The minute Gabe pictured the details of his sketch, the boy appeared like a ghost.

"Oh my God. What's that?" Rayne cried out. "That's… him. The guy you drew."

Gabriel relived one of his worst nightmares, except that he was awake. The guy looked dead. He could see through him, yet he didn't feel Death in this boy. He sensed a strong will to live and survive. The boy didn't speak. His image flashed his torment, the agony of being locked into the helmet, unable to see or feel anything. Gabriel heard his distant cries and knew it had been him. The essence of the boy existed in two realities, one here and one somewhere else. It looked as if every second of that duality pained him.

"Who are you?" he asked. "*What* are you?"

The instant that Gabe spoke, the screaming grew louder and unbearable, sweeping by his ear. He cringed and felt sick. His cries carried a jolt of electricity, like getting hit by a Taser, that made it hard for him to stand.

"No, stop!" He bent over in pain with his hands over his ears.

"Gabriel, what's happening?" Rayne rushed to him, yelling, "Stop! You're hurting him."

She stepped in front and blocked him from the guy in black. When she did, Gabe heard a loud zap and felt his ears pop as if a portal opened and closed to another existence.

"He's gone," she said.

He heard the relief in her voice, but for him nothing had changed. Whatever bond he shared with the boy in black, it went on. Gabe had to do something. He was under assault. He'd never had a vision come alive before his eyes and attack him. He sensed the kid had come to him for a reason, but his tortured soul had been filled with the injustice of what had happened to him, that he let Gabe feel his anger.

Gabe didn't know how to break a connection he'd never experienced before. He'd never been bombarded from inside. It came too fast, from all directions. *Make it stop!* On pure instinct Gabriel reacted. He stopped fighting. He had to defend his psyche and wasn't sure how until he willed his body to break the link. He hoped he could find his way back—and that it wasn't already too late.

Like flipping a switch, he shut down.

When he raised his chin to the heavens, he saw the night sky on a slow spin over him before his knees buckled and he hit the ground. Rayne's face wavered over him. Her voice became distant. He didn't even feel her hand when she touched him. Her face split into three and circled over him.

Rayne's sweet face was the last thing he saw. In a desperate move, he linked to her mind and his love for her, unsure he could even do what he imagined. She became his tether, his only way home. He clung to her as long as he could before everything went black.

It all happened fast. Rayne couldn't stop it. One minute Gabe was fine. The next he staggered like a drunk and collapsed, convulsing on the ground at her feet in a strange seizure. It reminded her of the time he'd connected to Lucas at the L.A. County Museum of Art and his link went horribly wrong—only there weren't any blue flames or freaked animals or scary quakes.

Who had he connected to this time? It couldn't have been Lucas again.

"Gabriel, can you hear me?" She clutched his face with both hands and tried to get his eyes to focus, but his seizure got worse. "Oh, please, no."

In the distance, she heard the SUV barrel up and screech to a stop. Lucas and Kendra jumped from the vehicle with doors flung open and headlights on.

"What happened?" Luke yelled as he knelt by Gabe.

"I don't know. Some b-bastard in a helmet and goggles came out of n-nowhere, looking like the Terminator. He never touched Gabe, but something happened." Rayne choked on every word. Nothing made sense.

"Whoever it was, I don't feel a presence." Kendra looked around before she knelt next to Gabe and touched his cheek. "Has this ever happened to him before? It looks like a seizure."

"Yeah, he did this once, when we searched for Luke after he escaped the hospital. Gabe told me that he made a connection, or whatever, that made him...sick." Rayne held down his shoulders. "We were just talking. He was fine, until ghost boy showed up."

"Don't restrain him, Rayne. He's too strong. You could get whacked or hurt *him* instead."

Gabriel moaned and thrashed on the asphalt. When his knuckles got scraped, they glistened with blood. Rayne didn't want to let him go, but she did what Kendra told her. The Indigo healer looked at her watch and took a quick look around.

"Kick that broken glass away from him, Lucas. Anything that can hurt him," Kendra said. "And cushion his head, Rayne."

Rayne shrugged out of her jacket and folded it under Gabe's head, but she wanted to do more.

"He's convulsing. Can he swallow his tongue? Shouldn't we…"

"No, people can't swallow their tongues, but let's roll him on his side. He's not breathing right. We gotta keep his airway clear so he doesn't choke or puke."

Lucas grabbed one of his arms and they rolled him over. After Kendra checked her watch for a second time, Rayne had to ask, "Why are you checking the time?"

"Longer than five minutes, we should call 911. But I'm afraid if we do that, they'll only take him to the closest hospital."

When she glared over her shoulder at Haven Hills, Rayne understood. She had her burner phone for emergencies. She could call for help, but that would put Gabe's fate into someone else's hands. "Yeah, good point."

"Besides, if Gabe is seizing, it's something psychic. We have to get him to his uncle. Maybe he'll know what to do."

"Gabe drew Terminator boy in his sketchbook, Luke. He was screaming, in the drawing and here too. Since you two are channeling dreams, he must've come from a vision *you* had. Do you remember him?"

"Yeah. Hard to forget something like that." Luke couldn't

look her in the eye. "If I brought this guy to Gabriel, I'm sorry."

"You and Gabe, you guys don't pick your visions." Rayne reached for her brother's hand and squeezed it.

"It's slowing down," Kendra said.

It didn't take long for Gabriel to quit shaking. The worst of his tremors had stopped—short of her five-minute window to call 911—but he didn't wake up. When Kendra touched his cheek, Rayne knew she'd tried to mentally connect with him.

"Anything?" she asked. "Can you reach him?"

The girl only shook her head and said, "Let's get him home."

With those words, urgency gripped Rayne by the throat. She didn't know how to help Gabriel, and Kendra didn't either. The Indigo girl put up a strong front, but she looked as worried as Rayne was. It took all three of them to get Gabriel into the Navigator.

They had a long ride ahead.

Near the Bristol Mountains
Hours later

Lucas rode the Harley and Kendra drove the SUV so Rayne could stay with Gabriel in the back. Cradling Gabe's head in her lap, she stared out the windshield from the backseat—numb—watching miles of center lane stripes roll by the Navigator. The vehicle's headlights caught the movement of swaying grasses and acres of fence posts as Kendra drove by, pushing the speed limit. The two-hour ride back to the Bristol Mountains felt as if it would never end.

Rayne held Gabriel and never felt so powerless. None of them could help him. His shudders had faded into something more frightening. He'd collapsed into a deep sleep that none of them could wake him from. After Kendra failed to connect to him using another mind link, Rayne even tried kissing him. That worked before in the museum library, but nothing woke him now.

In all the excitement, Rayne remembered that she hadn't called Gabe's uncle. She had her cell, but just thinking about what she'd say made her sick.

"I guess I should let his uncle know," Rayne told Kendra. "If he needs a doctor…"

"Already done."

"But how…?"

Rayne didn't finish her question. She doubted that she'd ever get used to how Indigos communicated. Once they got close enough to the Bristol Mountains, Kendra must've sent the equivalent of a mental flare to Uncle Reginald. Indigos had their own psychic "friends and family" plan.

"What did his uncle say? Is this…normal for kids like Gabe?" Rayne brushed her fingers through his hair and touched his forehead. He didn't have a fever, but that was little consolation. "Why won't he wake up?"

"His uncle's never seen anything like this before. He's worried." Kendra met her gaze in the rearview mirror. "He said that Gabriel has blown past being an Indigo and that Crystal kids are…complicated. They're sensitive and strange things come at them like a magnet from our reality and the other side. That's all he'd say, but it's enough to scare me. I've never known a Crystal."

Rayne shifted her gaze to the SUV's outside mirror to make sure she still saw the headlight of her Harley behind them. Lucas was like Gabe—complicated. She stroked Gabriel's cheek and willed him to open his eyes.

He didn't.

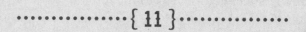

{ 11 }

Burbank
3:00 a.m.

Rafael felt sluggish, gripped by the drugs that still lingered in his system. He slowly opened his eyes and felt the chill of concrete under his shoulder blades and arms. He ached all over. Even his teeth hurt. When he could focus, he saw nothing but stark white and thought he had died. It took time for him to realize that he was in a locked cell with a painted floor, a white padded room no bigger than a closet.

The white room made him think of heaven…and Benny as an angel. But when the reality hit him—that he was a loser and would never see heaven—Rafael felt like a stain. The only color, to screw up the clean white, was him.

"Pendejos," he cursed under his breath as he sat up and leaned against a wall.

He felt sick and had a splitting headache that throbbed behind his eyes. His feet were ice cold. They'd taken his boots and jacket. All he had on were his jeans, his black *Dia de los Muertos* T-shirt and a fresh bandage over his gunshot wound that had broken open when they attacked him at the tunnel entrance. His cell was only four walls. No toilet or sink.

Whatever the purpose of this locked room, it wasn't meant for long-term visitors.

Kendra. Can you hear me?

Rafe thought of her and hoped she was close enough to hear him. That was a long shot, and his luck had never been good, except for the day he'd met her and Benny, but when he didn't feel Kendra, he had to move.

When he could manage it, he got to his feet without puking and went to the door. He didn't have to test it to see if it was locked. There wasn't a knob on his side. Only one of those secured doors that opened with a swipe of an ID card. A small wire-mesh window had been blocked from the other side. He couldn't see anything beyond his cell, but if they expected him to stay quiet until they came for him— well, screw that.

"*Mierda!* Open the door. *Me cago en tus muertos!*"

Rafe pounded on the door with his fist and yelled. No one came. He knew that telling these people what he'd do to their dead relatives wasn't a good way to win them over, but he didn't care.

Minutes later

O'Dell hated working the backside of midnight. The church didn't pay overtime and he had no ambition beyond the money. To kill time he'd eaten his second helping of General Tso's chicken and fried rice, a reheat from a take-out order that he had stashed in his minifridge. His office smelled like Chinatown and broccoli farts.

His operations bunker had only a skeleton screw on the graveyard shift. Three guys manned the computers and ran the church's Tracker facial recognition program that targeted Indigo kids in their database system, searching for them on the streets of L.A. Big screens projected flashes of color across a bull pen of desks cast in murky shadows, the command center located steps down from where his office was behind them. The only reason he was still there had been that Mexican kid, the one that Boelens had brought in, on his orders.

He knew the boss would give him special instructions. That's why he'd contacted the man using the encrypted phone he'd been given. He'd never seen the guy's face. Hell, he only guessed that the head of operations—his boss—was a man. The way he talked, the guy had to have a dick. Plus whatever he said in his disguised mechanical voice, he sounded like a RoboCop knockoff.

"That kid is awake and he's pissing me off." His number-two man, Boelens, poked his head into O'Dell's open door. The guy had a lizard stare. He never blinked.

"Have you heard back on what we're supposed to do with him?" his man asked. "I know what I'd like to do. That pain-in-the-ass freak is giving me a tumor."

Boelens had only one reason to be here at this hour. He hated Lucas Darby and Kendra Walker after they humiliated him and derailed his night raid at the tunnels. A rat's nest of Indigos had gotten the better of him, especially the unnamed rocker boy with the British accent.

O'Dell never saw the Brit. He'd been injured on that mission. He made himself a medal—his own version of the Purple Heart—that he'd hung on his office wall. He'd been shot in the foot. *His* weapon. *His* finger on the trigger. No one else knew that and he saw no point in shedding light on what really happened. Who would *believe* him? After that night he started treatment to have his snake tattoos removed from his forearms. No one would hear why he'd done that either.

"I haven't—"

Before O'Dell could finish, his encrypted phone rang with

the ring tone for the *Justified* TV show. He should have been happy to finally get the return call, but it always made him nervous to talk to the boss. O'Dell cleared his throat, picked up the phone off his desktop and turned his chair so Boelens wouldn't see him sweat.

"Hello?"

"I don't have much time. Tell me what you've got."

O'Dell gritted his teeth. He went from nervous to mad in two seconds. The bastard had kept him waiting for nearly a full day, as if he had nothing better to do. Now he expected him to spill his good news, pronto. That was bullshit.

"I had my men stake out those tunnels, like I told you I would. Just like I figured, one of those Indigo kids came back. The Mex, Rafael Santana. I got him with me in a Burbank holding cell."

There was silence on the line. He thought maybe the guy hung up.

"Is he connected to that...Crystal kid, Lucas Darby?"

"Yeah, he's linked to a whole nest of those mind freaks, including the Brit who sent you that message through Boelens. I figured you'd want to know. We could have a gold mine of Indigos if we play this right. Any special orders? We could work him over, see what he knows. My man Boelens has a way with these kids."

"No. Leave him to me. I'll make arrangements to pick him up, but I want you there personally to make the transfer. Do I make myself clear?"

O'Dell narrowed his eyes and spun his chair back around. Boelens was still standing at his doorway. Without a word, the guy shrugged and jutted his chin to prod him for information. Boelens would have preferred to make hamburger meat out of the Mex, but he wouldn't get the chance.

"Yes, sir. Crystal clear."

After O'Dell ended the call, Boelens had to know. "So? What are we supposed to do with this kid?"

"Nothing." O'Dell glared at his man. "Someone's comin' to load him up. I'm to hand him over personally. Guess the boss trusts me."

"Yeah, that must be it." Boelens smirked with a raised eyebrow. "Just promise me that I get to wrap the kid up in a nice bow, ready for pick up."

O'Dell rolled his eyes and said, "Don't leave any bruises they can see."

Boelens grinned and left. He was an easy man to please.

North of L.A.
Dawn

Belly-down, Rafael lay in the back of a moving van without windows. The vehicle vibrated against his bruised, aching ribs, a farewell token from an angry dude who never blinked. But Rafe couldn't do anything about his pain. His hands had been handcuffed behind him, and his legs were zip-tied together and trussed to his cuffs. He felt like a pig heading to slaughter.

He'd been beat before. Plenty. The worst part was where beatings took him. He relived the anger of his father, the screaming and the smell of alcohol on his old man's breath. He experienced every cut, bruise and broken bone in his past again, as if it were fresh. Most of all he felt like the loser he was—especially after what he let happen to Benny. All he had to do was keep the kid safe, but he'd fucked that up.

Shit.

The drive went on forever, plenty of time for him to dwell on his mistakes. Mostly he thought of Kendra. She'd never know what happened to him. When he left her behind, he only had one thing on his mind—feeling Benny's spirit. He never thought what leaving would do to her. He felt like a coward, a useless shit like his old man.

He drifted in and out of consciousness. Once he woke up to the sound of church bells in the distance and the road noise sounded as if they'd driven through the suburbs before they got onto another freeway and more miles. After the van got off the highway and slowed down, he heard the sound of water. It reminded him of a river and that made him sleepy, but parts of the road were rough and that hurt his ribs.

When the van finally came to a stop, he heard voices outside.

"Hey! Let me out, *pendejos,*" he yelled.

The vehicle rolled on. When no one came, he laid down his head and closed his eyes again, but this time the van slowed its speed and stopped after only a few minutes. The panel door opened and he felt hands yank at his body.

He grimaced in pain when they dragged him out, punishing his gunshot wound and his throbbing ribs. After they cut his legs loose from his cuffs, men in black uniforms hauled him to his bare feet, and his knees and ankles felt stiff and numb. He squinted in the early morning sun with his eyes watering. After he stumbled, two men held him by his arms and dragged him.

Rafael didn't let them see how much they hurt him.

The men lugged him into the shadow of a dark mansion, a fancy place almost as big as the Stewart Estate. That stone-and-brick house towered over him and looked more like a museum. Armed guards patrolled the grounds and manned the entrance where they took him, but Rafael noticed something strange.

Each man stared at him as if he had horns and a tail. That only made him mad.

"What are you lookin' at, *cabron?*" Rafe glared at one and

struggled against the tight grip of the guards. He tried looking tougher than he felt, being dragged by the arms.

"Some of these men haven't seen one of you Indigo freaks up close. Not here anyways," a gruff voice came from his right.

"But you have?"

"Yeah, I've seen enough to believe in the cause. Your kind, you're nothing but animals."

Rafe scowled at the man. Kendra had once explained the word *irony* to him. He understood what she meant now.

"Why is it that bullies with the hardest fists always point the finger at the other guy...calling *him* the animal?" Rafe asked. He didn't wait for an answer. "What is this place?"

"Shut up, head case."

The man was done talking. When he wrenched his arm, Rafe felt a jolt of pain shoot through his ribs. He winced but didn't make a sound. He had too much to think about. He didn't miss the significance of what the guard told him. He was the first Indigo brought here—to the kind of mansion built for powerful, wealthy men.

That meant Rafe was special for a reason. And since he hadn't been blindfolded, and they let him see the boss man's house, that meant something else too. He wouldn't be leaving here—breathing.

Knowing that should have scared him, but it only made him want to see Kendra one last time.

Stewart Estate
Dawn

Something woke Rayne. She lifted her head with a start. With her eyes wide, she gasped at the sudden noise of a dog's whimper.

"Hellboy? What is it?"

Gabriel's loyal dog whined and wagged his tail at the sound of her voice.

"Uncle Reginald?" she called out. The man didn't answer. Gabe's uncle had been in the room most of the night, but was gone now.

Bleary-eyed, Rayne yawned to clear the fog from her morning brain. She looked down and realized that she still wore the same clothes she had on yesterday. She'd stayed with Gabriel in his room. Nothing would have made her leave him. She'd slept in a large tufted chair that she'd moved close to his four-poster bed and used her arms as a pillow at the foot of his mattress. Hellboy had curled up near her and refused to leave too.

Now the ghost dog had his ears perked and his eyes on his unconscious master. Rayne searched Gabriel's room to look for any reason that Hellboy had his ears at attention. A clock ticked across the bedroom, and a wind off the mountains sighed outside, but nothing felt off except…Gabriel.

"Where is he, boy?" she pleaded. "Fetch him home. Can you?"

Hellboy only cocked his glimmering blue head. Rayne felt the remnants of a bad dream haunting her mind. After the twilight memory came to her in flashes, she remembered it hadn't been a dream at all. Her nightmare was still happening.

"Gabriel?" she whispered, but he didn't stir.

He lay in his bed, fast asleep, if she could call it that. He looked tanned and healthy, especially after he'd returned home to his uncle's estate and the Bristol Mountains, but Gabe slept as if he were in a coma. She moved closer to hear him breathe. His long eyelashes touched his flushed cheeks as his chest rose and fell. His breaths were steady. When she felt his forehead, he didn't have a fever.

She didn't understand any of this.

"Open your eyes, Gabriel. Can you hear me?"

Nothing had changed since Gabe had collapsed near Haven Hills. When she gazed across his bedroom to catch the first signs of morning, she desperately wanted the new day to bring hope. The soft flicker of a gray sunrise seeped into his chamber from tall windows draped in burgundy velvet. Photographs of his mother and uncle were in ornate gilded frames that hung beside colorful mementos from his circus life. His collection of L.A. rock band T-shirts hung in an open armoire. When she smelled his subtle cologne and the scent of his skin, Rayne reached for one of his scraped hands and held it. His inflamed knuckles were bruised. She hated to see him like this.

She couldn't lose him now.

"You're scaring me, Gabriel."

The cold trickle of a tear rolled down her cheek when she kissed his hand. Touching his cheek, she prayed he'd open his eyes.

"Please wake up."

Gabriel heard a distant sound, something quite familiar. It nudged his mind like a persistent memory. He knew he wasn't alone, but a thick haze lay between him and...

Rayne.

In a vast wasteland of never-ending shadows, he called her name and sent a message to the hive, until he realized she couldn't hear him that way. She had been his compass—his way home. When he thought of her, he pictured everything that he loved and the unshakable bonds that he had in his life—his uncle and his new Indigo family, the memory of his beloved mother, Hellboy and the collective of souls.

Most of all, he loved Rayne. She had brought him home once before.

After his mother died, he had felt lost. His father had his mother killed, trying to find him. He lived off the grid—hiding from the long reach of the Believers and his father—because he didn't know what else to do. He thought his uncle would blame him for being the reason his sister had died, but Gabe had been wrong.

He'd been wrong about a lot of things. Rayne and his uncle helped him see that having nothing to lose wasn't the thing that gave him an edge. What made him strong were people worth fighting for and freedom and the Indigos' right to survive. He had anchored to Rayne for a reason.

She would bring him home again.

When he thought of her, a pale light cut into his darkness and he smelled the faint lavender and rosemary scent of her hair and the warmth of her touch on his skin. *Wake up.* He wanted it to happen. *Open your eyes!* He felt like screaming but couldn't make his body move until he sensed soft skin and a gentle squeeze on his fingers.

Gabe blinked. He looked through the blur of his lashes until the shadows ebbed away and everything came into focus.

"Gabriel?"

A girl's face—cast in a soft light—moved closer to his. He felt the warmth of her body and breathed in the intoxicating aroma of her skin. *My precious girl.* As much as he wanted to speak to Rayne, he couldn't. He'd left a thing undone—dangerously unraveled. Something important, but Rayne wasn't a part of whatever it was—nor was anyone else. He had to be the one to finish it. Gabe realized that now.

He shifted his gaze and fixed on a dark figure in the room. Fainter than he was before, the guy in black hadn't left. He looked more like an eerie mirage that still shadowed him. This time the macabre vision stared at him with sad accusing eyes. Without words, he demanded something of Gabe that he had yet to figure out, but he didn't attack him this time. He vanished in a thin trail of smoke, but a part of him lingered—inside Gabriel.

What do you want?

The boy had gone and Gabe got no answer. He sat up in bed and shut his eyes to fight off a wave of dizziness. He felt sick, but he couldn't let that stop him. He threw off his blankets and got out of bed to find he was only dressed in boxers. That should have made him feel awkward around Rayne, but he didn't have time for that.

"I have to…"

He heard the words come from his mouth as he stood by his bed and he barely recognized his voice. He'd lost the echo of the other, but that left him feeling uneasy, as if he had suddenly lost something he should have held on to.

"What is it, Gabriel?"

When Rayne spoke, he turned his head and stared at her. Nothing she said sank in. Gabe had something else he had to do. He walked straight for the full-length mirror in his bedroom. He had to see what he knew would be there. After he saw his reflection, he couldn't move. His face looked back, but the image of someone else was there too—shifting and writhing underneath his skin.

A shadow stared out through his eyes—*the boy in black.*

"What's wr-wrong, Gabriel?" Rayne's voice cracked. "Please say something. Talk to me."

"You can't…see this?"

"See what?"

The way he glared into his mirror—fixated yet repulsed

by what he saw—scared the hell out of her. It was as if it wasn't *her* Gabriel. He acted as if he didn't see her—as if he weren't…

"Are you awake? Is this one of your…visions?" She'd seen him glaze-eyed before, whenever he hadn't fully awakened from his vision. "Do you need your sketchbook? Is that what it is?"

Gabriel needed the release he got from drawing what he saw. She'd seen him do that to break free of a vision before. A finished drawing meant he could wake up. Rayne didn't wait for him to answer. She rushed to a desk that he had in his bedroom and grabbed the artist's pad he used to turn his hellish prophesies into real Indigo faces.

"Here. Take it." She pushed the spiral sketchbook at him. When he still didn't look at her and kept his attention on the mirror, she tugged at his arm.

"Draw what you see, Gabe. Let me *help* you."

Rayne pleaded and when she grabbed his elbow, he finally blinked as if he saw her this time.

"No. I can't." He shook his head. "This isn't…a vision."

"What do you mean? What's happening to you?"

"I don't know, but you shouldn't be here. He could come back. I'm not sure I can protect you."

Gabriel didn't wait for her to say anything. He grabbed a pair of jeans from his armoire, pulled them over his boxers and zipped up. He looked spooked. While he rummaged through his clothes for a shirt and shoved his feet into un-laced boots, she pushed him to talk.

"That guy in the helmet? He's here?" she asked. "I didn't see him this time. Where is he?"

Before he walked by her without an explanation, she stopped him until he looked her in the eye. He touched her

cheek and heaved a sigh. She wasn't sure he'd tell her anything until he finally opened up.

"He's here, Rayne. In me."

Gabriel knew he had hurt Rayne when he shut her out.
He had to think, and staring into her beautiful gray eyes only
clouded his thoughts and flipped his guy switch to protect
her. He needed clarity and quiet and the freedom to sense
an answer—the Indigo way.

He had a place to go for that. Walking through the grand
hall of Stewart family portraits in oils with their gilded gold
frames, he barely looked up as he shrugged into an ivory
sweater. The long history of his proud family line, coupled
with the sense of duty he felt to protect the Indigos, had
been woven into a tapestry of commitment that weighed
heavier now, and rightfully so. The echo of his footsteps
mirrored the bracing beat of his heart as he navigated hall-
ways he knew well from his childhood, until he reached a
massive wooden door.

Gabe tugged it open and climbed the stone steps of the
tower to head for the rampart, the highest overlook of the
Bristol Mountains. He had to tap into his psychic instincts.
They'd served him well and he wouldn't abandon his faith
in them now. But he felt a blistering headache and an ever-
increasing weakness as he trudged up the steep flight of
steps, carrying the burden of another soul inside him—and
his doubt.

Had *he* done this or had the boy targeted him and won?
Perhaps it wasn't a question of winning or losing. He sensed
the boy's need might trump all that.

Tower stone radiated the morning chill, and the walls of
the spiral stairs smelled of humidity and the sweet pull of
childhood magic. The hiss of his footsteps echoed memo-

ries. He felt safe in these walls, as safe as if he were in his mother's arms.

Gabriel had always appreciated the solitude of early morning, the twilight between his two worlds colliding. He chose to believe that a new day meant that he had survived whatever dark world he'd dreamed, even though there were nights he wasn't sure which existence was reality.

He hoped he would be strong enough to deal with whoever he'd brought home from Haven Hills. Like what happened with Lucas, this kid had connected to him through a vision and hadn't let go—not even after Gabe had shut down his consciousness. He had to know how that could happen. Until he could, he didn't feel in control. His ability to protect these Indigo kids had turned into utter chaos. Even before Rafael went missing, he had a bad premonition that he had failed before he'd started.

He was missing something. He had brought this stranger home to his uncle's estate and put all of them at risk. Even though he hadn't done it deliberately, the dangerous connection had been made and was still with him. Why? How? He wanted there to be a reason that could help them all, but he didn't know how to turn things around.

When Gabe got to the top step, he heaved open the heavy wooden door and pushed through it. The parapet wall of the rampart circled around him as he gazed onto the Bristol Mountains from atop the tower. The lush hills were made more beautiful by the blush of dawn. He breathed deep as a faint breeze swept through his hair and made his eyes water. Gabriel walked to the wall and leaned his elbows onto the stone. He looked over the grounds and searched for the familiar, the hiking trails and gardens that he'd spent time with his mother and uncle as a child.

When he felt the extraordinary soul stir inside him, he

looked to the mountains for answers. If Gabriel had a death wish, he couldn't think of a better place to be.

Oliver never considered what might happen before he mind-shadowed the life force residue left on the book. He'd done it before, but after a strange voice invaded his head, he indulged his curiosity and went after it. He'd done it out of boredom, fear or whatever. It didn't matter now. He tripped through a one-way door and now drifted weightless through the rise and fall of a surging darkness, cut loose from everything he had known.

Only he wasn't really free and he knew it.

He missed Caila, but nothing else. The doctor had said the girl had used him. Any memory he had of her was a lie, so he'd be alone to face whatever would happen and he didn't know what to think of his reinvented gift.

At first he felt the attachment of his physical body and took comfort that he could always return—as if that was *normal*. His meat anchor kept him straddling two realities, but the longer he stayed separated, the more he realized that neither existence made him happy. Not even the power of his new gift gave him peace.

It only made him want more.

Until now he had never linked to another soul, except when he used his gift to feel an object that would trigger a vision, but that was different. He'd get a glimpse of a memory or sense where someone was and images would speed past him on fast forward. Only he would know which ones meant something. He'd pick out the things that made sense and pieced them together to tell a story. The way his ability used to work felt like making a movie.

Nothing like this.

Because Dr. Fiona had made him stronger and different,

this time he had crossed paths and marked the soul of someone more powerful. Maybe it didn't matter who did the tagging. What was done was done. He got pulled into the boy's existence and he'd never seen or felt anything like it before. One minute he'd been in an alley, the next he was—

Where, exactly?

He drifted and stared across a cosmic passage. When everything shifted to shadows and slowed down, colors became more vivid. Brilliant glimmers of light oozed across a vast expanse like the Northern Lights through the night sky. He sensed other souls like him and felt rooted to something bigger. He didn't know how he understood this. He just did.

Perhaps his link to the boy gave him insight they shared.

But when the hypnotic beauty of the light came to an end, he felt his soul surrender to gravity as if he had a phantom sensation of the body he'd left behind. Oliver wasn't sure he liked how that felt, but he didn't have time to brood over it. After a dim glow intensified and nearly blinded him, the streets of L.A. were gone as the shadows lifted. He passed from one reality into another in the blink of his eye.

Unlike his first meeting with the boy in the alley, this time he saw through a body not his own. Gabriel's body. He remembered the name that the girl had called him. Once Gabriel had opened his eyes, Oliver felt him rush to a mirror. He knew what the kid saw because he saw it too. The freak show of looking through someone else's eyes scared him, but something else shocked him more.

Gabriel radiated a pulsing cobalt blue with spears of crystal that magnified the light. Oliver had heard other kids talk about seeing an aura. Every human being had one, but not every Indigo saw them. He hadn't been able to—until now. Maybe Gabriel had something to do with his new ability. Indigos had an aura of cobalt blue, but he'd only heard rumors about those who had a different kind of light. That's how he realized what Gabriel was.

A Crystal child.

Oliver had been hit by something he never saw coming. He was in the process of becoming a more powerful Indigo than he ever thought he'd be. Whatever Dr. Fiona had done to him, it had triggered a change that was still evolving. But he didn't feel strong enough to stir things up with a Crystal child and he didn't know how to break the connection. From the look on Gabriel's face in the mirror, he didn't either.

Oliver had to figure it out. If his old gift still functioned, he would've known where Gabriel was by now. The information Dr. Fiona promised would earn him his freedom, but something was off. He had to stay focused and keep his eyes open—Gabriel's eyes—to get what he needed and move on.

Just do it. You didn't ask for this, any of it. Oliver gave in to his dark thoughts. *You don't owe this kid anything.* The truth was that he didn't have much to go back for—except a girl who had filled him with lies—lies he wanted to believe, yet couldn't now.

But as he stood atop the world, inside Gabriel, and stared across a picture postcard of mountains in perfect stillness, he wanted more than the life he had before Caila changed everything.

Gabriel made him *want* more…*feel* more. He had opened a door to an infinite way to live and made him realize that Indigos didn't have to live in fear—or die as victims. As Oliver gazed over the most beautiful mountains he'd ever seen, he didn't feel alone for the first time in years. He felt connected to the earth and to a consciousness he'd never experienced before.

He wanted to breathe in hope for a new freedom and feel the warmth of his Indigo family in this place where he felt others like him. But when he suddenly realized—that he couldn't breathe or feel anything—a sudden panic hit him hard.

He was thrust back into the dark isolation of the helmet and couldn't catch his breath. Trapped inside Gabriel's body felt like sinking into a crushing quicksand. His senses were gone. Even his eyesight was borrowed as long as Gabriel let him see. He felt empty and dead. This wasn't *his* body. *How long could he exist like this?* If he died with his consciousness inside Gabriel, who would know—*or care?*

He *had* to find a way back. *Had to.*

Ward 8
Morning

Fiona dodged traffic in her Mercedes as she listened to Beethoven's "Ode to Joy." She pulled into the parking garage at Haven Hills and waved through the guard station without slowing down. With more important things awaiting her, Fiona screeched to a stop in her assigned spot nearest the elevator that would take her to the basement and Ward 8. After she clipped her ID badge to the lapel of her navy suit, she took one last look in the car mirror.

She had intended to check her lipstick, but seeing the accusing doubt in her own eyes made her turn away. She'd gotten a disturbing phone call from the night-shift nursing staff. Oliver Blue had been found—collapsed on the floor of his cell in a coma—with a book clutched in his hands. He held the book so tightly that it took two nurses to pry his fingers loose.

Fiona got out of her car and headed for the bank of elevators. Her heels clacked on the cement and echoed in the garage as her mind raced with dire thoughts about what might have happened to the boy. It didn't take long for her fleeting concern for Oliver to turn into her *real* worry. She pictured Alexander Reese's face. Others on staff could talk about a boy slipping into an unexplained coma and word could get to Alexander. If she couldn't turn this situation around, she'd have to answer to him and explain why she hadn't told him about Oliver—or asked his approval for her deviation from church protocols.

She reached for her ID badge and fingered the key that hung with it. That key locked away all her secrets. She had downplayed it to staff, saying it was archived materials from a previous work assignment. No one had questioned her. The records she kept there went back years, files on the kids she had performed unusual procedures on or marked as special—kids like Oliver.

Her cutting-edge experiments would be revolutionary to anyone with half a brain. Unfettered by conscience, she had made better progress without anyone looking over her shoulder, second-guessing her with their mundane morality.

"Come on," she muttered as she hit the elevator button several times.

When she got to the ward, a nurse greeted her at the double doors.

"We have him in ICU. He's unresponsive, but stable…for now." The nurse handed her a clipboard with Oliver's updated condition. "Awaiting your orders, Doctor."

In step with the nurse, Fiona read as she moved. When she entered the ICU, she saw the activity in Room 4. Oliver was the only critical patient. The intensive care unit was small and well equipped. Of late it had mainly been used for patient recovery after her experimental surgical procedures. The new direction she'd taken with Oliver had put a hold on surgeries.

The overnight emergency would get noticed, especially since she hadn't been on duty to do damage control.

The night doctor on call had started the initial diagnostics, ordered lab work and performed a brain scan to assess the severity of the boy's condition. With Oliver's eyes closed and no verbal or motor responses, he had scored a three on the Glasgow Coma Scale. More tests would be coming on her orders now, but with Oliver in such a deep coma, his body functions would have to be managed. At the sound of a steady beeping heart monitor and the hiss of a respirator, Fiona knew what she would see when she entered ICU 4.

Oliver had a tracheal tube in his mouth. His narrow bed had electrodes and colored leads snaking from his body that were plugged into the equipment that would monitor his condition and keep him alive if his body failed.

"Clear the room while I examine my patient." Fiona stared down at Oliver with her jaw tight until every nurse left the room. When she was alone with the boy, she did a quick exam that shed no light, but she had a theory.

"You found him, didn't you, Oliver? This Crystal child." She stroked fingers through his hair. "What did he do to you?"

She'd seen the aftermath of what the other Crystal child had done at the L.A. County Museum of Art. Complete annihilation. Perhaps this boy had done the same to Oliver's mind. If he did, her lab rat would be useless to her now.

Fiona seethed with anger. She'd been beaten again—outsmarted—by an unnamed kid she had to get her hands on. He existed. She had no doubt, even if Alexander didn't believe he did. She'd prove it to him. Fiona pulled open the door to ICU 4 and gave an order to the first nurse who walked by.

"Bring me Caila Ferrie. Strap her into a wheelchair and bring her here. Now."

"Yes, Doctor."

Fiona crossed her arms and stared at Oliver from the door. If there was a chance to read his memory in his condition, the strange Indigo girl, who bartered in memories, might be her only hope to discover what had happened to the boy. With any luck, she'd get what she really wanted—a Crystal child worthy of her attention.

Stewart Estate
Hours later

Rayne had tried to help Gabriel, but he looked miserable and refused to talk. He'd turned down food, even though he hadn't eaten since yesterday, and looked exhausted. His face flinched as if he had a splitting headache, but he didn't complain.

Gabriel went to the great room, drawn to the fire. He gazed into the raging flames in the hearth, mesmerized by them. Rayne had followed him there but gave him space now. He had a comforter around him even though the room was stifling hot, and he kept tossing logs onto the blaze. Gabe finally quit stoking the fire when his uncle went to talk to him.

"We have to do something." Rayne paced the floor and kept her voice to a whisper, as she watched Gabriel and his uncle from across the large room.

Lucas and Kendra were with her. They all watched from a distance to give them privacy. None of them were close enough to hear the conversation, but when Uncle Reginald was done, he had a dour look on his face as he joined them.

"I don't mean to alarm any of you," his uncle said. "But

I noticed something odd about how Gabriel spoke to me a minute ago."

Rayne had seen Gabe shift from annoyed to angry, something she'd never seen him do with an uncle he loved like a real father. Sure, he had anger issues when it came to his bio-dad. Who wouldn't? The man had something to do with the death of Gabe's mother. That would wreck any father–son relationship, but the mood swings she'd seen from Gabe today looked as if he was suffering from a migraine that was getting worse.

"What did he say?" Rayne asked his uncle.

"It wasn't what he said. It was more the way he said it." Uncle Reginald fixed his worried gaze on his nephew. "He lost his accent. It came and went, actually. He's fighting whoever is inside him, but I can't be sure if he's winning."

"I've noticed something too," Lucas said. "Whenever I'm around Gabriel, I get a steady buzz of energy. It jacks me up, in a good way, but I haven't felt it since he collapsed at Haven Hills. I thought it was because he'd passed out. Guess I was wrong. I didn't notice it missing until now."

"He's weak. I can feel it." Kendra fixed her gaze on Gabe's uncle. "We have to stop this...or slow it down. Any ideas?"

Rayne looked to Uncle Reginald. They all did.

"One, maybe, but I'll need all of you." Gabe's uncle shifted his gaze between them. "I have no idea if it'll work."

After Uncle Reginald told them what he had in mind, Rayne agreed to do her part. When they left her alone with Gabe, she knelt in front of him with her arms crossed over his knees. His face looked flush and tinged with misery as he stared into the fire with his honey-amber eyes reflecting a soft glimmer of golden heat. When he turned to her, she touched his cheek.

"I'm s-sorry to be such a—" he said in a whisper.

Before he went on, she touched his lips with a finger and shook her head so he'd stop. "You're having a bad day, times two. You didn't ask for this."

Beautiful, generous Gabriel had tried to apologize for something he had no control over. He had a hitchhiker onboard, a guy who looked as if he'd walked off the set of a *Road Warrior* remake. Rayne wanted to hate the guy in black for what he'd done to Gabriel, but he could be another innocent victim of the Believers. She feared that was why Gabe had been so lost and conflicted. He wouldn't hurt this kid if there were any chance he needed help—no matter what that meant for him.

"I need you to come with me," she said.

Gabriel looked as if he'd refuse, but when Rayne held out her hand, he took it.

North of L.A.

Rafael stared at his naked reflection in a tall mirror. If he gritted his teeth any more, they'd fuse together. Strands of his damp hair hung in his face and he didn't care. His skin was flush from exertion and still carried the marks of red handprints where the bastards had grabbed him.

"Don't he smell pretty?" one guy said.

He blew Rafe a fake kiss in the mirror with a stupid smirk on his face. The other one only shook his head and kept toweling him off.

"Asshole." Rafe glared and spoke in English this time. He didn't want the guy to misunderstand his meaning.

"Orders, kid. Nothin' personal."

The two guys with no necks had stripped him of his clothes and tossed them into the trash like garbage. They hauled him into a steaming-hot gym shower with his hands cuffed behind his back. If the guys had been naked too, he would've killed the sick fucks, but they only scrubbed his skin raw, manhandled him with a soapy rag and washed his hair. While they did, he cursed their mothers for giving birth to them, but nothing stopped the abuse.

They'd cleaned him up. *Now what?* Rafael didn't want to know, but when one of them opened a locker that had a garment bag hanging in it, he grimaced. After the bag got unzipped and he saw what was inside, he shoved back.

"No way." He shook his head. "This is bullshit!"

One of the jerks hauled him back by the hair. "Sorry, kid. Orders."

Twenty minutes later

Rafael couldn't breathe and everything pinched. He craned his neck trying to get comfortable, but nothing helped. He sneezed at the smell of the spicy cologne they made him wear, but that wasn't the worst of it. They'd forced him into a damned suit and tie.

"*Pendejos,*" he muttered under her breath.

The jerks from the shower handed him off to the next guys, who hauled him handcuffed through the mansion, past fancy paintings like in a museum and chandeliers that looked like diamonds. They probably were. He ended up in a dining room bigger than his whole apartment in the projects where he had lived with his old man before he ran away, after the bastard almost killed him.

One man sat at the head of a long shiny table, dressed in pricey threads. He'd already started eating, but glanced up when Rafe came into the room.

"Excellent. Glad you could make it."

Rafael scrunched his face and looked behind him. *Who is this clown talkin' to?*

"I've set a place for you. Eggs, ham, potatoes. I hope you like coffee."

Rafael stared at a man who looked as if he could run for president. The suit couldn't look him in the eye and he had businessman hair, not a strand out of place and gray at the temples. He smiled without a scrap of sincerity and Rafe didn't trust him. The guy could run for Congress.

"Take off his cuffs and leave us. I'll be fine." The man didn't have to say it twice. His men did as they were told and Rafe sat, looking down at a plate of warm food.

Rafael had every intention of letting pride get between him and the ham and eggs on his plate, but since he'd already lost whatever dignity he had in the shower, he changed his mind and grabbed a fork. He knew better than to screw this up with talking. He kept his mouth shut, except for when he ate.

"When was the last time you had something to eat?" the suit asked.

Rafael only shrugged and kept eating. The coffee looked good, but he grabbed the tall glass of water instead and sucked it down as if he'd been lost in the desert. He ate in silence, except for the sounds of his fork hitting the plate, until the suit ruined it.

"My name is Alexander Reese…in case you're curious."

Rafe stopped his fork midshovel and glared at the man. He'd recognized the name. Gabriel had said it first. This guy was in charge of the Believers here in L.A. The man smiled when he noticed his reaction, but grinned more when he realized Rafe hadn't tried to cover up his hatred. The guy thought he knew why he reacted the way he did, but he didn't know a damned thing.

This son of a bitch, with his fancy clothes and house, had

been the one who killed Benny. He was in charge and had given the order. Nothing else meant jack shit to Rafael.

"I understand you know Gabriel Stewart. Don't bother to deny it." The man cut into a slice of ham and ate it without looking at him. "Give him up and I'll quit pursuing the others. He's the only one I want. You tell me where he is and I secure him, you're free to go."

Rafe already knew he wasn't leaving this place alive. The guy had punched his ticket for sure when he told him his name. *Free to go, my ass.* He put down his fork and slipped it into his sleeve to hide it. If the guy was stupid enough to give him something sharp, he'd be dumber not to take it.

"You expect me to believe you," Rafe said.

"I don't care if you do or not. I'm just giving you a chance to do this the easy way."

A snake in a suit, that's what the man was. Rafael smiled.

"Mister, I wouldn't know *how* to do things easy, so bring it. I'm not telling you *anything* about Gabriel or anyone else."

Rafe had had enough bullshit. With the fork gripped in his hands and under the table, he shoved back his chair to brace for a fight. But before he made his move to stab the guy, a shadow stopped him. Rafe felt a familiar chill and knew what it was before anything happened.

The room faded to a blur and time slowed to a sputtering stop. Rafe sensed a displacement of air as if a door had sprung open to another dimension, but shut with a sucking stillness that almost hurt his ears. Alexander Reese drank coffee as if he didn't notice what had happened behind him.

A wooden panel in the corner of the dining room rippled until it bulged like an ocean's wave. The wall gave birth to a horror that Rafe had never seen. The bloodied body of a woman popped from the wood until it was free, dressed in jeans and a T-shirt. Dark veins laced under gray skin pulsed and throbbed as if the ghost still had a beating heart. Black hair in a tumble was crusted in blood from an open head wound. Tendrils of pitch-black hair curled into twists as if a preternatural wind caught the strands. Her eyes were fixed on him.

When the dead woman realized he could see her, she glided to the table in a sudden rush. He swallowed, hard. Couldn't breathe. *Damn!*

The spirit lingered behind Alexander Reese and glared at the man with eyes that turned to bloodred embers. That's when Rafael recognized her. The ghost of Lady Kathryn, Gabriel's mother. It *had* to be her.

Rafe had heard the story after Benny's funeral. Gabe wanted the truth out, about how he knew the name of the man in charge of the Believers. He had to admit that he was mad at first, but after he thought about how no one gets to pick their fathers, Rafe listened to what Gabe had to say. That's when he found out about how Kathryn had died. A car accident, courtesy of Alexander Reese, bought and paid for.

"Gabriel loves his mother, even still," Rafe said. He fixed his gaze on the dead woman, looking over Reese's shoulder as the man ate. "Not a day goes by, that boy doesn't think of her. She's still his source of power. His love for her will always be his strength. Gabriel and his mother will bring you down. I'd bet on it."

Rafael felt his eyes fill.

"Bet on the dead? You're a fool…and you don't know anything about his mother." Reese wiped his mouth and couldn't look him in the eye.

"I know enough. Every child's heart carries its own memory of the first heartbeat it hears. Mothers never leave their children—*ever*—not even in death. That kind of love…*stays*. I've never had anyone love me like that…except for Benny."

It took Gabriel's dead mother—and the voice of his own heart—for Rafe to realize he still *had* Benny. It wasn't the way he would've wanted, but it would *have* to be enough. Someone like him, he'd been blessed to love Benny at all.

"Who's Benny?"

Rafe didn't know if he could talk about him with the one who had ordered him dead, but before he could answer, Kathryn turned into ice crystals. From the top of her head down, she crackled and changed until she was encased in ice. When she was done, she let the crystals thaw. In seconds a wash of colors melted down her curves and turned her back into the beautiful woman she had been in life. She wore a long velvet robe and had a glittering tiara on her head. Rafael recognized the image he'd seen of her on the circus billboards at the Stewart Estate. *Lady Kathryn.*

Rafe's throat wedged tight. She let him feel her pain of not being with her son to see him grow up. He felt the same thing about Benny and let her suffer his loss in a way he couldn't have shared it with anyone else. The dead don't need words. He released his grief in her care and knew she'd understand. After Rafe saw a tear trickle down the dead woman's cheek, she nodded. In that moment he believed that she cried for Benny too.

Seeing Kathryn standing over Alexander Reese, she let him sense why she was there. The dead woman had every intention of screwing with the man who killed her. If he could help her do that, he'd be willing to try. He was as good as dead anyway. It didn't hurt him to have friends on the other side.

"Tell me something," Rafe said to Reese. "Do you believe in heaven?"

"I'm a religious man. Of course I do."

"Guess that means you believe in hell too." Rafe glanced

at Kathryn with a smile only she would understand. "You better get *real* comfortable with *that* idea."

Alexander Reese stopped eating.

"Tell me something else, Believer. How do you justify killing innocent kids if you believe in God?"

"You're neither innocent nor human, that's how. You're a plague on mankind. I'm doing God and humanity a service."

Some people were a waste of skin, but this guy had taken hate to a whole new level.

"You fathered one of us. Gabriel is your son, but no one in your church knows that, do they?" When the man flinched, he knew he'd hit the bull's-eye. "Is that why you had your men leave us alone? No one else knows about Gabriel. That's why I'm here instead of Ward 8."

"You must be psychic," the man said, sneering. "Yes, I'm sorry to say that Gabriel is indeed my son. How did you know?"

"It explains why he never talks about you." Rafael yanked off his tie and threw it on the floor. He'd had enough, of everything. "I got a father like you. You remind me of him, only you carry a different kind of bat."

Kathryn drifted over Reese like a darkening storm and spiraled into the frightening and angry ghost she had been. The robe and tiara were gone. When a strong scent of perfume filled the air, it looked as if Reese must've smelled it too. His head jerked and he shifted his gaze around the room. Real paranoid.

The dead woman had sent Rafe a clear message that he now understood. Whatever the guy had done, he wouldn't get away with it—*not in this world or the next*. Rafe wanted revenge for Benny's death, but that wouldn't bring him back. Knowing what it took for Gabriel's mother to appear to him—to let him know she had chosen to haunt her killer rather than be with her son—how could he take what was rightfully hers?

"He's all yours," Rafe said. "Make it count for Benny too."

He kept his eyes on Kathryn when he tossed the fork onto the table. After she mouthed the words *Thank you*, Alexander Reese stood and threw his napkin down. By the look on the man's face, he knew what Rafe had intended to do with his makeshift weapon. If he had known why he'd given up on the idea, he might've been more scared.

"Guards!" Reese yelled. After his men rushed into the room, he said, "Civility is wasted on someone like you."

"Funny. I was thinking the same thing," Rafe said.

As two men in suits grabbed his arms and hauled him from his chair, Rafael shouted at Reese, but what he said was meant for Kathryn.

"You wanna know about Benny? You gave the order that killed him. He was a ten-year-old kid. He wasn't even one of us," Rafe yelled as they dragged him from the room. "Don't think heaven is waitin' for you. Your next suit should be made of asbestos, asshole."

Alexander Reese waved his hand in disgust. "Take him to a cell, gentlemen. I'll be down shortly," the man said, but before Rafe got out the door, he called out, "What's your gift, boy? I'm curious."

The men stopped dragging him and Rafael looked over his shoulder with a smile.

"You recognize that perfume, *cabron?*" When he saw that the man did, he said, "That's Kathryn sending her regards. She's here...for *you*."

He knew he'd made things worse, but Rafe didn't care. Seeing the shocked look on Alexander Reese's face made it worth whatever would happen to him now.

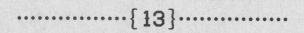

{ 13 }

Haven Hills Treatment Facility
Ward 8

Caila hated seeing Oliver so broken. A tube had been taped into his mouth, and his beautiful eyes, which she *always* wanted to see, were closed. His skin looked ghostly pale and his lungs filled through a pump. The incessant beeping of machines and flashes of lights had replaced everything that made Oliver human. Had the same thing happened to Zack before his brain ended up in a jar? Seeing Oliver unconscious and hooked to machines made Caila sick.

I'm sorry, Oliver. I'm so sorry. She repeated those words in her head, hoping he'd hear her, but he looked dead. What had they done to him?

"He's in a coma. If you can reach him, there's still time to save his life," Dr. Fiona said. "But it's up to you now."

Caila fought the restraints on her arms. She wanted to touch Oliver—to see if he was still in his body—to know if he was alive, but they had tied her to a wheelchair. Strangling this arrogant doctor came a close second for what she wanted to do with her hands. This woman had done something to

Oliver that put him in a coma. Now she made it seem as if she were the only one who could save him.

"What do you w–want...me to d–do?" Caila choked on every word. It took all her willpower to hide the hatred she felt for this woman.

"Like Oliver visited you, he did the same with someone else. That boy is the one who hurt Oliver. *He* did this. I'm sure of it."

Caila gritted her teeth. "Who is *he?*"

"I don't know his name, but Oliver had tracked him with his gift. I know he found him. This boy is a danger to any-one who crosses his path. Unfortunately, until he attacked Oliver, no one had known *how* dangerous. He's an Indigo who hurts his own kind."

Hurts his own kind? Caila wondered if this woman ever listened to the spew coming out of her mouth. "Why would Oliver go after this guy? Did you ask him to?"

"I think Oliver was trying to protect other kids like you and him. That's the only thing I can figure. He did a brave thing." Dr. Fiona stroked Oliver's hair and stared down at him. "I thought that since you were friends, you might fin-ish what he started, because it mattered to him."

"You say that like he's already beyond saving, like this is his last wish, or something." Caila felt heat rush to her face. "Are you keeping him alive only so I can...help you?"

"What kind of monster do you think I am?"

Caila shut her eyes. She didn't want to look into the smug, lying face of Dr. Fiona, but she had no choice except to do what she said. Touching Oliver, even if it was only to say goodbye, was all Caila had left.

"Tell me about this guy you want me to find," she said.

"What did you tell Oliver about him? I have to know everything."

Dr. Fiona smiled. "Yes, of course. I'll tell you everything you need to know."

Stewart Estate

Rayne held his hand as she led him toward the serenity room. Gabriel saw the door had been left open. Soft lights flickered into the corridor with laser beams piercing the darkness. When he heard the mock sound of a *Star Wars* light saber, he knew his uncle had the planetarium show equipment ready to go.

Gabriel stopped at the threshold to see projections of beautiful images rotating in layers across the dome over his head. In the darkness, he saw silhouettes below and the Indigo boy's soul stirred inside him. On the steps down, Gabe clutched his chest and held on to a railing until the pain subsided. Although he couldn't be sure, he sensed fear that wasn't his own.

"Are you okay?" Rayne asked, and squeezed his hand.

"Yeah," he lied.

When he got to the base of the steps, Gabe stared at the concerned face of Uncle Reginald. He wasn't alone. Lucas and Kendra stood at his shoulders and in the shadows of the dark room, the other Indigo children had gathered too.

"What's the occasion?" Gabe forced a smile.

"A coming-out party, of sorts," his uncle said. "At least I hope that's what it turns out to be."

Uncle Reginald led him to a reclined seat in the center of the room. Gabe sprawled into the chair and watched as the shadows of the other Indigos closed around him. Their brilliant blue auras bled together as they closed ranks, and on cue, stunning images of a rain forest filled the circle over him. Glistening raindrops on vibrant green leaves, colorful exotic animals and rushing rivers told a story across the domed ceiling, with the soft patter of rain as white noise playing in the background. His uncle knew how much rain meant to him and his mother— and how much that would relax him.

Uncle Reginald stood over him. "I've never seen a case like yours, Gabriel, but I'd like to meet our guest, wouldn't you?"

"I'd prefer to buy him cab fare and send him home, uncle."

Despite the severity of the situation, Uncle Reginald fought a smile. "Yes, of course. In due time, but let me explain what I'd like to try."

"Okay. I'm ready." Gabe burrowed his back into the plush seat, fighting the torment of his worsening headache. "Explain away."

"Not to you, Gabriel. I'm hoping to speak to our visitor… through you. This is an intervention. With your permission, I'd like to begin."

After Gabe nodded, his uncle called for the others to lay a hand on him. When they did, he felt a surge of energy from the hive and closed his eyes, embracing the feeling. Each hand carried its own signature that he felt even with his eyes shut. The fingers of the Effin twins tickled and made him hungry. Kendra soothed him with her healing gift. Lucas bolstered his strength with his own and Rayne's small hand nudged a smile from him. Each face projected their presence into the darkness of his mind, but the Indigo boy inside him didn't have the same reaction to their touch. Gabe had to fight his negativity and the dark specter of his life force.

Uncle Reginald placed his hand on Gabe's head and said, "We mean you no harm. We're here to help you, if we can."

Amid the soft rhythms of the rain, Gabriel heard faint music come through Lucas and Kendra. Some Indigos heard haunting melodies in their heads. It made them calm. Lucas had told him that when he was a baby, he hummed a song before he ever said the word *Mama*. Now Kendra's and Lucas's gifts sent the sweetness of two violins in harmony to quiet the boy they had come to reach.

"What's your name, dear boy?" Uncle Reginald asked. "Can you tell us that much?"

Gabe's belly clenched. He winced with the pain.

"Are you all right, Gabriel?"

"Don't mind me. Keep…t-talking." He felt sick. "I think he hears you."

Gabe felt the life force from the hive standing around him, but something dark lurked inside him too. The soul of the other Indigo boy swept low and prowled like a shark in deep water. When he felt the heat of him rise to the surface of his skin, Gabe's face grew hot and he panted for every breath. Feeling this presence in him carried the agony of shotgunning his soul into the Indigo expanse, except that he couldn't find comfort in the release of the blast.

An odd sensation rippled up from his toes and jolted through him until he opened his mouth to speak. He had no idea what he would say. It wouldn't be him doing the talking.

"My name is…Oliver Blue."

Gabe heard the words come from his mouth, but he sounded like someone else. His voice was lower and he'd lost his accent. That sent chills over his skin until Oliver's struggles sent heat raging through him that felt like a sudden and intense fever.

"Can you…hear me? I can talk?"

"We can hear you fine. It's truly remarkable how you can speak through Gabriel," his uncle said. "I'm sure you have questions. We do too."

"What happened? How did I…?"

"That's what we'd like to know too. My nephew thinks you crossed paths at Haven Hills. Is that where...your body is?"

It took a long time for Oliver to answer.

"I don't...kn-know that...name," the boy told them.

Even though the voice came from Gabriel, it carried an echo that sounded far away. Gabe tried to speak louder, but straining made things worse. He had to give over control to this boy.

"It's a mental hospital, run by the Church of Spiritual Freedom," his uncle clarified.

"Oh God. Hang on." Gabe grimaced. "Something's... happening."

Like the other night in the alley, when he first encountered Oliver, he got bombarded with too many images and thoughts to filter through it all. Every flash of this boy's memory, every word spoken in anger, punched Gabe from inside and pummeled him as if he were under attack.

Fucking soul vampires.

His first instinct was to protect his psyche. It took all his self-control, and his Indigo intuition, to relax and let Oliver speak through him.

Fear is a drug.

He let the boy say what he wanted and show him stuff. Gabe flashed on locked rooms and evil experiments from people wearing white. Hours of isolation and the panic of unbearable torture raged through him in seconds, forcing him to endure. Oliver wanted him to know and feel what had happened to him. When he felt his body sweep through ventilation shafts as if he could fly, the vertigo made him want to puke, but he held on.

Gabriel held it all inside...for Oliver's sake.

No one else heard his confusion and anger. If Gabe allowed Oliver's startled thoughts to escape into the hive, the others might not understand his need to rage. Oliver simply couldn't contain his hatred and had to release it, something Gabe had sympathy for. He refused to be distracted by Oliver's behavior when he saw only what they had in common. The guy raged against the injustice of being abducted and tortured by adults who should care, while Gabe had suffered the murder of his mother at the hands of a father who should have loved them both.

Gabe resisted showing what he saw and felt from Oliver because he couldn't risk exposing the children, or anyone, to his torture at the hands of the Believers. If he let the others sense his torment, they wouldn't see what Gabe was beginning to realize.

Somewhere at the heart of all Oliver's pain was a girl. Gabriel sensed her presence through Oliver, who let him see a scared face with ice-blue eyes.

Caila.

The instant he sensed the girl's name, Gabriel couldn't breathe. He gripped his hands on the armrests of his chair and gasped. Suddenly he was inside the black helmet, suffocating. It felt as if he were drowning. Gabe fought the panic and forced his trust in this boy.

Otherwise he could too easily believe that Oliver intended to kill him.

"He understands...the reference," Gabe panted. "It's made him...angry. Tell him m-more."

"We think the Believers are hunting Indigo children." Uncle Reginald raised his voice, feeling the urgency. "They're experimenting on them in a place they call Ward 8. Does *that* sound familiar?"

The boy didn't answer. Gabe felt stabs of pain that pulsed at his temples. When he winced, Lucas jumped in.

"I'd like to try something. It could help," Luke said.

Gabe opened his eyes and stared at Rayne's brother like everyone else. Luke had never spoken up like that before. It surprised him. The guy's lack of confidence came from being young and inexperienced after he'd spent years in a mental hospital, but he was smart and a quick learner.

"Let him try." He nodded. "Go for it, Luke."

"You and Gabriel, you're more alike than you realize," Rayne said. "I know you can help him."

After a shaky smile, Lucas heaved a sigh and moved his hand to Gabe's head. He placed it alongside Uncle Reginald's. The blistering headache had become unbearable for Gabe. Gambling on Lucas, when everything hurt, had its risks.

But it was the right thing to do.

Haven Hills Treatment Facility
Ward 8

Caila felt the eyes of Dr. Fiona on her as she reached for Oliver's cheek. Her fingers trembled, giving away how much it tortured her to see him like this. She couldn't help feeling that he'd never find his way back. Her gift had gotten him into this, but she had no hope that it would bring him back. Her psychic ability worked more on its own, when she felt threatened or scared or painfully alone. Although she felt all three as she stared down at him now, she'd been emotionally violated by this cruel woman who watched her. She wanted her words to be only for him, but she had no hope for privacy.

"Oliver? I need you," she whispered. "Please...hear me."

When she leaned close, she kissed his cheek and trailed a finger down his pale cheek. *All my fault.*

Memories of him flooded her mind, notions that she had planted, but that didn't make them less real for both of them. In her mind she pictured him smiling, she felt the warmth of his hand in hers, and she imagined that kiss happening again, but none of those memories would bring him back.

Oliver. The doctor says you're in a coma…that a boy hurt you. Show me what you saw. She says that's the only way to help you get better. She willed him to hear her. *Show me the boy. Tell me about him.* She closed her eyes tight, to block out the horror of seeing him struggling for every breath through a machine.

Nothing. She got *nothing.*

"Dig into his memories. I didn't bring you here to whisper sweet nothings in his ear. Do it."

The ugliness in Dr. Fiona's voice pulled Caila from any closeness she had with Oliver, but when she opened her eyes, she saw it. Caila gasped when his eyelids fluttered. Had she imagined it? She had wanted to reach him so badly that maybe his reaction had been only her wishful thinking. When his head moved and he winced at the breathing tube in his mouth, he looked as if he was choking.

"What's happening?" Caila backed off and glanced over her shoulder at the woman in white. "Is he dying?"

"Keep trying. Tell me what you see. I have to know about the other boy," the doctor insisted. "What did Oliver see?"

"But he could tell you himself, if he comes out of this," she argued. "Isn't that possible?"

"Your gift works best when you're scared. That's what you said." Dr. Fiona grabbed her hair and yanked her head back so she'd have to look at her. "Well, try this. If you don't do what I say, I'll make room for you next to Zack."

Stewart Estate
Minutes later

When Lucas had seen Gabriel wince, he sensed something through his body. It had come from the strong connection they had, ever since they shared visions and haunting dreams. This time he felt an intrusion from another soul.

Luke had to test his instincts. Uncle Reginald had been right about trust being important, but the first person he had to trust had to be *himself*. After he moved his hand closer to Gabe's uncle, he felt the energy in a different way. A strange psychic push came from inside Gabriel's body and shoved him back.

Oliver, I presume.

He didn't know if the guy sensed him there, but he felt his stress and anger radiate up his arm. He had to mind-shield it down to manage it. He shut his eyes and forced an attack on Gabriel, at least enough for him to break through to Oliver. This time Gabe made it easy to get past his defenses, not like the way he'd tricked him at the pond.

Once he got in, Luke let his mind drift to a memory from his own childhood that he made into an illusion for all of them. The wind blew against his face, and his stomach lurched when his father barreled the Harley into a turn. Lucas grabbed the handlebars tight and grinned. He'd never felt so free and happy—and loved.

Riding the Harley with his dad, as they restored the vintage bike, had been his favorite memory. He shared that joy—and his father's love—with Oliver to give him something to unleash his soul and calm him. Like waves ebbing on the shoreline at dusk, Luke felt Oliver's anger retreat.

"Thank you, Luke. Much better," Gabriel said as he breathed deep and relaxed in the illusion. It didn't take long for Oliver to become active again, but something had changed.

"He's getting too weak. I can barely hear him now." Gabe had to speak for Oliver this time. "He's sending me a rush of images, with a few words. I have to decipher it. It's like one of our visions, Luke."

Lucas could feel the rush of Oliver's story at the same time as Gabe told them about it. Through Gabriel, Oliver shared how he'd been abducted in an alley and a hood had been placed over his head. He didn't get a look at the hospital, but he'd used his senses to "see" another way. When Gabe told them about that, his uncle smiled.

"Smart boy," Uncle Reginald said.

Oliver loaded Gabe with details about elevators, muggy basements and turning corners, but when he talked about double doors and a security code, *that* made sense to Lucas. It matched his dreams, the ones that always started his nightmares of seeing through the eyes of other Indigos who'd been tortured there. He lived their experiences as if everything had happened to him too.

"Those double doors," Lucas said. "They're the same ones I see in my visions. If Ward 8 is in the basement of Haven Hills, I think I can find it."

"If it's there." Kendra was the first one to cast doubt on what Oliver had shared. "We don't know anything about this guy. It would be better to assume he's lying than to risk getting tricked into an ambush."

Lucas hated living in a world where human beings had to distrust each other in order to feel safe, but after the Believers had killed Benny, he saw the need for a healthy dose of skepticism.

"I'm all for being cautious, but I can feel this guy dying inside me," Gabriel said. "He's getting weaker. I don't think he's faking that."

"It would appear that Oliver Blue can teleport his consciousness," Uncle Reginald said. "I've never known anyone that could do that. Apparently the distance between him and his body has grown too far. That's probably why he's waning, poor fellow."

"I have to help him," Gabe insisted. "I can't listen to him die in me, and I don't know what that would do to me either. I *have* to do something."

"What do you propose?" his uncle asked.

"He jumped into me near Haven Hills. Get me close enough. *Us,* close enough. Maybe he can make the leap back."

"It may not be that simple." Kendra had an edge to her voice. "If this is a trap, they could be expecting us at the hospital. Even if he's telling us the truth, that doesn't mean the Believers aren't using him to get to us. All of this… The stuff that happened in that alley…could've been a trap."

"A trap that we sprang on ourselves?" Gabe shook his head. "I don't think they could've known we would take home a hitchhiker. That would make them far more diabolical than I'm willing to give them credit for."

"So what do we do?" Kendra asked. "Rafael is still missing. If he's alive…"

"I know and I hear what you're saying, believe me. I have my doubts too," Gabe said. "But I can't risk Oliver's life because I'm paranoid or in a rush to find one of ours. I couldn't live with that. Choosing between two lives isn't right, and doing nothing is as good as killing Oliver."

When everyone fell silent, Lucas felt the gravity of any decision they would make. He didn't envy Gabriel. He'd be the one who'd have to live with the consequences the most, if anything happened to Oliver or Rafael.

"Maybe the girl can help us," Gabe said.

"What girl?" they all said in unison.

Haven Hills Treatment Facility
Ward 8

Caila gasped. She yanked her hand back as if Oliver were on fire. "What happened?"

Not even Dr. Fiona's gruff and demanding voice could distract her from the rush of sensations Caila felt when she'd tried to retrieve Oliver's memories.

The doctor had removed his breathing tube. He'd stopped choking and the artificial inflation of his lungs made the room quieter. That helped her to connect with him. But even though she was inches from his face, she had the sense he was far away and slipping from her mental grasp.

She'd never felt anything like it. *Ever.*

"What did you see?"

"Give me a second. This isn't like getting email," she snapped.

The doctor had told her that Oliver had been tracking a boy after she'd given him a library book, something the kid had touched. That part of the doctor's story felt true. Caila could picture Oliver doing that the way she'd seen him track Zack, when he used a can of Cheez Whiz. Once she got past the memories she'd planted in Oliver, the ones she shared with him, it was easy to read his new experiences—the ones from the dark alley. She'd never seen those memories before. They hadn't come from her.

Show me, Oliver. Please, she had begged him.

She didn't beg him for his memories because the doctor had ordered it. She felt Oliver's urgent need to share them with her. He let her see flashes of what happened. She had to hide her reaction from the doctor. The searing evil off the woman would always be hard for her to ignore, but what Oliver let her see next shocked her.

• 186 •

There wasn't just one boy with Oliver. There were more Indigos and one had the blue aura of a very powerful Crystal child. She didn't know how she knew this. Oliver had let her *feel* it, but as quickly as he had let her in, he shut down his mind until only his voice came to her.

Give Dr. Fiona a message for me. I know she's there.

Caila shoved back from him with eyes wide in shock. She heard his voice as if he had whispered in her ear, but when she pulled from him, he still had his eyes closed. He was unconscious. Her skin rippled in goose bumps.

"Oliver? Are you...?" She couldn't say it, not in front of this doctor. She would sound crazy to believe that he wasn't unconscious at all.

"What happened?" the woman asked.

"Nothing. I got a little confused." Caila replayed what Oliver had said in her mind. What he told her now didn't make sense, but she couldn't stall any longer.

"I don't know what he means," she said. She let the doctor hear her, because Oliver wanted her to do something for him.

"Just say it. Now!" Dr. Fiona ordered.

"Oliver wants me to give you a message," she told the doctor. "He says you'll understand."

Caila felt crushed. Oliver had taken the doctor's side and shut her out. He was treating her like a stranger, one that he didn't trust. The pathetic part was that she couldn't argue with him.

"Just tell me what he said. Exactly."

Caila stood back from his bed and wrapped her arms around her shoulders to ward off a sudden chill. She didn't know if she'd be doing the right thing, but Oliver had been adamant.

"He said...that he has the guy you want." A tear slid down her cheek. "He says he'll meet you where he did the first time…where he saw you in the mirror. No one knows about that place…except you, he says."

"Yes, I know the place. Go on."

Caila struggled with every word Oliver shared with her. She felt him blocking her. He kept his sentences short, so she wouldn't have time to think, only repeat what he had meant for Dr. Fiona.

"Oliver says that it's the only place he didn't let the boy know about…and that his name is Gabriel." What Oliver said next made her feel as if they'd both betrayed their own kind.

"He says that…he didn't let me read his thoughts. That's why he had to speak in riddles." Caila felt heat rush to her face. Oliver had been talking about her as if she were the enemy now. "He asked if you'd keep your promise…since he kept up his end."

Dr. Fiona smiled. Her lips curled, but there was no humor in her eyes. "Oliver? If you can hear me, I understand. I'll wait for you there," the doctor said. "I'm a woman as good as my word."

The doctor walked to the door of the ICU hospital room and called out to her security guards. They came running.

"Take this girl back to her cell. When I return, I'll have a decision on what to do with her." The woman took a step out the door but stopped and told one of the guards, "Put a call in to Mr. Boelens. Tell him I'll have a pickup for him after visiting hours. He'll know what I mean."

Dr. Fiona turned and smiled at her, but not in a good way. Caila didn't need the gift of second sight to see she didn't have a future in this woman's eyes. She'd run out of time.

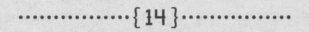

{ 14 }

Outside L.A.
Dusk

Riding in the very backseat of Uncle Reginald's Navigator, Rayne couldn't get close enough to Gabriel. He held her in his arms as she sat on his lap at the start of the trip, but as they neared L.A., she had to hold him closer to her heart. She breathed in the smell of his skin and wrapped her fingers in his dark hair until she had to kiss him.

She wanted to *be* with this boy—to feel his body on hers— to share the intimacy of making love for the first time, with Gabriel. No matter what happened between them, she would never regret loving him. He was so beautiful, inside and out. As she kissed him, and felt the urgency growing in them both, tears filled her eyes.

Her body wanted more. She had to have *more,* but she stopped. Breathless, she pulled her lips from his. Without a word, he looked into her eyes and with a shy smile and blushing cheeks, she knew he understood why. They weren't alone. He mouthed the words *I love you* and brushed a tear from her cheek.

Loving Gabriel would always be special. She held his face

in both hands and kissed him one last time. Every second of holding him felt precious. After the incident in the alley, where he was attacked by a strange Indigo boy, it felt as if she'd almost lost him. She still could. The fight with the Believers was real. She'd seen how strong he was—a powerful Crystal child—yet Oliver had shown all of them that if Gabe was vulnerable, they all were.

They were nearly to L.A. The closer they got, the more she worried. She wasn't sure why, but she didn't have a good feeling about what they were about to do.

"Are you all right? You look pale," she whispered as she sat up and grabbed his hand, entwining her fingers in his. "How's your headache?"

"That headache has a name." Gabe forced a halfhearted smile. "Oliver."

She knew that he wanted to lighten the mood, but the mention of Oliver's name made Rayne's stomach clench into a knot. Even though others were quiet, she felt the tension. Lucas had an iPod in his ears. Kendra stared out her window, not talking to anyone. The Effin brothers never said anything to anyone…ever. They all looked withdrawn into the same stillness as she felt. Even Uncle Reginald hadn't spoken much since they'd left the Bristol Mountains.

"What's happening with…?" She spun a finger toward his chest and made a face. "…your evil twin. Does he get carsick?"

"You better pray he doesn't. You'd be in the splatter zone." Gabe smiled, but quickly frowned. "Good Lord, so would I."

"Is he…chatty in there?" she asked. "Because that would weird me out."

"No. He feels stronger, but he's been oddly quiet."

"What do you think *that* means?"

Gabe's eyes turned dark, and any humor on his face disappeared. "The guy could be on death's door. Merely being apart from his body this long, he could be conserving what life he's got left, but we could still be too late."

When Gabe saw the concern on her face, he kissed her cheek. "I feel this strange urgency to...help him. Now that we share the same body, it's uncanny how his feelings become mine. I have no idea if that works in reverse, but I suppose if he develops a craving for Yorkshire pudding and afternoon tea with scones, I'll have my answer."

"God," she gasped with eyes wide. "We just kissed. Did he...feel that too? I don't like this, Gabriel."

"If he felt it, he was a perfect gentleman. He didn't give me pointers, if that's what you're thinking." Gabe cocked his head and said, "Wait. Should I be jealous?"

Rayne grinned and nudged him with an elbow, but something else bothered her. She looked down at her hand in his and asked the question that had weighed heavy on her mind ever since she heard Oliver's voice coming from him in the serenity room.

"Do you still feel that you can trust him?"

Rayne had the same doubts as Kendra. Trusting Oliver meant all of them would risk losing everything, on his word. Even Rafael would have skin in the game. When she saw the look on Gabriel's face, she knew he felt the same.

"I hope we can trust him," he said. "I surely hope so."

Rayne held Gabe and stared out the window of the moving SUV as it sped toward L.A. The dying rays of the sun torched the horizon as they approached the city. It wouldn't be long now.

Soon they would *all* know the truth about Oliver.

West Hollywood
Forty-five minutes later

Fiona paced the floor of her living room, waiting. After the sun went down, her imagination took over and she needed a drink to settle her nerves. She tossed back the last dregs of her second glass of red wine and poured another. It was the only thing that took the edge off.

She wouldn't admit this to anyone else, but Oliver Blue frightened her. She'd created him, but knowing that he could simply appear—anywhere, anytime—unnerved her. The last time he'd popped in unannounced, she'd been naked, ready to take a shower. He'd come to her at the worst possible time. Had he done it on purpose...to scare her?

"This is my show. I'm in control."

She repeated those words in her head as she gazed out the floor-to-ceiling windows onto the glittering skyline of West Hollywood. When the alcohol got the better of her judgment— and her nerves— she had gone through her house and flipped on every light. In the end, that looked ridiculous to her. It felt like an admission that she was a nervous and vulnerable woman, not the scientist that she was, on the verge of greatness.

Fiona turned out the lights and waited. She'd set the mood as if she were expecting a date...or had planned a séance. Shadows stretched across her living room, avoiding the pockets where she had candles burning and her gas fireplace flickering.

Darkness suited Oliver. The boy had a disturbing nature that she had seen from the first time she looked into his eyes. More than what she had turned him into, Fiona feared the boy he had *always* been—a fighter and a kid with an arrest record. It's why she had found him, but she had no idea it would come to this.

Oliver. Where are you?

She dreaded seeing him, but she wanted this over. His condition had put him in a coma, yet what had it done to his mind? Would he be...*sane?* She had proven her hypothesis that if she sense-deprived the responsive Indigo mind, she could force their abilities to reach new heights—push them into new powers the way the brain compensates when it's injured. She'd amassed a thick file on Oliver Blue.

Fiona knew that she'd have to be careful who she told about Oliver now. The information would have to be managed and disseminated to a chosen few, so she could continue her work in the church's name.

That's why she had files locked away in Ward 8. Her research was too important to be scrutinized by a prosaic mind. Her work was visionary. The magnitude of her discovery could benefit the advancement of mankind in a controllable way, not in the random chance of the fornicating masses. Many of these Indigo kids came from the streets, unwanted by their own parents because they couldn't be controlled. Since few people understood the gifted mind, some of these children had criminal records like Oliver.

Even imagining what she could do with someone of *her* intelligence. To enhance God-given gifts like hers, it staggered her with possibility. Under the right circumstances, the church could handpick the future evolution of man and she could play her part in that. Fiona never would have attained such knowledge with Alexander holding her back or people with wearisome moral principles.

She gazed into the fire and let her mind wander, toward a future she'd always known would be hers. When she raised the wine to her lips, she caught an odd reflection in the wineglass.

The glimmer of a face.

Oliver.

"Hello, Doctor."

His low voice gripped her heart. She recognized it and turned, but he wasn't there. "Oliver? Is that you?"

She'd heard his voice as if it came from inside her ear, as if he crowded her head. When she didn't see him, her eyes peered into every shadow, searching for him. Fiona felt the weight of his presence. The hair on her neck prickled as if she were being watched.

She drew a ragged breath and masked her raw nerves by going for a refill of wine. When she got to her liquor bar, she grabbed a shot of something stronger and tossed it back. The bourbon burned her throat and churned hot when it hit her stomach. Fiona glanced at her reflection in the mirror behind the bar. She finger-combed her hair and took another deep breath. The alcohol had given her liquid courage when she needed it and she had another.

But when she looked up, Fiona saw Oliver's dark eyes in the mirror.

This time she screamed. When she turned, she knocked her wine decanter off the counter and cringed when it shattered. Shards of cut glass glistened across her tile floor and carpet.

"Oliver?"

Her voice quivered. She stared into the shadows and saw a dark shape.

"Step into…the light…so I can s-see you."

She squinted into the darkness, waiting. When he stepped toward her, she staggered back. She had her bedroom door to her right and her front door wasn't far. Her mind raced with what she would do, if she had to.

Run.

Lock a door.

Call 911.

But with Oliver, she'd have no place to hide. He could find her—*anywhere.*

"Talk to me, Oliver. That's what you came to do, right?" She cleared her throat and clutched her hands to keep them from trembling. "I'm…impressed. You can…talk now."

Oliver Blue came into the light from her fireplace. The blaze reflected off the gelatinous sheen of his body.

She sucked in one long breath and couldn't let it out. Her body shook, but she prayed he wouldn't see her weakness. Unlike how she'd seen him in her bathroom, he didn't have the black binding on, which she had used on his body to prevent bedsores. He stood before her—strong—as she had first seen him in Ward 8.

He wore the same jeans and a black T-shirt with a bloody smiley face that she remembered when she cut it off him. His shirt had been cut into provocative strips across his chest. The slashes showed through to the skin of his muscled chest. She marveled at how the boy had become a hellish chameleon, but after she realized she'd thrown that shirt away, she felt the hairs on her arms slowly rise. How could he be wearing it now?

Oliver drifted like a lifeless spirit. A horror conjured from a nightmare.

"I learned how to talk…" Oliver struggled to speak. "…but it's hard."

Fiona fought back her fear by taking comfort in one thought—that it was too bad Oliver wouldn't get a chance to improve. His brain would make an excellent addition to her life's work.

She would kill the monster she'd created.

"You told that girl about the boy. You said his first name is Gabriel," she said. "Do you have…a last name now?"

"Yes, Gabriel Stewart. I know where he is." Oliver spoke every word as if it took a great deal of effort. "You promised. I deliver him. You let me go."

"But…" She dared to step closer to him. "You haven't *delivered* him yet."

When Oliver smiled, her heart froze. She could see the glittering skyline through his viscous skull. When the boy drifted toward her—until he stood inches from her face—she gasped. Oliver's fierce stare hit her like a slap to the face.

"Careful…what you wish for."

In that moment, the fire did nothing to stop the chills that skittered across her skin when Oliver shifted his gaze. He looked over her shoulder and she slowly turned to see a boy with long dark hair and striking eyes.

"I'd say it's lovely to meet you, but it would be rude to lie."

The boy's British accent carried a chilling edge. When he raised his arms and clenched his fists, heat came off his body until he burst into blue flames. The fire didn't burn him. Fiona felt the Crystal child's loathing and saw it in his unnatural eyes.

She couldn't breathe…couldn't *move*.

The boy radiated a brutal heat, but Fiona still felt the icy grip of Oliver's forceful presence until both boys vanished into a suffocating darkness—replaced by images of torture and cruelty that blistered her mind. She recognized them from Ward 8. Terrified kids she had seen before, yet barely recognized. This time she saw them. *All of them.* Their tortured expressions melted into oozing replicas of *her* face. She breathed in their fear and sensed every cut of the scalpel. Brains that she had extracted, she was forced to feel the pain as if it happened to her without anesthetic. Wave after wave of horror pummeled her until she collapsed and emptied her stomach.

The last thing she remembered before everything went black was looking up into the faces of Oliver Blue and the Crystal child.

Fiona knew she would die.

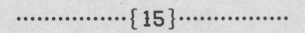

{ 15 }

Outside Haven Hills Treatment Facility
7:15 p.m.

Gabriel stared down at the security badge with a key that he'd taken from the doctor's purse to get them into Ward 8. He stared at her photo ID and name—Dr. Fiona Haugstad. She looked scholarly and refined in her photo, but that's not how he would remember her.

He gritted his teeth and slouched against a brick wall with his eyes on the Haven Hills facility below. He had laid out a plan for them to get into the hospital basement. Between Luke's visions and Oliver's sense memory, they had pieced a strategy together and spent the last two hours scoping out the facility for access.

The others were waiting for him. He could see them in the shadows of the alley where he had first "met" Oliver. They stood next to his uncle's Navigator and Dr. Fiona's Mercedes. They'd stolen the doctor's car to have an extra vehicle in case they needed room for kids they'd have to rescue from the ward. Gabe felt their eyes on him, but he had walked away to be alone. He was sure the others thought that whatever came next, they would cross a threshold in their fight for freedom, but Gabriel had already crossed that boundary.

Are you okay? Kendra reached out to him. Luke had too, but he hadn't responded to either of them.

He still felt riddled with anger from his psychic assault of the woman. Violence of any kind carried a price. Even if the doctor deserved the same heartless treatment she had heaped onto innocent kids, that didn't make him feel any better for doing the same to her.

Gabe thought of Rayne's brother when he couldn't shake the feeling that he'd proven Luke's point on killing after the guy argued, "That would make me no better than them." Not much separated him from the merciless doctor once his rage took over.

But Gabriel had another reason for wanting to be alone—Oliver was still inside him. He'd retreated there again, after their confrontation with the doctor.

I know you're there. Why haven't you left? he asked the Indigo boy.

In truth, now that Oliver was stronger and not such a burden, he didn't mind the company, especially after they'd shared what happened. Oliver was the only one who could truly understand the darkness that had seized his soul and still lingered. Rayne had seen him manifest his power from a distance, but Oliver had a unique front-row seat that left Gabriel with no secrets from him.

What you did...to Dr. Fiona. I'd never felt anything like that. She helped me...become who I am now, Oliver told him.

Gabe felt like shit. He wanted to hit something. After he took a deep breath, he shoved his hands into his jeans and stared into the night sky. Oliver only knew what he'd remembered of his experience with Dr. Fiona Haugstad. The mind often blocked terrible things or twisted them into something more tolerable. Oliver hadn't seen his visions, the nightmares he and Lucas had endured. He hadn't even seen his *own* torture at the hands of this vicious woman when she locked him into a sensory-deprivation helmet to see if he'd survive. The sick experiment of a soulless woman.

She didn't help you, Oliver. She tortured you.

When Oliver fell silent inside him, until he almost didn't feel him at all, Gabriel had to reach him, to make him understand.

That helmet was Machiavellian, sick and depraved stuff. She wasn't doing it to help you…or your girl.

Oliver interrupted him.

Caila isn't my…girl.

Despite the gravity of their situation, Gabriel had to smile and shake his head. Oliver denied Caila meant anything special to him, yet he'd insisted on keeping her in the dark on the secret meeting he had with Dr. Fiona. He had Caila pass on his message and do nothing more. He didn't want to put the girl at risk or give the doctor something to torture out of her. Oliver clearly wanted to protect her. Gabe had sensed that and more.

You protected her. You did the right thing. When we get to Ward 8, you'll see what the Believers do to Indigos. You don't have to believe me.

When Gabriel glanced at the others standing at the SUV and the doctor's Mercedes, he knew it was time to go.

Now let's get your body back…and find your girl.

Gabe headed to the vehicles and muttered, "That's something a guy doesn't say every day."

"What's up with Gabriel?" Kendra paced the alley behind where they parked the Navigator and the doctor's Mercedes. "Do you think he killed her? That doctor?"

Rayne wanted to tell her no, but the truth was that she couldn't be sure. Gabriel was complicated and the Indigos were about to break into Ward 8. No one knew what had happened at the doctor's place and no one asked him. They only saw Gabe drive up in her Mercedes. He didn't want to talk about it and Oliver was still in him. Rayne felt like shit that she couldn't help him, but she had to trust Gabriel when he told her that he wanted to be alone...to think. He'd talk to her when he was ready.

Kendra was complicated too. She looked wired and wouldn't stand still, but Rayne suspected she had another reason for being wound tight.

"I think...things are gonna get ugly. Gabriel is trying to spare us, but he won't be able to. He's just beginning to see that." Rayne touched her arm to get her to stop and listen. "You still can't sense Rafe here?"

Kendra couldn't look her in the eye. She only shook her head. When she stopped pacing like a crazy woman, she stared at the hospital.

"The truth is...I think I've lost my gift. I used to hear Indigo voices through my garden, but I don't feel other Indigos as much anymore," Kendra told her. "God's punishing me. I'm not worthy and Rafael is paying the price."

"What do you mean?" Rayne closed the gap between them and stroked her hair, but Kendra pulled away.

"What if he's in there and I can't feel him? He can block me. He's done it before, but what if I'm weak? I could be failing him. He could be in there and dying. Or maybe they killed him already."

Rayne heard the fragile break in her voice and knew she was crying.

"We have to find him, Rayne. He's got to be here. Even

if I can't sense him, if we don't find him soon…" The girl broke down. "I can't lose him. Not now."

"I know."

She didn't know what else to say. Telling her that *Everything will be okay* or *We'll find him, you'll see* sounded like bullshit. Something personal had happened between Rafael and Kendra. She felt it every time she saw them together. Benny's death had forged a bond between them, whether Kendra wanted to admit it or not. She only hoped the girl would get a chance to tell Rafe how she felt.

Until that happened, all Rayne could do was hold Kendra while she cried over the things she may never get to say.

7:20 p.m.

"Okay, once more. Since Lucas has been inside and knows the layout, he'll be our eyes and ears in the hospital," Gabe told them. "Kendra will back him up outside. She'll have the twins with her."

Luke had volunteered to be the first one in. He'd insisted on being the one to locate the right elevator that matched Oliver's descriptions. Gabriel wasn't sure he liked the idea of Rayne's brother going back to the hospital that still caused his nightmares. It would be hard on him, plus the guy had been a patient and someone on staff might recognize him. But Lucas had promised not to take any undue risk and had worn one of Gabe's hoodies to cover his face.

Kendra would make a strong backup, but if things went to hell, Luke would have to rely on the Effin brothers and use their abilities the same way *he* had. As a Crystal child, Rayne's brother could magnify what the twins could do, if he didn't doubt his power.

"If something doesn't feel right, pull back and we'll find

another way," Gabe said. "We'll have forty minutes to locate Ward 8 and get in there. That's when visiting hours will be over and access to the main floor will be closed to the public, but once we locate the ward, it won't matter if the main floor gets shut down. We'll find a way out, even if it's the hard way. They won't be expecting an uprising from kids drugged and locked away."

Gabriel stared into the faces of the Indigo family he had grown to love. They stood around him in a circle.

"If anyone senses Rafael, we all want to hear about it," he said. "Does everyone know what they're supposed to do?"

The Effin brothers looked up at him and smiled. Their white-blond hair shone blue under the moon. Kendra placed her hands on the boys' shoulders. She knew the key role they would play and would keep them safe.

Lucas was harder to read. He kept a poker face, but Gabe knew him well enough to know what he'd be thinking. The kid had heart and would do his part, even though he hated violence and wished he lived in a world where it wasn't necessary. Despite his strong beliefs, he'd taken up the cause of these Indigos when he could've lived a proper life of privilege. He had a legal battle ahead of him, to regain control of the trust fund money set up by his dead parents. His older sister, Mia, had power of attorney now, but Luke could fight for his independence in court, as Rayne had done. The guy had options. Gabriel respected Luke's choice to take a stand. He made doing the right thing look simple and easy, when it often amounted to an uphill scramble with unseen perils.

Uncle Reginald winked at him with his usual charming smile. He looked dapper, dressed in a summer tweed suit, a bow tie and a Ripley newsboy cap in herringbone that made him look like an Oxford professor. All he lacked was a vintage Sherlock Holmes calabash smoking pipe. The man had opened his home—and his life—to these children. Now he risked everything to defend their right to live free. He could've refused their need for a safe haven or stayed at home and taken an easier path of apathy, but here he stood. Gabriel couldn't have been more proud to call him blood.

When his eyes glanced at Rayne, his heart filled with everything he felt for her. He wanted to protect her, but she had chosen to be here—alongside her brother and these children she now called family, as he had done. He loved her more than his own life.

Looking into her eyes, he said what was in his heart.

"The Believers see us as children. Let them dismiss us. Let them believe that we will act as children and run in fear when they show force. We will prove them wrong." Gabriel shifted his gaze to Lucas. "Trust your gut and your Indigo heart to tell you what to do. It will be enough."

He put his hand in the center of the circle, and the others did too. When they all touched, and the blue auras melded into one, he said, "For Benny...and Rafael."

They bowed their heads in silence, and without prompting, the hive filled with images of the little ten-year-old they'd lost and the guy who had loved him like a brother. It was as if Benny and Rafe were with them now. The Effin twins never said much aloud, but they didn't hide their tears now. They'd lost their best friend and the boy who had replaced him in their hearts, Rafael.

Gabe noticed that Kendra wore two infinity bracelets, hers and the one that Rafael had left behind on Benny's grave. Benny had been buried with the third one. Rafael had meant those infinity bracelets for the family he always wished he had. Gabriel understood what it meant to lose everything.

They were ready, as they ever would be.

"Let's go."

Gabe gripped Dr. Fiona's ID badge in his hand as he headed off into the darkness with the others. He didn't feel Rafael in this place. Kendra had told him that she didn't either. If Rafe wasn't here—dead or alive—they'd have to keep searching. But for Benny, they would take the first step in shutting down Ward 8.

Rafael would've liked that.

Outside Haven Hills Treatment Facility

Lucas had been inside ten minutes. Using binoculars, Kendra had a good view of the rear entrance of Haven Hills from a grassy knoll, a landscaped fringe of the hospital parking lot located near a garage loading bay. She and the Effin brothers would be only steps away if Lucas got into trouble.

She watched for any signs of danger and kept an eye out for uniformed security, something to do while she slowly went crazy with worry. Kendra felt every second ticking down until visiting hours would be over. They'd purposefully picked the timing, even though it would be tight. At the end of visiting hours, they could be in the building without drawing attention, while security staff would be distracted by making sure visitors left and the hospital was secure again. But if they didn't find the right elevator, they'd lose their window of time to get into Ward 8.

What's happening, Luke?

When he didn't answer right away, she glanced over her shoulder to the Effin twins. They looked anxious too.

I sense more Indigos here, somewhere inside, but I can't pick out one voice. It could be that they're drugged like Lucas was. Kendra sent a message to the twins and the hive before she directed her next thought to Lucas.

Talk to me, Luke. Tell me something.

I'm here. Gimme a sec.

They'd lost two more minutes. Kendra shut her eyes and listened hard, praying Lucas would come through. She had a bad feeling and it had to do with Oliver. Rafael's life hung on Oliver.

They had to do this—now. That's all she knew.

I've hit three elevators to the basement, but none of them matched Oliver's description of the turns and steps. I'm not feeling it either.

Kendra felt the stress in Lucas's message.

Maybe there's a private entrance down. If Ward 8 is secret, that could be an added security measure, she told him.

Kendra thought more about what Oliver had told them.

He said they brought him into a garage loading bay that had sliding doors into the building. This rear entrance is the only place that fits that description. It has to be right. Stick with it, Luke.

Three more minutes went by.

I'm down to the last two. I'm going as fast as I can, but it's gonna be tight.

Kendra looked at her watch. Visiting hours would soon be over.

You got fifteen minutes, she told him. *We're coming in. We can't get caught out here if they close the doors early.*

Kendra stood and brushed grass off her jeans and the twins before they headed for the rear entrance. She held the boys' small hands as they walked toward the hospital. The last place she wanted them to be would be Haven Hills. It broke her heart to be the one to walk them through the door, but the Effin brothers had a unique gift that Gabriel knew how to maximize.

Understood, Luke told her. *Get to the gift shop. It'll still be open. Gabriel is there.*

What about you?

I'll catch up. Don't worry. Take care of the twins.

Kendra didn't like deviating from the plan, but she didn't see any other way. When she saw a man in uniform standing at the door, she squeezed the hands of the twins and held them firm.

"Visiting hours are almost over," the guard said.

"We're just here to pick up my grandmother. She's in the gift shop and needs a ride. We'll be right out. Promise." She smiled and the guy waved her on.

She breathed a sigh of relief as they stepped through the glass doors, but when she heard the sound of a fast-moving vehicle behind her, she dared to glance over her shoulder.

A dark van pulled up. It didn't have windows or markings. Kendra tensed. She'd seen a van like it before—the first time she'd actually set eyes on Lucas—when a group of mercenaries had beat him into a concussion on the rooftop of a parking garage.

Kendra rushed the boys inside and looked for the gift shop. She spotted it right away, near a bank of escalators.

You boys get to that store. She pointed. *Look for Gabriel.*

After the twins nodded and left her, she hid behind a column and watched the van. Terrible images flashed through her mind as she waited to see who would get out. A bead of sweat trickled down the back of her neck and felt like unwanted fingers.

Like a waking nightmare, Boelens jumped out from behind the driver's seat, the leader of the Believers security. The man knew her and Lucas, and Gabriel too. He hated them enough to kill them on sight.

"Oh God."

The twins would freak out if they saw the man again. They'd recognize the cruel mercenary, the guy who never blinked. One of the twins had been injured in the blast that had killed their best friend. It had taken the boys weeks to sleep through the night after Benny died. She'd held them in her arms when they cried. Fear like that shouldn't be on a kid's face...*ever.*

Boelens had shattered their lives—and now it looked as if he would ruin everything.

Kendra stuck around long enough to see that the mercenary didn't have anyone else with him. He parked the van at the door and stopped to say something to the guard. Odds were that he was headed to Ward 8, but she couldn't afford to let him see her. She could jeopardize everything by confronting him without knowing where the others were.

She gritted her teeth and did the only thing her gut told her to do. She had to stick to the plan. Kendra ran for the gift shop to stay with the Effin brothers and she warned the hive by letting them hear the message she sent to Luke.

Lucas, watch your back. Boelens pulled up in a van. If he heads for Ward 8, we're screwed. When she didn't hear from him, she sent Luke another message.

Lucas, did you hear me?

He didn't answer.

{ 16 }

Haven Hills Treatment Facility
7:55 p.m.

Earlier in the evening, Dispatch interrupted his patrol assignment and sent Boelens a message to make a hospital run
after visiting hours. They had no other explanation except
that they would have a pickup by eight o'clock. The order
had been issued during his dinner hour by Dr. Fiona Haugstad. If *he* got a message like that, it usually meant one thing.

She had a body to dispose of.

Since it took hours to do the job proper, he had an agree-
ment with the doctor to give him a heads-up by scheduling
body dumps ahead of time. That allowed him to manage his
day better. Because she hadn't given him the usual notice,
it made him wonder what was up. When he got to Haven
Hills, he parked at the rear entrance until he checked things
out firsthand. If the doctor wasn't ready for him, he wouldn't
waste time waiting around. He'd bag the pickup and leave
it for his boss, O'Dell, to deal with. The guy was a real desk
jockey. He'd figure it out and send someone else.

"I'll be in and out. Watch my ride, will ya?" he told the

security guard standing at the door. The guy recognized him and nodded.

Boelens rushed through the automatic doors and hit the head before he did anything else. In the hospital lobby, he didn't have to go far. A private elevator, marked for restricted access, was located behind a small chapel. He swiped his ID badge into the security reader, punched the down button and paced until his ride came.

At this hour the main floor had few people. Anything that moved caught his eye. Being alert paid off in his line of work. When he saw a kid in a hoodie on the mezzanine, Boelens did a double take. He recognized the boy's face. He'd know Lucas Darby anywhere.

"Holy shit."

The mind freak hadn't seen him yet. The kid was looking for something. His eyes searched the lobby as he walked. Boelens looked for a place to hide, but it was too late. The little bastard spotted him and ran. On instinct, Boelens felt for his weapon and took off after the boy, with a smirk on his face. He ran up the moving escalator, taking it three steps at a time.

"Stupid. Real stupid, kid."

Darby had returned to the Believers' stronghold, a mental hospital that had him locked away for years. Boelens would make him regret that decision.

Gabriel and his uncle had been in the gift shop with Rayne, waiting for Lucas to tell them how to get to Ward 8. They had kept a low profile while they waited, pretending to be visitors. But with visiting hours nearly ended, the small shop had made another closing announcement.

Gabriel held Rayne's hand as he glanced at his uncle. He didn't need to send a telepathic message. He saw in one glance that Uncle Reginald was worried as they headed for the gift shop exit.

"Come on. We gotta..." Gabe stopped when he heard Kendra's message about Boelens and saw her and the twins heading toward the store.

They had run out of time.

"Shit. Boelens is here," Gabe told Rayne.

"What?" She gripped his hand harder and looked over his shoulder into the lobby.

Gabriel intended to warn her to stay calm and not draw attention, but all bets were off when he saw a man bounding up an escalator to the mezzanine outside the store. Boelens had spotted Lucas and was chasing him.

Oh God. Luke.

Gabriel didn't think twice and he didn't wait for his uncle and Rayne to catch on. He went after Boelens when he saw the bastard close in on Luke. His anger fueled his adrenaline. No way he'd let the guy hurt him. Gabe kept his eyes on Rayne's brother to see which direction he'd turn on the next level up, but he slid to an abrupt stop when Luke vanished before his eyes.

His body shrank to a pinpoint and disappeared with an ear-punishing zap that left Gabriel standing at the base of the escalator, dumbfounded. A night-crew janitor took an interest in his sudden change of heart and an older woman in a walker smiled at him, but nothing looked out of the ordinary. Visiting hours were over and stragglers were heading out the main entrance. No one looked alarmed.

"What the hell?"

Gabe turned where he stood and searched the hospital lobby for any signs of a commotion. Everything looked quiet and he'd lost track of Boelens. He didn't hear running. No one looked startled, except for him. His uncle shrugged and headed toward him and Rayne looked confused.

What happened, Gabriel?

Where's Lucas?

Uncle Reginald and Kendra had questions.

So did Rayne. "You freaked me out. Why'd you run? Did you see Boelens?"

Gabe didn't know what to say. When nothing looked dodgy, he suddenly knew what had happened and felt rather foolish. Rayne's brother had created an illusion for Boelens to chase. He'd apparently stretched it to include him, most likely a payback for the pond incident.

Very clever, Lucas.

He heard a guy clear his throat on the mezzanine level above him and looked up to see Luke staring down at him from a railing. He didn't gloat. He looked...grateful.

Thanks to Boelens, I found the right elevator, Luke told him. *It's behind the chapel and it looks like you'll need the ID badge to operate it. I'll meet you there.*

What did you do with Boelens?

He's chasing me to the front parking lot. We won't have much time.

Gabriel nodded. Lucas would keep Boelens busy with an illusion that would have him chasing his own tail—at least for as long as he could. He hoped it would be enough.

"We gotta go. Now." He grabbed Rayne's hand. "Our timetable just got shorter."

As they headed for the elevator, his uncle asked, "Did our Lucas pull a rabbit out of his Indigo hat?"

"I would say he learned a valuable lesson at Mother's pond. Never underestimate the influence of a heaping pile of elephant excrement."

"Ah." His uncle winked. "Truer words have never been said."

* * *

The minute Gabriel got off the elevator and stepped into the basement that would lead them to Ward 8, he stared into narrow corridors that snaked through the shadows with old machinery and ductwork in every direction. If Oliver hadn't been firm on which way to go, they would've wasted valuable time searching.

Oliver sent him abrupt messages that sounded more like orders. Gabe counted his steps and turned where Oliver told him.

What about surveillance cameras? Lucas asked.

Got it covered, Gabe told him without breaking stride.

Before Gabe had gotten off the elevator, he'd taken care of any surveillance cameras by using his affinity with animals and insects. He conjured his power and enlisted the help of a few well-chosen friends to mess with any security guards watching the recording live. Roaches and mice found every lens a curiosity and blocked the view with their sudden infestation. He counted on his vermin army keeping hospital security repulsed long enough for them to get in and out. He hoped it would buy them time.

Although Uncle Reginald had been keen on the idea of his revolting distraction, something different bothered him more.

"Are you sure you should have your eyes closed? It's unnerving and you look positively nutters."

Despite the tension, Gabriel smiled at his uncle.

"Oliver says keeping my eyes closed helps him," he whispered. "He had a hood on, remember?"

"Why are you whispering? It looks like we're alone...except for you know who," his uncle said.

"*Shh.* You know who is counting." Gabe felt another telepathic nudge inside him and pointed. "Oliver says make a turn here."

"Good Lord, this is *most* peculiar."

"He says we're close," Gabe said. "Keep an eye out for—"

Uncle Reginald stuck his arm out to stop him and finished his thought. "A red-and-white sign?"

Gabe opened his eyes and looked up. "We're here."

Lucas stood at his shoulder and stared at the sign that had haunted both of them. No one spoke, not even his uncle. The Ward 8 sign had triggered the cold grip of every nightmare. Seeing it sent a shudder through Gabe. There had been a piece of him that wished this place didn't exist, that it had all been bad dreams, but he couldn't hope for that now. The real Ward 8 was a reminder that everything he and Lucas dreamed had been true. Those nightmare visions could be happening to Rafael. It made him sick to imagine it.

Soon they would all know what the Believers did to innocent Indigos behind these doors.

{ 17 }

Ward 8

Gabriel held Dr. Fiona's security badge in his hand as he stood outside the entrance to the ward. Every failed attempt to find Rafael had deflated him. Kendra and the others counted on him. They were feeling the tension and the frustration of coming up empty. Rafe had to be here, but after seeing the horrors in his visions, he wasn't sure that wishing the guy would be here was a good thing.

He didn't know what lay beyond these doors, but his war against his father and the Believers had to start here—the source of his nightmare visions.

You gotta find Caila. Oliver's low voice jolted him with adrenaline. It sounded as if the guy had yelled in his ear.

Easy, Romeo. We have to find your body first. This is where you get off, remember?

The power stirred inside him and Gabe felt the burn in his belly as he swiped Dr. Fiona's badge through the reader. The door buzzed a warning and he yanked it open, before he handed the passkey to his uncle.

Please tell me the minute you find Rafael. Use this to free him,

Caila and any others. I've got a long-overdue rendezvous to meet Oliver.

Gabriel walked through the door and down a corridor until he noticed activity ahead. A nurses' station served as a hub, with signs pointing to a surgical wing, patient exam rooms and the ICU. He saw enough of the remaining wing to know there'd be locked cells where the Indigo children would be held against their will.

They would have to split up.

But when he got to the end of the hallway, he came face-to-face with three uniformed women who stood behind the counter of the nurses' station, glaring at him. A security guard had noticed the commotion and came running.

"Stop right there," the uniformed man yelled. "How did you get in here?"

"Who are you?" a nurse asked.

Gabriel felt Uncle Reginald at his side. Lucas, Kendra and Rayne fanned out. When the Effin twins shoved their way through to stand in front of him, he put his hands on the boys' shoulders. He drew from the power of their blue aura burning in him—and he felt sure these people had never seen the likes of them.

"Sorry for the intrusion. I suppose it would be rude of me not to make introductions. My name is Gabriel." With a sweep of his hand, he beckoned his faithful companion and said, "And this is my dog, Hellboy."

When his phantom dog materialized from thin air and crept through a portal of glowing mist that now swirled at his feet, he snarled and bristled and bared his teeth. One nurse cried and made the sign of the cross and the guard swallowed, hard. He approached with more caution, his hand on the butt of his weapon.

"You can't have a…uh…dog in here," the guard stammered. "Hospital rules."

"I'm pretty sure dead dogs are the one exception. Look it up."

Gabriel narrowed his eyes and stared into each of their faces. None of them looked him in the eye.

They knew what he was.

"Look at you, in your pristine uniforms, pretending to be caregivers. You think you're normal, law-abiding citizens who pay your taxes and contribute to society, but what you do for a paycheck is drug and torture children." He shifted his gaze to each face. "Well, for you, that will end here. You've drawn the short straw."

Gabriel conjured every nightmare he had—the most vile and disgusting—and amassed it inside him. Like a fast-acting poison, it made him sick, but he didn't care.

"You've been the source of my worst nightmares. I'm here to return the favor."

When he stepped forward with Hellboy, the Effin brothers wouldn't let him go alone. They came with him, like the many times they had trained. He looked into the intense blue eyes of the small boys and understood what they wanted.

They were done hiding and wanted to be seen.

After Gabriel nodded, the twins raised their thin arms—in slow unison—and pointed their small index fingers at the guard. The man looked sick and took a step back, but didn't take his eyes off the boys. The simple act of pointing their fingers had spooked the man into believing they were evil demon children.

"Stay where you are. You're not authorized to be here," the guard threatened.

"But we would have your *permission* if you abducted us off the streets and brought us here in shackles against our will?

Is that how it works?" Gabe yelled. "Where is Rafael Santana? I'll spare the first one to tell me."

When no one spoke up, Gabriel thought he knew why.

"Do you even know their names...these children that you torture, mutilate and kill?" He shook his head. "You are *all* cowards...and bloody criminals."

Gabe saw the fear in their eyes, but these people wouldn't understand the power of the Indigo soul without a demonstration. The only experience they had came from their dominance over scared children who didn't realize what they could do to defend themselves. Many Indigos were like Lucas. They were quiet by nature and intelligent, peace-loving human beings. But because of his mother, Gabriel had evolved from an Indigo warrior to become a powerful Crystal child.

It was time the Believers met another breed of Indigo.

When he felt the rising heat of his connection to the Effin brothers, it was as if they'd plugged him into an electrical socket. The twins juiced him up and turned their abilities over to him.

"Now it's my turn."

Gabriel flung his arms and hurled the worst of his fury. He shot a fireball at the guard and it blasted his body. The force of it smashed him against a wall. In shock, the man shrieked as if he were on fire. He collapsed to the floor and clutched his arms and legs into the fetal position, swatting at the blue flames that fed off him.

One nurse screamed at the sight of the armed guard fighting demons she couldn't see. Another woman cowered behind the counter, but none of them would escape. Using the gifts of the twins, Gabe attacked the hypothalamus, the gland in the human brain that controlled every human being's base instinct. He made these people desperate to run, yet they were too afraid to move. For good measure, he filled them with insatiable hunger and confused them by making them horny. The next time they craved pizza or felt the urge to have sex, they would be reminded of their sins.

Being able to use the power of both Effin brothers and magnify it made these Believers puppets in Gabriel's hands. He drew from his psychic attack on Dr. Fiona and gave them each a taste of the nightmare he had concocted especially for the doctor. They all deserved a share. They would feel what they'd done to every child, and that memory would plague their nights forever.

"What you're doing to naive children, you don't deserve mercy." Gabriel hesitated long enough for them to wonder what he'd do to them. "But I don't want to kill you and you don't want to end up on the wrong side of dead. Cooperate and no one will get hurt."

Gabriel thought he would feel better about shutting down Ward 8, but destroying it was only walls and locked cells and the patient files of blameless children who had died to satisfy the Believer's cruel vision of the future. The real evil still existed in the minds and malicious hearts of those who had conceived and built the ward.

All he felt was an aching emptiness and a grief that would always be a part of him.

Lucas had been right. Killing for the sake of killing wasn't the answer and revenge wouldn't bring back his mother, or Benny, or any other child who had died at the hands of the Believers—and starting a war might never bring Rafael back. If there was any hope for a future where Indigo children could live as equals, Gabriel had to find a different way to stop the bloodshed and the genocide.

Destroying the ward meant no more nightmares would come from this place. He'd have to settle for that.

Minutes later

With the situation contained and relatively stable, Gabriel sent Hellboy away. The presence of a ghost dog might scare any new Indigos they might find, and Hellboy wasn't meant for stealth.

"Lock the Believers in one cell and tell me the minute you find Rafael...if he's here," Gabe said. "Free any Indigos and tell 'em we'll get them out of here. We won't leave anyone behind."

At the mention of Rafael's name, Kendra's eyes flared in anger, but she stayed in control. She and Rayne grabbed ID badges off the nurses and ushered them down the hall while Uncle Reginald went looking for Caila. Lucas had already taken care of the guard and confiscated his gun, but the twins wouldn't be denied. They stayed with him because they were too curious about Oliver.

"I know what you want. Come on," he told the twins.

When Gabriel set eyes on Oliver Blue, lying unconscious on a bed in ICU 4, he looked better than he had expected. He had color to his cheeks and he breathed on his own, without a respirator. It wouldn't take much to unplug him. The beeping equipment and the leads coming off his body that fed data into machines to monitor his heart and operate the brain scanner didn't intimidate the twins. It was as if they knew he was in there and all right, playing a mad game of hide-and-seek.

The boys ran up to Oliver, poked his arms and giggled. One of them squeezed his nose shut until Oliver's body gasped for air.

"I wouldn't piss him off, boys. Have you seen the size of this guy?" When Gabe looked at Oliver, he smiled and said, "Time to wake up and carry your own weight, Sleeping Beauty."

Gabe knew he wouldn't have to ask twice. Oliver had every intention of seeing Caila with his own eyes, but when the Indigo boy stirred inside him, it felt as if his internal organs were being rearranged.

"Ah, easy now. That's my liver." Gabe winced.

A wash of gelatinous blue pulled from his skin. The ooze looked stark against the white sheets of the hospital bed until it melted and spread over unconscious Oliver.

So cool. One of the twins refused to be quiet as the transformation took hold.

That was in you, Gabriel? the other said. *He looks like... boogers.*

"I heard that," Oliver mumbled in a gruff, graveled voice. After he opened his eyes, he squinted into the light and said, "Never admit that you know what boogers look like."

Both the Effin brothers laughed. The sound felt peculiar in this place, but Gabriel liked it.

After he pulled Oliver free of the hospital equipment, he helped him sit up. The guy was shaky and although he winced in pain, he didn't make a big deal about it. One of the twins gave him water to drink, but when Oliver was ready to say more, Gabe was surprised at the first thing out of his mouth.

"I gotta get out of this pastel shit." Oliver stared down at the hospital pajamas he wore and grimaced.

"Your makeover will have to wait. We gotta move."

Gabriel still had Boelens on his mind. The guy was on the loose somewhere and could still cause trouble, but Gabe wouldn't leave Ward 8 operational. He had to hit the Believers hard and send a message to his father—that he'd be next.

"Thanks for the body loan, Gabriel. And for what you did

here, there are no words, man." Oliver stood with his help. "Where's Caila? Is she okay?"

When Gabriel heard a commotion outside and saw a girl rushing to ICU 4 with his uncle, he knew who she was.

"Oliver?" she cried. "I thought I'd never see you again."

The girl ran into the room and didn't hide how she felt about Oliver Blue. Caila wouldn't have broken stride until she held him in her arms, but the guy stuck out his hand to stop her.

"Hold it. Don't get near me," he said. Oliver stared at her as if he were seeing her for the first time. "None of you should let her touch you. She's a user. She messes with your head."

Caila stumbled back and looked crushed. Her face turned bloodred and she cowered from Oliver's stare. She couldn't look any of them in the eye. By her reaction, Gabriel saw there was truth in what Oliver said. The girl didn't deny or justify whatever she'd done to him. But after Gabe had shared his body with Oliver, he knew something about the guy that even *he* didn't know.

Fake or not, Oliver had real feelings for Caila.

"Can we have some privacy?" Oliver shifted his gaze to Gabriel and waited.

"Yeah, you got two minutes." He didn't apologize for making things harder. It's just the way things were.

"That'll do. Thanks."

Gabriel shut the door behind him and the twins after they left. With their two-minute clock ticking down, he looked through the observation window and saw Oliver stare at the girl. Neither of them looked in a hurry to say a word. Whatever had happened between them, it was complicated.

Oliver wanted to hate Caila for what she did to him. She'd hijacked his life, no different than what the Believers did when they kidnapped kids off the street. This girl came to him and used his relationship with Zack to force him to help her. He still didn't understand why, but that didn't matter now.

After today, he didn't have to see her again—but that's not what his heart wanted. *Shit!*

"Whatever you did to me, it wasn't real," he said. "The doctor told me that. Don't deny it. You used me."

"No, that's not—"

"Dr. Fiona said you don't even know what the truth is. I can't trust you."

Caila's face glistened with fresh tears. "I thought I was doing the right thing, but…I was wrong. I almost got you killed, like…"

The girl was falling apart. She looked thin and frail. Her body shook and she couldn't look him in the eye. A normal human being would've walked away and let the sins of her past catch up with her, but no one had ever accused him of being normal.

Despite how she had betrayed him and put him in the crosshairs of the Believers, she'd also given him something that meant more. She'd given him *hope*. The weeks of torture strapped into that helmet, his mind held a lifeline buried in it—his memories of Caila. When he wanted to die, she had given him a reason to live.

Even now he had to fight his thoughts that he would have a future with her in it. He knew the memories she'd planted in him were lies, but what the hell was he doing, fighting something he should want too? He also had to deal with his unhealthy appreciation for what Dr. Fiona had done *to* him and *for* him. She'd made him stronger and turned his gift into something more powerful, but she'd done it through her cruelty.

Damn it, he hated the way he felt. All of these thoughts confused him—but none more than his strange feelings for this girl, conflicting emotions he might never shake.

"Did you find Zack? Is he here?" he asked.

Caila stared at him with tears welling in her eyes. She looked like a lost little girl. When she finally broke down, she sobbed so hard that Oliver wasn't sure she'd ever tell him anything. The mistrust had festered in him too long. Her tears could be part of her act. He wasn't sure he could believe anything she told him, but he waited for her to talk and didn't push.

"He's...he's dead." She grabbed her stomach and slid down the wall, crying. "That doctor...has his brain in a jar. We can't even bury him. The doctor said he died...because of me."

Oliver's eyes grew wide and he couldn't catch his breath. The doctor was a liar. Caila lied too. He didn't know what to believe, but if Zack's brain was in a jar, the girl hadn't been the one to cut it out. All he could do was trust his gut instincts.

His mind raced with memories of his friend and somehow he knew what the girl said was true. When he touched the Cheez Whiz can and used his ability to scry for Zack, a trail of darkness lingered. He'd chalked it up to his own shitty outlook on life, but now in this place, he felt the hole where Zack had been.

Oliver knelt down with Caila. He didn't touch her. He wasn't sure he could, but he missed Zack and knew she did too. That part had always felt real. He reached out his hand

and touched her hair. When she broke down in his arms, he finally gave in and held her.

He didn't fight the lies she'd planted in him. All he felt was his crushing grief over Zack.

Haven Hills Treatment Facility
Lobby

Boelens had chased the Darby kid through the mezzanine before the boy hit the hospital lobby. When the little freak got to the front entrance, Boelens thought he'd get help from the night-shift guards.

"Stop the little bastard!"

When he'd yelled at them and pointed, he got only weird looks in return. They acted as if he were a frigging lunatic.

"What the hell is *wrong* with you?"

He barreled through the automatic doors and ran into the darkness of the parking lot where few vehicles remained. The kid would be easy to spot. And outside, he'd make sure there were no witnesses. He could shoot him and say he had a weapon. Killing the mind freak and claiming self-defense—against a disturbed mental patient who had escaped the hospital—would cure all his problems. The church and the hospital would back him up.

Worn out from the chase, Boelens felt like shit. His lungs burned and his legs were giving out. Like the first time he set eyes on the kid, Darby would pay the price for making him run. Only this time, Boelens would get to finish it, without interference from Kendra Walker.

He heard Darby's footsteps and saw his back. The little bastard had stretched his lead. Boelens knew he wouldn't catch him if he didn't stop him soon. After he left the parking lot, he'd lose the security lights.

Heaving for air, Boelens stopped and pulled his gun. He racked the slide and took aim.

"Adios, motherfucker."

Boelens pulled the trigger and felt the gun buck in his hands.

"What the hell? No way."

Darby kept running. He'd missed. Boelens wiped the sweat from his eyes and took aim again. This time when he fired, the kid disappeared like a ghost. One minute he was running scared, the next he was...*gone*.

"This ain't over, Darby." Boelens gritted his teeth and swore under his breath. "You're mine, you little shit."

Ward 8
Minutes later

Uncle Reginald and Rayne brought the freed Indigos with them as they came toward Gabriel. Their blue auras were a bit dim but still with them. The kids looked scared. There were five and one looked no more than six years old. What had the Believers planned to do with *him?* Gabriel fought hard to control his anger at seeing such an innocent child in this place.

"This little guy is named Noah." With tears in her eyes, Rayne fought hard not to cry as she ran her fingers through the kid's mussed brown hair. "He's...shy."

The boy didn't react and looked in shock. His steel-gray eyes were the color of midnight blue and were glazed over. Gabriel knelt in front of Noah. He wanted to smile, but he couldn't.

"You're safe, Noah. We'll get you home. Promise."

Little Noah finally looked at Gabe. He didn't smile, but seeing the boy stare into his eyes felt like a small victory.

"And here we have two strapping young lads, Sam and

Quinn." His uncle rested his hands on the heads of the two boys who looked to be about Lucas's age.

Gabriel stood and said, "Good to meet you, boys."

Quinn had blue eyes the color of a spring sky and auburn hair. Sam was his dark opposite with olive skin, pitch-black waves and pale green eyes the color of desert cactus. Both boys looked as if they'd bolt the minute they hit the night air. Gabe hoped they would stay, but that would be up to them.

"These two heartbreakers are Denise and Debbie." Uncle Reginald pointed as he introduced them. The girls were the mirror image of each other, both with dark hair and eyes, and a spray of freckles across their noses.

"They're sisters," his uncle said. "Twins, to be exact. One of them is quite bossy."

"I am *not*," Debbie said.

Denise only rolled her eyes.

"We're Indigos, like you," Gabriel told them.

He didn't bother educating them on the difference between Indigo and Crystal children. That would come if they stayed.

"We have no time to explain why we're here," he told them. "That will have to come later, if you're interested. I only ask that you follow our orders until you get outside, when you'll be free to go, but I hope you'll come with us. There's so much we can teach each other."

"If you need a home, we can give you one where you'll be safe and among your own kind," Uncle Reginald said. "But that will be your choice, always."

His uncle made sure that Gabe knew he could bring them home.

God, he's not here. Rafael is not here.

When Gabriel heard the sound of Kendra's voice in his

head, he turned to see her running toward him. Seeing the misery on her face, he knew she was hurting.

Kendra had a strength she wielded in her eyes, a fierce determination, but after the Believers destroyed everything she had built and reminded her how vulnerable they *all* were, she carried a sadness that he saw now. After Rafael went missing, she'd pulled away from them. She did what she had to do for the children, but her heart wasn't in it. She'd lost the brightness of her spirit that always shone through her eyes.

"I didn't find him," she said. "And I don't *feel* him here."

Her lips trembled and she looked away. Gabe knew the longer it took for them to find Rafael, the more hopeless they all felt. When the door to ICU 4 opened and Oliver and Caila came out, the girl looked worn out from crying. Oliver didn't look much better.

"Who's Rafael?" Oliver asked.

"He's one of ours. They have him. We just don't know where," Gabe said. "It's why we came here in the first place."

Oliver glanced at Caila and she nodded her encouragement.

"If you have something of his, I can help you find him," Oliver said. "It's what I...do."

Kendra narrowed her eyes with a shocked expression on her face. When she stepped forward, it looked as if she was gauging whether or not she could trust him.

"I had a...feeling about you." With her eyes fixed on Oliver, she touched the black leather bracelet with a silver infinity charm that she had on her wrist. "This is his. When we get out of here, I'll give it to you...to try."

Gabriel knew that bracelet meant much more to all of them than something Rafael wore. It meant home and family and hope for a future they could share. When Oliver looked down at the bracelet, Kendra stroked the leather with a finger.

"If he's still alive, he's…in a dark place. I can't reach him," she said. "Please…help me find him."

Kendra didn't have to tell the guy why Rafael was special to her. Everything she felt for Rafe was in her eyes. She didn't hide it anymore.

"Count on it." Oliver nodded.

Before Gabriel could intrude on the moment by reminding them the clock was ticking and they had to go, Lucas did a fine job of it.

Fire in the hole!

After Lucas sent a message to the hive, Kendra and Uncle Reginald reached for the new kids and shielded them with their bodies. When they heard a loud crash of glass and a grunt, Gabe knew that Rayne's brother had found another way to exorcise his Ward 8 demons.

"That's just our Lucas, doing a little…demo work," Gabe told the new kids. "Nothing to be alarmed about."

Luke had used his powers to destroy the computers and short-circuit every piece of equipment he found. Gabe suspected the Believers would have a network with backup protocols, but it didn't hurt to annihilate whatever they found. Ward 8 would be a heaping pile of destruction when the morning shift arrived.

The Believers would know their secret wasn't a secret anymore—and they'd have to wonder what had been compromised.

"We can't leave until we destroy her files. That doctor has information on Oliver and me… Others too." Caila had been quiet until now. "She keeps records of her sick experiments and how they tracked us. They're in a locked room. I know where it is, but she's the only one who has a key."

Uncle Reginald raised an eyebrow and held up the ID badge for Dr. Fiona Haugstad. "You mean this key?"

Caila's tearstained face melted into a sad smile.

Gabriel sensed the significance of unlocking the door to a file room and office that Dr. Fiona had kept secret. It felt like the reason they had come to destroy the ward. Everything else could be replaced by the church, but whatever evil this woman had conceived, she had locked it away for a reason. If there was anything that would cripple the Believers and set them back, perhaps it would be here.

Keep the new kids back, uncle. I have a bad feeling. Gabe sent his message to the hive as a warning.

When his uncle nodded, Gabe walked into the small room. He saw a desk, a computer for Lucas to fry beyond all repair and two metal file cabinets. The office looked like any other. He wasn't sure what he had expected, but this wasn't it. Everything looked too normal. Whatever she hid behind the locked door would have to be in the files.

But to his right, he saw shelves that had been blocked by the open door. What he saw staggered him. "Oh my God."

Gabriel shook in disgust and his stomach clenched. When Kendra came into the room, he put a hand out to hold her and the others back, but it was too late. She tried to stop the Effin brothers from looking at what he'd found, but the twins shoved by her.

The hive went silent.

Dr. Fiona had a shelf of jars containing brains and body parts of the children she had killed in the name of science and her faith. The stark reality of seeing human beings reduced to nothing more than lab experiments revolted Gabriel. His father must've known about this. How could he not? This vile woman slaughtered children and carried out her carnage in secret, but his father had to be a part of it.

Kendra crept toward the shelves and clutched her stomach when she got close. Rayne rushed to her.

"Don't do it," Rayne said. "I'll look for you."

She moved Kendra away from the atrocities—marked with the names of the dead. Rayne looked at every jar for the name of Rafael Santana. When she didn't find it, she took a ragged breath. Not finding him didn't make her search any easier.

No one spoke until Caila pointed a shaky hand to a jar filled with a murky viscous liquid and a human brain.

"That's Zack… What's left of him," Caila said. "He was my…friend."

"Ah, hell." Oliver didn't hide his pain. He pulled Caila into his arms and held her. "I'm not leaving him here."

Gabe felt bone-deep shame. Oliver and Caila didn't know of his connection to the head of the Believers in L.A., Alexander Reese. Gabriel couldn't help feeling responsible for the sinister acts. He steeled himself for what would come next.

He had to stop his father.

"We're not leaving *any* of them," Gabe said.

To the hive, he sent the rest of his message.

We're taking these damned files too. Maybe we'll find out more about how they hunt us. And we can make contact with others they've marked. Warn them.

Gabriel could barely finish. Seeing the dead eyes of Kendra made him feel worse. He backed out of the room, struggling to breathe as the nightmare of his visions came rushing back. Hellboy nudged his leg and whimpered, but the only thing that made the horror tolerable was Rayne.

She held him when he needed her strength—*and her humanity.*

When he heard the soft sobs of her crying, he knew what plagued her heart. Lucas could've ended up in a jar and become nothing more than a footnote to Dr. Fiona's data. What had started with the search for her missing brother had turned into a fight for survival and hope for a future where Indigos wouldn't be hunted like animals, but the darkness of what they found in Dr. Fiona's sociopathic science made him see the hopelessness of what they had naively tried to do.

Seeing this locked room reminded Gabriel that Ward 8 was only one location. The Believers had a worldwide organization of followers and resources. What kinds of atrocities were locked away in other secret rooms? How many Dr. Fionas did they have doing God's work?

To stop the killing on a global scale, Gabriel considered the unthinkable—revealing to the world and law enforcement authorities what the Believers were doing to children—but the answer always came back the same. Revealing what they were would only increase the hunters looking for them. More children would die. It was a vicious cycle that had no end.

He held Rayne tighter—his precious girl—and cradled her head to his chest, feeling like a drowning man. She was the only thing that kept him from sinking into a darkness that was slowly swallowing him.

After Lucas found insulated boxes marked for organ harvesting and a supply cart to wheel out what they planned to take, the guy quietly got down to the morbid business of dealing with the body parts floating in jars. Oliver watched him work, but he kept one eye on Zack's brain. The girl helping Lucas, the one they called Kendra, stared at him but didn't push him to help. As respectful as they were with the dead, Oliver couldn't let anyone else touch his friend.

"I'll do Zack."

"You sure?" Lucas asked.

"Yeah...I'm sure."

Lucas handed him a container and left him alone to deal with it. Oliver could've used rubber gloves as they had done, but with his gift, he had to touch Zack one last time. His hands shook when he reached into the jar and he almost couldn't do it. The minute his fingers hit the cold liquid, a chill ran up his arm and the room went dark. He knew what would happen, but he had to do it for Zack.

The instant he touched the brain, images flashed in his head to fill the darkness.

Oliver saw how Zack died. He felt everything.

Frantic pants turned into heaving sickness. The darkness of Zack's death sent him into a gruesome tailspin that felt as if it would never end. He saw through Zack's eyes and knew what it felt like to die alone and scared, at the hands of merciless people who didn't even know his name. No one should die like that—*no one*.

He heard a steady thump that ran a cold shiver through his body and shredded his nerves. Oliver listened and held his breath, not wanting the beating to end.

Until. It. Did.

He knew the beating had been Zack's heart. In the shadowy darkness of his friend's last minutes, Oliver heard a distant cry—a gut-wrenching wail. At first he thought it had been Zack. It took a while for him to realize that the cry had come from him. When his shadowy vision faded, he opened his eyes and felt the chill of tears on his face. He pulled his hand from the jar and saw the others were looking at him.

He didn't give a shit.

Oliver felt belly-punched and exhausted. When the others quit staring, they left him alone, but someone had been with him through it all. He hadn't felt her touch him, but Caila must've known what would happen to him the minute he reached for Zack's brain. She had used her gift on him again—only this time she saw and felt what he did.

"I had to...kn-know," she choked. "I'm sorry."

"You didn't have to...go through that."

Oliver held Caila and she held him back.

What happened to Zack would never be forgotten now, but the horror would crowd any of the good things that either of them would remember about the way Zack lived. Knowing how he died was Oliver's way of dealing with his own grief, but this girl had a choice. She didn't have to witness Zack dying from inside his skin.

The girl had guts.

Minutes later

When Oliver helped clear out Dr. Fiona's office, he found a cardboard box of shoes and handed them out to the kids who needed something on their bare feet. He found a pair of running shoes that would work for him and tried not to think about why the doctor had the box in the first place.

He noticed that Lucas and Kendra had sorted through the files in the cabinet and tossed most of them into boxes that they'd loaded onto the pushcart, but a few folders were thrown onto the desk. He didn't have to wait long to find out why some files were being singled out.

"We've pulled the files they had on us. Oliver and Caila's too," Gabriel said. "I figured you'd want to see what they had on you, but that's up to each of you to decide. The rest of the records we'll take with us to study later. If we can warn others that the Believers have them on their sick radar, we'll do that too."

He told them how they'd leave the hospital. All the deception that had gone into sneaking in was no longer necessary. Gabriel and the others weren't concerned about any confrontation with security guards. From the expression on the Crystal child's face, he looked fried—and something dark had a hold of him, something Oliver understood.

He still wanted to help them find Rafael, but after that, he'd be on his own. He wasn't sure how he felt about that.

"You curious about what they have on you?" Oliver asked Caila.

"No, I can't look. I don't wanna know. That doctor told me enough," she said, without hesitating. "I'm gonna burn mine. I don't want *anyone* seeing it."

"I can understand that." He nodded.

After an awkward moment, she said, "I'm going with Rayne. She's got...Zack."

"Yeah, I'll catch up, as soon as we're done here." Oliver watched her leave, but Caila never looked back.

"Grab those files on the desk, will ya?" Lucas called out to him. "We'll put them on top."

"Yeah, sure."

Oliver made one final pass through the empty room to grab the handful of files stacked on the desk. There were folders on him and Caila, Lucas, the guy named Rafael Santana and one for Kendra Walker. When he saw the sketchy surveillance photos Dr. Fiona had shown him of Gabriel Stewart, he realized how much she had manipulated him. If she lied about the Crystal kid, he couldn't trust her on anything else.

Instead of grabbing his own file, he reached for the one

marked Caila Ferrie. He didn't have a right to pry into her private information, but something made him read the file.

What he saw surprised him.

"Well, I'll be damned."

Oliver stuck the contents of Caila's file in the back of his, where it wouldn't be easily spotted. After he handed the stack of folders to Lucas and saw where he'd put them, he felt like an ass. Lucas and the others were ready to leave. He couldn't change his mind now, even if he wanted to.

There were days he hated having a conscience.

"Shit," he whispered.

Oliver didn't know what to believe anymore, but if Zack wanted to protect this girl, he had his reasons. He had to find out the truth about Caila—for Zack's sake and his own.

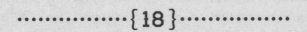

{ 18 }

Haven Hills Treatment Facility
9:10 p.m.

What they'd done to cripple Ward 8 should have felt like
a small triumph, but coming away without finding Rafael
and seeing the wall of jars left Gabriel feeling empty. Even
though leaving Haven Hills had gone off without a hitch,
he thought it had been *too* easy. The lobby had been quiet
and the lights were dimmed for the evening hours. Only one
guard had stopped them from going out the rear entrance.
and the man didn't put up much resistance after the Effin
brothers took care of him.

Rayne and Caila wheeled the cart that held Dr. Fiona's
macabre collection of body parts, and Uncle Reginald took
charge of the Indigos they'd rescued and held little Noah in
his arms. The boy had fallen asleep. When none of the new
kids bolted, Gabe took that as a positive sign when everything else felt hollow.

But as his eyes searched the darkness, something felt off
and he wasn't sure what.

He didn't feel the usual psychic push, like when the Believers were closing in. As he glanced over his shoulder, he

saw the look of worry and tension on Kendra's face and knew she must've had the same feeling. She caught up to him and spoke in a low voice. No doubt whatever speculations she had, she didn't want to scare the hive by passing her fears on to them.

"Boelens was here earlier. I saw him," she muttered under her breath. "He had his van parked at the rear entrance, but I didn't see it anywhere when we came out. I don't like it. He's not the kind of guy to roll over and play dead. He wouldn't do us the favor."

"That's a guy I'd like to see fitted for a coffin," he said. "Don't tell Lucas I said that."

Even in the dim light, Gabriel saw the faint twitch of her lip.

"Your secret is safe with me. I swear, if he took Rafael…" She didn't have to finish for Gabe to know what she would do.

"We won't quit until we find him, Kendra. The Believers have him somewhere else, that's all. Maybe Oliver can make a difference. We're lucky to have him with us."

Gabe stole a glance at the others and saw Rayne. Her brother had taken over pushing the cart for her and Caila. Lucas had done the gentlemanly thing, but the boy didn't have the instincts of a warrior like the rest of them. He should have stayed alert and been ready to fight if they were ambushed by Boelens or anyone else. He'd chosen to help his sister instead.

Luke would learn, but Gabriel envied his innocence.

"You feel anything?" he asked Kendra. "'Cause I don't, if you don't count the hair on the back of my neck crawling up my skull. Can't put a finger on why I'm on edge, but I am."

"Yeah, I know what you mean."

She kept her eyes alert as they slipped into the shadows beyond the hospital parking lot, heading for Uncle Reginald's Navigator and the doctor's Mercedes.

"To be safe, we shouldn't dawdle at the vehicles. We'll pack up our dead comrades and move out," he told her. "Oliver rides with you and me."

"I hoped you'd say that." She dared to smile, but she looked more worried than happy. "I've gotta know what he can do to find Rafael."

"Yeah, me too."

Gabriel prayed Oliver would help them find Rafe, but he had another reason for wanting to see how the guy worked.

If Oliver found Rafael, he could also help him locate his father. What he would do when he found the man had been festering in his mind. After seeing Dr. Fiona's unchecked cruelty under the watchful eye of his father, a man he'd grown to despise, Gabe no longer feared his dark thoughts. There would come a time he'd have to embrace them.

He wasn't noble like Lucas—and never would be.

Minutes later

Gabriel approached the vehicles they'd left behind with caution. He half expected to see Boelens jump from every shadow. Oliver must've sensed his tension, because the guy stood at his shoulder with his eyes alert. Gabe liked Oliver's instincts. He didn't talk much, but he felt connected to the guy. He was certain he'd known Oliver in another life and they'd been close.

But a warning from an unlikely source caught Gabe by surprise.

"Hold up, you guys," Rayne whispered, and grabbed his arm. She looked spooked. "The Mercedes… It's rocking. I saw it move."

They all stopped a safe distance from the Navigator and the Mercedes. Gabriel had been so distracted—waiting for Boelens to mess up their exit strategy—that he forgot about the vehicle they'd stolen from Dr. Fiona.

"You hear that?" Caila looked at Oliver. "I hear someone…screaming. But it sounds far away."

Even the Effin brothers got quiet. Considering they didn't talk, that was saying something. Gabriel glanced at Oliver and raised an eyebrow. Oliver only shrugged.

"Wait a minute. Everyone is freaking out…" Kendra narrowed her eyes at him and Oliver. "…except you two. What's up?"

Gabriel rolled his eyes and heaved a sigh. Without any more drama, he reached into his pocket and pulled out the key to the Mercedes. The rocking got worse and the screams Caila had heard became louder. The noise came from the trunk.

When he unlocked the cargo hold, the interior light came on and Gabriel backed away to let them see. Caila and Rayne gasped and Lucas looked confused. The twins snorted a laugh—*twice*.

Kendra was the only one who found the sight mildly amusing. Dr. Fiona was duct-taped in the trunk looking like a prize sow with her eyes bugging out of her head. Her hair hung over her eyes and made her look like a madwoman.

Fitting.

When all eyes shifted to Gabriel, he winced and said, "Surprise?"

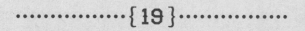

{ 19 }

West Hollywood

"It's not like I took her…as a souvenir, exactly. I had a rea-son," Gabriel said.

For a stunned moment, no one said anything. They stared at him in shock. Dr. Fiona wiggled and screamed and fought the duct tape that bound her hands and legs and covered her mouth. Her pale skin glowed red under the trunk light, and streaks of makeup ran down her face and made her look like the monster she was.

"It would be in your best interest to shut up," he told her. "You can trust me on *that* one."

Gabe saw the whites of her eyes. She looked plenty scared, but she quit struggling.

"I thought you'd…killed her. I think we *all* did." Lucas had a hard-to-read expression on his face. Gabriel couldn't tell if he was disappointed or pleased.

"Well, it's not like she didn't deserve a little killing." He shrugged. "I didn't know what to do with her. I thought we could decide after we hit the ward."

"But why didn't you tell us she was *in the trunk?*" Kendra asked.

They stared at him, waiting.

"To be honest…" Gabe flinched. "I forgot."

"Oh God." Rayne muttered.

Gabe thought he saw her smile, but surely he'd been mistaken.

"Well, I've had a lot on my mind." He raised his voice. "I was…*busy*."

"So, what *are* you gonna do with her, now that this place is history?" Caila crossed her arms. "She killed Zack…and tortured Oliver and she had these kids locked up. In those files, you'll see what a psycho she is. We *can't* let her live. She'll only keep doing it."

Lucas looked as if he would take a stand against killing the doctor, but when he stopped, Gabe wasn't sure what to make of his change of heart. If it had been only the two of them, he would talk it out, but he wouldn't do that in front of the others.

"Shall we flip a coin?" he asked them. "No matter what we decide, there will be consequences. I don't believe killing should be our *only* answer, not even with her, but we can't drop her off at the next bus stop either. Anyone with a brilliant idea, please. I'm all ears."

No one said anything, but the tension was suffocating. Gabe had said enough. He didn't want the decision to be his, but he wasn't sure what else to do. Even Uncle Reginald kept his silence as he watched him. It felt as if his uncle was waiting to see what he'd decide on his own, but the problem with growing up and becoming a man was that a guy didn't always *feel* grown up. Sometimes he felt more like a kid. And waging war—against the Believers or anyone—came with a price he wasn't sure he was ready to pay.

Gabe stared into the precipice of the bleak decision he knew was ahead. Letting the doctor go—or killing her—

either way would cost them and he knew it would fall on his shoulders, squarely. He couldn't see anyone else paying that price, but when Oliver stepped forward, the guy got his attention.

"I've got an idea," he said. "But I'll need Caila to make it work."

Gabriel stared at him and let out the breath he'd been holding.

Oliver stared down at Caila after he'd made his case. The girl didn't look convinced.

"You don't understand. My gift doesn't work like that. I can't flip a switch and make it happen," Caila told him. "I have to…be threatened before it…protects me."

What she said made sense. Oliver remembered how scared she had looked in the alley, when the Believers had abducted them.

"Look at her, Caila." He pointed at the squirming woman tied up in the trunk of the Mercedes. "She killed Zack. Doing the same to her is off the table. We gotta find another way, but she'll keep killing kids if you don't figure out a way to make her stop. If that doesn't make you feel threatened, I don't know what else will."

The girl stared at the doctor and finally nodded. "I'll try."

The other Indigos cleared a path for her to do her thing with Dr. Fiona. The girl stood over the woman who had killed Zack. Oliver could see her whole body shaking, especially when she reached out her hands and grabbed the woman's head. The doctor fought the girl but couldn't break free of her grip. Dr. Fiona's eyes rolled back into her head, and her body convulsed until she collapsed and Caila took a step back.

JORDAN DANE

Oliver felt his body tingle, just standing next to her. His memory of their kiss stirred in him too.

"Something happened. I could feel it." The girl half smiled, as if she'd surprised herself. "She's someone else now. I replaced her memories and planted new ones. This place and what she's done? She won't remember it."

Oliver felt proud of her, but Gabe wasn't as convinced.

"How will we know if it worked?" Gabriel asked. "I'm not sure I feel comfortable with leaving her here…without knowing for certain that she can't hurt anyone else."

The girl didn't hesitate. "It will take a little time for the full thing to manifest in her mind, but it's in there to stay. Believe me. I know this firsthand."

"What did you do to her?" Rayne asked.

At first, Caila only smiled and shook her head. She looked painfully embarrassed for some strange reason. Oliver wasn't sure she'd tell them anything, but these kids had a right to know.

"Come on, Caila. Spill."

"I made her a Disney character."

"You what?" Gabriel grinned. "Which one?"

When the girl told them, Oliver laughed harder than he'd done in a long time. There hadn't been many funny things in his life. It felt good to laugh, and hearing the others do the same made him happy.

He tugged a strand of Caila's hair, grinned at the girl and said, "Gabe? Promise me that we're coming back to L.A. to see the doc when she embraces her new life."

He helped Gabe cut the woman loose and pulled her from the trunk of the Mercedes. They left her sitting on the curb, staring into the night sky, humming a tune.

"Yeah, this I gotta see," Oliver whispered as he climbed into the SUV.

Twenty minutes later

With adrenaline still rushing through her veins, Kendra struggled with a warrior nature that kept her on edge and her random need to laugh like the kid she was. Every time she pictured the British-proper Gabriel telling them that he'd forgotten he had a woman in the trunk—a woman who deserved "a little killing" —she had to bite her lip.

It felt good to almost laugh again, but she knew her nerves were worn to shreds over Rafael. In the shadows of her haunted mind, she saw Rafe staring back at her. She even smelled his skin and felt his presence with her until she remembered she might never see him again. Any smile she had on her face vanished.

After the *doc in the trunk* incident, Gabriel had them pack up what they'd taken from Ward 8 in the back of the SUV. Gabe rode shotgun with his uncle driving the Navigator. They wanted to get a safe distance from the hospital and make sure they weren't followed.

Kendra kept her eyes on the Mercedes behind them.

Rayne had volunteered to drive Dr. Fiona's car and took the new kids, minus one. Noah rode with the Effin twins in the Navigator. Lucas went with them, as the least likely to kill the woman.

Kendra hadn't shaken the bad feeling she'd had ever since they left Haven Hills. Boelens didn't strike her as the kind of guy who would forget…ever. She kept her eyes on the mirrors and caught a glimpse out the back when the Effin brothers and Noah weren't looking. She didn't want to make them worry if they saw how paranoid she was.

But the real reason she'd been on edge sat next to her with Caila—Oliver Blue. He'd promised to do his best to find Rafael. She thought she'd have to wait and every second had been pure agony, but when Gabriel mercifully glanced over his shoulder and met her gaze, Kendra knew what he wanted her to do.

"It's time. Give Oliver the infinity bracelet," Gabe said. "Please."

Kendra hated being the center of attention. She felt eyes on her in the SUV. They bored holes into her that she felt like heat under her skin. Even Uncle Reginald stared from his rearview mirror. She'd grown to love them all, but they knew too much about her now. She couldn't hide how she felt about Rafael. She'd let them see into her heart.

When she unfastened the leather bracelet from her wrist, a duplicate of the one she wore, her fingers trembled. She couldn't stop them from shaking.

Oliver sat too close to her. His eyes. They were intense and unrelenting. He was a virtual stranger, yet he had a magnetic pull that made it hard to hide anything from him. He would know she had skin in the game, that finding Rafael was as important to her as breathing.

"This is his. Rafael's."

Kendra hesitated.

She wanted to hand him the black leather bracelet with the silver infinity charm, but she had a hard time looking him in the eye. Oliver could break her. If he sensed Rafe was dead—and saw every gruesome detail of how he died— that would kill her. Handing over the bracelet wasn't only about finding Rafael. It could mean an end to her faith that she'd find him alive. She clutched the leather in a tight fist.

Oliver locked eyes with her.

"I'll find him," he said. As if he'd read her mind, he whispered, "If you're ready for the truth."

Kendra slowly nodded. When a tear rolled down her

cheek, she gave him the leather strap and held his hand in both of hers, knowing she had to trust him.

Whatever had happened to Rafael, Oliver would know—and soon she would too.

Oliver had seen the look in Kendra's eyes before. Anyone that came to him, looking for someone, always dug into him with that same desperation for answers. Not knowing what happened to Rafael was bad, but finding out the truth could make things worse—and final. He understood that better than most. Not every vision carried good news. It didn't for Zack.

Some people say that the truth sets you free. Well, those people should shut the fuck up and mind their own business.

"This won't be like me watching a video of what happened to him." Oliver clutched the bracelet and felt the heat of a stirring fire in his belly. "I get...glimpses of stuff. Sometimes it won't make sense to me, so I may need your help. You good with that?"

Before Oliver heard what she said, his insides got yanked into a twist. It felt as if he'd been gutted like a fish. "Ah, shit. I can't..."

Kendra, Gabriel and Caila, they all got swallowed by an ominous shadow that covered them in inky black. He couldn't see anything, yet he felt his body drift end over end. He flailed his arms but couldn't stop the feeling that he was falling.

Being inside Gabriel, he'd sensed the serenity of his Indigo soul and had seen dazzling colors that looked like the Aurora Borealis strafing the night sky. But in this dark place where he'd gone looking for Rafael, he felt mired in a thick viscous existence, without hope.

I can't be here, he screamed. *Get me out.*

He felt as if he were drowning. *Breathe! I can't breathe.*

Death surrounded Rafael. It clung to him. It possessed him. Oliver got battered with images he didn't understand. They slugged him like brutal fists, one more savage than the last.

Pictures flooded his mind. Some he could sense. Others he saw as if he were there. A bloody tiara. An old Spanish mission in the hills was awash in the fire of the sun. He didn't know what any of it meant. He only knew he had to remember everything. He could smell the stench of gasoline and saw a car wrecked in a ditch. And the ear-piercing shriek of an elephant in a circus suddenly switched to the calming peal of six bells at an evening church service. A baseball bat in the grip of a drunken old man made him flinch until he got swept away in a rushing river that cut deep into a canyon. The cold water felt like ice.

Under the flashes of memory, there was a steady unrelenting pounding that haunted him, like something he didn't want to remember. He listened harder, yet couldn't make out the muffled sound.

Whatever it was, it felt important. He shoved aside everything he pictured to *feel* it, to understand what he heard. When he realized what it could be, the eerie throbbing grabbed him by the throat and squeezed until he couldn't breathe.

Just like with Zack, Oliver listened to the beat of a heart. It had to be Rafael. Oliver sank into a never-ending darkness that he'd never seen before. After the memories stopped, all he felt was empty.

North of L.A.
10:10 p.m.

When Boelens called O'Dell, he expected to be the one with news, but the guy sounded pissed and let him have it.

"Where have you been?" O'Dell's voice grated on his nerves, especially over his cell. "Didn't you make a stop at the hospital?"

"Yeah, but wait'll you hear—"

Before Boelens finished, the guy butted in. He only caught bits and pieces, but he'd heard enough. He knew something bad had happened inside Haven Hills, but nothing like what O'Dell told him.

"You don't sound surprised," the guy said.

"I'm not. I was there. I saw who did it."

"What?" he yelled. "Why didn't you stop them?"

Boelens didn't know how to explain what happened to him, so he didn't. "There were too many of 'em, but I did you one better. I'm following them now."

He smiled when O'Dell yammered on with one question after another, before he got quiet.

"Where are you? At least tell me that."

"You can track my GPS in the van. They're playing it cagey, but they haven't spotted me."

Boelens gripped his steering wheel and glared at the Lincoln Navigator and the Mercedes he'd been following since West Hollywood. They'd made evasive turns and strange stops to be sure no one had followed them, but all he had to do was hang back and stay patient.

"Call the boss man on your Bat phone and tell him I recognized Lucas Darby, Kendra Walker and that little prick, the British rocker." He described the others too. "You tell him I've got 'em in my crosshairs and that I'll need backup."

"This shit went down on his watch. If anything goes worse now, he's gonna be looking for someone to hang. Those kids hit the ward hard."

O'Dell told him more about the attack.

"He can't pin anything on me. You tell him these little

bastards got into Ward 8 on their own. That's a secured facility. He can start by asking how they did *that*. Check the card reader security logs. They got in after visiting hours."

Boelens knew the church would do everything in its power not to become a headline. To cover up the attack on Ward 8, they'd have to call in favors to keep it out of the news. The last thing they needed was an investigation from the legit police or a reporter with too much curiosity. What went down was worse than he thought. The freaks hadn't just freed other kids. According to O'Dell, they'd annihilated the ward and maybe even stolen secrets that the church couldn't afford to have leaked out.

But to Boelens, this attack went down under his nose. This was personal.

"You tell him who I've got hooked. This little traveling freak show isn't getting away from me a second time," he said. "I know they want the Darby kid, but I'm not making any promises. If I get him in my sights, I'm taking him out. This time I want all of them. We gotta end this."

"I'll call you as soon as I talk to him. Wait for orders."

Boelens didn't care about any orders. He didn't give a shit. He was the guy with his boots on the ground

Minutes later, he had O'Dell on the phone again.

"The boss is tracking your GPS signal," the guy said. "He wants you to keep following them, but don't stop them. He thinks he knows where they're going."

"Is he sending backup?"

"He says if he's right, he's got that covered."

"If he's right? What the hell is that? My ass is on the line and he's flipping a coin." Another armchair quarterback. Boelens hated getting second-guessed. "I don't know about this. He's not telling us something."

O'Dell surprised him by chuckling before he said, "He's

talkin' bonus money, but he wants this thing to go down *his* way. All you gotta do is not lose 'em. Can you handle that?"

Boelens almost didn't answer. "Yeah, money works."

He ended the call and clenched his jaw until it hurt. O'Dell and his boss thought that money solved everything, but some things went beyond the almighty dollar.

If these mind freaks wanted a war, they'd started one.

{20}

Outside L.A.

It took all Kendra's willpower not to touch Oliver when he collapsed into a strange trance that left him mumbling peculiar words. With his knuckles white and his hand shaking, he clutched at Rafe's leather bracelet as if it were his lifeline back. In seconds, his thrashing was over. He fell into a deep sleep and didn't move. Now his head lay on her shoulder, but she didn't dare wake him. Visions were tricky. She was afraid that interference from another Indigo could screw things up or taint what he'd seen. She'd never witnessed anyone scry to find someone before.

Caila must've had the same instinct. She shoved back from Oliver when he tensed his body, even though the girl looked in agony at having to watch him suffer. Gabriel kept his eyes on the road, and the Effin brothers and Noah were deathly still and didn't move.

Gabriel watched the rearview mirror. When he shifted his eyes to her, Kendra only shook her head. *He looks rough,* she told him. *I hate this.* Gabe only nodded.

When Oliver finally cracked his eyes open and sat up, he stared through the front windshield in a stupor, as if he were mesmerized by the headlights. He looked as if he'd awakened from a deep sleep. No one spoke.

Once Oliver had something to say, he finally opened his mouth.

"I'm hungry." He blinked. "I could eat. I mean seriously chow."

"Help us find Rafael and I'll buy you anything you want," Kendra said.

"Deal."

Oliver still looked in a fog, but when he shut his glazed eyes as if he had a terrible headache, he started talking.

"Prom queen Carrie, monks with sandals, NASCAR, *Dumbo, Saved by the Bell,* seventh-inning stretch and shrinkage." Oliver narrowed his eyes before he finally smiled. "Yeah, that's it. That's everything. In order too."

"Shrinkage?" Gabe raised an eyebrow.

Oliver only shrugged and said, "Yeah. *That* shrinkage. It's how I remember what I see."

"Your junk shrinks?" Gabe asked. "My condolences."

"No." Oliver ignored the twins giggling in the back. "When I have a vision, I get bombarded with images. The way I remember them, and the order I see them, is with association. I give each one an image that I can remember and I picture them in a familiar setting, like when I go into the warehouses I've been living in. The prom queen greets me at the door and she's been doing the nasty with some monks. You get the idea."

"Good Lord," his uncle said. "That's…"

"Bent and twisted?"

"Brilliant, actually."

"Absolutely," Kendra said. She used something similar— minus the monk perverts—but had never tried to explain her process to anyone else. Oliver's way was pure genius.

"Walk us through it." She shifted in her seat to look him in the eye. "You said you might need our help in deciphering what you saw. Start with the first one, prom queen Carrie. Are you talking about that old scary movie, *Carrie?*"

"Yeah. At the end, she gets named prom queen and gets doused in blood," he told them. "I saw a bloody tiara. The diamonds glittered like they were real."

"That means nothing to me." Kendra shook her head. "Anyone else?"

No one spoke up, but when she glanced at Gabriel, he looked stunned.

Oliver's description had shocked Gabe—a bloody tiara could only refer to his dead mother, Kathryn. The blood came from the way she died, the violence of it. The authorities had ruled her death a car accident, but he knew better.

She'd been run off a cliff. There was evidence of another car's paint scraped on her bumper, but with the rain and the condition of the road, the authorities took the easy way out. He couldn't even come forward to question the ruling. His father had men hunting for him. They still were. He had no doubt his father saw an opportunity to murder his mother and had hired the men to do it, cruel men with pliable ethics.

"He's referring to my mother. She died in a car crash. Troopers ruled it an accident, but she was…murdered," Gabe said. "But what does our search for Rafael have to do with my mother and how she died?"

Gabe had told the others, but he didn't know how much to share about his father with Oliver and Caila. He needed their cooperation to find Rafael. If he told them about his father and his connection to the Believers, their cooperation could end. He didn't want to lie, but holding off on the whole truth seemed like a good idea. At least, for the moment.

"Monks with sandals," Oliver said. "In my vision I flashed on an old Spanish Mission in the hills. The adobe walls were lit by the sun."

Gabriel shook his head. The guy's vision was a puzzle with pieces that had to fit together.

Oliver went on to explain the rest. He'd associated NASCAR with the smell of gasoline and a bad car crash, both strong references to his mother's death. Dumbo was the image he'd chosen to recall an elephant in a circus. "That part has to do with my mother again."

"I have a theory on that, Gabriel," his uncle said as he drove. "But I'd prefer not to speculate until we've heard the boy out. Please, go on, Oliver."

"Saved by the bell." Oliver scrunched his face and put up both his hands. "Please, no Screech jokes. I've got a headache."

"I'll try and resist," Gabe said.

"I saw six large iron bells. After the elephant shrieked and nearly made me jump out of my skin, the bells did a Zen number on my soul. I think they had something to do with that Spanish mission and the monks, but I don't know."

"The seventh-inning stretch? What's that all about?" Gabriel asked.

"Baseball. A bat to be exact." Oliver crossed his arms and sprawled in his seat. "I saw an old drunk guy with a nasty temper. He unleashed on some poor kid. Hurt him bad too."

"Rafael and his father." Kendra didn't hesitate. "I saw... something in his past when we did our mind-shield exercise. That part has got to be about Rafael."

When she didn't explain, Gabe felt certain that her silence was for Rafe's sake, and he knew plenty about an abusive father. His dad never used a bat, but there were other ways to scar a kid.

"Okay, so let's talk shrinkage," Gabe said. "Stick to your vision."

"I got swept away in a fast-running current. A river. I remember seeing steep canyon walls rushing by. Definitely cold water, man. Ice cold." When Oliver got done with all his visions, he shrugged. "That's it. That's what I saw."

Besides the vision connection to his mother's murder and Rafael's father, Gabriel didn't have a clue what the imagery meant, but his uncle must've had a notion.

"If I can get you close enough, Kendra, do you think you'd feel where Rafael is?" Uncle Reginald asked, watching her in his rearview mirror.

"If he's still alive…yeah, I think so."

"His heart was still beating. I felt it." Oliver glanced at Caila. They both looked sad, but what he said made Kendra happy.

"Do you know where Rafe is?" she asked his uncle. The hope in Kendra's voice was undeniable.

"The San Gabriel Mountains are a big haystack, but if I'm right, I believe I may know where we can find a needle or two."

Forty minutes later

"Do you know where you're going?" Gabriel asked his uncle.

"Yes. Have faith, nephew."

Uncle Reginald changed direction and told him he was heading for the northern L.A. suburbs of San Gabriel, located between Alhambra and Temple City. After he got off the Foothill Freeway, his uncle told him that he would have to rely on his memory to get him to the mission. It didn't take long for them to arrive.

Gabe saw the historic site ahead.

"I've visited many of the old Spanish missions," his uncle said. "I find them quite charming. When Oliver mentioned six bells, I recalled one mission had a *campanario*. In Spanish that means a wall of bells. At Mission San Gabriel Arcángel, there are six beautiful bells, set in arches. It's dark now, but they look particularly stunning in the morning light. Have you seen them before, Oliver?"

"Not for real, sir."

As Uncle Reginald turned his SUV onto the mission grounds, Gabriel gazed out his window at a piece of history. Tall palm trees lined the street in front of the old mission, and the entrance to the cathedral had a massive arched wooden door. The *campanario* of six bells had lights shining on them. The old stone and adobe Spanish mission would've looked almost ghostly at night, except that it was located on a busy street with businesses nearby.

"The mission name, it means Saint Gabriel the Archangel? Does anyone have chills like I do right now?" Kendra said.

"I'm more afraid of getting struck by lightning, actually," Gabe muttered.

"It does seem that we have come full circle," his uncle said. "All I can do is get you close, my dear. You'll have to do the heavy lifting from here, I'm afraid. Do you sense Rafael, Kendra?"

When she didn't answer right away, Gabriel had a bad feeling the mission would turn out to be another bust. He didn't know how a mission would tie in to Rafael's disappearance. It wasn't a Believers' stronghold.

"I feel...something. It's like I'm retracing the steps he took. The essence I feel of him is weak. It's like I know he's been here, but he's not here now," she said. "I've never felt anything like this before."

By the strain in her voice, Gabe knew she was trying hard to *feel* anything. He hoped her inkling wasn't just wishful thinking.

"I think that he...heard those bells. It's like they're in my head too. Yes, I'm sure of it."

"I'll make one more pass, but this is good news. Don't lose faith now. This is more than we had. You didn't feel him at Haven Hills at all. This is *something*, Kendra." His uncle's excitement was contagious. "If you can't get any more, I have another location to try. It's not far. I promise you. If you're retracing his steps, we could be onto something."

For the first time in days, Gabriel saw a smile on the girl's face. He dared to send a telepathic message to Lucas, to let him and the others know why they'd come here and what Kendra sensed.

"Where to now?" Gabe asked his uncle.

"San Gabriel Canyon Road isn't far. It will take us by a reservoir, but I believe that I know the cause of Oliver's shrinkage."

Oliver rolled his eyes and sighed. "Okay, for the record, I never said it was *my* shrinkage."

"Yes, of course. If you insist, dear fellow." His uncle smirked. "But I believe the ice-cold river that Oliver referred to is actually the Cold Water Canyon. It's worth a try."

Uncle Reginald looked too sure to be guessing.

What aren't you telling me? Gabe sent a message to his uncle and blocked out the others from hearing it. *What does Rafael's disappearance have to do with my mother?*

His uncle didn't look at him. He kept his eyes on the road and clenched his jaw.

There's only one reason I can think of that Oliver would link your mother and her death to Rafael, the man told him.

Uncle Reginald finally looked at him with a sad expression on his face. He'd seen the look before.

Your mother must be with Rafael.

That made no sense to him. His mother had never haunted him or his uncle. Gabe had never felt her in any way. Why would she be with Rafe? Gabe narrowed his eyes at his uncle and wouldn't let it go. A part of him wasn't sure he wanted to hear the rest.

But why? he asked his uncle. *She didn't know Rafe.*

The only thing that makes sense to me is that Rafael wasn't abducted by the Believers for their usual agenda. That's why we haven't been able to find him. If I'm right, Kendra is taking us to your father, Gabriel. Your mother is with him.

Gabe stared at his uncle before he sat back into his seat, stunned. He glared out the windshield, but his uncle wasn't done with his theories.

Your father may have taken Rafael to get to you. There could be a reason getting out of Ward 8 appeared too easy. I can't be sure, but this could be a trap.

It didn't matter if his uncle was right or not. Gabriel knew he'd have to face his father one way or another. He couldn't keep running from his nature—or the man who despised him for it. Staring into the night sky, he stirred the fire in his belly and gave in to the dark side of who he was.

11:15 p.m.

When the road turned into two lanes and signs for Cold Water Canyon became easier to spot, Gabriel sensed a malevolence that went beyond his dark gift. His growing awareness of evil had nothing to do with sensing Rafael.

Thoughts of his mother got muddled with his hatred for his father and confused him. He couldn't shove out the hurt that she might have chosen to haunt the man who killed her rather than be with *him*. He shouldn't have wished that for her—either way—but in the hour before he would end this fight with his father, he couldn't stop obsessing over those bad feelings.

It felt as if he'd betrayed her, but he couldn't stop.

He's here…somewhere. Kendra sent the hive a message. *But something's wrong.*

I feel something off too. Gabe didn't take his eyes off the shadowy ravine as his uncle turned down a side road that paralleled the deep gorge, with the Mercedes following them.

Uncle Reginald drove slower and the chassis rocked as the road turned into nothing more than rutted gravel. Gabriel hit a button and the passenger window rolled down. He heard the sound of rushing water and smelled the dust and humidity of the canyon.

"This could be it. It's too dark for me to be sure though." Oliver broke the silence in the vehicle.

The guy would have to learn how to speak to the hive if he stayed, but Gabriel was glad he was with them now.

"Look. There's a light." Gabriel pointed toward the horizon.

The glow ahead became more intense as they got closer. When the narrow road made a hard right and became asphalt again, Uncle Reginald pulled onto a shoulder and waited for Rayne to park behind him.

Gabriel couldn't take his eyes off the horizon. A large estate that rivaled his uncle's was lit by security lights. A stone wall surrounded the mansion with a main entrance that appeared to be guarded by armed men. They couldn't get much closer without being seen.

"Rafael is down there. I'm sure of it." Kendra didn't have to confirm what Gabriel already knew.

They had found Rafael Santana—and his father.

He trusted Oliver's vision and the sense that his mother would be with Rafael. In his heart, he knew that felt right and if any part of Oliver's vision had got them here, then it had to be right. Seeing his father after all these years, and knowing the man had killed his mother, would be hard enough. He still didn't know if he could kill him for what he'd done, but one thought plagued him more than seeing his father again.

Whatever he decided to do, his mother could be watching. She would see what he'd become.

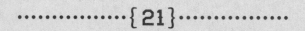

{ 21 }

The Estate of Alexander Reese
San Gabriel Mountains
11:35 p.m.

As Gabriel watched the mansion on the horizon with binoculars, the estate looked mired in secrets. The armed guards were a telltale sign there was something to hide. Beyond the potential danger, Gabriel felt a sense of urgency that gripped him hard. He couldn't explain it, but when he glanced at Kendra and saw the look in her eyes, he knew she had the same feeling.

Whatever he sensed, it had to do with Rafael. He hated thinking that Rafe was in the hands of his father because of him, but he had a dark belief that they'd run out of time. If they didn't go in soon, Rafe could die.

"I want to go with you," Rayne said. "I know I'm not like you, but I can help."

She'd come to him, knowing that breaching the walls and rescuing Rafael would be more dangerous with so many armed guards.

"I know you can, but we have the safety of these children to consider," he said. "And there's something else."

After seeing the potential danger of his father's small army, he never would've wanted Rayne here at all. She wasn't like them, and a gun would only make her a target for cruel men without souls. He didn't want *any* of this, but he didn't see a choice. Worst of all, there were the lives of more innocent children to consider, the kids rescued from Ward 8. The pressure of making the decision on who should stay behind or come with him could mean a death sentence, either way.

When he looked in Rayne's eyes—he didn't want her here and carrying a gun at all—but he had another reason for asking her to stay behind.

"If my father is in there, I don't want you to see...what could happen between us. I know I already scare you, but this will be...worse."

"I love you, Gabriel. Nothing can change that." She touched his cheek. "Whatever you need from me, I'll do it."

She put on a brave face and he saw the love in her eyes, but he wouldn't change his mind. He hoped she understood. He'd come to stop the Believers, but the fight here was personal too.

"I need you to hide the vehicles. Get them off the road and wait. If we don't come back..." He ran a finger down her cheek. "...take them home."

He could tell that Rayne knew what he'd meant by them not coming back. It was the reason she didn't argue. When she nodded, he pulled her into his arms, lifted her off the ground and held her. He shut his eyes so he could feel what it meant to be in her arms. After he put her down, he kissed her and ran his hands through the soft strands of her hair.

He wanted this to be over. He wanted a day where all he had to think about was making her happy.

"Stay alert. They could have patrols outside the walls,

watching this road," he told her. "Keep your gun handy and be prepared to move out if you see anything suspicious."

Gabe hated leaving her behind, but he didn't have a choice. He made sure she had the keys to both vehicles and watched as she backed the cars out and hid them off the road. When he turned to find his uncle and the others, he saw Oliver instead. The guy had been no more than a shadow in a stand of trees.

"What are we doing, Crystal?"

Before he could tell him anything, Oliver had to know the truth. There was no way around it.

"I can't ask you to go with us," Gabe said.

"Then don't ask. I volunteer."

"No, there's something about me that might make a difference. The others know the truth, but you don't."

"Gabriel, there's nothing you can tell me that will change my mind."

Oliver stepped out of the shadows and stood in front of him. When the guy looked determined to go, Gabe blurted out what he wanted him to know.

"My father is Alexander Reese," he told him. "He runs the Believers in L.A. That's his house."

Gabriel pointed at the mansion on the horizon. "He killed my mother because of me. I'm sure he'd rather see me dead. That would allow him to bury the secret that he fathered an abomination like me. I've got a target on my back, put there by him, and he's probably taken Rafael to get me here. This could be a trap. Does that make a difference?"

Gabe waited for Oliver to say something.

"Man, you've got more baggage than Samsonite." The guy crossed his arms. "Father's Day must suck for you."

"Yeah. You could say that." Gabe took a deep breath and ran a hand through his hair. "It's hard to explain what I do, except that I can magnify other Indigos' capabilities. I could use your means of unconventional travel, but I would understand if you'd rather sit this one out."

Oliver didn't answer right away. He stared at him as if he was making up his mind. "I have to admit that you scare me, Gabriel. I've seen what you do and I don't understand it, but I'm with you. On your orders, I'm there."

"Just stick close to me."

"You got it."

Gabe didn't bother to explain why he'd asked that. There simply wasn't enough time, and saying anything more would make the guy feel like odd man out. Because Oliver didn't communicate with the hive well enough—messages only seemed to come one-way—Gabe had to keep him close and remember to say stuff aloud. He'd find a way to make that work.

Heading for the overlook with Oliver, he heard two voices in his head.

We wanna go. Rafael is in there. We can feel him too. The Effin twins ran toward him, hitting him with messages before he even saw them. When they stood in front of him, he put his hands on their shoulders.

"Not this time. I need you to protect the others. I'm counting on you. We all need to do our part, or this won't work."

When the boys looked at him, their eyes filled with tears, but they didn't complain or even push to go. Their stone-faced silence said more than any words they could have chosen. He knew why they wanted to go.

"Don't worry. We'll find him. I can feel him here too."

He hugged the brave boys and breathed a deep sigh. The truth was that he trusted the twins to hold their own, whether they stayed or went with them. But they were still boys. If he envied Lucas his innocence, how could he push the twins to do more against so many armed men? The brothers were powerful Indigos. They'd have their day soon enough, when they got older.

But he had the same personal reason for leaving them behind as he'd asked of Rayne. He didn't want them to witness what he might have to do when he confronted his father. He never had a brother or sister, and no experience with younger kids, but it felt wrong to unleash his pent-up rage—the lifelong contempt he felt toward his father—in front of these children.

As Gabriel walked away from the Effin twins, Oliver said, "Don't second guess. Trust your gut."

"Easier said, my fine friend."

Gabe joined his uncle, Lucas and Kendra on the ridge and gazed at his father's estate. When they had attacked Ward 8, they had the benefit of Lucas's experience and his dream visions to guide them. On his father's estate, they would have none of that. No one knew the layout of the grounds or the mansion. They would have to rely on their instincts to find Rafael and use the hive to get through it.

Not much of a plan.

"Kendra, give Oliver the bracelet," Gabe said. "When we get inside, he can help another way."

"Yeah, sure." She handed over Rafe's leather bracelet and Oliver took it.

"Stick together." Gabriel fixed his gaze on each one before he turned to head down a short ravine that would take them to the stone wall that surrounded the grounds.

"What a minute. What's the plan?" Lucas asked.

Before Gabe could answer, Oliver did it for him.

"Don't get killed. That's the plan." Oliver put his arm around Lucas's neck. "That goes double for anyone wearing pastel pajamas that make them look like the fuckin' Easter bunny. No way I'm buyin' it, lookin' like this."

"You sayin' it like that, I guess I've got it easy," Luke said. "I wasn't gonna say anything, but yeah."

Ten minutes later

The closer he got to the stone wall that bordered the estate, the more Gabriel realized what it all would mean. He would find his father here. The day had finally come. He'd been haunted by the man and what he'd done to his mother for so long, his father seemed more of an invincible monster in his mind. He'd only been a boy when his mother took him and ran away from a man she feared would've killed him for what he was. Gabriel couldn't outrun his past anymore.

When he got to the perimeter wall, he didn't have to tell Oliver what to do. The guy offered his clasped hands and a bent knee. After Gabe gave him his left foot, he hoisted him over the wall in one motion. He did the same for Kendra and Lucas. Uncle Reginald had been less graceful. When it was Oliver's time to scale the wall, Gabe and Luke gave him a hand from the other side with Kendra's help while Uncle Reginald caught his breath.

Gabe felt his way through the shadows, sensing the presence of the armed guards who patrolled the grounds in pairs. The men were dressed in black uniforms, like a military unit. Gabriel sensed every turn they made and even anticipated their moves in advance. He avoided the security lights and sought the darkness. The guards needed the light. *They* didn't. Through shrubs and the long shadows of trees, Gabe guided the others as he maneuvered in the dark. He trusted his instincts to get them through it. It felt like a peculiar choreography with lethal intent.

Because he had the others with him, he didn't push it by being reckless, as he might've done on his own. The whole thing felt like a game, but it wasn't. Thinking of it as sport allowed him to put off imagining what would come next.

The others came to rescue Rafael. He wanted that too. But now that he suspected his father might've set a trap for him, Gabriel wouldn't ignore the challenge. He came to confront the man.

When he got to the west corner of the mansion, he pressed his back to stone and glanced at Oliver. "You trust me?"

"Fine time to ask," the guy said. "But yeah. Why? Are you planning to cure me of that?"

"You'll see."

Minutes later

Rayne felt the weight of her Glock in a holster that she wore under one of Gabriel's jean jackets. He'd left her the binoculars. As she paced the ground near the vehicles, she kept one eye on the kids who sat inside the SUV and the other on the lit estate on the next rise. She'd moved the Indigos to one car, the larger SUV, so they'd be together and easier for her to watch over them.

She listened for every sound and jumped at the hoot of an owl. The night creature had been alarmed at her intrusion and flew away on silent wings while her heart pounded out of control. When she heard the soft thud of the SUV door closing, it didn't take long for Caila to join her.

"Are they asleep?" she whispered to the girl.

"Sam and Quinn are too wired, but the rest of them are quiet." Caila crossed her arms and stared across the ravine to the home of Gabriel's father. "But quiet is good, right?"

Rayne knew she wasn't talking about sleeping kids anymore.

"Did you turn off the interior lights in both cars?" she asked the girl.

"Yeah. No worries."

Going stealth in the dark, the last thing she needed was for one of the kids to open the door and make them a target.

"You're not like us, are you?" Caila asked.

"No, but Lucas is my brother. He's like Gabriel, sort of. I'm in this, for them."

The girl nodded, as if she'd said something perfectly normal. Rayne liked her and she liked having company, but when the girl gasped, everything got edgy.

"Hold on." Caila grabbed her arm. "I'm getting a push."

"What's that?" Rayne whispered.

"Someone's coming. And it's not one of us." Caila pulled her toward the SUV and they both crouched behind it.

Rayne pulled her weapon and racked the slide.

"Stay behind me," she said.

She moved in tandem with Caila, staying low and shadowing her. Rayne listened and heard the soft crunch of gravel and the low hum of an engine in the distance. Sound echoed across the canyon walls. When she didn't see headlights, not even with her binoculars, she knew that wasn't a good sign. Anyone driving in the dark without lights didn't want to be seen.

"Maybe they'll drive by," the girl said.

Rayne knew it was safer not to assume that. She had parked the vehicles far enough off the road that they wouldn't be noticed, but she had to prepare for the worst. "Crack the door and tell the kids to stay quiet."

When Caila opened the door and whispered to the kids, Rayne saw the Effin brothers shove from their seats and move to join her. She knew they wanted to help. The brothers had Indigo powers and she trusted them, but letting them take on danger felt wrong to her. If anything happened, when she was supposed to be watching over them, she'd never forgive herself.

"Stay put until I know what's happening," she whispered to the brothers. "Caila, get inside and stay with them. Keep their heads down until you hear from me."

Rayne shut the door and moved closer to the road to listen. The car without lights must've stopped. She couldn't hear the engine, and the tires had stopped rolling. That didn't make her feel any better. Not hearing the noise only made her more worried. Rayne held her breath and searched the shadows for anything that moved.

With a two-fisted grip, she held her weapon as she listened and waited. When she heard the soft snap of a twig behind her, she turned and aimed her Glock at the shadow of a man, but it was too late.

He had a gun aimed at her face.

"Hello, little girl."

Even in the moonlight, Rayne knew who it was. She'd recognize Boelens anywhere.

Inside the estate of Alexander Reese

Channeling Oliver's gift, Gabriel traveled like a drifting mist and fused into every shadow. Even though his real body hadn't moved, he vanished into the house and stood in a foyer under a crystal chandelier before he floated through the main floor and up a massive curved staircase. Even moving in the mansion, he still felt Oliver next to him outside—a most *peculiar* sensation. Kendra and Lucas were harder for him to sense, but he had a definite connection with his uncle.

He wasn't a stranger to seeing through different sets of eyes. When he shotgunned through animals, he became them. He felt his body change from a wolf on the hunt of prey to an eagle soaring over the earth with its keen eyes. Now adrenaline pumped through his blood and doubled his excitement. He sent messages to the hive and told them where he was and gave them the location of rooms in the house.

Tell me what you sense about Rafael, Kendra. Have Oliver scry for him too.

His father's home had security measures in place. In his present state, Gabe got by them undetected, but once they located Rafael that would change. Since they wouldn't have the finesse of cat burglars, Gabriel had to know who lived in the house, to determine the threat once they broke in.

He didn't know the layout of the manor, but he followed his instincts when he recognized a scent—the smell of his father. The aroma triggered voices from his past. The sound of his mother and father arguing over him in the middle of the night, those yelling matches had scared him when he was a kid. Some nights they *still* lingered in his sleep.

At the end of the hall on the second floor was a suite with double doors. As he drifted toward the room, he felt colder. He sensed evil, but maybe that was his mind playing tricks on him or his past catching up.

When he got to the door, he pushed his body to take shape as he'd seen Oliver do when he transformed into *boogers,* as the twins put it. If there were security cameras, he would become visible now, but a part of him wanted his father to see him. To be afraid of what he saw. Gabriel reached for the knob to turn it, but his fingers slipped off the metal. His hands had substance, but they were more gel than flesh and bone. It took time for him to make his fingers work. When they did, he opened the door and eased into the room.

As he crept toward the large bed, he barely felt the carpet under his feet. Every ounce of control took effort. His body was a foreign instrument he had little experience with.

Trying what Oliver had done, he marveled at the guy's accomplishment as an Indigo. Being a Crystal child didn't give Gabe any advantage.

When he got closer, he saw the shape of a man under the covers. The face of his father—the man's angry eyes—haunted him in the dark. Gabriel couldn't stay in the moment. The way he was, he had a hard time distinguishing between the past and present. The nightmares of his childhood had become a barrier that left him as good as crippled.

He fought it, but in the grips of his past, he was a boy facing his father. He stood over the bed and glared at the man who had ruined his life and murdered his mother.

He battled his emotions and the strange state of his body as he dug deep to stir the fire of his power and channel it through the essence he was now. He felt the heat well up. The process had started. His father would know what he had become. On the verge of adapting Oliver's power with his, Gabe let the surge take over until he heard a soft click behind him.

"Hello, Gabriel."

Gabe stopped dead still. The sound of his father's voice sent a shudder through him. When he turned, the man held a gun aimed at his heart and didn't wait for him to speak.

Alexander Reese pulled the trigger.

Something woke him.

Rafael opened his one good eye and searched the dark room for anything that moved. Nothing did. His lip had started bleeding again and it stung. He wanted water but wasn't sure he could drink it. He felt sick.

Because there were no windows in the room, he kept track of the time of day by the chill. It was cold now. It had to be nighttime or early morning.

Are you here? He let his mind reach out to her.

The lady sometimes came to him—Gabriel's mother—whenever the men who beat him stopped. He didn't know why she came to him. Maybe the dead felt a duty to the living whenever they sensed the end coming. It made him think of the old man's spirit who was always with Benny at the dead train in the tunnels, watching over him like a guardian angel. Rafe had to stop thinking about that. He wasn't dead yet.

He struggled to move, but the weight of his body made his pain worse. Wearing only the suit pants they'd given him, he hung from a steel bar and ropes cut into his wrists. Whenever he went unconscious or fell asleep, the warm blood trailed down his arms until it dried and stuck. He couldn't stand anymore. They'd kicked one of his legs. He thought they'd busted it again, the one his old man had broken years ago with his baseball bat.

They beat him to find out where Gabriel was. He'd die before he said anything—and not just for Kendra's sake. Gabriel deserved to live.

Rafe tried using his mind shield, as Uncle Reginald had warned them about if they got caught by the Believers, but the beatings only numbed the hurt. The pain stayed on the fringes of his mind but was getting worse now. He knew his body would fail him. He had nothing left. He couldn't fight them anymore. His shield had weakened and he couldn't concentrate.

All his energy went to one effort. The only thing that worked was when he thought of Kendra. Sometimes it would only be the way her skin smelled, or the scent of that coconut shampoo she used sometimes, the one he'd stolen for her. Other times he imagined her whispering to him in the dark, the way they used to talk when neither of them could sleep. When the pain got bad, he retreated to her arms until she was the only thing he felt. He trained his mind to find her in his memory.

When he died, that's where he wanted to be—with her and Benny.

He was with Kendra now, when the shadowy room got brighter. He lifted his head and tried to stand taller. If they'd come to bruise their knuckles again, he'd stare them in the eye one more time, but when he looked up, he saw the lady.

Cinder block walls bubbled and spears of light shot through the cracks in the shape of a woman. A beautiful woman, dressed in a long robe. Her skin glowed as though she had a light inside and when she smiled at him, he thought he smiled back, because his lip hurt. She always made him feel warm and safe, but when he heard a noise that echoed through the mansion, he knew what it was.

The sound of a gunshot.

Lady Kathryn faded into dust and he heard the patter of her ashes hit the floor in front of him, before the shouting and the sound of more gunfire took over.

Something bad had happened. He felt it.

{22}

With the gunshot still ringing in his ears, Gabriel gasped for air and grabbed his chest, rolling in pain. *What the hell happened?* He didn't have time to figure it out.

The gunfire had scrambled the guards. Alarms went off and spotlights strafed the grounds with his father's armed men on full alert. A small unit hit the front door and went inside, as Gabriel took cover with the others. He stared at everything around him, stunned. He couldn't make sense of what happened. He breathed fresh air and felt the night's chill on his face, but his father's bedroom was gone.

Only the pain had stayed.

Oh God, it hurts.

An agonizing burn shot through his body. It tore into him like a hot iron. When he could, he ran his fingers over his clothes and expected to feel the warm stickiness of blood, but he didn't. His chest hurt as if he'd been hit by a battering ram. He was bruised and ached all over, but mostly it hurt where his father shot him. The bullet must've gone straight through him.

Worse than the pain, something else obsessed him. The cold-blooded eyes of his father bored into him the same way that bullet had. The man wasn't in front of him now, aiming a gun at his chest, but it all felt too fresh.

Oliver was with him. It took time for Gabe to clear his mind and realize what had happened. He was outside the mansion with the others, where he'd left his real body. Gabriel had never been so grateful to be alive.

"What happened?" Oliver pressed a hand to his chest and said, "Just breathe. You're here. You're safe. Sort of."

"He shot me. My father...*shot* me."

Not even saying the words made it real. Gabriel didn't know what he had expected. His father had shot him. If he had walked into the mansion on his own, without using Oliver's gift, he would be dead. It had happened so fast, not even his powers could've saved him. A shudder ran through him and he fought the tears that stung his eyes.

What had he expected? His father hated him. Now he knew how much.

"Gabriel, are you hurt?" His uncle crawled over to him and looked as worried as he'd ever seen him. He ran his hand over his face and leaned over to kiss his cheek. "That bastard. He's a killer, but I still expected...something between a father and his son. Not *this*," his uncle cried and clutched at Gabe's clothes, unwilling to let him go.

"We're not leaving here without Rafael," Gabe told him. "My father has got to be stopped. It ends here."

Kendra and Lucas looked as ready for a fight as he was, but when Oliver held up Rafael's infinity bracelet, all eyes were on him.

"I know where he is," Oliver said. "Follow me."

Rayne felt the weight of the Glock in her hands. It was heavy and the muscles in her arms burned from holding it steady. A bead of sweat trickled down her cheek. She wanted to brush it away, but she couldn't move.

All she had to do was pull the trigger. Why couldn't she do it?

"You must be having a déjà vu moment..." Boelens said. "...'cause we've done this before."

The mercenary looked bigger than she remembered. Under the dim haze of the moon, the shadows of his face made him look crazy and the barrel of his weapon was a cannon.

"Where's your freak brother...and the rest of his circus?" the man asked.

Rayne didn't see the point of talking to him, except that it meant he might not pull the trigger. All the range shooting in the world hadn't prepared her for confronting this man with his gun aimed at her face.

"We heard there've been sightings of Big Foot in the canyon. Thought we'd take a look, but maybe they only saw *you*," she said.

"You think that gun gives you a smart-ass license?"

"Nope. That's genetics, I'm afraid."

Rayne's mind raced with what to do. The kids were hiding in the SUV. Boelens didn't seem to know they were there.

"You alone?" she asked. "I thought wolves like you traveled in a pack...or did you wear out your welcome with the church?"

Boelens ignored her question. He gripped his weapon tighter and gritted his teeth. "Last chance. Tell me where the others are. Or I got no reason to talk to you."

Rayne fought to keep her breaths steady. Her adrenaline was off the charts.

"The others are gone. They left me here to watch the cars. In case you didn't notice, I'm not like them," she said. "You're wasting your time. I'm not telling you anything."

"There's no one here to protect you…like before." He took a step closer and grinned. "You're right. You're not one of them. Drop your weapon and I'll let you go. You don't have to end up like the freaks."

Rayne couldn't take her eyes off him. He actually looked as if he enjoyed this, as if he knew how things would turn out. Maybe he did. If he shot and killed her, he'd get his hands on the kids. Even though the twins might hold their own, from what Luke had told her, they'd be no match against a gun, not like Kendra.

But when the man winced with a pained expression, he lowered his weapon with a gasp.

"Those little mind freaks are close by. They're messing with me again. I can feel it." Boelens grabbed his head and stumbled.

The Effin brothers were up to something. Rayne knew it. They were inside the SUV, targeting their psychic attack on Boelens where he stood.

"Where are they?" he yelled.

"I don't know what you're talking about. No one's here except me." She tried to distract him, but he only got madder.

Whatever the twins were doing to him, his pain must've gotten worse. When the man lunged toward the SUV and made a move to grab the door, one of the girls inside screamed. Boelens knew they weren't alone and he wouldn't stop. Rayne had no more time. She had to do something. She tensed her grip and felt her finger on the trigger. When she heard gunfire and alarms blaring in the distance, her muscles tensed and she pulled the trigger.

She didn't even remember doing it. It just happened.

"Oh God. I'm…sorry."

Boelens clutched his chest and stumbled back, still holding the gun in his hand. He wasn't down. His eyes grew wide with shock before his face turned mean. When he aimed his weapon, the gun wavered between her and the children in the car. He could still hurt them.

With tears in her eyes, she shot him again until he fell to the ground.

"Stay down. Don't make me do it again," she yelled.

Sick. She felt sick.

Blood pooled on his chest and glistened under the moonlight, thick like black oil. Whenever he choked for air, his throat gurgled and blood trickled from his mouth and drained down his face. After he quit struggling, his chest heaved once before it finally stopped. She listened hard for his next gasping breath, but it never came. His dead eyes stared up at the moon. Rayne wanted to look away, but she couldn't

I killed him.

She didn't know if she said the words aloud, but in her head, it sounded as if she'd screamed it. Rayne couldn't move. Numb and shaking, she dropped to her knees with her ears ringing. She couldn't catch her breath. When she saw the shadows of the others, they knelt by her, but she couldn't feel their hands touch her.

She felt...*dead*.

Minutes later

On the trail of Rafael, Oliver mind-shadowed the life force residue left on the leather bracelet. It led him to the back of the mansion and he felt the energy signature pull his awareness to a spot beneath the foundation. If he had been in an open field, he might've thought that he'd found a buried body, but this close to the stone walls meant Rafael was inside and belowground.

There had to be a basement. Oliver felt the guy's heart

beating. He knew he was still alive, but it sounded weak. Knowing that Rafael needed their help made him pick up his pace and the others followed.

"He's in the basement...and he's still alive." He glanced at Kendra. "We gotta find a way down there, but I'll get you close."

A terraced back patio glared in floodlights. It blinded him as he rounded a corner. He stuck to the shadows that came from bushes and trees. Oliver crouched low and ran toward a metal grate that jutted out into a flower bed and was flush to the ground. When he got closer, he saw the glint of glass under the metal. A window. He'd seen them before, in old warehouses he'd broken into. It was an escape route in case of fire, for anyone caught in the basement.

"Help me take this off," he said to the others.

The metal screen lifted without much effort. It had been designed for that. Beneath the grill was a small well, shored up by terraced stone. There was enough room for someone to crawl through it. If they broke the glass window, they'd have their way into the basement. Oliver didn't hesitate. He sat on the edge of the opening and used his feet to mule kick the window. It broke on the second try. If he'd had his boots on, instead of the secondhand sneakers he'd found in Dr. Fiona's office, it would've only taken one shot.

"They'll have alarms on this. We won't have much time."

Lucas and Gabriel helped him kick out the shards of broken glass and they walked into a dark room. The only light came from behind them, off the terrace. Alarms were still ear-piercing and he heard the muffled shouts of men that echoed through the house and the grounds outside.

"This way."

It got darker as they went down a long corridor lined with doors. As Oliver crept through the hallway, he tried turning a few doorknobs. Gabe and Kendra helped too. None of the rooms were locked, but they were empty. Each had a large drain in the floor. This section of the basement seemed more like a storage locker, but storage for *what?* Oliver didn't like the feel of it. The rest of the mansion screamed of money, but this part felt like something they hid and could hose out.

By the third unlocked and empty room, Gabriel looked at him sideways, as if he were full of crap and had taken them to the wrong place. But when they got to the fourth door, they found a kid trussed to a metal bar. His hands were tied over his head. With his chin down, he looked almost dead. The faint glow from a high basement window made his skin look like raw hamburger meat.

Oliver smelled the unmistakable odor of blood and saw the kid's bare chest was covered in streaks of it. Where his hands were bound, blood trickled from cuts on his wrists. When he'd become too weak to stand, his own body and gravity had done the damage.

Kendra shoved by him and rushed across the room. The guy must've been Rafael. Oliver was happy they'd found him.

What he didn't like was that it had been too easy.

Before Oliver cut Rafael down, Kendra rushed to him. She held his battered face in her trembling fingers and kissed him.

"I can't believe it. You're alive," she cried. "I love you so much."

He winced when she touched him, but he kissed her back. Luke and Oliver had to help him stand. He was too weak to do it on his own.

"*Mi vida.* I thought I'd never see you again."

Kendra wanted time to help him heal, both inside and out. She hoped they would have it, but when she felt a psychic push, she knew something was wrong. From the look on Rafe's face, he did too.

Gabriel saw Oliver and knew he thought the same thing. Rafael was tied to a bar and looked too weak to move. He couldn't escape in his condition, but an unlocked cell made their rescue too simple.

When he heard the scuff of a shoe behind him, Gabe knew who would be there. Alexander Reese blocked the door with several of his men. His father had more armed guards standing in the shadows in the corridor. He expected the man to act smug, but he had a shocked expression meant for him.

"I shot you. I know I did."

"Gracious of you to let me turn around before you pulled the trigger. You always were a coward," Gabe said.

"You really *are* a monster. What *are* you?"

"That's rich, coming from you, but I am what you made me, *Father.*"

Gabriel should've been more hurt by what the man said, but after all these years of nightmares where he was forced to relive his father's accusations, he only felt numb. He still couldn't imagine what it took to kill the woman he'd once loved and hunt his own son, fully prepared to take his life too.

Monster indeed.

"You hired men to kill my mother and you hid behind your church and corrupt law enforcement officials to get away with it. And for what? To hide that you fathered me?"

One of the uniformed guards flinched and took a quick look at Reese. If Gabe had any doubts that his father had wanted to keep his freak son a dark secret, those doubts were gone now.

"Your kind is a plague on humanity. A test of our worthiness to survive. When I saw what you were, I had to do something, but I don't expect you to understand. You're the enemy."

Gabriel felt the fire in his belly. He felt infinite and powerful. His body shook with the mounting force of the Indigo collective, souls alive and dead. But this time when he tapped in to his gift, he felt something…different.

He felt…*her*.

His uncle had been right. His mother *was* here. He sensed her for the first time since she died, and his eyes burned with tears he couldn't hold back.

Oh God. She's here. Do you feel her, uncle?

Gabriel fought the emotion of seeing his uncle's face. They both had dreamed of seeing her again, but in the presence of his father, it felt wrong.

"Justify your choices all you want, but I'm ashamed to call you my father." His voice sounded deeper and it echoed off the walls. "*You* are the animal here, not my mother or me or the innocent children you have killed in the name of your twisted doctrine."

Although his father's face had been stern before, now he looked frightened. He stared at him as if he had two heads.

"You've said enough." His father's voice cracked. "This ends. Now."

Gabe didn't hesitate. In a low, contempt-filled voice, he said, "Agreed."

Something gripped Gabriel. A jolt of energy surged through his body until he thought his chest would burst. Pressure built in the room that made it hard for him to breathe. When the door shut behind Reese, it slammed so hard it sounded like a gun blast.

One of the guards tried the knob.

"It's locked. It won't open," he yelled.

Gabriel hadn't shut the door. When he looked at the others, he knew they hadn't either. From the corridor outside, he heard men crying out and the sounds of a scuffle. A strange light stabbed through the darkness under the door, eclipsed by the shadows of someone running. A sudden burst of gunfire echoed in the hall and sent his father's men lunging for cover anywhere they could find it.

Lucas, Kendra and Oliver did too, but Gabriel and his uncle stood their ground. Gabe held on to the rush of power that he'd built up. When he shotgunned and felt the fragments of his essence blast into the room, he saw the light shoot from his eyes and felt the burn of blue flames rising off his body. He sensed the strength of his uncle and the others when they stood and joined him. Weak as he was, even Rafe did what he could.

Their energy melded with his into one force and he magnified their abilities.

Gabriel thrust his hands at his father and two of his men, hitting them with the full strength of his power. One man's chest caved in and he dropped where he stood. His father's body smacked against the back wall and collapsed to the floor in a heap, and another guard got pummeled beside him. He cracked his head on stone and when he slid down the wall, he left a bloody trail.

Lucas hit those left standing with an illusion that made the room spin and buck under their feet. More than one door tempted them to save their sorry asses, but the openings slammed shut when they tried to run. Every time they got to their feet, they stumbled like drunks. Gabe had to block Luke's illusion from his mind. It felt too real and made him sick.

He sent a message to Kendra. *Look out! Ten o'clock.*

A guy to her left lunged with a knife, but Kendra didn't back down. She glared at him and dominated his brain with the power of suggestion that left him cowering. She'd manipulated him into turning the knife on himself. His hands shook as he fought not to stab his chest.

We gotta get Rafe out of here. He's too weak for this. Kendra shot a glance toward Rafe and Gabe knew what she meant. Rafael and his uncle conjured the dead in these men's minds. Dark spirits screamed across the room in a flurry of terrifying visions that never ended. Rafe's body shook with the effort. With his blood loss, Kendra had been right to worry.

Gabriel gave her a nod and went where he was needed.

Oliver had multiplied his body and created an army of dark warriors in sinister black helmets. Their glistening bodies looked ghostly in the pale light as they fought, but the real Oliver had a brawl on his hands. Two of Gabe's father's men had him cornered and were using their fists.

Gabe could've finished it using his powers, but with too much adrenaline flooding his veins, he balled up his fists and gave Oliver a hand. He had to hit something. *Anything.* With Oliver at his shoulder, Gabe threw punches until his knuckles felt raw. Oliver pounded the guy next to him so hard that the man's feet came off the floor. His new friend had seen his share of street fights.

Even with the room in utter chaos, Gabriel sensed a dark presence. He landed an uppercut that sent his man to the floor and looked over his shoulder to where his father had fallen. The man wasn't there.

His father had grabbed a gun and slowly aimed it at him, but before Gabriel mounted a defense, he heard a shout.

"She's here," Rafael called out to him. "The lady."

Rafe struggled to stand and stared across the room to a dark corner. Even his father turned and lowered his weapon. He must've seen what Rafe did—what they *all* could see now. The wall undulated into a blur. Its porous surface punched through with stabs of light until a blinding ball of energy emerged. It vibrated the air and sent tingles over his skin and the hair on his arms stood on end.

"Mother?"

Gabe felt her love in the dazzling light that hurt his eyes, but he couldn't look away. His mother flooded him with memories. In a rush, they hit him until he felt as if he'd lived a lifetime of loving her.

She must've glutted his father with images too. Gabe could only imagine how dark they must've been. His father looked terrified. When his mother drifted between him and his father, the man raised his weapon again and aimed for Gabriel.

"You want your freak son? He's yours," his father shouted.

When Gabe heard the gun blast, he expected to be hit. He had stood in the bullet's path. There was no way his father could've missed, but he felt nothing.

His mother swallowed the man with her light and he cried out in a bloodcurdling scream. A gut-wrenching crush of bone sent shivers over Gabe. When a dark pool oozed across the floor, it leached out from under the brilliant glow. The sight sent the remaining guards scrambling for the door. They scattered and ran, leaving their dead and wounded behind.

"Mother?"

When Gabe knew his father was gone, he reached toward his mother and her light changed into the soft flicker of candlelight. She appeared to him dressed in her velvet robe and tiara, as he would always remember her. She reached for his hand and her fingertips touched him, sending a jolt of extraordinary power through him, coupled with her love. When a sad smile graced her face, a tear rolled down her cheek that glistened like a diamond.

I'm so proud of the man you've become…but I couldn't let you take the life of your father. I had to protect you, the only way I could, his mother's voice whispered inside his ear. *I will always love you, my precious boy.*

Before he could say what was in his heart, she vanished with her light and the room went dark. She left a ghostly image of white on his eyes and the energy sucked from the room with a noise that popped his ears.

"Mother...please. Stay with me," he called out to her, but she didn't return. "I love you."

His mother had come to protect him—and be the one to exact revenge on a man who had wronged them both. She'd blinded him so he wouldn't see her do it. Stunned, Gabriel felt numb. His eyes burned with the tears he'd been holding back.

In the sudden stillness of the room, no one spoke. No one breathed. Gabe sensed the others standing next to him and felt their eyes on him. He stared down at what remained of his father—nothing more than a stain to be cleaned.

Whatever he had felt toward his father, it was over now.

The grief and the mind-numbing loss he had for his mother would never bring her back. Nothing would. He'd have to find a way to live with that. He hurt inside and out, but with his father gone, how would he channel the hate that had become part of his nature now? Hate and love were opposite sides of a coin. Filled with both, he wouldn't find it easy to stop either one, but he'd have to find a way if he wanted to reclaim his life.

As the energy drained from his body, he felt the void his mother's love left in his heart and all he wanted to do was fill it with Rayne.

{23}

Outside the Estate of Alexander Reese
After 1:00 a.m.

It was eerily quiet as they walked through what was left of his father's mansion after his dead mother had ended the fight. Gabriel smelled the coppery stench of blood. Splatters of it marred the once-pristine walls, and boot prints in smears of crimson soiled the floors. Lucas and Oliver helped carry Rafael. He had a bad leg and was too weak to hold up his head, even though he tried. Kendra never left his side.

But before Gabriel had made it through the front gates, he'd heard what had happened between Rayne and Boelens from the Effin brothers. He ran to her, not waiting for the others. Nothing could keep him from her.

He pictured what had happened and every step became a punishment. When he came upon the spot where she'd parked the vehicles, he spotted her in the shadows with Caila. When she saw him, she broke into a run and landed in his arms, crying.

"Did he hurt you?" He cradled her and whispered in her ear, "I never should've left you."

"I killed him. Oh God, I killed a guy."

"Not just *any* guy, Rayne. You did what you had to. You're alive and you protected these kids." He couldn't let her go. Tears ran down his cheeks and he ached over what she'd been through, but he kept his voice strong for her. "You're safe now. I'm taking you home."

Rayne's body shook and she kept talking, almost not hearing him. He could tell she was in shock. When he looked up, he saw Caila. She shook her head, letting him know it had been bad.

"She's taking it really hard. She doesn't deserve this," Caila said. "She was so brave. I couldn't have done what she did."

Rayne listened to the girl's voice and calmed down long enough to stop sobbing and look him in the eye.

"I'll be okay. We've *all* been through a lot. I'm just glad we found Rafael and that you're all right." Rayne put her hand to his chest. "I don't know what I would've done if I'd lost you."

Gabriel brushed the hair from her face and kissed her tears. He wanted to be alone with her, but Caila had stayed for a reason.

"I know this isn't my place. I don't know you very well, but…" the girl said. "…if you want to forget what happened, I can help you do that."

It had been such a simple offer. Gabe didn't know what to make of it and Rayne looked confused too. When she pulled from his arms and went to the girl, he wasn't sure what she would say.

"Your gift… It's amazing, really." She took Caila's hand and held it. "I have to admit that a part of me wishes I could wipe away what happened, but forgetting it won't change what I did. That man would still be dead."

Rayne fought a fresh round of tears, but she pushed through it.

"It's so hard for me to say no...especially about *this*." She cried harder. "When my parents died, I was hurting. I *still* ache for them. I'm sure Lucas does too, but I wouldn't erase them from my mind, or want to pretend that they went away and would never come back. The pain of losing them is part of me now. It makes me appreciate the people that I love even more."

Rayne hugged the girl tight and said, "Thank you for caring, but I'll find a way to deal with what I did."

When she pulled from Caila's arms, the girl stared as if she had a million questions, but didn't ask one.

Gabriel couldn't take his eyes off Rayne either, but for a very different reason. His brave, precious girl was the strongest person he'd ever known.

Hours later

The two-hour trip home to the Stewart Estate had been a quiet one. Whenever Rayne closed her eyes to doze off, she saw Boelens pointing his gun and she jerked awake. The sound of the blast, the feel of the weapon bucking in her hands and the way the bullet sounded when it hit his body—she couldn't imagine that ever leaving her.

Rayne couldn't get warm and couldn't stop shaking. She fought hard not to cry. She was afraid that if she started, she wouldn't stop.

"Boelens was a bad guy. Caila and the twins said you didn't have a choice. You did what you had to do. You saved them." Gabe stroked her hair and kept talking to her, quiet so no one else would hear.

He held her close and whispered in her ear that she was safe, that they'd be home soon. But in quieter moments, when he thought she'd dozed off, she caught him staring out the window of the SUV, plagued by his own demons. He hadn't said much about what had happened in the mansion. That would come. Gabe only held her hand and hadn't let go.

Noah was the only one who slept. She thanked God for that. The little boy had a sweet snore that made her smile when he got really loud. Dawn was still a couple of hours away and they all were hurting. Gabe had bruised knuckles, something she hadn't expected to see. Oliver had a busted lip, but on him it looked good.

When she heard Kendra whispering to Rafael, it pulled her from her dark thoughts. Knowing Rafe was alive and with Kendra made her feel better. He'd been injured the worst, but he was in good hands. The Effin brothers sat close to him and ran their hands through Rafe's hair and touched him to let them know they were there. Kendra had done what she could to make him comfortable. The Indigo healer would do more for him when they got home, but Rafe let her hold him, even though he winced in pain. And when things got real quiet in the car, she sometimes heard Kendra crying, but she knew those tears weren't from her being sad.

After ribbons of asphalt turned into two-lane roads with the city lights behind them, Rayne saw the signs for the Bristol Mountains and it made her cry. She was happy to have a home, but when she saw that Oliver had taken a special interest in where they were going, his excitement reminded her of the first time she had seen the Stewart mansion.

"How far is this place?" Oliver asked.

"Not far now," Uncle Reginald told him. He sounded tired.

When they got to the estate, Gabe's uncle unlocked the main gate and maneuvered the SUV up the winding and narrow road to the mansion. Lucas drove the Mercedes behind them, a car they'd have to ditch or scrap for parts.

On the crest of the hill that overlooked the manor, Gabe's uncle slowed down. Rayne had remembered how it felt to see the impressive estate for the first time, when she rode in on her Harley with Gabriel. She smiled when she saw Oliver and Caila on the edge of their seats, staring onto the sprawling estate and its grounds.

"Holy…" Caila gasped. "…shit."

"Yeah," Oliver said. "Ditto."

"You have a home here for as long as you like…if you need one," Uncle Reginald said. "But nothing has to be decided tonight. We can talk about that in due course, when you're ready."

"Yes, sir."

Uncle Reginald pulled up to the main entrance with the Mercedes behind them. He welcomed the children to his home and Rayne did her part. Helping out had calmed her nerves. She even smiled when she saw the new kids react to the posh digs. The massive staircase, the chandeliers and tapestries and the artwork made the mansion look more like a magical museum.

The place might have looked intimidating, except for one thing. Little faces stared through the staircase banister, each kid sitting on a step to get his or her own view. When Bethany, Sarah, Little G and Domino saw Rafael, they yelled and came running, dressed in their pajamas.

Seeing them made Rayne grin. Gabe did too.

Oliver and Lucas helped Rafe walk in as the children rushed them. Kendra didn't fuss over their enthusiasm at seeing him. Hugs were good medicine. So was being home.

Once they crossed the threshold, Rafael was greeted by another dear friend. When Frederick made a grand appearance, Rayne slipped into Gabriel's arms and held him. Seeing Frederick brought back good memories, even if the man was dead. The butler didn't care if the new guests saw him. He'd come because he'd been worried about Rafael. Frederick spun like a whirling dervish made of silver glitter and exploded like a series of small fireworks. He'd turned into the Fourth of July in tux tails.

"Oh my God. Who's that?" Caila pointed. "Is he...dead?"

Oliver raised an eyebrow and smirked, but Rafael was the first to answer.

"That's Frederick. I call him Dead Fred. He's my..."

When Rafe didn't finish, Frederick did it for him. "Your butler, sir?"

"I was gonna say my friend."

Frederick placed a hand over his heart and smiled. Rayne didn't know if ghosts blushed, but *this* one did.

"I'm touched, Rafael," Frederick said.

Rafe curled his cut lip into a grin and winced when he said, "Don't be. Who'd believe I got a butler? Alive or dead."

Frederick raised an eyebrow that eventually turned into a smile after Rafael went to his room. Rayne didn't have to be a ghost whisperer to know what the butler thought.

It was good to have everyone home again.

Stewart Estate
Days later

Oliver Blue could have claimed any number of empty bedrooms as his at the Stewart Estate, but he chose a small room near the tower door. It suited him, he said, but Gabriel thought there might be another reason he'd chosen such a modest accommodation. Gabe didn't mind sharing his favorite spot on the estate—the rampart tower—but he had a feeling that Oliver had picked the small, unassuming room because he might not stay.

With a guy like Oliver Blue, it was wise not to take anything for granted.

Gabriel found that he needed the solitude of the rampart after what had happened, but he also was determined to spend time with Oliver. He shared his morning tea with him as they watched the sun rise over the Bristol Mountains from the mansion's stone tower. Oliver had a habit of straddling the parapet wall, dangling his feet precariously as he bathed in the warmth of the rising sun, like a tomcat assured of his footing.

But one morning, when he found Oliver perched on the wall, his morning companion appeared more solemn—even in his black Zombie Hunter T-shirt. It took time for him to open up.

"I'd like to borrow a car and some money. There's something I have to—"

"I'll ask my uncle. Anything I can do to help?"

Oliver shook his head and said, "No. Something I have to do...with Caila and Zack's ashes. She doesn't know yet. Can we keep it our secret until I ask her?"

"Yeah, sure."

When the morning breeze tossed his hair into his eyes, Oliver squinted and faced into the wind.

"Will you be coming back?" Gabe asked.

It might've seemed an odd question, but he felt a restless spirit in Oliver. He was a guy who could be content on his own, but he hoped he would stay.

"You're both welcome here as long as you need. You know that, right?"

"Thanks." Oliver fixed his gaze on him, and a slow, lazy smile curled his lip. After he got quiet again, he eventually had more to say.

"I felt dead inside, Gabe. I thought that living on my own,

I was free, but hiding out and being afraid isn't living. I didn't see that until Caila."

Gabe had to smile. Rayne had dug him out of his hole too.

"She came to me to save Zack, but she saved me instead. I gotta return the favor," Oliver told him. "I have thinking to do, but thanks to you and your uncle, I feel like I have time now…and a purpose."

Gabe grinned and raised his teacup. "You're welcome. Now shut up so we can enjoy the dawn."

Oliver smiled and eased into a very familiar and comfortable silence. Gabriel knew how to be patient. When he was ready, Oliver would talk to him about Caila and his plans—and he would listen. He didn't need to be a psychic to know his friend.

After all, they'd been acquaintances in another lifetime. Gabriel had never been more sure of it.

The next day

Gabriel picked up his pace as he raced down the hall, heading for the great room. Before dinner, the children often gathered there, waiting to eat. He was looking for Oliver and Caila, but as he saw the others, he told them to follow him. When he walked into the room, there was a fire in the hearth and he spotted Oliver in a chair, reading. Caila sat in the love seat next to him.

"Just the two I wanted to see," he shouted.

"What the hell did *I* do?" Oliver asked.

"It's more like what *she* did." He nudged his head toward Caila. "I know you wanted to pay a visit to Dr. Fiona to see how she was getting on, but I'm afraid you're too late."

Gabriel held a laptop under his arm and pinched his lip to fight a smile.

"What are you talking about?" Oliver asked, and put down his book.

"I took the liberty of setting up a Google Alert in her name. I thought it would be prudent to monitor any recent hits on the internet." Gabriel couldn't stop smiling when he told them, "It seems she has gone viral with over three million hits and counting. She's been arrested, actually."

He opened his laptop and set it on a table. When they all gathered around, he clicked the play button and a video started. It was a news story from L.A. that made it on YouTube. Dr. Fiona had not only embraced her new life, but she had transformed herself.

She had dyed her hair pitch-black on one side and on the other, her hair was stark white. As police hauled her from her home in handcuffs, she wore large sunglasses, a tight-fitting lacy black dress and an elaborate fur coat—spotted black and white. Her lips were painted in cherry red and she never stopped hurling insults at the cops who'd arrested her and at the angry PETA protestors carrying signs.

"Meet the new Cruella De Vil. It seems she has been hording puppies. Dalmatians, to be exact."

Caila gasped. "She didn't hurt any of them, did she? I didn't think it would go *that* far."

"It seems her homeowners association didn't approve of the barking at all hours and the smell of poop." He grinned. "She had one hundred and five at last count, but I'm sure they will all find nice homes, ones where they won't end up as a coat."

Gabriel told them how the late-night talk shows had made her a joke, but Dr. Fiona made an even bigger splash when she hit *Tosh.0*. According to reporters, she'd been committed for psychiatric evaluation and her medical license was under review.

"I propose we celebrate," Gabe said. "After dinner, let's stream *One Hundred and One Dalmatians* on Netflix. It should be spectacular in the serenity room. Who's game?"

The little ones jumped and raised their hands with a heavy dose of giggles.

"That's settled. Let's eat. I'm starving," he said.

Gabriel let the others leave, but he stayed behind to talk to Caila.

"I wanted to thank you. Things could have turned out much worse. After what Dr. Fiona did to you and Zack, Oliver and so many others, it would've been easy to want to see her dead, but you found another way. She's a viral wonder and a laughingstock for comedians. If she had any clout in her profession, that's over now. She won't hurt kids anymore, and if she keeps channeling Cruella, she may stay locked up for a long time. Thank you."

Caila only smiled.

"What made you decide on a Disney character anyway?" he asked.

The girl shook her head and walked with him. "I don't know, actually. Guess I've got a thing for cartoons."

Gabriel let her join the others. The girl had saved him from a difficult decision and found a solution that even Lucas could appreciate.

What Gabriel couldn't share with anyone, except his uncle, was that he'd been monitoring the news on police activity in the Cold Water Canyon area and in West Hollywood. He hadn't seen one report of gun violence, an attack on the hospital or dead bodies found in the San Gabriel Mountains. His father's estate had been remote. It wasn't likely that gunfire would have been easily reported since noise echoed in the canyon, but he had a different theory that made more sense.

The Believers had done their own cleanup.

For the sake of the other Indigos, and especially for Rayne, that meant it wasn't likely that their involvement would be known, but it meant something else too.

The Believers had covered their tracks. They would live to fight another day.

Five days later

Oliver had to lie to Caila to get her to come with him. He didn't feel bad about it. He only knew she could hate him after.

Being alone with her, for long hours on the road, might've felt weird, but he found that he liked it. He took his time and didn't push the speed. He stopped more often and even hit some historic markers and ate in small towns. A part of him didn't want their trip to end, but it had to.

When he crossed the border into Wyoming and watched the miles tick down until they were nearly to Casper, he knew he'd have to prepare her for the truth. He hadn't brought her to Wyoming to spread Zack's ashes in a place that Oliver swore was special to their dead friend.

He'd brought her file, the one the Believers had kept on Caila, the very one he had memorized.

When he got out of the car to fill up the tank in Casper, he stretched his long legs and breathed in the cool mountain air. After Caila went inside to freshen up, he turned his face toward the sun and gazed at the mountains. The town stood at the base of Casper Mountain and had the North Platte River winding through it. Something about Caila fit this place.

She had been a small-town girl in the big city and she'd held on to a sweet innocence that made her vulnerable in L.A. That's what Zack had seen in her and wanted to protect. She didn't have to be an Indigo who'd used her gift to make him feel the same. In the end, that's how he justified how he felt, and would always feel, about her.

When he got done filling up and paying, Caila came out and she looked pretty. Real pretty.

"Do you know where we're going?" she asked.

He only nodded and got in the car.

Oliver had run out of time with her, yet that had been inevitable. Part of him dreaded what had to happen next, but those feelings of his had been part of the lies she'd planted in him. He should stop calling them lies. Whatever she'd done to him was now the truth. He'd accepted it. He hoped she would find a way to live with it too.

When he pulled onto a side street near town and drove down a quiet block, he looked for the address and found the home. He parked at the curb and kept the engine running.

Before she asked him any questions, he told her the truth.

"This isn't Zack's house. It's...yours."

Caila flinched when he said it. She turned and stared at the ranch-style home at the end of a cul-de-sac.

"No, you're wrong. I don't remember this place." She shifted her gaze back to him. "What are you doing, Oliver? You're scaring me. I thought you said—"

"I knew you wouldn't come with me if I told you the truth."

"What are you saying?"

He reached behind the front seat and pulled out her file that he'd stuffed in a small bag of his. But before he told her what he'd found in the folder, he had to reason with her.

"Dr. Fiona said stuff about you. I thought she'd been lying to manipulate me into doing what she wanted."

"She *was* lying. All of it was a lie."

"Not all of it. What she told me about you? It was mostly

the truth." He shrugged after he saw her reaction. "Yeah, that shocked me too. She told so many lies that I don't think she knew what was true anymore."

When Caila turned from him and wouldn't look him in the eye, he kept talking.

"You had a good friend. Ashley Baker. You grew up together, went to the same schools, but she wasn't a happy girl. Her parents divorced and she took it hard. You tried to help her...like you did me."

"Ashley? No, you're lying." She stared at the house. "I had a half sister named Ashley, but Dad made her leave. Why are you doing this?"

"This time, instead of planting happy memories in her, I think you took the bad ones away, like you offered to do for Rayne. You thought you were helping her, but you were hurting yourself," he told her. "You ran away from home, thinking your parents didn't want you, but that wasn't... how it was. Those were Ashley's bad memories, not yours. Your parents have been searching for you, Caila. They never *stopped* looking."

Oliver sighed and wasn't sure he could finish.

"You helped Ashley for a while, but she couldn't dodge her life. She committed suicide, Caila. That's when you ran away from home. You couldn't deal with what happened to her."

"No, that's just...wrong. Ashley's not dead. She just... moved away." She shook her head and refused to look at him.

"You took her bad memories and thought they were yours. You didn't think you had people who loved you and a home, but you do." He held out her file and waited for her to take it. "It's all in here. Your gift has a name. It's retrocognition. You can see past events, but you can also manipulate them. You plant memories like you did in me. Ashley's death triggered you into a spiral you couldn't get out of, but you can control it."

Oliver handed her the file, but she didn't take it.

"Your gift is why the Believers targeted you. They tracked you in L.A., especially after you crossed paths with Zack. After that, they backtracked where you came from and made this folder on you. It was only a matter of time before they picked you up, but now that we have your file, you'll be safe here, Caila."

Oliver didn't know how safe *any* Indigo was with the Believers still operating in secret, but that was *his* battle now.

His quiet morning talks with Gabriel had settled his mind on any lingering loyalty he might have felt toward the doctor who had altered his gifts. Dr. Fiona hadn't given him anything that wasn't already in him. He didn't owe her anything, not even the hatred he should've felt. He let it all go.

He'd made up his mind to help Gabriel and the others, so kids like Caila could live a normal life. Even if he wanted to stay in touch with her and see how her life turned out, he couldn't. That wouldn't be safe for her.

Caila took the file from him with her hands trembling. She saw the police report her mother and father had filed. She looked at photos of them in newspaper clippings. After Oliver had read her file, he went online to do more research and printed the pages for her. Her parents had even started a Facebook page and told her story in countless comments and prayers and pictures. That's how he'd found out about Ashley.

"My parents aren't divorced?" She asked the question but didn't wait for an answer.

She pored through the records the church had carefully put together when they wanted to abduct her. They'd studied what they thought she could do, made notes in her file and taken surveillance photos. The pieces were coming to-gether for her. He could see it.

"Oh my God. My dad used to work in L.A. before we moved here. He was a freelance animator and worked for Disney. That's why I hear the songs. I grew up hearing them. It's why I did that thing to the doctor."

"Maybe those songs reminded you of home. Your *real* home."

As the puzzle of her life clicked into place, he saw it in her face and heard it in her voice. Hearing her say the words *my dad* and *we* meant that she'd found nuggets of truth in the information she read. Tears hit the paper until she finally stopped and looked at him.

She was so happy. Her eyes were the color of a summer sky in Wyoming. In that moment, he saw the little girl she must've been—the sweet girl who only wanted to help her best friend, Ashley.

"I love you, Oliver." She hesitated. "I'm so…sorry for—"

Oliver didn't let her finish. He touched a finger to her lips and shook his head until she stopped. He couldn't take his eyes off her. He wanted to remember her exactly like this. Caila reached for the jacket he had on and poked a finger through one of his button holes with her eyes shut tight.

When she opened them, she said, "Please don't get out of the car. Saying goodbye will be hard enough."

She didn't wait for him to say a word. Maybe she didn't need to know he felt the same…about everything. He took that as a good sign, that she'd accepted how things would be. If he had been standing next to her, not knowing what to do with his hands, he'd be too tempted to hold her and kiss her. That would make things worse. The girl didn't need strings to start her new life, in a place that he hoped would keep her safe.

After she got out of the car, she pulled her small bag from the backseat and set it on the curb. When he handed her Zack's ashes, she placed her hand over his and took the small tin box.

"Zack would've loved it here," he said. "Find him a beautiful spot on the mountain and set him free. He really loved you, you know? I felt it."

He didn't know if the love he felt for her had been Zack's or his. That didn't matter now.

With shaky fingers pressed to her lips, she said goodbye to him without another word. Her eyes were filled with tears and his were too. When one broke free and rolled down his cheek, he didn't wipe it away. Caila closed the car door and picked up her bag and Zack's tin before she headed to the front door. Oliver waited until she knocked and the door opened.

"Have a good life, Caila," he whispered. "I love you too."

He waited until he saw Caila's mother pull her missing daughter into her arms and bring her inside before he drove away and never looked back. He would have the love— and the life—she'd given him in a kiss. It would have to be enough.

Caila was the first girl he ever loved. That's how he always wanted to remember her.

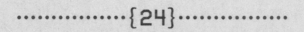

{24}

Stewart Estate
Days later

Kendra had gotten up early, too restless to sleep another minute without seeing Rafael. Every morning was like that for her now. Ever since they'd found him alive, she felt as if she'd gotten a second chance to turn her life around—and she wanted Rafael to be more than a friend.

She rushed to get ready. After her shower, she dressed in jeans, a lacy tank under a large plaid shirt and hiking boots. The clothes weren't very girly, but they were comfortable. Instead of pulling back her hair, she let it fall loose to her shoulders and spent time in front of the mirror. She even put on a touch of makeup that she'd borrowed from Rayne. The last thing she put on was the infinity bracelet he'd given her.

As she walked down the hallway, heading for Rafael's room, she had nervous knots in her stomach. They felt wonderful and terrible all at the same time. She'd never felt more alive—and happy—but as she stepped softly by his room, she found his door ajar. She expected him to still be asleep, but his room looked empty.

Rafael hadn't fully recovered from the beating he'd endured at the hands of Gabriel's father and his men. He walked with a limp and had a cut lip and a bruise under one eye. With Rafael, the outside would heal.

It was the inside of him that would take longer.

After getting a glimpse behind his mind shield—the frightening look he'd been brave enough to let her see—she knew he had good reason for how he would always be. She also knew that he was the strongest person she'd ever known because of it.

Kendra pushed open his bedroom door and stepped inside his room. Rafael's bed had been made and he was gone. He'd taken a shower. The air carried the aroma of herbal soap and the natural scent of Rafael that she'd grown addicted to.

She sat on the edge of his mattress and grabbed one of his pillows. Kendra held it in her arms, breathed in the smell of his skin and thought of him. Closing her eyes, she sensed him with her and almost felt his warmth and the way his lips touched hers. But she didn't have to imagine what that would feel like. She could have him, for real. After she put his pillow back, she ran her hands over the bed linens to fix what she'd messed up, and went looking for him.

When she got to the dining room, she found the Effin brothers. They had huge bowls of cereal in front of them, filled to the top, and spoons the size of shovels.

"Have you seen, Rafael?" she asked them.

They looked at each other before they shrugged. Kendra narrowed her eyes at the twins. The boys usually knew everything going on in the house, especially at this early hour. For them to only shrug, without their usual telepathic chatter, meant something was up. They didn't make very good liars.

When she plopped down next to them and stared them in the eye, they totally caved.

Minutes later

The twins only told her where she could find Rafael. With milk dribbled on their chins and lips pursed, the brothers refused to tell her anything else.

Kendra ran out the first door she found and hugged her body against the morning chill of the Bristol Mountains. She crossed the stone patio and walked past the fountain where she'd first kissed Rafael after Benny's funeral. The rush of memories quickened her steps, and her eyes searched for him as she followed a dirt path at the rear of the estate.

With every step, she heard the lilt of a new melody that wrapped around her heart. As an Indigo, she felt the music had become a part of her since she was a child. But today the haunting unforgettable song was different from anything she'd ever heard before.

After she stepped through an old stone archway that led beyond the walls of the estate, she found Rafael. When she saw what he was doing, she stopped to watch him. He wore jeans and a blue tank. His dark hair shone in the morning sun and his body glistened with sweat. He was hard at work, digging into the soil. From the looks of the ground and the shed nearby, she finally realized what he must've been working on for days.

Rafael made a garden—*for her.*

When she gasped and covered her mouth, Rafe turned.

"I wanted it to be a surprise."

"It is," she whispered. "Oh God. It is."

Kendra's eyes filled when she saw what he had done. Hurt as he was, he'd spent hours cleaning up the old greenhouse on the estate and now was turning over the dark, rich-looking soil, preparing the ground to plant seeds.

She'd been lost without her garden. Plants were her connection to the other Indigo souls she heard in her head. She sensed them best in her medicinal herbs and vegetables. After the Believers had destroyed the beautiful garden she had in the tunnels, she didn't know where she would start a new one. Wherever it would be meant she'd found a new home.

If anyone understood how much home meant to her, it was Rafael.

"I'm gonna paint the greenhouse tomorrow," he told her. "Now that you know about it, maybe you can go with me to Ludlow. You can help me pick out the color."

She could only nod as tears rolled down her cheeks.

"When we're in town, we can pick out seeds too. Uncle Reginald says he has special ones, from when Gabriel's mother had the garden."

Kendra sensed the love already deep in the earth. Lady Kathryn's legacy would be in every plant.

"This is...perfect," she said.

Rafael took off his work gloves and grinned at her. In the morning light, his handsome face lit up and he looked happier than she had ever seen him. She knew he had to be hurting, but he looked healthy and strong. His aura was dazzling in the sun.

Kendra walked toward him with one question on her mind. She didn't want to ask him, but she had to know.

"Does this mean that you've decided to stay?"

Her voice sounded fractured and weak, but only because Rafael was the one boy who could crush her. She stood close enough to feel the heat off his skin and touched the infinity bracelet that he wore on his wrist—the one she had returned to him.

"You left before. I know you did it because you missed Benny, but I..." She swallowed, hard. "I *need* you. You're my home, my family. I want my future to be with you. You belong here with me…with us. I love you, Rafael."

"I love you too." His low voice sent shivers over her skin.

This time when he kissed her, she didn't pull away. She knew exactly what she wanted. His body felt good next to hers and he kissed her with such tenderness that she sensed how special this moment was for him too. Rafael had loved her in his quiet way. He'd been her rock without expecting anything in return. Any future that she could ever hope for, it would begin with him.

Kendra never believed that she deserved to be happy. She'd started a rebellion for the future of all Indigos. She still believed in her cause with all her heart, but now she wanted something for *her*. She *did* deserve happiness—and so did he.

Only one thing stood in her way.

She had to tell him what she'd done. *Her* secret. She still felt unworthy of being loved. If anyone understood that, it was Rafael. She'd sensed the way he felt when he'd let her past his mind defenses. But if she expected a life with him, she had to be honest. He had to know *her* sins. He'd been brave enough to show her every bad thing that had ever happened to him. Rafe had given her the courage to do the same.

She reached for his hand and pulled him with her until they sat on a low stone wall that surrounded the garden. A large oak sheltered them from the morning breeze.

"Te amo, mi corazón," he whispered in Spanish as he kissed her cheek. The intimacy of his voice felt like making love.

Kendra nuzzled her forehead against his as she struggled to find the words.

"There's something I have to…*show* you."

She told him what she wanted and he nodded without saying anything.

Whenever she thought about the moment she would bare

her soul and tell the guy she loved about what she did, she'd always envisioned it with her saying the words that would forever change the way he would look at her. But with Rafael, she wanted him to see it, to feel her shame.

Kendra closed her eyes as Rafael held her in his arms. When she let him past her mind shield, the tears came. They would have no more secrets between them.

She hoped he wouldn't hate her.

Rafael held Kendra as if she would break. He breathed in the scent of her hair and kissed her neck. Being with her like this, he felt as if any minute he'd wake up from a dream and things would change back the way they were. He wasn't sure he'd ever get over the feeling that he didn't deserve her, but the one thing he could give her was a garden. He knew what it would mean to her—*and to him*.

Kendra was an Indigo healer. Growing things would always be a part of her nature. It was the way she stayed connected to her Indigo soul and her gift. From the day he met her, she'd planted roots in him. She made him care about something more than the misery of his own life. She taught him how to love Benny. He hadn't realized that until he'd lost little man, and the only anchor he had left was Kendra.

It had been easy to steal Rayne's Harley and run away from the pain. He didn't give a shit about anything. Losing Benny had thrown him into that dark place, the hole his old man had dug for him the night he almost beat him to death. But after Rafe had been taken by the Believers, he thought he would die and not see Kendra again. That's when he learned something different.

Sticking around and caring what happens to other people—and loving someone—took *real* courage. That's why he had to fix a garden for Kendra. He wanted her to know that he would stick now—no matter what happened—and he would love her, even if it meant she didn't love him back.

I have to show you something.

When her voice whispered inside his head, he shut his eyes and pulled her to his chest.

You don't have to. Nothing will change how much I love you, he told her.

Please… Do this for me. It was the last thing she told him before she touched his face and the darkness took over.

Kendra didn't block him with her shield. She unraveled a story she wanted him to see. His mind flashed on two girls arguing in a small bedroom. Two beds meant they shared the same room. It took him a moment to recognize Kendra as a little girl, no more than ten. She looked Benny's age when he died.

"Daddy said you couldn't go by yourself and I'm busy doin' homework."

"But I don't have milk for my cereal. I'm hungry."

"Eat it dry. I do."

Kendra turned up the music she'd been listening to on the radio and ignored her younger sister as she wrote in a notebook. After a while, she got up to see where the girl went. When she wasn't in the kitchen, she searched the house and went to another bedroom. She pulled open a drawer and took out a box that had cash in it. Money must've been missing, because she looked mad. Kendra ran outside. When she spotted her sister down the street, she yelled at her.

"I'm telling Daddy." When the girl still didn't come back, she shouted, *"I'm not coming after you, Lily Grace. You're a brat."*

Kendra went into the house and slammed the door. She lost her temper and messed up her sister's bed, but when Lily didn't return after the sun went down, she got scared and didn't know what to do. She went looking, but never found her, and the store clerk didn't remember seeing her. When Kendra called her father, she had to leave a message. By the time he got home from work, it was too late.

She'd be haunted by the sight of her sister walking away—and her doing nothing—but the accusations of her father hurt worst of all. He blew up and blamed her for everything.

"I didn't mean to do it, Daddy. It just…happened. Please don't hate me."

After the vision ended, Rafael felt drained as if he'd lived it. Kendra stared at him and her eyes welled with tears.

"She was only eight," she said. "How could I *do* that? She was a little kid."

"So were you."

When she kept talking, he knew she hadn't heard him.

"Daddy worked two jobs so we could go to school and have a house to live in. He did that for us. All I had to do was watch her till he got home," she cried. "The grocery store was only three blocks away. I should've taken her. I should've been a better sister."

Kendra was beyond listening. She pushed him away and turned her back on him, saying, "Please don't look at me. I can't do this if you're looking."

"It wasn't your fault."

She stared into her past in a daze, saying anything that came to her mind.

"The police never found her…or her body. Daddy finally bought a coffin and we buried it empty so people would quit asking about her," she told him. "But he stopped…loving me. That's when I left. I knew he wouldn't care anyway. I only reminded him…of what I did to her."

Rafael wrapped his arms around her and pulled her to his chest, respecting her wishes not to look at her. When she stopped sobbing, he whispered in her ear, "It wasn't your fault. You have to quit blaming yourself, Kendra. You were a kid."

He rocked her and kept saying the same thing until she got quiet.

Guilt was a terrible thing. Rafe had a lot in his life that had been out of his control, like the father he got, and even how Benny had found and changed him forever. He saw the same things in Kendra. Whoever took her sister, *they* were to blame for what happened, not a little girl who was too young to be responsible for the evil in others—or a father working two jobs who couldn't afford day care.

He had to find a way to forgive himself for what happened to Benny, just like Kendra had to feel worthy of a second chance. He felt closer to her now than he ever had before, but when she pulled from him, she looked worn out and sad. *Broken.*

"Do you blame me for what happened to Benny?" he asked her.

"No, of course not. The Believers did that."

She held his hand. Her skin felt good next to his.

"I'm glad you said that, because then maybe you'll believe that what happened to your sister isn't your fault either. Someone *else* took her. Someone bad." He held her face in his hands. "We can't keep doing this. We're living in the past. I'm tired of feeling bad all the time, but I don't feel bad when I'm with you."

He didn't wait for her to say anything.

"If you forgive me and I forgive you, maybe one day we can look in the mirror and forgive who we see," he said.

She smiled, in that fragile way that always broke his heart and made him love her more.

"No more secrets between us," he said. "That's a good start."

"A start?"

Rafael tucked a strand of her hair behind her ear and grinned.

"Yeah, like starting over Help me finish our garden," he said. "We got good soil here, don't you think?"

New tears rolled down her cheeks, but Kendra didn't look sad anymore. Rafael wasn't stupid enough to think that one brave confession and a good cry would stop the hurt, but it was a start—for *both* of them.

{25}

Rayne had told Lucas where Mia lived. He'd gotten the information from her and avoided sounding as if he was interested in reaching out to their older sister, but he knew that day would come. It *had* to.

That moment was now.

He stood outside her home across the street and watched her move through her living room. She'd become colors and motion through slated blinds. The room was dark. The only flicker of light came from the TV. When he got closer, he saw that she had a small bowl of popcorn in her hand as she'd settled onto a sofa.

Gabriel had dropped him off and he'd made plans to rendezvous with him later when he was done. Luke hadn't told Rayne. He knew she'd want to come, but confronting Mia for what she'd done to him had always been personal. This wasn't about disintegrating their grieving family. It was about a big sister making devastating decisions for a younger brother she believed to be mentally unstable.

If his sister called the cops to have him arrested, he didn't want to risk Rayne's freedom for something he had to do on his own. Lucas stuck to the shadows and went around to the backyard. He found a darkened window that was open a crack. He felt like a criminal as he crawled into his sister's home, but he didn't trust her to greet him like long-lost family. In her mind, he'd be a mental patient on the run.

As he walked toward the faint noise and the light from the living room, he felt his heart race. He didn't know what he wanted to say to her. Only anger welled inside him. In the darkness, he wanted to picture Mia as the girl he'd grown up with, but he couldn't.

Too much had happened and she'd nearly gotten him killed.

When he couldn't stand it any longer, Luke blurted the first thing that came to his mouth.

"I want my life back." He stepped out of the shadows of a darkened hallway. "I'm tired of running from my own sister."

Mia jumped at the sound of his voice and she shot to her feet and turned to face him.

"Lucas?" His older sister's eyes grew wide and her gaze darted to the cell phone on her coffee table. "Are you...?"

"Am I stable? Is that what you wanted to ask me?" He didn't wait for her to answer. "I was always okay. I was just different. You never understood that."

What he'd said had hurt her. He saw it in her eyes. She'd always been tough. Confident. Tonight, with her scrubbed face and hair in a ponytail, she looked small without her high heels...and worn out.

"You forgot how it was with you. You kept saying you saw our dead parents. That's not right, Luke. You needed a doctor's help. You were hallucinating things that didn't make sense."

"To you maybe, but to kids like me, it makes *perfect* sense. Ever hear of a Crystal child...or an Indigo? Look it up on the internet. We're psychic. We feel things differently than you do, but that doesn't make us animals or something to be afraid of."

When he stepped closer to her, she backed away and her body tensed.

"I won't hurt you, Mia. Not like you've hurt me…and can *still* hurt me."

His sister crossed her arms and in the dim light, he saw her eyes filled with tears. He didn't know what to expect from this confrontation, but her crying wasn't it.

"I thought I'd done the right thing…for you…for us as a family. I didn't know what else to do. I was practically a kid myself when Mommy and Daddy died. I had to do what was right. I love you, Lucas, but even now you scare me."

"You scare me too. What happened to you? You turned on me and Rayne, all for that lame church. Do you know what they do to kids like me? They're killing us…torturing us with their weird experiments…in the name of their twisted religion. You're a part of that, Mia. You chose *them* over our family."

"I don't know what you're talking about. Killing? Torture? I've never heard or seen anything like that."

"Open your eyes, Mia. I'm your brother. I've seen what they do. You almost got me sent to Ward 8. They would've killed me there."

"I didn't know. I swear."

"So who do you believe? If you don't trust me, we're done as a family, but I intend to fight for my trust fund money in court if I have to. I need to move on with my life. I'm with Rayne. We're okay…if that still matters to you."

Tears flowed more easily now. When she wiped her face, he watched how her fingers trembled.

"I won't fight you, Lucas. The money is yours. I'll see to it." She sighed and chewed her lower lip. "I quit my job at the church. Something didn't feel right about the way they were searching for you. I trusted your doctor, Fiona Haugstad. I thought she would help you, but I was wrong."

Mia clutched her arms tighter across her stomach and inched closer to him. Her eyes were wary, but he felt something had changed in her.

"I tried to get in touch with you and Rayne on her cell until her voice mail got full. I don't know how to make it up to you…and to Rayne." She shook her head. "I want us to be a family, but I don't know how to do that. Maybe it's too late."

For once Mia didn't have all the answers. Lucas considered that a good start. She looked fragile, like a bird with a busted wing.

"Come here."

When Luke pulled Mia to his chest, she let go. She sobbed and collapsed into his arms. He couldn't remember the last time she'd touched him. Luke had no illusions that they could be a family again.

He only knew that for the first time, he wanted to try.

Stewart Estate
The next morning

Drinking tea and sitting atop the parapet of the tower in his jeans and a T-shirt, Gabriel watched an unusual glow move closer to the gates of the estate. He straightened his slouch and narrowed his eyes toward the horizon. In the dawn's pale light, the headlights of a caravan of cars looked hazy in a morning fog as thoughts raced through his head.

The Believers had found them.

He set down his cup on the ledge and ran for the tower door and down the spiral stairs with the sound of his boots echoing off stone. Uncle Reginald's suite wasn't far. Gabriel prayed that he was wrong about the unwanted early morning intrusion when he pounded on his uncle's door.

"Gabriel? What is it?"

"We've got visitors coming to our gate. Four or five cars."

His uncle didn't ask any more questions.

"I'll be dressed in two shakes. Pull the SUV in front. I'll meet you. We'll confront them at the gate. Go. Now."

Gabriel ran to grab the keys and head for the estate garage. On his way he sent a message to the hive through Kendra, Lucas and Rafael. They'd know what to do.

We have company. Evacuation plan. Stay put until you hear from me, he told them.

What? Shit!

I'm on it.

Will do.

The voices of the others filled his head. He didn't want to send a panic to the little ones—waking them from a dead sleep after the devastating attack in the tunnels had happened in much the same way—but he didn't have a choice. They might need to take cover and hide in the stronghold his uncle had made of a reinforced panic room. Reginald had made sure to drill them on what to do for emergencies.

As Gabriel barreled up to the front door in the Navigator, he screeched to a stop for his uncle to get in. Uncle Reginald's face looked pale, but his eyes were determined.

"I'll do the talking. They'll expect that."

"And when they're done talking, I'll take over."

"Agreed." His uncle glanced toward him. "Let's hope it doesn't come to that."

The ride down the mountain jostled his empty stomach as the SUV navigated through ruts in the road and sharp turns down the switchbacks. When they got close enough to see the front gate in the early morning light, four vehicles were lined up in front of the gate with engines running. The silhouettes of people without faces stood in front of blazing headlights.

"If this was the Believers, they wouldn't have waited. They would've stormed the gate and rushed us, Gabriel."

As they got near enough to see faces, Gabe shot a perplexed look at his uncle. "They're kids."

More than a dozen kids stood outside the gate in a line, waiting for them. When Gabe and his uncle got out of the SUV, he left the engine running in case they had to make a quick getaway, but something in the young faces made him more curious than fearful. Their thoughts beckoned and embraced him.

One girl stepped forward as they approached the locked and secured metal gate to the grounds. She was thin and dressed in sweats and a hoodie.

"If you're who I think you are, you won't find it strange that we're here," she said. "Indigos all over are talking about you... What you did."

She stared past his uncle, straight at Gabriel.

"You're him, aren't you?" The blonde girl pointed at him. "Your aura, it's...stunning. I've never seen anything like it."

"That's him." A whisper rushed through the kids, and every gaze turned toward him. "He's the one."

A girl who could read auras explained the eerie sensation he had felt at the assault on his father's mansion. She must have sensed the negative energy of the fight and his powerful impact on the hive. He didn't know such a thing was even possible.

"How did you know where to come?" Gabriel asked.

"A few of us just knew," she said. "We'd never felt anything like you before. We came to see for ourselves…to see if we can help."

"Yeah." A young boy stepped forward and his voice cracked. "Like, you woke us up, dude. For real. What are you…exactly?"

"Good question." Gabriel smiled.

He didn't know what to make of these kids knowing where they were and feeling his presence as if he'd left a signature on the hive collective that others sensed. They had found their way to him because of it. That felt dangerous and risky, but something more hit him.

Indigos outside of L.A. had sensed the fight. They'd instinctively known what had happened and even knew where to come. The more they pushed the boundaries of what they could do as a collective—together—the stronger the hive could become. Something had happened. They were becoming what they had always been meant to be.

"I wasn't sure we'd accomplished much…until now. We took out some of their leaders in L.A., destroyed one of their torture wards at a mental hospital, shredded their computer system and records and we rescued some Indigos. But the Believers are massive, yeah?" After the kids nodded, Gabe went on. "But you being here, that's amazing. I've got to know how you did that."

"I'd say breakfast is in order." Uncle Reginald winked at him and opened the gate. "Please…join us."

Before the Indigos climbed back in their cars for the ride up the mountain to the mansion, they lined up one by one and shook hands with Gabriel and touched him, telling him their names. No one ordered it. They did it without prompting.

Gabe's face flushed with heat.

"I'm Gabriel. Welcome."

They had started more than a fight against the Believers in

L.A. and retaliation against his father for what had happened to Benny. With each handshake and smile, Gabe felt tears burning behind his eyes. All the emotional pressure he'd felt over being responsible for his new Indigo family came rushing to the surface and hit him hard. He fought the lump in his throat as the realization hit him.

They hadn't just survived the fight. They'd started…a movement.

Stewart Estate
Days later

Despite the energized buzz that came from knowing that Indigos outside L.A. were hearing about what had happened and spreading the word about the success of their fight against the Believers, in the days that had followed the attack, Rayne couldn't stop the dark spiral that had started when she pulled the trigger and killed Boelens. Each day brought new ordeals. The first few nights had been the worst. When she couldn't stand to be alone, she'd slept in her brother's room. Lucas gave her his bed and he slept on the floor.

The nightmares felt as if they would never end. Flashbacks filled her nights and loud noises gave her the shakes and sometimes brought her to tears. She found it hard to concentrate and there were days she wouldn't get out of bed. It felt as if she were slowly sinking into quicksand, and very little made her feel better.

Uncle Reginald offered to take her to a doctor so she could talk it out. He'd offered the same to any of the Indigos who needed help to deal with what had happened, but what could she or any of them possibly admit to an outsider?

But as time went by, small things became tolerable. Gabriel never gave up on her. He slept on the floor in Luke's room when she let him and he held her when she needed it. He seemed to intuitively know what she needed and quietly took care of her.

What helped most was him telling her about the others, when she didn't have to dwell on her misery. He knew she would care and he made her feel a part of the clan they were building. Gradually she filled her days helping Uncle Reginald get the new children settled into a routine. If she had any downtime, the dark memories came. They were never far from the surface.

Her dark days had kept her from saying goodbye to little Noah. She missed him, but he had a family of his own. Uncle Reginald saw to it that Noah found his way home. He had to do the job discreetly, of course. He didn't want to be blamed for taking the child, but through trusted friends, he made sure the ten-year-old got home to his desperate parents. There had been an AMBER Alert, but since the Believers had taken the boy across state lines and hidden him in their hospital ward in a basement, Noah's trail had grown ice cold. Uncle Reginald had to settle for watching the little boy's homecoming on the television.

If Noah talked about the magical home in the mountains where he'd been taken by nice people and a dead butler, who would believe him?

After time went by, Uncle Reginald asked the new Indigos what they wanted to do. If they had families or other places to be, he didn't want to stop them, but being around other Indigos and learning from each other had made for a strong incentive for them to stay.

When he had an idea who would stick, he asked her thoughts on homeschooling and Rayne volunteered to help. Whatever hurt she still felt over killing Boelens, she decided to turn it into a positive and help the kids. They were building a haven for homeless at-risk Indigos and she wanted to be a part of it. She signed up to take online courses for the kids and for herself. Kendra offered her time and Debbie, one of the new Indigos, told them she'd always wanted to be a teacher. Her twin sister, Denise, had the gifts of a healer and made a fine apprentice for Kendra.

With more Indigos reaching out to them in different ways, they'd started a movement that carried its own momentum. They'd become an inspiration to an underground resistance. Fighting against the Believers worldwide meant they'd have to get organized. A group like theirs had started in Canada with another one in Mexico. Who knows how many would follow in other countries? They were developing secret ways to stay in touch online and through the hive collective that was growing, according to Gabriel.

The pressure and responsibility of their newfound movement weighed heavy on Rayne, in a good way. Her life had taken on a deeper purpose than she would ever have believed possible on the day she went searching for her missing brother and met Gabriel at a deserted zoo.

She wouldn't be a kid on her own anymore. She had a bigger family than the one she'd lost.

Sam and Quinn became inseparable friends with Lucas. Seeing the boys happy made her feel better. They were Indigos, but Luke had taken them under his wing and pushed them on their abilities. He had a theory that Crystal children were another level in the evolutionary journey, not a final destination. If he'd learned anything from the Believers, it was that no one should feel superior being the top of the food chain. Time made all things possible.

They were becoming a family and thanks to Gabriel, he helped her feel part of it, even though the bad days still haunted her.

The next day

When Rayne didn't come down for breakfast, he knew she'd had another bad night. Sitting in the great room, he listened for the sound of her footsteps on the stairs, but they never came. He'd lost his appetite anyway.

Lately, her good days outweighed the bad and he'd been grateful, but on days when she wanted to be alone, he had a hard time knowing what to do for her. After his mother died, he had slid into a dark hole. On the run from his father, he had dealt with his grief and anger on his own. He didn't have much of a choice, but he'd made sure Rayne knew she wasn't alone. He talked about the others, when she was ready to listen.

He had told her that Rafael and Kendra had started a garden and that the children helped fill it. He talked about how it warmed his heart to see his mother's fertile soil flourish again. It made him feel closer to her. When he wasn't thinking about Rayne, his thoughts turned to his mother, usually on nights when he couldn't sleep.

But Gabe had grown tired of feeling bad and he hoped Rayne felt the same.

"Enough is enough."

Gabriel got off his butt and went into the kitchen. He had things to do.

Afternoon

When Gabriel knocked on Rayne's bedroom door, she answered wearing a pink bathrobe and with her hair damp. With her skin flushed, she reminded him of the stillness of dawn on the rampart.

"It's a beautiful day. I hoped you would join me," he said.

A smile lit her face. "Wow. You look amazing."

He came dressed in a proper suit coat, a dress shirt and vest, his best jeans and clean boots. In his hand he carried a wicker picnic basket. Truth be told, he had fireflies in his belly. Seeing her always made him a bit jittery, especially when she looked at him the way she was now. Her smoky gray eyes drifted over his body, top to bottom, and he felt the heat under his skin.

He had to admit that a part of him wanted to drop the basket in the hall and have a different kind of picnic indoors. He'd dreamed of Rayne that way now, but nothing would happen between them until she was ready.

"I need to get dressed. I'll only be a minute." Rayne closed the door to her room and he took a seat outside her door.

She had lied about the "minute."

While he waited, his right knee developed a bounce and his hands behaved like strangers. He raked fingers through his hair and straightened his jacket. But every second he had to wait proved to be worth it.

When Rayne came out from her room, she stole his very breath. The light had come back to her eyes and she smelled bewitching, like an exotic flower. She wore tight jeans with wicked slashes across her thighs, a pale pink sweater that made her look quite small and brown ankle boots. Her gray eyes had taken on a different shade and looked like a fragile robin's egg. When she opened her mouth to say something, he touched her lips and shook his head.

He wanted to remember…everything.

Gabe pulled her into his arms and felt the heat of her body against his. One hand pressed the small of her back. With the other, he laced his fingers through her hair as he kissed her. Her lips tasted like sweet fresh berries.

He closed his eyes to feel lost in her. That's where he

wanted to stay, but the hallway outside her door wouldn't do. When he pulled his lips from hers, he breathed in the warm scent of her skin and kissed her forehead.

"Come with me," he whispered in her ear.

"Where are we going?" Rayne asked.

He loved the velvet touch of her breath on his cheek.

"You'll see."

Holding Gabriel's hand meant everything to her. The warmth of his skin and the quiet way he looked at her, she felt loved without words. With all the powerful things he could do, he acted a little nervous around her today and that made her feel special too.

When he took a familiar path behind the estate, she knew where they were going—the high meadow—a place that had been special to him and his mother...and now her. A cool breeze tousled her hair, and the sun warmed her skin as she gazed across the rolling hills that faded to a pale blue in the distance. Hellboy joined them and ran ahead, chasing butterflies. It felt as if they were the only ones on the planet.

She ran a hand over the tops of tall flowers that lined the path and filled her lungs with the crisp mountain air. When she let out her breaths, she imagined letting go of her nightmares and the fear. Being with Gabriel, she felt strong again, but that strength had come from inside her too. The tragedy of her parents' death and the fight to find Lucas had taught her how strong she could be.

When they got to the big boulder in the meadow, he surprised her by walking beyond it. He took her to the beautiful pond, the one that had been cut from the forest and mirrored the sky. The late afternoon sun pitched a thick stand of trees into darkness and made the setting a perfect blend of light and shadows.

After Gabe spread a blanket for them to sit, she smiled and asked, "What's in the basket?"

"Open it and find out."

On top he had a fresh bouquet of flowers. She breathed in the scent and dug deeper. Every morsel had a special note from him secreted in the folds of cloth napkins. Personal, private messages written in his hand, telling her how much he loved her and how brave and strong she will always be. With each note, she read them quietly and fought the tears.

She never knew love could be like this.

"You thought of everything," she whispered, and kissed his hand.

"I thought you'd be hungry," he said. "You haven't eaten today, but all I needed is you."

Gabriel had packed foods that made her mouth water. She didn't realize how hungry she was. Exotic spreads and cheeses, stuffed olives, crusty bread, a small bottle of white wine and something amazing for dessert—chocolate drizzled strawberries. She pictured feeding them to him and kissing the juice from his lips.

"I love you so much," she said.

She pulled him to her and kissed his sweet lips. Nothing could've been more perfect.

As shadow fingers stretched across the pond and the chill of the mountains closed in on them, Rayne helped him pack up their picnic. They had to get back before it got too dark to see the path. Even before the day was over, Gabriel replayed every moment he had with her. He didn't want to forget anything. He'd spent the afternoon feeding and kissing Rayne, but he wasn't done.

He had more planned and wanted to surprise her.

Before he would escort her back to her bedroom door and kiss her one final time, he planned to take her to the rampart tower. He'd downloaded his favorite songs on his iPod, slow songs that made his heart bleed and music that made him feel stronger. He wanted to share them with her and dance under the moon. In the days that had followed the shooting, Rayne had told him how she felt and shared her fears in measured doses, but today had been about healing…and hope. He had needed it too.

After he packed up the picnic basket and headed home, something made him stop and gaze across the pond. Hellboy must've heard it too. His ears stood at attention and he sniffed the air, whimpering.

A faint whisper drifted on the wind.

Gabriel.

Someone called his name. When he turned, he saw a glimmer of light on the far side of the water. His mother appeared to him, dressed in jeans and a sweater, looking like when they'd picnicked in the meadow. She smiled at him and raised a hand.

She was saying goodbye.

Gabe held up a hand to his mother. He sensed it would be for the last time. In the dying light of the sunset, she faded into the shadows of the forest until she became a beautiful shimmer on the water and was gone. Hellboy stayed where he was and howled the lone cry of a wolf before he vanished for the night. The sound of the phantom dog's bay sent chills over his skin as it gradually died.

When he turned, Rayne reached for his hand and said, "Let's go home."

Gabriel took a deep breath and let his past go.

★ ★ ★ ★ ★

····ACKNOWLEDGMENTS····

The inspiration behind Indigo Awakening and Crystal Fire of the Hunted series came from researching Indigo children. Query "Indigo Child" on the internet and you'll get millions of hits. Real life and headlines often inspire my books, and this time is no exception. For the purposes of fiction, I took liberties in my portrayal of Indigo and Crystal children and supersized their powers, but some people believe that the next evolution of man is already walking among us. Indigo kids are generally described as highly intelligent, gifted teen psychics with a bright "indigo" aura and a mission to save the world. They have high IQs, see angels and commune with the dead.

At the start of this series, I depict Indigo teens as victims being hunted by a fanatical church until Gabriel Stewart—a powerful psychic boy—comes out of hiding and commits to the fight. The Indigos uncover their growing abilities and awaken the powers of the hive mind. Together, they are more powerful, but in *Crystal Fire* (book #2 in the Hunted series), the darker side of wielding such psychic power emerges and they must reconcile the Crystal child's peace-loving nature with the warrior spirit of the Indigo.

Special thanks goes to Caila Ferrie, a Canadian author

who entered a contest of mine and was named a character in this book. She gave an evocative answer to what psychic power she would want to have, and as winner, she sent me a fun list of personal traits to incorporate into the book. Apparently she is a big fan of Disney. Thanks also to O'Dell and Boelens, the real guys, who became my evil villains. Two nicer people you will not find, but in this book, I portrayed their dastardly twins.

Personal thanks to my support net—my family and dear friends who understand that writers are weird. My brainstorming buddies, Denise and Dana, helped grease the rusty wheels when I needed it—over sushi. And a special hug to my best friend and the love of my life, my husband, John, for his support and peculiar sense of humor.

I also want to thank my designer Goddess in the trenches, my agent, Meredith Bernstein. Sometimes I think she's psychic. My gratitude to Natashya Wilson and the creative team at Harlequin Teen and the best PR person I've ever worked with, Lisa Wray. You make everything fun! To my amazing editor at Harlequin, Mary-Theresa Hussey, you are a dream to work with and make every book stronger because of your insights. I secretly believe you are a Crystal child, but I won't tell anyone. Promise.

The Clann

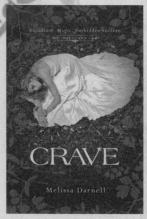

The powerful magic users of the Clann have always feared and mistrusted vampires. But when Clann golden boy Tristan Coleman falls for Savannah Colbert—the banished half Clann, half vampire girl who is just coming into her powers—a fuse is lit that may explode into war. Forbidden love, dangerous secrets and bloodlust combine in a deadly hurricane that some will not survive.

AVAILABLE WHEREVER BOOKS ARE SOLD!

www.HarlequinTEEN.com

HTCRTR6

 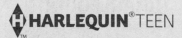